WHITE SEA RISING

MJ KEPHART

Printed in the United States of America
ISBN 978-0-9961098-0-2

Defiant Books
www.mjkephart.com

*For Diane,
Will and Laura*

WHITE SEA RISING

PART 1

Delayed-Critical

"As the Imam said, Israel must be wiped off the map."

— Mahmoud Ahmadinejad, President of Iran

"Masada shall not fall again."

— Concluding declaration to the swearing-in ceremony for Israeli Defense Forces soldiers, referring to the Roman siege of the Jewish fortress in AD 73, which resulted in the mass suicide of the 960 defenders.

1

Sada Di-Nur heard the long tone in her earpiece as she waited in the staging room. That was the signal. When she looked through the peephole in the door, the hallway was clear.

She wore the same cover-up she'd put on by the pool of the Al Batinah Beach Resort, but had added a wide-brimmed straw hat and large sunglasses to obscure her face. Leaving the hotel room, she used the fire escape exit at the end of the hall and climbed the three flights of stairs to the eighteenth floor. A large bag with the resort's logo was looped over one forearm, and a towel obscured her hand. No one she happened to pass would notice the small device in her palm.

Sada stopped halfway down the corridor at a door on the right. She inserted the interface card of the lock programmer/interrogator into the electronic door lock. The LPI was the size of a smart phone, with a large keypad and a cable to the interface card. This particular brand was used by hotel chains around the world, including this resort in the United Arab Emirates. Just like the upscale hotels where she'd practiced in Tel Aviv. With a few memorized keystrokes, she queried the lock for its code and programmed the interface card to replicate the occupant's keycard. The lock, thinking it recognized the legitimate key, whirred and flashed three green lights.

Sada slid inside and closed the door behind her. First, precautions. Taking a rubber stopper from her bag, she wedged it into the gap above the threshold. She studied the room. A suitcase lay opened on the bed, a few clothes draped over a chair back. No briefcase or papers in sight. She put the LPI and the towel in her bag and removed another small black device. She paused and checked her earpiece.

This was not the way to conduct the operation. They'd been scrambling, reacting, ever since the report that the other team was delayed in Madrid. Then those two men had shown up unexpectedly at Alizadeh's side. Even now, late in the afternoon, the rest of the surveillance element was pinned to the resort's pool and lounge areas, making sure they kept eyes on the bodyguards. *Go* or *No-go*. The heated debate had lasted into the early morning hours, but in the end Jacob, the team leader, could not be dissuaded. They needed to know when Alizadeh was in the room by himself and when he was on his phone.

Sada knelt on the carpet next to the nightstand. The listening device in her hand was as small as a camera's memory card, but with two short wires trailing out of one end. She pulled the backing off the double-sided tape and slid her hand beneath the nightstand, attaching the bug to the back of the kick plate.

She retrieved the beach bag and put her hat and glasses on, quickly surveying the room to ensure she'd left nothing behind. She removed the wedge from under the door.

To her horror, muffled footsteps stopped just outside.

Sada grabbed the beach bag and darted into the bathroom. She was easing the door shut when the heavy handle of the room door thudded down.

She cursed at the trap she was in. It was madness trying to do this without the right personnel. And now? Options and probabilities flashed through her mind. Death, possibly. Compromise and mission failure, more likely.

An image and snatch of conversation surfaced from her frantic swirl of thoughts. Early in her selection training, her class gathered under a camouflage netting shielding the Negev sun, an instructor speaking to them:

Success will depend on preparation and discretion more often than courage. But when your preparations fail, act boldly.

She set the beach bag down and slipped out of her cover-up and bathing suit, making sure the spandex made no sounds. She found a folded towel in the dark and wrapped it around her head.

You must not hesitate.

Sada said a quick prayer.

Act.

She turned on the bathroom light and ran the sink faucet for three seconds.

She was Susan Hempstead again, British schoolteacher on holiday, when she walked out of the bathroom with her hands rubbing the towel into her hair. She saw the man in the far corner, the shock registering on his face. Broad features, Central Asian characteristics. This man was not Alizadeh, the target. That was good, perhaps. More options.

Her gasp was not entirely feigned. The man was still an unknown threat. He had dropped his backpack and managed to pull a 9 mm pistol from under his sports jacket. He was clearly not a professional—which could be more dangerous. He shouted something, but it wasn't

Farsi or Arabic.

"No, no, no, no. Don't hurt me!"

Susan, the British tourist, pleaded for her life. She pulled back in terror, crouching, trying to cover her nakedness with one arm, the other outstretched to ward off the man.

"Who are you?" the man shouted, this time in heavily accented English.

"Don't hurt me," she said. She repeated that refrain again and again between her sobs.

"What are you doing here?" the man shouted.

"Please, leave my room."

She saw the doubt form in the man's eyes. She continued to back away. The man approached, but the weapon was lowered, no longer pointed at her chest.

She spun on her heels and reached for the door handle, her shoulders hunched, a victim fleeing.

A leopard coiled to strike.

The man closed the distance while she fumbled with the door handle and grabbed her arm.

Sada let the man's pull initiate her spin. She rotated through her hips, slamming her fist into the brachial plexus of the man's shoulder joint. He grunted in pained surprise and the weapon fell from his deadened hand. Her kick to his groin had so much force she came up on the toes of her foot. He doubled over, retching, his head hanging near her waist. Stepping forward, she swung her arm under the man's neck, locking it down with the other arm. When she straightened her legs and arched her back, the man realized his predicament—the crook of her arm was a vice, bicep and forearm pinching his carotids shut. He slapped at her naked flank for a few seconds before blacking out.

Sada let the man's bulk slump to the floor and took several deep breaths.

The operation was falling apart. Everything after this would be an improvisation. A series of reactions that could snowball out of control.

She snapped back to the present. She was in the target's room with an unconscious body. Alizadeh had given this man access to his room, which meant he was expecting to meet him here.

Soon.

2

The Al Batinah Beach Resort dominated the strip of land at the base of the Western Al Hajar Mountains. Two white wings of tiered balconies spread from a glass spine twenty stories tall, in brilliant contrast to the barren foothills and jagged brown peaks behind it. On the far side of the coastal highway spread long stretches of undeveloped beach.

Barrett Ross was ready for a desert oasis. It was in the mid nineties when they'd left Dubai, and after a two and a half hour ride across the desert, folded in the back of his friend's Audi, his legs were cramped and his T-shirt was clinging to his back.

"Not bad, huh?"

Barrett caught Dave Allen's smile in the rearview mirror. His friend was happy to conjure up a first-class resort in this Martian landscape.

"It might work," Barrett said. "Let's see what the mini-bar looks like."

Amy Caldwell turned around in the front seat and smiled. "You'll love it," she said in her broad Australian accent. "It's perfect for unwinding."

Which was the point. To get away from D.C. and the think tank, the endless meetings, talking point papers, and dry reviews of foreign military expenditures. For the next week he was going to forget about work—lie in the sun, drink during the day, and read whatever he wanted to. The valet ran over as they pulled beneath the overhang, and Barrett pulled himself from the back seat as soon as the car stopped, stretching his arms skyward. The searing heat brought back his days in the 82nd and sandy drop zones under the North Carolina sun. Parachuting had been a hell of a lot more interesting than what he was doing these days.

Inside the foyer, the staff greeted them with tall glasses of iced juice and moist cloths. Dave and Amy dealt with the reservations they'd made, and Barrett strolled around the large circular lobby. An evening breeze was blowing onshore, ruffling cocktail napkins before circulating through opened French doors to sway the palms beneath the domed ceiling.

Barrett stepped out onto the verandah and took in the view. A series of pools stretched around the back half of the resort, connected by shaded paths and wooden footbridges. Beyond, a row of sun umbrellas marked the beach, and he could make out a line of dark smudges on the horizon. Oil tankers, he decided, plying the Strait.

He was walking back to join his friends when he noticed one other person was waiting to check in. The man was a large Middle Easterner wearing slacks and a blazer over a mustard-colored shirt. He wasn't very patient, because he was standing so close to Dave and Amy that he was almost on top of them. As Barrett joined his friends, he caught the big man's glare.

The man said nothing, though, and with their keycards in hand, they drifted towards the breeze coming through the doors.

"Let's get a drink," Amy said. She led the way to a large tiki bar that overlooked the pool area. A Filipino in a floral shirt took their orders as soon as they sat down. They formed a plan—a few cocktails, an evening swim, and then time to chill in their rooms before dinner. The bartender put a pilsner down in front of Barrett.

A loud and angry voice suddenly welled up inside the foyer and carried through the open doors. Barrett swiveled partway on his stool and saw Colonel Mustard, the big angry man from the check-in line, berating the young woman behind the front desk. A senior manager rushed to the desk to rescue his colleague and placate the ugly customer.

What an ass.

"Flamin' galah," Amy said, exaggerating her Aussie accent.

Dave nodded. "Idiots are a global problem."

A man slid onto a stool a couple of places from Barrett. "That's the answer, mate."

Barrett lifted his glass in silent salute.

"Right. Do you have Tetley's?" the man asked the bartender.

The newcomer was short and fit, with a certain look, and Barrett pegged him as a soldier.

"Where're you from in the U.K.?"

"Banbury," the man replied. "Near Birmingham. You?"

"Pennsylvania."

"Excellent," the British tourist said, and then stuck out his hand. "Peter."

"Barrett. These are my friends Dave and Amy."

The Brit's bearing reminded Barrett of the good NCOs he'd worked with in the past—sure of themselves, used to being in charge.

"What brings you to the UAE?" the Brit asked.

"Dave works for the airline. He's been telling me for years to come visit. So here I am. This time in flip-flops."

Peter looked at him in an appraising way. "Military?"

"Army for a few years, before I decided to try something else."

Peter nodded. "I was with our Para Regiment in Afghanistan."

Barrett smiled. "Small world." He'd traveled halfway around the world, and the first foreigner he met was a paratrooper. "I started off in the 82nd. We had a Colour Sergeant from 3 Para serving on exchange in my battalion."

"Excellent." Peter raised his beer. "Ready for Anything."

Presumably, that was the motto of the Para Regiment.

"All the Way," he replied.

Maybe it was the beer, or the other man's straightforward pride, but in either case Barrett didn't feel as corny as he expected.

He and the Brit started to swap war stories, comparing the shit-holes they'd been posted to in Iraq and Afghanistan, confirming that the inconveniences of a soldier's life are common to every army. As Barrett put his empty beer down on the counter, a startlingly attractive woman walked up behind the Brit. Maybe beautiful, if she'd been smiling. She wore a cover-up and carried a large sun hat in her hand.

She stopped next to Peter and the man looked surprised to see her.

"We need to talk about our plans for tonight," she said.

"Sure," Peter said. He made brief introductions. The woman's name was Susan.

The woman nodded toward Barrett and his friends, but her gaze floated somewhere over Barrett's head.

Her hair was shoulder length, almost black, and straight except for the ends curling in to frame her face. Her skin tone was olive, what people called *warm*, and the nose was aquiline—almost too sharp. Her eyes were direct and intelligent as he realized when she caught him staring. He jerked his gaze away and looked out across the bar. He noticed a young man by the pool, scanning faces around the pool.

Damn. The British woman had been looking past him toward this guy by the pool. He was sure of it.

"Excuse me," the Brit said, and stood to follow the woman, who was already walking away towards the hotel. *That* didn't sound like a cocky British soldier on holiday.

Had the man just raised his guard? Or dropped his guard?

"What was that all about?" Amy asked after the Brits left.

Barrett shrugged.

"She didn't want hubby drinking away the afternoon at the bar," Dave said.

"Women can be so unreasonable," Amy said.

The three friends ordered several more rounds of drinks as they caught up with each other. It was late when they settled the tab and decided to head up to their rooms. They were waiting at the bank of elevators when Barrett heard his name called.

"Mr. Ross?"

The hotel manager, a short, impeccably dressed man, rushed over with a conciliatory smile.

"Sir, I'm very sorry," he said in crisp English. "I am afraid my colleague has made a mistake. We have maintenance scheduled on the eighteenth floor this week. I'm going to change you to a room on the sixteenth. Same amenities, you can be sure."

"You guys go ahead," Barrett said as the elevator door opened. "I'll see you at dinner."

Amy frowned, though, as the manager scuttled back to the desk.

"That's odd," she said.

"What's up?" Dave asked.

"My Arabic may be a bit dodgy," she said, "but that barney at the front desk earlier—the loud bastard—he was shouting the number eighteen."

Barrett urged his friends to go ahead, and walked back to the front desk. The manager fumbled at the computer and swiped the keycard three times before he managed to reprogram it for the correct room.

"Again, I apologize for the inconvenience, sir. I do hope you enjoy your stay with us."

"No sweat," he said. "If this is my biggest hassle for the week, I'll be just fine."

Barrett caught the next elevator, but the beer must have affected him more than he thought—or he was jetlagged after his Dulles to Heathrow to Dubai flights—because he pushed the wrong button for the floor. As he stepped out of the elevator and started down the long corridor, he realized he had hit 18 instead of 16.

He knew that because of the construction. In contrast to the deep maroon carpets and the rich green print on the walls, along with low yellow lights in ornate sconces, he saw up ahead something ragged, out of place. It looked like the wallpaper was peeling off.

A few steps from the end of the hall, he saw the wallpaper was torn and peeled back around a series of holes. A few were little black circles, the others white gouges of missing drywall.

Not construction. He knew what little black circles could mean. He flexed his hands as he moved around the corner, wishing he were carrying something more than his room key.

Almost instantly he lurched to his right to avoid

stepping in a mess.

Blood, jelly-thick, spread across the carpet, the edges of the puddle still rounded on top of the fibers. The blood framed a bald white head. The head was face down— destroyed, he could tell—and attached to an awkwardly fallen body. A tourist, stout calves protruding from khaki shorts, sandals on the feet. Yet the tourist was holding a handgun, his wrist bent back awkwardly as if by the fall. Barrett pressed himself against the short wall in front of him, blocked from the view of the rest of the corridor, looking back at the body. The weapon in the dead man's hand had a suppressor screwed onto the barrel.

Get help. Get security. Don't be stupid.

As he worked on controlling his breathing, he made a decision. He peered around the corner—and jerked back. There were more bodies, plus a disconcerting flit of movement he couldn't place.

You can't do anything here. This is not your job.

Despite the cover afforded by the corner, he crouched and moved back away from the wall. Shifting his feet, he inched to the left, opening his line of sight into the straightaway. Pie-ing the corner, they used to call it. Seeing more, but exposing himself, too. What the fuck was he doing? A couple of doors on the left-hand wall, nothing else. Closer to the right hand wall, white running shoes and the cuffs of blue jeans. Indexing left, slowly. Carefully. Right around the corner, two men were down, not moving. Tan slacks, Arab, or Middle Eastern, faces pressed to the floor. Closer to him, slumped against the right wall, was an Arab, neatly trimmed beard, chin resting on his chest. Blood on the wall above the man, smeared downward to his sitting position. A half dozen doors down on the left, a door was blocked open by the legs sticking through it, the torso hidden from view.

He was about to get shot. On vacation.

Would it be a crime, or terrorism?

Where were the bad guys?

He was trying to figure out where to start. He knew the rules for triage—if he could make his brain function. At least help anyone who had a chance of living.

Stutter-stepping, he moved around the bodies, trying to find signs of life—when a form rushed through the open door on the left. The man tripped over the legs of the casualty sprawled on the threshold and fell into the hall, landing on one knee with his hands splayed to catch himself. The man froze, his head turned to meet Barrett's stare. He was young, in western dress, dark skin with delicate features and a receding hairline. A pair of bookish wireframe glasses had slid down on his nose. Barrett had never seen a look of such naked fear. The man scanned him up and down for two seconds. Fear became confusion, then relief with the realization he was not about to die. The young man scrambled to his feet and sprinted to the stairwell exit at the end of the hall.

The door to Barrett's right yanked open and his attention was focused like a laser on the black hole of a gun barrel pointed at his head.

He realized it was only a pistol, but the muzzle bore seemed to take up the entire doorway, like a cannon. The faint lines of the rifling spiraled out from the dark recess until they faded away at the silver lip. Just above this, the shiny rectangle of the rear sight post reminded him that a straight line lay between his face, the sight, and the shooter's eye on the other end. He allowed his view to shift from one end to the other.

Holding the gun was Peter, the Brit from the bar.

3

The PA system crackled to life, and the feedback shattered the stillness of the Iranian desert. A voice issued strident commands and began a countdown in Farsi, as soldiers ran to their assigned positions and vehicles moved outside the danger area.

The command of *Launch* was clipped by the ignition of the first rocket engine. The roar of solid-fuel combustion grew as the missile slid along its guide rails, and the noise continued to crescendo as another engine ignited, and another. Six green-tipped medium-range ballistic missiles raced away from their mobile launchers, obscuring the vehicles in roiling clouds of dust and exhaust.

The observers craned their necks to follow the plumes arcing up from the desert floor toward a point high above the southern horizon. The contrails began to diffuse into smears, tugged by the winds at altitude, as the barrage of Shahab-3 missiles flew to their targets a thousand kilometers away in the Gulf of Oman.

A tall, broad-shouldered officer in desert-pattern camouflage stood among the crowd of dignitaries and media observers, watching with a large measure of impatience. He felt some pride, surely. It was good that the world was watching his country today. But, despite what would be said, he knew the truth. A military man should not confuse fact with fantasy.

Colonel Rostam Safavi kept his expression even. The clean-shaven face, with its hawk-like nose, betrayed no emotion. It was an ability long practiced. He wondered, though, if another bystander were to turn to share congratulations, would he see the anger in Safavi's eyes?

A stocky officer stepped before the lectern set up in front of the reviewing area.

"Today, our *Great Prophet* exercise proves the capability of the Islamic Republic of Iran to protect its people and our willingness to strike back at the Great Satan."

The brigadier general stood before a thicket of microphones. The flat bill of his dark green fatigue cap was festooned with the gold embroidered insignia of the Aerospace Forces of the Islamic Revolutionary Guard Corps. A trace of smugness played across his features.

"The Shahab and her sisters will rain death on the Zionists if they violate the sanctity of our borders. It is no secret that America and Israel collude to attack our peaceful nuclear facilities. With these forces," the general made a grand sweep of his arm toward the launcher systems arrayed behind him, "the enemies of the Revolution cannot do so without seeing the desert run red with their blood."

As the general warmed to his task, Safavi stepped back from the crowd. He could stomach only so much of the fat general's preening before the cameras. Propaganda had its uses, but not for him. As he turned his back and walked away, he thought of the countless tasks needing his attention. He had a unit to train.

"Colonel Safavi."

General Masoud Roghani had stepped away from the crowd and was walking to catch up. The commander of the Qods Force led the special operations wing of the Islamic Revolutionary Guard Corps. Safavi saluted his superior as the older officer neared.

"My dear colonel," the general said. "You didn't enjoy the show?"

Safavi had little use for humor, but the general liked to needle his protégé. Having ordered Safavi here against his will, the general knew the officer was impatient to leave.

"I tire of empty boasts, General," Safavi replied as the other officer fell in step beside him. He tempered his tone to show the proper deference, and his respect was genuine. Roghani might look like a fat politician now, like so many of the senior IRGC officers, but he was a true warrior. He was among the handful of men who shaped the Qods Force into what it was today, and his victories against Iran's foes were legendary: Beirut in 1983; Buenos Aires, 1994; Khobar, 1996; Karbala, 2007.

"The Israelis see through these charades," Safavi continued. "Our missile forces don't frighten them."

"Not yet," Roghani said. "The Supreme Leader understands that."

The invocation of the Supreme Leader was a subtle warning. Safavi knew he was considered arrogant and headstrong. But he also knew Roghani prized his ability to think. And to take risks. Very few in the IRGC were willing to do that, and Roghani had plucked him from the mass of young sycophants in the officer corps and groomed him for a unique role.

"Besides," Roghani continued, "we *want* the Americans and the Jews to think they are seeing nothing new."

"I understand." In a lowered voice, Safavi added, "Still, this posturing is nothing but a waste of time."

"Listen to me," Roghani said. "The operation is in motion. Curb your impatience. You and your men may soon play the pivotal role in putting the truth into the boasts of men like that." Roghani cocked his head at the missile force commander. "If the Supreme Leader decides it's time."

May. If. For all their talk, the clerics were weak. When it came to building a greater Iran, they vacillated. Like old women wringing their hands.

He wouldn't waver, if given the chance.

"Alizadeh should report within a few days," Roghani said. His tone indicated that the discussion should be left at that.

Safavi bit back a sarcastic comment at the mention of the civilian's name. Another weak man.

"If it's God's will," he replied instead.

"Just be ready."

Safavi saluted his commander and strode towards the vehicle park, yelling for his driver.

It was time for more than sham displays. It was time to change the calculus of what was possible for his country.

If only the task would be given.

Peter lowered the pistol toward the floor. Barrett, freed from his lock on the business end of the weapon, saw it was a .45. The Englishman was dressed in sharp casual, as if he'd just come from a club. Yet his entire right pants leg below the upper thigh was soaked, and blood was pooling around his shoe. He fell against the doorjamb, ashen-faced, staggered backward into the room, and crashed to the floor.

Barrett took the weapon from Peter's hand, leaving it to one side. He inserted his hands under the man's armpits and dragged him out of the vestibule and into the room so he could better assess the damage. The door slammed behind them.

He found the bullet entrance on the inside of Peter's pant leg, high up near the inseam. He squeezed a finger through the hole in the fabric, then another, pulling and gripping until he ripped the fabric apart. Blood was pumping from the wound. The femoral artery was nicked, maybe severed. That wasn't a good sign. Barrett clamped down on the entry wound with one palm and squeezed the other one underneath the man's thigh. The exit wound was worse.

Barrett hurried to the bathroom, dripping blood on the tiled floor and sink basin, and grabbed all of the hand towels and washcloths in one swipe. Kneeling beside Peter, he formed a compress over the entry wound and forced wads of the terry cloth material into the cavity on the backside of the leg. Peter stared at the ceiling.

"Hang in there. I've got you."

Barrett had seen this done. He'd trained for it.

He clamped down on the wound as hard as he could and looked around. *That'll work.* He let go of the bandages long enough to dive the length of the bed, grab the lamp off the bedside nightstand, and yank it toward the Brit. The cord ripped out of the wall socket and upset the nightstand in the process. The lamp fell, crushing the shade and shattering the bulb, but he pulled it close enough to the man's thigh so he had the whole cord to work with. He slipped it around Peter's leg and pulled it into a half knot, cinching it as tight as he could. The cord dug into the man's flesh. Barrett looked around and grabbed the TV remote from where it'd fallen off the nightstand. Placing one end on the tourniquet, he tied a square knot in the cord and cranked the remote around in circles, ratcheting the vice around Peter's thigh. The remote's plastic case gave way with a crack, but the innards held firm. Barrett cranked the makeshift handle in circles, while wiping the blood away from the wound as best he could until he could see the flow was stopped. He secured the remote against Peter's thigh with one of the man's shoelaces.

He dipped a forefinger in the blood on the carpet and finger-painted a red "T" on Peter's forehead. Maybe civilian doctors didn't care about this, but it was what he'd been taught long ago.

"Peter. Can you hear me?"

The man was conscious but unresponsive. Barrett loosened the man's clothes to help treat for shock.

"Listen to me," Barrett stood to grab the phone, "help is on the way."

The man's eyelids fluttered. "Wait," he said. His breathing was labored. "Wait—"

"We'll get you a doc asap," Barrett interrupted.

"Listen to *me*."

He was half-listening to the wounded man as the phone rang unanswered in his other ear. The man was in shock. Why wouldn't the desk answer the goddamn phone?

"Take the backpack." Peter was on the verge of passing out.

"I don't understand," was all Barrett managed before the desk finally answered.

"Hello? I need help, a doctor, paramedics on the eighteenth floor. There's a shooting. What…yes! At least five bodies. I'm with a man who needs a hospital now. I don't know what room… I'll open the door. Hurry." He dropped the phone back on its cradle.

"Take it to your intelligence people."

Barrett heard the voice but didn't understand. "What?"

"On the chair."

He looked around. He had no idea what the man was

talking about.

"Please," the man said as Barrett knelt beside him. "You're a soldier. Take the backpack. Go to your embassy." The Brit lost consciousness.

He was not going to let this man die. The others he hadn't been able to help, but this one he could.

Barrett heard running steps and muffled shouts in the corridor. He advanced to the door to open it but hesitated. What was the Brit talking about? What did being a soldier have to do with anything?

A small blue and silver backpack lay in the desk chair across the room. *Intelligence people,* the man said. Take the backpack to the embassy. Intelligence.

Barrett stood with his hand on the doorknob. Something clicked, images popping unbidden into his mind. Another hotel in Dubai. A couple of years ago. Barrett knew what his next choice should be, but the little voice he'd spent the past six years learning to ignore was hammering away inside his head.

Barrett rushed across the room, grabbed the backpack and slung it over a shoulder.

He opened the door onto pandemonium. Hotel staff and security personnel were bumping into each other, everyone shouting into hand-held radios with little effect. No one was sure what to do other than call for the police. Several employees were bending over the bodies in the hall, but Barrett already knew how little could be done for those people.

He'd wait and make sure the EMTs found Peter. At least the former Para stood a chance of living.

All the while the pack on his back felt more and more conspicuous. He was getting involved. That's the way he'd always gone. Taking the extra step to help a buddy. Only this buddy had somehow gotten himself shot in a fancy resort, for a reason that Barrett had yet to determine.

4

B ack in his room, Barrett slammed down two glasses of cold tap water. As he set the tumbler on the bathroom counter, he saw the bloody fingerprints wrapping around the glass. He turned on the hot water and scrubbed his hands.

What the hell had he stumbled on?

Medical personnel had arrived and taken charge of Peter. They were followed by the police, who eyed him with suspicion, seeing the blood all over his hands and clothes. One of the EMTs said something to the cops as they wheeled Peter past on a stretcher, and that seemed to keep Barrett from getting cuffed and frisked. With a hotel staff member translating, he explained to an officer that he had found the bodies in the hall and helped the Brit. *That was it*. The policeman and his partner were young, nervous, and clearly overwhelmed by the responsibility of securing a crime scene with multiple bodies. After an hour or more, and reiterating several times through the translator that Barrett stay in his room, they let him come down to his floor.

A man he met that afternoon over a beer was bleeding out from a gunshot wound. Five other victims—victims or assailants?—that he could see, lay in the hall. The man gave him a backpack to take to the intelligence people at the embassy.

So, what was the intelligence?

Barrett dumped the contents of the blue and silver backpack onto a circular table in the corner of the room. Maps and guide books—some English, others in Arabic— an opened roll of snack wafers, a bottle of headache pills, and a kidney-shaped travel pillow. He turned the pack upside down and shook, but that was it. Turning the pack over again, he noticed the small zippered compartment on an inside wall, sized just right for holding a passport. The fabric formed a small lump. He unzipped the pouch and pulled out a small red computer flash drive.

Taking his laptop out of his own pack, he inserted the drive into a USB port. The drive contained no files, and all two gigs of memory were still available. He felt around in the side pockets of the backpack, double-checking, but came up with nothing else.

None of the contents strewn on the table in front of him seemed worthy of calling the United States embassy, let alone visiting it. He could just picture the encounter with the Marine security element.

Uh, yes, Sergeant. A strange man who said he was British, but I don't think he was, who got shot last night, told me to give this backpack to you. Actually, to the intel guys. Can I come in and talk to the Chief of Station?

He threw all the items, including the red flash drive, back into the pack and zipped it up.

His thoughts circled back to the moment of recognition that swept over him in Peter's room. Violence, with an international flavor, in a Dubai hotel. He wasn't technically in Dubai, but close enough.

Two or three years ago the Israelis had assassinated a top Hamas leader traveling in the UAE. A diplomatic uproar ensued when the Dubai police released hotel security video and the forged passport photos of the suspected Israeli agents. It caused a media sensation for weeks. Even if Barrett hadn't been a think-tank analyst, he would have followed the story like millions of other people, fascinated at the voyeuristic peek into real-world spy craft.

So what was this? Another Mossad hit? A botched one? Maybe Hamas's security goons weren't sleeping this time.

He was pretty sure of one thing. Peter was no British tourist.

Barrett took the blue and silver backpack, compressed it and shoved it into the bottom of his own backpack.

The idea of waking up Dave and Amy was not one he relished. His friend would be sound asleep, curled up in bed with an intelligent, beautiful woman. He, on the other hand, was alone in his room. But he needed to talk this through with someone.

The clock on the nightstand read 12:34 when he picked up the phone and dialed Dave's room.

"Dave. Come down to my room right now."

"Okay…"

"I need your help with something."

"Sure."

"Make sure you're dressed to go out," he said. "Wallet, keys, passport."

Three minutes later, Dave phoned back. "What the hell's going on?"

"What happened?"

"You wake me up at oh-dark-thirty, and when I try to leave my room, everyone's going ape-shit. A hotel staffer is yelling at me, and when I start to push my way past, a cop comes running up. Very high-strung."

Barrett gave his friend a rundown of the events from the time he stepped off the elevator on the eighteenth.

"What do you want to do?" Dave asked at last. "I'll get to your room, one way or another."

Barrett needed to think. It didn't sound like the cops were going to allow them to make an early morning trip to the U.S. embassy.

"I don't know. There's no reason for me to trust this guy. Except he gave me that backpack out of desperation. It wasn't planned."

"Maybe he was just desperate to get it out of his room," Dave said. "You sure there's nothing in it? Drugs?"

"Nothing I can see."

"So we forget about it. Toss the bag in a dumpster."

"Dave, if this Peter works for who I think he does, then the people on the other side aren't exactly friendlies. I don't want this backpack, but I don't think I can just leave it lying around."

Dave was not a complicated soul. "Okay. We take it to the embassy," he concluded.

Barrett had his laptop open and was searching the Internet. "The embassy's in Abu Dhabi. But there's a consulate in Dubai, in the Bur Dubai."

"I know the area. It'll take us two and a half hours to get there."

That seemed like a long time to be exposed with material that was potentially incriminating. Barrett shifted gears from his earlier plan. "I'm expecting a visit from the police. I'm the closest thing they have to a witness. Let's see how that goes. Maybe the right thing is to turn the bag over to them."

"That's an option," Dave said. "I'd say trust your instincts."

"Maybe when we get the all-clear, we'll take that ride to the consulate."

"Sounds like a plan," Dave said. "In the meantime, get some sleep. And Barrett?"

"Yeah?"

"Try not to walk into any more firefights in this nice hotel tonight, okay?"

Dave's inclination to be a wise-ass, no matter the circumstances, was reassuring in its familiarity. It was good to know that his old Army buddy was with him on this.

Barrett went back to the bathroom and started the hot water in the shower.

It was still a pathetic commentary on his life that right now he had no one else to turn to. Dave had told him to bring someone along, but Barrett didn't have anyone special to invite on this trip. He hadn't had one for a long time.

He turned the water as hot as he could stand, and stood there as it drummed on his scalp.

Even though the time difference made it daylight in the States, reaching out to his family was not really an option either. Not with his father gone. And not after his last discouraging visit with his mother and siblings.

Barrett stepped out of the shower and toweled off. He picked his bloodstained clothes off the floor and threw them into the tub. He'd just put on a pair of jeans and T-shirt when someone knocked on the door. He opened to find four police officers standing on the threshold.

"Mr. Ross?"

The first man wore a pressed uniform of a tan blouse and matching trousers, with a red cord looped through the epaulette on one shoulder. A dark green peaked cap with gold insignia sat on his head. He was a trim man in his late forties, with intelligent eyes and a sharp black goatee and mustache.

"My name is Colonel Al-Hashimi," the man said in

fluent English. "I am chief of the Department of Criminal Investigation. I represent the chief of the Dubai Police, as well as the prime minister, his majesty Sheikh al-Maktoum. May I come in?"

Barrett stepped aside. They had really pulled out some big guns for this investigation. Then again, it wasn't every day that six people were slaughtered.

"This is Captain Rafai, my acting deputy on this investigation," Hashimi said. Rafai looked rumpled in comparison to Hashimi's crispness, with a paunch to boot. The chief didn't introduce the two officers wearing dark green berets.

"Mr. Ross, I need to ask you about what you saw tonight. Also, I request your cooperation in allowing us to search your room."

"Of course. I have nothing to hide."

As the words came out, he remembered his backpack, set right out in the open on top of the bedspread. Maybe he should have hidden it. Nothing should make the police suspicious. Except the fact that he had one backpack shoved inside another.

He realized, as he mulled over these thoughts, that he was already planning on keeping the pack and turning it over to the American authorities as the Brit requested. He wasn't going to volunteer that information to the police.

"Thank you," Hashimi said with a quick nod to the two junior officers. They began going through the closet and chest of drawers.

The police chief pointed at the two chairs opposite the writing desk. The other officer, Rafai, hovered, seemingly unsure whether to follow the interview or supervise the searchers.

Hashimi asked what brought Barrett to the UAE, and he explained the invitation from Dave, and how he came to be on the eighteenth floor.

Hashimi listened, but Barrett could tell he wasn't in danger of being a prime suspect. The policeman seemed to be thinking of the thousand other things he needed to accomplish after this interview.

When he explained about finding and treating Peter, Al-Hashimi asked, "Did you know this man?"

"I met him today, at the pool-side bar," he replied.

Al-Hashimi's placid expression changed, as if startled by an unanticipated confession. He took out a small leather-bound notebook as Barrett described the chance meeting with the British tourist, their brief conversation, and then Peter leaving with his wife, or girlfriend, he wasn't sure which.

"The British woman," Hashimi asked, "had you seen her before? Or since?"

"No."

"Besides the man named Peter, to whom you gave medical aid, did you recognize any of the bodies upstairs?" Hashimi asked.

"I don't think so," he replied. "The first body I saw in the hallway was a Westerner, and bald. I saw two men in the hallway, but they looked like Arabs. Another body lay in the doorway, but—"

Hashimi looked up from his notebook.

"Wait," Barrett said. "There was another man." Barrett described the bookish man with the receding hairline who stumbled out of the room and fled toward the emergency exit.

Hashimi's quiet grunt was noncommittal. Barrett wasn't sure if the man was pleased to have a clue, or upset to have another identity to track down. "Is there anything else you can tell me, Mr. Ross?"

A professional law enforcement officer, a polite and intelligent man, representing a nation with whom the United States had good relations, was asking if he had anything to add to aid a criminal investigation.

"No, sir. I can't think of anything else."

Hashimi said that in the morning all the guests would be free to attend breakfast in any of the hotel's restaurants, but the police were asking everyone to remain on resort grounds until further notice. By this time the junior officers had completed their search and were standing at parade rest, awaiting their boss.

He realized that the policeman named Rafai had moved somewhere behind him during the interview. He glanced over his shoulder. Rafai was zipping up the backpack with a bored expression.

As he stood to leave, Colonel Hashimi scrutinized his primary witness.

"Mr. Ross, this incident is not without precedent. It is not the first time the sovereignty of the United Arab Emirates has been violated by the extra-judicial activities of foreign parties. His Majesty has lost all patience with this."

Hashimi paused, searching Barrett's face. "Among the dead is a senior official from a neighboring state. As I think you have already reasoned out, your friends from the pool were not British tourists on holiday. This investigation has the highest priority within my government. If you remember anything, contact my office immediately."

"I understand."

"Good morning."

As he closed the door after the policemen, Barrett felt a small resurgence of his former adrenaline. He was committing to a course of action without understanding where it was taking him.

Yeah, the intrigue was exciting. He had a conflicting idea, though: *this is above my pay grade*. That's what soldiers said when they got stuck with a hot potato that put them between two higher-ups who were vying for control. He needed to put his *duty first* instinct in check. This was most definitely not his fight, and he was kidding himself if he thought he had any business getting involved. He wasn't a soldier anymore, and he certainly wasn't a spook.

He'd do what the spy named Peter had asked, but the sooner he got rid of the pack, the better. He was supposed to be enjoying some R&R.

5

Safavi saw the mistake before anyone else.

He'd returned to the Iranian military base he commanded north of Qom earlier in the evening, just in time for the night's training at the live-fire complex.

From a vantage point on the catwalk that ran along the thick walls of the shoot house, he watched through his night-vision goggles as teams cleared the rooms and hallways. They flowed through the complex, the men leapfrogging each other in a lethal choreography punctuated by gunfire and grenades blasts.

In the room directly beneath Safavi, lifelike mannequins in American-style camouflage uniforms were propped against walls and seated in chairs. In the hallway outside, a four-man team staged in a line against the wall. The student-leader gave a hand signal, and the number one-man shotgunned the doorknob before kicking it open. The team poured through the breach, engaging targets in their sectors, then proceeded to the next room. Safavi walked along the catwalk, following the team through the maze.

He watched through the metal grating beneath his feet as the students reached another room. Confusion broke out this time as the four soldiers jockeyed for position near the door. He turned his head away as a soldier tossed a flash-bang. The one-man and two-man burst through the door, engaging targets and moving to their points of domination in opposite corners.

The three-man charged through the door and stepped to his right, the four-man behind him, moving to the left. The four-man stopped with his back against the wall, engaging the mannequin on the opposite wall with two shots. He swept his AUG A3 to the right, engaging a target in the farthest corner, then swung the assault rifle farther right to shoot a target just off the corner.

The trainer following the team caught the mistake. A whistle blast halted the exercise, followed by shouts and confusion. The overhead lights were thrown on, and Safavi pushed the night-vision goggles on top his head.

A round had blown through the one-man's neck. He was bleeding out, staining the plywood floor. Medical personnel rushed in, surrounding the casualty. The man hadn't stopped where he was supposed to, but continued a few feet along the next wall. In the haze and dust kicked up by the flash-bang, using his night-vision goggles, the four-man mistook his team member for a target mannequin. Some of these soldiers had made the same mistake with blank ammunition. Now they were seeing firsthand how unforgiving reality could be.

Instructors escorted the rest of the shaken trainees from the complex.

Safavi found his deputy hovering just beyond the circle of medics working on the dying man. "Colonel Hessaby. Who is it?"

Second Colonel Ali Hessaby blanched at the sight of his commander overhead. "Hamandani, sir," he reported.

"A new man."

"Status?"

Hessaby pursed his lips and shook his head.

"Bring the others in and have them see this. They need to understand the cost of mistakes."

"Yes, sir," Hessaby said. He conferred with the senior medic before hustling out of the room to track down the team leaders.

Safavi climbed down the ladder on the exterior of the shoot house and made his way in the dark across the compound to the low-slung building that was his headquarters.

He listed in his mind the points he would make to his junior leaders at the morning meeting. They would watch the infrared video from inside the shoot house; they would see the recruit die. He would show them video of other armies doing the same exercise, correctly.

Entering his office, Safavi logged onto his computer. He had unrestricted Internet access. His force, Ansar-ol-Mahdi, was to be patterned off the special operations units of the West. Especially the Americans. General Roghani had given him unprecedented leeway to equip and train the unit as he saw fit. Being practical, Safavi knew better than to start from scratch. What was the American expression? Don't reinvent the wheel?

Ansar-ol-Mahdi's existence was barely known among the most senior men in the IRGC, even within the Qods Force. The Americans, on the other hand, bragged about everything they did. If Safavi could not find what he needed on websites of the American government, he searched among the many paramilitary "SWAT" forces, all eager to swagger and show off their skills on YouTube. Some of the videos were laughable. But others were very instructive.

Books, too. The Americans loved to write about their

exploits in "secret" units, and he read everything they published about Iraq, Afghanistan, and—

Colonel Hessaby knocked on the doorframe, interrupting his thoughts.

"Sir, may I come in?"

"Certainly." Hessaby was a methodical officer. He could even be hesitant and plodding. But Safavi appreciated the man's careful approach as a complement to his own aggressiveness. If Hessaby was conventional, he was also smart. Safavi made a point of always considering his counsel.

"Sir, Hamandani makes the second man in three weeks. That's eleven fatalities and seventeen injuries in six months."

"Colonel Hessaby—" Safavi began, but checked himself. "Tea?" he asked.

"Yes, thank you." Hessaby sat in a chair opposite his commander's desk.

A small table near the wall held the samovar. Safavi placed loose tea and a pinch of crushed rose petals in a metal infuser and poured the boiling water over it. The beautiful scent wafted up to him. He replaced the lid of the teapot to let it steep.

"It is unfortunate," he said.

"My concern, Colonel, is the loss of another man who has received substantial training, for whom much time—"

"I know," Safavi cut him off. "But I have a schedule. One which may not accommodate every man's individual abilities."

Safavi glanced at his second in command as he poured the tea into glass cups. The man's brow was furrowed.

"Sir, is it not counterproductive to lose these men—"

"Most of the men are not getting themselves killed, that is my point."

He could see his deputy was struggling with what tack

to take as he accepted the cup of tea.

"Let me ask you," he continued. "Do you believe in the mission we train for?"

"Yes, of course."

"What it means to our people?"

"Yes, but—"

"I believe in it. That is why I am willing to push these men as hard as I can. We need quick learners. If Hamandani and the others are part of a culling process, so be it."

"But—"

"These men who die, they die as martyrs. They know it. They embraced this risk." Safavi set his cup down too hard, sloshing the tea across the desk. "If any of the others want to return to their old units, let them go. They can goose-step through the next Sacred Defense Parade in white spats. Like simple-minded chimps!"

Hessaby rose from his seat quietly, thanking his commander for the tea. He departed, closing the door behind him softly.

Safavi mopped up the spilled tea with an old paper. He then worked through more video clips, selecting the ones to show to his leaders to reinforce the proper technique.

Hessaby's concern, his fear, was indicative of the issues Safavi faced in forging an elite unit within the larger Qods Force. They were to be a unit comparable to their Western enemies, but with a most unique mission. The men had shown they could adapt to new weapons, new skills, and new techniques. Successful tactics at this level, though, required men who could also think for themselves. Act decisively and rapidly, without a senior officer directing every move.

Safavi was willing to do this. He would do it, when necessary.

He locked his computer and went back outside.

Standing in the shadow beneath the entrance's overhang, he lit a cigarette. Far in the distance, the white tip of Damavand Mountain rose above a strata of moonlit clouds. Legend said Arash the Archer, at the end of an ancient war, shot his bow from the summit of Damavand. The arrow traveled a thousand leagues to mark the border of Iran.

Where would the borders of greater Iran be five years from now?

Pleased with the vision, Safavi marched across the nighttime compound. Passing the motor pool, he headed for the concrete tunnel system he'd built beneath the sand at great expense. A muffled explosion greeted him as he drew near. His most experienced teams were working with precision charges and cutting torches inside the tunnels. They needed to master the difficulties of working with high explosives and deadly gases in confined spaces.

They had many skills to perfect in a short amount of time.

In her room on the third floor of the Millennium Dubai Airport Hotel, Sada vaguely registered her reflection in the blank television screen. She wished she could make her mind go blank as well. She wished she could un-imagine the horror of what happened in that hallway.

Three hours ago, the secured call awoke her. The detached voice from Ops-Relay in Austria gave the SitRep. The target was intercepted and eliminated, but the team was compromised. Aaron had managed to call in while fleeing with Nuri and Kaela to a safe-house in Abu Dhabi. Dov, Gil, and Yoni were down, presumed dead. Jacob was wounded and in police custody.

Sada was to proceed with her outbound flight as scheduled.

She'd left the Al Batinah Resort the evening before and checked into this hotel five minutes from the main terminal, scheduled for an eight a.m. flight to Frankfurt. After her encounter with the man in Alizadeh's room, Jacob insisted she depart before everyone else, even if they were short a team. If someone looked, the hotel security cameras would show her activities several hours before the rest of the team's movements.

Jacob. Why didn't he abort? Was it his sense of duty? Or overconfidence?

The other two Iranians were bodyguards, after all. Two experienced shooters, and not the perfunctory security usually assigned to Alizadeh in Tehran.

The third man, the one she subdued and hustled to Jacob's room, was not Iranian, or a bodyguard. He was a complication, though. They couldn't interrogate the man, not under the circumstance, so Jacob simply sedated him. But her team leader couldn't hide his concern. Despite his practiced, cool demeanor, she knew he feared the mission was unraveling. He should have listened to his instincts.

Sada's cellphone rang again. The voice from Austria said, "Stand by," followed by a series of clicks. Then, "We have more information." A new voice this time. Male, middle-aged, but she couldn't place the face. It didn't matter. Another shift had taken over the operations center at the Institute.

Sada remained silent.

"Your man is from Kazakhstan. Timur Ismagulov, as his passport says. It's interesting."

Her team was decimated. The people she had come to think of as family. She could have done without *interesting*.

"How?"

"Ismagulov was a low-level KGB officer based in Astana. When the Soviets dissolved in '92, he transitioned to the KNB, Kazakhstan's National Security Committee.

He left in 2004 on a small pension."

"Why was he meeting Alizadeh?"

"We're not sure. But the Kazakh came to the our attention over the winter."

"Yes?"

"We intercepted chatter. A Central Asian source was trying to contact AQ to sell something. We tracked this to Ismagulov. Then everything went cold. No more communications through the intermediaries we knew of. Either AQ didn't trust him, or he found another middle man."

"Suddenly he's meeting with the head of Iran's nuclear weapons program. What use would he be to the Iranians?"

"Jacob might know."

"I don't know if he found anything. We had to sedate the man quickly. We called in the passport, and I left."

"You said before the man had a bag. Where is it now?"

"I assume the police will have found it in Jacob's room. Unless there were more Iranians we don't know about."

"A friend at the hotel tells us someone was with Jacob when the police arrived," the man said.

"Who?"

"An American tourist. He gave Jacob first aid until medical personnel arrived."

"Do we know who he is?"

"The police questioned him. His name is Barrett Ross."

Why did she know that name? It was an unusual name—

He'd been one of the men at the pool bar. Not the big one. The other one, the sandy-haired American with the slimmer build. The one Jacob had forced her to talk to when all she wanted to do was figure out who the men by the pool with Alizadeh were.

What was this American doing in the operation? Was he following Jacob? Was he drunk? Was he an operative?

"I should find this man."

"No. You leave on your flight as scheduled. The police are already combing through the security footage."

"Maybe this American compromised the team."

"Eight a.m. Be on that flight. Report in when you reach Frankfurt."

The line to Ops Relay clicked dead.

Her stomach turned again. Sure, she was afraid. But she was almost physically ill with the thought of getting on that flight this morning. She would be giving up on an assignment, making the others' sacrifices meaningless. Even if Alizadeh had been eliminated.

Sada understood what an order was. She also knew that following orders blindly could get people hurt. She was the one in a position to accurately assess the situation. Not Austria. Not the Institute. If she ran, they might never know what happened or why.

Sada began pacing the floor. She must get a grip on her anxiety level. She had to be able to function efficiently, now more than ever.

Is this what had happened to Avigail? Had the stress become overwhelming? Her best friend, the one person she could always turn to, had been pulled from operational duty two months ago. She was only the most recent in a series of female operatives who were currently undergoing psych evaluations and counseling. The halls at headquarters were rife with rumors, and Sada had heard the whisperings. Some said the standards had been lowered, and the younger generation wasn't tough enough. *Especially the women.* Other voices, sympathetic, said the demands of constant operations in recent years was a strain the old guard, neither men nor women, had ever had to suffer.

Avigail had been in her training cohort. The girl was as strong as any of them. And now she was just trying to regain some semblance of control.

Sada's first few years with the Institute had been exciting. Her missions in Europe helped keep tabs on the front organizations of Hamas and Hezbollah. But the extremes between stultifying boredom and panic, always leavened by a constant state of high tension, it wore on a person. A decade after her recruitment, and six years after joining the kidon, she was realizing the pressure was not sustainable. Not for her. If she managed to escape from Dubai, she would not let herself come to the point Avigail and the others had.

That worry was one she must put in the back of her mind. For now, she needed to salvage what she could of the situation. The mission was not complete, as far as she was concerned, and she was the only one on her team who wasn't dead or running for her life.

She would find the American and do what she needed to get the information. He might become just one more American who'd regret venturing into the Middle East.

6

$\mathbf{B}$arrett pulled himself out of bed at seven o'clock. As he splashed water on his face, he thought about checking to see if Dave and Amy were awake but decided to leave them alone. Although he was not hungry, he headed off to the breakfast buffet with hopes of grabbing a coffee and walking out to the beach.

A smattering of guests sat at tables throughout the dining room. The coffee urn at the end of the buffet was empty, and Barrett flagged down a waiter to see if he could get it filled.

"I can spare some while you wait." A large man in a business suit addressed him from a nearby table.

The man was about sixty years old, with a full head of white hair and wire-rimmed glasses. His substantial girth filled the chair, and he held the *Financial Times* in a meaty hand. He indicated the chair across from him with the other hand.

"You sure you don't mind?" Barrett asked.

"Not at all," the man said with a southern accent. "I saw your Penn State shirt."

"You went to Penn State?" Barrett asked, pulling a chair out.

"Oh, no," the man chuckled. "Tennessee Volunteer, born and bred. But you're a fellow American—and you looked like you could use a cup of coffee."

"Thank you." Barrett took the offered coffee pot. He savored the taste of his first shot of caffeine and, putting the cup down, asked, "Where in Tennessee?"

"I live in Knoxville now. What about yourself?"

"I'm originally from a small town called Titusville. Far northwestern corner of Pennsylvania, up by Lake Erie."

"Way up north. You're a serious Yankee."

"We probably have more in common than you think. Where I grew up, people call it Pennsyl-tucky."

"A fellow redneck. Bless you," the man said. He extended his hand across the table. "Tommy McCowan."

"Barrett Ross. Pleasure to meet you."

Redneck—the man didn't know the half of it. The small towns and hilly country of Crawford County could be anyplace in the foothills of the Appalachians, north or south. The hills of North Carolina or the backwoods of West Virginia. The kind of place most people never left if they were born there.

Like his brother and sister.

Life was hard enough in the area, even for the people who were smart and hard-working. Nothing came easy in a region that hadn't seen any real prosperity since the country's first oil boom petered out in 1900, and Standard Oil and everyone else moved on to Texas. Opportunities for making a decent living were hard to come by. It didn't help if your primary pursuit was partying, or if your choice of life partner was an absolute deadbeat.

Jamie was in relationship that was going nowhere, having settled for the lowest common denominator the area had to offer. Nate, now twenty-seven, was still "the kid" to everyone. Welcomed at all the bars, and doing absolutely nothing with his life. Dad had given up on both kids, while his mother made excuses for them, which put a constant strain on their relationship until the end.

You could carve out a decent life if you tried. His dad had made the effort, working thirty years as a skilled machinist in the plant over in Franklin. Life had looked good for a while, especially to the son who got to be the first one to go off to college. When the family started to go sour, Barrett had been caught up in his own life in Happy Valley, PA. His siblings were six and nine years younger than him, and by the time he took notice, they'd already made their important decisions. Or not.

"Business or pleasure?" the man asked, bringing Barrett back to the present.

"Vacation," he replied. "Yourself?"

"Work, mostly."

"What type of business?"

"MENAC 2013. The Middle East and North Africa Nuclear Construction conference."

That caught Barrett's attention. At work, he focused on conventional capabilities: how many soldiers, tanks, and planes countries had. More important, whether they knew how to use them. But he followed all issues related to national security. Nuclear proliferation was a hot topic currently, with tons of mainstream news stories about sanctions, failed diplomacy, and preemptive strikes.

"That must make some people nervous," Barrett said.

The man chuckled. "This is all about peaceful uses of the atom." Then he dropped his voice as if to share an inside scoop. "Nuclear power is big business in the region. The market here for new plants will top $350 billion this year."

"That's big."

"The UAE, Jordan, Saudi Arabia, Kuwait, they've all

got projects in the pipeline."

"What about nonproliferation concerns?"

"The IAEA—that's the International Atomic Energy Agency—has its people all over the place. Half the conference is about licensing requirements and import restrictions. And security."

"Where do you fit in?" he asked.

"My company manufacturers precision components used inside the plants' equipment. The conference's a chance to meet and greet the bigwigs building the projects."

The man handed him a business card. Tommy McCowan was the founder and CEO of CarbonTec, a company headquartered in Knoxville. The card indicated a specialization in something called carbon fiber composites.

Tommy put his paper aside, and they chatted. Barrett learned Tommy had worked for the government at Oak Ridge National Laboratory before venturing out years ago as an entrepreneur in the private side of the nuclear industry. He'd flown his corporate jet to a nearby regional airport to spend a day of relaxation at the resort before the conference in Dubai.

"What do you do, Barrett?"

"I'm a military analyst in DC. I cover some of the people in this part of the world. But this trip is strictly R&R."

"Good for you," Tommy said. "Ex-military?"

He gave Tommy a quick synopsis of his eight years in the Army. He skipped his time at the bank.

Tommy was impressed, but Barrett tried to deflect the praise. Civilians always confused service with heroism. He hadn't slugged it out through Fallujah or places like that.

Tommy checked his watch, and Barrett realized he was on a schedule.

"Look's like you're headed out," Barrett said. "Police

aren't giving you any trouble?"

"When I heard what happened, I came down and spoke to the liaison they set up at the desk. Showed him my conference agenda and reservations in the city. The Emiratis can be down right helpful to people looking to do business."

As Tommy stood up to go, he asked, "Did you hear the commotion last night?"

"I saw it," Barrett replied as he poured another cup. "Or the aftermath, at least."

The businessman sat back down, in rapt attention. Barrett told the story, including the police questioning, and his own speculation about the similarities to the exposed Mossad operation back in 2010.

"I doubt these folks were Hamas," Tommy replied. "If the attackers were Israelis, I'd bet my bottom dollar the target was Iranian."

Barrett was about to ask why, but Tommy was standing again. "Hope this doesn't ruin any plans you had."

"Not really. I may have to stick to the hotel for a while, being a witness of sorts."

"Mind your p's and q's," Tommy said. "The Dubai police are competent. You don't want to end up in a Dubai jail cell, from what I hear."

Barrett grunted in assent and took the man's offered hand.

"Thanks again for your service."

Then the older gentleman strode through the restaurant toward the lobby.

Barrett finished his coffee with a swallow and headed upstairs. The businessman had a point about staying on the authorities' good side. But Barrett wasn't keen to piss off the other interested parties, either. He'd let someone at the embassy decide how much to tell the police.

* * *

The Dassault Falcon 900B business jet approached from over the coastline and landed on Runway 29 at Fujairah International Airport. The pilot throttled back the engines as the plane touched down just past the yellow arrows marking the runway's leading edge.

Safavi was pleased, given the circumstances. They'd made the 1,200-kilometer trip from the Revolutionary Guard airfield northwest of Qom to the east coat of the UAE in an hour and a half. No other element in the entire military could do this.

Safavi was part of the new order, though. He'd learned much from General Masoud Roghani, Commander of the Qods Force, and used that knowledge to hone to his skills in battle against the Americans in Iraq. The Arabs were tiresome, but the munitions and training Safavi had given them served a greater cause.

For too long the Iranians had suffered the insolence of foreigners. The British, the Russians, always the Arabs, and now the Americans. Didn't his own family bear the scars of these wars? His grandfather died fighting British troops when they and the Russians plundered his country under the pretext of fighting the Germans. Forty years later, his father, an old man, died liberating Khorramshahr from the Iraqis. One of millions of lives wasted by the bumbling clerics in the early days of the Revolution.

He felt a deep sense of satisfaction, a feeling in his gut that things were moving in the right direction. His father and grandfather died expelling foreigners from Iran; he had fought to expel the Americans from Iran's backyard. Now he and his men were taking the next step.

The plane reached the end of the runway and turned onto the parallel taxiway. He was just fifty kilometers south of Alizadeh's hotel.

It helped they were on heightened alert since the day before. General Roghani called to inform him when the Kazakh failed to make the meeting with Alizadeh. Safavi pulled his leaders from training and gave them contingency orders. At 12:30 in the morning, two o'clock Dubai time, Roghani called again. The Scientist had called in, beside himself with fear.

Attackers had killed Alizadeh, along with Safavi's two men. The Scientist claimed the Israeli assassins were all dead, too, except for one man, who allowed him to flee. The Scientist was not a strong man, and Safavi didn't trust his judgment. In his haste to flee, he'd probably bumped into a bellboy. If it had been a Mossad agent, he wouldn't be alive to report in.

The question was, how much did the Israelis know? Was this assault merely aimed at Alizadeh, taking advantage of his travel outside Tehran? That was the likely scenario—another of his country's nuclear officials assassinated by the Zionists.

Or did the Israelis know about Ismagulov?

Safavi should have been the one who met the Kazakh in the first place. Alizadeh was never important to the mission, but he insisted the conference in Dubai provided the perfect cover for the meeting. In reality, Safavi knew the man just wanted an excuse to travel outside Iran, and maybe find himself an expensive European whore. The fat civilian bristled when Roghani stipulated that two of Safavi's own men would accompany him as bodyguards. Now Alizadeh's stupidity had drawn the Israelis into the situation. Safavi was left to pick up the pieces.

The three-engine Falcon taxied to a square area of tarmac surrounded by corrugated steel hangars. It was the smaller of three parking areas off the main runway. A dozen planes, business jets as well as a number of small commercial airliners available for charter were parked across it. The Dassault fit right in.

The flight plan filed with the airport would show his jet was the property of the Damavand Export Bank, Plc. What the Arabs didn't know was that Damavand Export Bank was a subsidiary of the Islamic Revolutionary Guard Corps. They had become adept over the years in creating shell businesses, mostly for buying foreign weapons while evading American-led sanctions. Damavand Export Bank was unique. It had been created solely for the purchase of this plane and to provide a cover for the movement of Safavi's unit.

The crew completed their shutdown procedures while Safavi's men waited in their seats. He had with him fifteen of his most experienced operatives. They were dressed in business casual, ready to disappear among the wealthy tourists, or don a jacket and tie to pose as businessmen in Dubai's financial district.

A white pickup pulled up outside. Colonel Hessaby walked down the passenger steps and met the Arab who got out. The customs man. Their customs man, who would take a cursory look at the cargo hold, sign off the paperwork, and walk away richer.

Another Arab got out of the passenger side of the pickup.

"Ah, Amir. Come in," Safavi said as the man poked his head into the cabin.

"Colonel," the man said.

They exchanged pleasantries, and he made a show of affording the Arab the proper respect, for Amir led their allied forces in the UAE.

"Sit," Safavi said, pointing at a nearby swivel chair. "Our visit is unexpected, I know. I have an important mission for you."

"We are ready for anything, Colonel."

"Once we get to your compound, I will explain in

greater detail. For now, I need you to do three things."

"Anything, of course."

"First," Safavi said, pushing a manila folder with a copy of a passport photo to the Arab. "This man—his name is Ismagulov. A Kazakh. I need to know if the police have him in custody. If so, we need to talk with him immediately."

"Yes, sir. Our man is well situated in the chief of police's office."

"Good. Second, I need to know the status of the investigation into the hotel shooting. As it unfolds. And I want the passport photos of the assassins before they are released to the media."

The man nodded.

"Finally, I need police vehicles. At least two. Five or six uniforms as well."

"Sir, I don't—" the man began to protest.

"Do what you have to," Safavi snapped. "This would not be a good time for your first failure."

"I understand."

"Good."

Safavi looked out the window. The team had gathered on the tarmac, and Hessaby was supervising their loading of the cases of weapons and equipment into three white Toyota panel vans pulled up alongside the plane.

"Amir, beyond your soldiers, how many active sympathizers can you mobilize on short notice?"

"Thousands and thousands, Colonel," the proxy force commander answered.

Safavi smiled. He knew the man exaggerated, in typical Arab fashion. By thousands, he meant hundreds. Still, he might need a useful core around which to build.

Safavi stood.

"Let's go. My team needs to set up, and I need to find my Scientist."

* * *

Back in his room, Barrett cleaned up and called Dave and Amy about meeting for breakfast. When he sat down twenty minutes later in the restaurant, Amy pumped him for all the details of the previous night. She sat stunned as he told them everything. He lowered his voice, feeling silly even as he did so, when he got to the part about Peter asking him to take the backpack.

"Barrett, it must have been awful," Amy said, "seeing all of that, I mean."

He didn't respond but instead studied his grapefruit and eggs. The incident last night felt abstract, like he'd been watching it from outside himself and acted on autopilot. Sometimes when you were thrust into a bad situation, and forced to react, you could handle things that might otherwise seem overwhelming. He'd learned that early on, thanks to the Army.

"This Peter guy, I wonder where his lady friend is," Dave said.

"A hospital or a police station, I assume."

"I wonder when they'll let us leave," Amy said.

"I met an American businessman over coffee this morning. He got permission to leave," Barrett answered.

"Do you want to take that drive over to the consulate now?" Dave asked.

"I'm not sure I want to draw attention to myself."

"We are booked here for the week," Dave added.

Barrett didn't know if he should wait for the police to let everyone go about their business, or if he should take measures in his own hands. Where was the certainty he felt last night?

"If we can't go anywhere, then let's do what we came here to do," Amy said. She had a sense of purpose and was taking charge. "Your vacation has had a setback, Barrett.

We need to get it back on track."

The day was mainly a repeat of the one before, although the pool was more subdued. Barrett spent a good chunk of time in the afternoon reading in a lounge chair. Dave only shook his head when he saw Barrett reading Thucydides. If it wasn't the Greek historian's *Peloponnesian War*, it was some other ancient text on military or political history, and Dave was long past trying to needle his friend about it. Dave had asked him about it once, when Barrett had lugged the book on an off-duty excursion.

"This should be required reading for every American citizen," Barrett had responded.

"Why?"

"So we'd all realize that we're not any smarter than people who lived three thousand years ago. Even if we have computers. And to understand that there's nothing new under the sun."

"I think that last bit is from the Bible, though," Dave said.

Later, when they headed up to dinner, the conversation turned to work.

"How do you like your new job?" Amy asked.

"It's good. The people are smart."

"Not the same as jumping out of airplanes for a living?" Dave asked.

"Nope." He hesitated, then added, "Beats selling mortgages, though."

"Dave mentioned you worked for a bank, after the Army," Amy said.

"For about five years."

"Did you like it?"

"The bank made lots of loans to Florida condo developers."

"Is that good?" she asked.

"The bank thought it was. Until no one could pay the

loans back."

"Did you get in trouble?"

"I wasn't a lender," he explained. "I was in another part of the bank. We bundled the loans together and sold them off to people who thought they were savvy investors."

"Sounds exciting," she said.

"It was a soulless experience."

"That bad?" she asked.

He thought about what to say next. He almost said *I was making really good money, but....* Instead, he verbalized only the second half of his thought: "It took the downturn for me to realize I hated what I was doing." The truth was, for five years he'd helped the bank make obscene amounts of money over questionable deals, doing well for himself in the process. Somehow he'd moved a long way from the idealistic young man who was thrilled to be leading a platoon of soldiers.

The meal was winding down, the waiter clearing plates. Dave and Amy said they were going to stroll down to the beach. Barrett thought about finding a bar for a nightcap but decided to head up to his room instead.

With the activities of the previous night weighing on him, and a heavy dinner in his stomach, Barrett fell into bed as soon as he closed the door.

The oddest ringtone raised him to consciousness. Only hotel phones sounded like that, the short buzzes repeating, repeating, until you remembered where you were.

He groped for the clock-radio, turning the display to see the red digits blazing 3:24 a.m. *Christ Almighty.* What was it going to take to sleep through the night around here? He found the handset for the phone.

"Barrett Ross?" a woman's voice asked.

"Yes."

"Mr. Ross, did my friend Peter give you anything?"

His mind raced, but was blank for any adequate reply.

"Mr. Ross? Last night. The man you helped, did he tell you anything? Give you anything? This is important."

"Who is this?"

"My name is Susan. Peter introduced us at the bar."

An image of the woman's face flashed into his mind. His first thought was that Peter was only her friend. The woman was calling about her wounded friend. Almost as quickly, he felt stupid. Grogginess was no excuse. Peter wasn't a British tourist, and neither was this woman. She wasn't calling about a wounded friend. She was asking about the backpack.

He thought about his conversation with Tommy, and the idea of walking an imaginary line between the local police and the other, less obvious forces.

Hadn't he made his decision? Whether it was intuition, gut feel, or the circumstances of the request, he'd decided to trust the man who called himself Peter. He was going to take the bag to American officials. Could he by extension trust this woman? He wanted to.

"Yes," he replied, answering the woman's question. "He asked me to take his backpack to the American embassy. I'm going to the consulate in Dubai as soon as the police let us leave."

The woman didn't respond for several beats. He remembered she wasn't much for small talk.

"Mr. Ross, listen to me carefully. You need to leave the hotel and go to your consulate now."

"Why?"

"You saw the carnage on the eighteenth floor. Do you have somebody with you? Someone you can trust?"

"I do."

"Take them with you."

She fell silent again. What would have been an awkward pause was welcomed, because his mind was spinning through the permutations of what might happen from this point on. Jail, likely. At a minimum.

"Leave now?" he asked, stalling for time to think of the questions he should be asking.

"I'll try to help if I can. Take the bag and go. Now."

The emphasis on the last word hung in the air, even after the line went dead.

7

Dave negotiated the Audi through the parking lot with the headlights off, as his friend requested. They'd snuck out a side door to the veranda at the back of the hotel, and followed the footpath around to the parking area. Barrett insisted they avoid the front doors. Personally, he thought his friend's caution might be erring on the side of overkill. Then again, after being woken in the dead of the night by a mystery woman, maybe Barrett wasn't overreacting.

Turning onto the coastal highway headed north, Dave switched on the high beams and mashed the gas pedal.

He glanced over at his friend. Barrett was staring straight ahead. The reason for this excursion, the pack from the supposed Brit, was crammed inside the backpack at Barrett's feet.

He'd known Barrett Ross for twelve years. Whatever the woman said to him on the phone—and it didn't sound like there were many details—had galvanized his friend. Barrett wasn't a man to overreact. When he said they had to leave, Dave trusted his judgment. Barrett Ross thought things through. That's why people listened to him. Amy, still half asleep, hadn't questioned Dave's running out to help his friend either.

Barrett was always the thinker. That was the big differences between the two of them. Not that he was an idiot, or anything, but Dave preferred to dive into a mess and see what shook out. You could always adjust fire from there. Different in a lot of ways, but that's why they'd worked well together.

Dave showed up in the battalion as a cherry second lieutenant, a brand-new rifle platoon leader. By that time Barrett was the most experienced lieutenant in the unit. He had the respect of the men and NCOs, more than most officers could ever hope for. He'd earned it by consistently doing the tough jobs and, unlike many young lieutenants, doing it without showing his ass.

Dave was the loud-mouthed newcomer, annoyed at his newbie status. He didn't care much for the unofficial pecking order among people of the same rank. The only way he kept out of hot water was by being good at what he did. Barrett, to his credit, treated him as a peer from the get-go.

They shared the same sense of humor, too. Barrett, quiet by nature, could be the life of the party if given a push. Two years of road trips with the other junior officers had proven that. But at work he was a professional. An overachiever, but not resented, because he did it in his own low-key, quiet way.

Right now his usually steady friend was amped. Understandably. Whatever was going on, it was crazy. Iranian officials and Israeli spies—crazy shit, with his friend in the middle of it all. All the more reason to get to the consulate in Dubai asap.

"Thanks for the lift," Barrett said. "Hope Amy's not upset."

"No sweat. But you're buying the road sodas."

It was a shame that this was interrupting Barrett's time off. Dave had been surprised when his friend took up the offer to fly out for the visit. Dave knew his friend had been in a protracted funk for a couple of years. He'd left the Army for some reason, although Dave would never understand why, then worked himself to death at the bank, and had now switched again to a totally different profession. A think tank, for chrissakes. Dave wasn't sure what his friend was looking for.

He'd also made a point of telling Barrett to bring someone along if he wanted, but as far as he knew, there hadn't been anyone serious in Barrett's life since the girl in North Carolina.

"How are things on the woman front?" he asked.

"Nothing much happening. Few dates here and there."

"You never got serious about anyone in New York, either, when you were at the bank."

"No," Barrett said. "The women around me had a certain picture of what the perfect life in the city looked like. I think they could sense my attitude about that."

"What's going on back home?" Dave asked. "How's your family?"

His friend was quiet for too long.

"My dad passed away five months ago."

Dave concentrated on keeping the car on the road. He couldn't believe it. He'd met Barrett's parents once when they visited Fort Bragg years ago.

"Barrett, I'm so sorry. I had no idea." Why the hell didn't his friend tell him when it happened?

"He took his own life, Dave."

"God, Barrett, I really am sorry. I don't know what to say."

"You don't need to say anything. Sorry to drop this on you. I should have told you long ago."

They rode in silence until Barrett had gathered his thoughts.

"We think it was depression, undiagnosed. Everyone just chalked it up to the way he grew more and more withdrawn as he got older. I knew a lot of things were pissing him off, but no one ever saw any signs of being suicidal."

Dave's impression of Barrett's parents had been that they were good people. Obviously loved their son. His dad had seemed on the quiet side, compared to Mrs. Ross. Dave had a better sense of Barrett's siblings, because they were a constant source of frustration for his friend. He knew that Barrett's brother and sister were included in the things that had depressed Mr. Ross.

"How's your family doing?"

"Mom's coping. My siblings have moved on. Jamie's still married to the idiot-loser. Dad only visited his granddaughters when the father was out of the house, so that's a shame. That he didn't see them more often. Nate took Dad's death harder. But it sounds like he's back to his old self. Just happy to have a car and a license. No serious brushes with the law, recently, that I know of."

The car compressed the suspension hard as it leaned to the outside of the turn. He took that roundabout faster than was prudent, but the tires held. The Emiratis loved their traffic circles, even out here in the middle of nowhere. They were speeding southwest along Route 89, having bypassed the rocky heights of the Al Hajar by circling around to the north. Highway 88 would be coming up soon, and that was a straight shot across the rolling sand dunes into the capital. A small town flashed by on the right.

He was still trying to process his friend's revelation when, cresting a slight rise in the highway, he saw flashing blue lights a mile ahead of them. He immediately eased back on the accelerator.

"What the hell?"

It was clear, even in the dark, that the lights were in the center of the highway, not off on the shoulder.

"Looks like a checkpoint," Barrett said. "Do you normally see these out here?"

"No, we don't." He downshifted and slowed as they drew near. The flashing lights reflected two SUVs pulled nose to nose across the two-lane southbound side of the highway, leaving a narrow gap between the vehicles. Sawhorse barriers extended on either side of the vehicles into the median and shoulder. In addition to the SUVs, patrol cars were parked on the far side of the traffic stop with their lights going as well. Traffic was light at this time of the morning, and the Audi came to a stop behind a short line of cars and a tanker truck. Policemen with assault rifles slung across their chests were talking to the drivers of the first two vehicles. Additional men milled around the barricades. He nosed forward as the first car up front was waved through.

"I really don't want to explain what we're doing," Barrett said. "Can we turn around?"

"Without getting shot?" he asked, looking over at Barrett. That might be the most reckless thing he'd ever heard his friend suggest. Maybe he was shook up about the night before. Or he didn't understand how the police operated over here.

"Let me know, Ranger buddy," he continued, "and I'll whip us around. But I'm pretty sure you don't want to spend time in police custody. Every couple of years a tourist dies."

He could see his friend thinking it through. They weren't guilty of anything. Except leaving the hotel against police orders, and not telling the police chief about taking a bag from a foreign agent.

The line of cars and trucks advanced as another car was waved through. He hesitated instead of pulling forward, continuing to search Barrett's face. This attracted the attention of a plainclothes policeman standing at the barricade, who looked at them hard.

"Shit," he muttered, and rolled the car forward.

"All right," Barrett said. "We haven't done anything wrong."

"Right," he said, thinking the opposite.

"Pull up and smile," Barrett said. "Chances are, this has nothing to do with the resort."

Dave really, really doubted that, but he eased the car forward again.

The man in civvies, the one staring at them, was talking into a hand-held. Each of the cars in front was now getting a perfunctory glance before being sent on its way.

Finally, the tanker truck in front of them was waved through the makeshift barricade without even stopping, and the officer motioned Dave to pull forward and stop. As he did so, three policemen with automatic rifles emerged out of the gloom in the median and spaced themselves along the side of the car. As Dave rolled down his window, the man in civvies was already striding forward from the barricade.

"Get out! Get out of the auto!" he yelled.

The police manhandled Barrett and Dave into the back seat of an SUV as the plainclothes officer hopped into the front and barked an order. The driver whipped the vehicle around the barricades, bumped across the narrow median to the northbound lanes, and accelerated to what had to be over ninety miles per hour. They were heading back in the direction they'd come. Barrett stole a quick glance over his shoulder. One of the sedans, lights off, was following.

Staring out into the dark, Barrett wondered why he hadn't told Dave about his dad. They'd talked a few times in preparation for his trip to Dubai. Probably because talking about it forced him to dredge up things he didn't what to think about. Like the question of why, for the five years he lived in New York, he'd managed to visit his family a grand total of three times. The most recent trip had been the disastrous return for the funeral, when he had succeeded in channeling all his guilt into an attack on his brother and sister.

In truth, going home always reminded Barrett he hadn't been much of a big brother. He'd been the golden child, excelling in school and sports, and going off to college. As far as people back home knew, he'd served a good stint in the Army and then switched careers to make a lot of money.

All the while things fell apart back home, and his father shriveled up into a dried-out husk of his former self. Barrett should have seen it. He should have helped his dad the way his dad had always helped him.

Soon they were approaching the palm-lined entrance of the Al Batinah Resort, but the two-vehicle convoy shot past, continuing south along the coast road. Dave caught his eye.

"Fujairah police station," Dave muttered.

The Boss, as he was beginning to think of the plainclothes officer, turned and barked something in Arabic that must have been "Shut up."

The section of the highway between the resort and the city of Fujairah to the south was void of towns, and they encountered almost no traffic. The dark waters of the Gulf of Oman lay just fifty meters beyond the left shoulder of the road. To the right, sandy flats stretched for a couple hundred meters before rising to rolling dunes and, beyond that, the mountains.

A burst of chatter on the police radio broke the silence. The driver responded, listened, and passed the hand-mic to the Boss. A short, sharp conversation ensued. The Boss turned to look through the rear window. Following the man's gaze, Barrett saw two police sedans in the distance, lights flashing, were gaining ground.

The driver pulled over to the shoulder. One of the new arrivals swerved in, braking hard, and shuddered to a dust-raising halt. The other pursuer pulled in behind the original trail vehicle. Through the headlights a tall, thin policeman walked toward them and the Boss lowered his window.

The tall officer was agitated, but he addressed the Boss in a deferential manner. The Boss was having none of it, though. Barrett could feel the palpable tension even from the backseat. The volume of the two men's exchanges rapidly ramped up.

Soon, the men were shouting and gesticulating. The Boss indicated the Americans in the back of his car were his charges, and kept pointing in the direction of their route. A jail cell in Fujairah, Dave seemed to think. The other man had different orders, it seemed, and he punctuated his argument by repeatedly jabbing a forefinger into the palm of his outstretched hand.

The Boss yelled in exasperation and flung open his door to confront the Tall One. *They're going to duke it out.*

A staccato burst of gunfire ripped through the air around them.

Barrett threw himself down in the seat, just missing Dave's head as his friend ducked. More shots exploded around them. He half heard, half saw Dave mouth, "Holy shit," his face also pressed to the seat. From his lowered position he saw the Tall One shouting, backing away from the Boss's door, fumbling with his holster. Another burst rent the air, and gunfire erupted all around the vehicles.

The Boss, jumping out of the SUV, started firing his sidearm. The driver of the SUV was opening his door when the windshield and driver's side window exploded, glass tinkling and blood misting the interior of the vehicle. The Boss popped up into view and fired three rounds over the hood at someone. Another short burst of automatic gunfire came from the vehicles parked behind them, followed by several, spaced, single shots.

"What the fuck!" Dave had found his voice.

"We need to get out of here!"

Barrett peeked around the edge of the driver's seat, not wanting to raise his head. He couldn't see far over the front of the vehicle. The driver was slumped over. He unsnapped the man's holster, pulled the weapon out and checked the safety. Dave was peering over the back seat.

"Shit."

The windshield and windows of the vehicle behind them were shot out. The driver was still in his seat, unmoving. In the dark, Barrett could make out bodies sprawled in the sandy shoulder along the two trail vehicles.

The Boss's door was yanked open, and a form bent in under the frame, reaching to the floor. A hand came up with his backpack, and another pointed a pistol into the backseat. Four shots exploded, the form slumped down, and slid backward out of the door. Through the side window he saw the Boss kneeling in the sand, weapon held with shaking arms.

"My side! Let's go!" Barrett's own words sounded far off, like his ears were stuffed with cotton.

He opened the door, looked to the rear, saw nothing more than they'd seen through the rear windshield. He flipped the safety off the pistol and swung his arm around the door as he stepped onto the ground, crouching. A policeman lay dying a few yards off the front wheel, knees pulled up to his midsection. No movement from the sedan in front, which had the driver's door open, lights still flashing.

"C'mon!"

Sprinting around the hood of the car, he gave a wide berth to the slumped Boss, who was now down on all fours. Barrett turned, aiming the pistol back toward the line of vehicles, making sure Dave was covered. His friend ran past, tapping him on the shoulder. "I'm good!"

Three or four more shots rang out from the far side of the trail vehicles, followed by shouts of pain.

He counted to three and sprinted after Dave. His friend was fifty meters in front, hard to pick out in the gloom. Dave's form rose up—the ground was sloping, the first of the small dunes—and disappeared. Seconds later, Barrett hit the top of the sandy mound and threw himself down next to his friend. They lay on their stomachs, breathing hard. He made sure to rest the pistol on his forearm, keeping the muzzle out of the sand.

He tried to swallow and realized how dry his mouth was. An involuntary spasm shuddered through his torso. They'd been awfully close to death. How many rounds just passed over their heads?

"What the hell?" Dave muttered. His breathing was ragged.

"The woman calls. We leave. We get arrested, then ambushed."

"Police killing police?" Dave asked.

"I don't think so."

They were both quiet except for their breathing, which was coming back under control.

"Somebody tried to grab the backpack," Dave said.

"It's still in the car."

They watched the highway. A car drove past the scene and didn't stop. As they watched, a panel truck approached. It slowed down before the driver thought better of what he was doing and sped away. The one body on the left side of the SUV would become visible in the dawn light.

"Do they have 9-1-1 out here?" Barrett asked. "How long until more cops show up?"

Dave shook his head. No guess.

"We should get the backpack and another weapon. Until we figure this out."

"I'm with you."

"I'll stop short and cover. You grab a weapon and the packs. We come back here."

"Wounded?" Dave asked.

"We don't risk it. I don't plan on being in anybody else's custody tonight."

"OK."

"Let's go."

The two covered the distance to the vehicles at a jog. Dave stayed ten meters to his side and slightly behind, out of any potential line of fire. He pulled up short of the Boss's vehicle, took a knee, scanning for movement. Dave hesitated, then dashed to the front of the vehicle and pulled an automatic rifle and a pistol off a body. He swiftly careened to the passenger door, found the backpacks, and returned to his friend's side. Armed with the assault rifle, Dave provided cover now. Barrett shouldered his daypack and pushed off into the desert. As he passed the Boss, he saw the man rolled onto his back, unconscious or dead, the lower half of his sports jacket stained with blood.

The cascading sound of crunching gravel stopped him in his tracks. A pair of headlights had Dave pinned in the no man's land of the shoulder. Dave had the weapon up, leaning into a firing stance. The vehicle swerved to a stop between the Boss's SUV and the pursuer vehicle, but Dave didn't fire. Barrett moved forward and to the side. He selected his aim point on the windshield and slipped his finger into the trigger guard.

The passenger side window slid down. The driver leaned across the seat and yelled, "Get in!"

He lowered his pistol.

It was the woman from the hotel bar.

8

The woman drove them south toward Fujairah. After several miles they passed a settlement of low buildings surrounded by a crumbling wall. She slowed, then veered off the highway onto a dirt road leading toward the mountains.

It was surreal, Barrett thought. They were being driven across the Emirati countryside by a spy. A member of the Israeli Mossad, if he was putting the pieces together correctly.

Barrett spotted the dark forms of animals at the side of the road just before the woman jerked the wheel and missed plowing into a small herd of goats and a stooped figure rushing to corral them.

They passed a communal trash dump and continued following the road for several miles as it climbed into the foothills. It petered out at the top of a small plateau. Off to the left, the Al Hajar mountains stood silhouetted against the starry sky. Ahead of them, the plateau butted up against the base of a cliff, and a wall of rock and scree rose a hundred feet over their heads.

The woman turned off the car.

"Thank you for helping Peter," she said.

"You're welcome."

"Why are we getting shot at?" Dave asked.

The woman ignored him. "Where's the flash drive?"

"There's nothing on it."

The woman remained waiting impatiently.

"Look." He pulled his laptop out and propped it open on the center console. He fished the flash drive out of the backpack and inserted it.

"Here," the woman said, turning the keyboard toward her. She clicked on the flash drive's icon and pressed a combination of buttons. Control-Alt-something-something, all in a blur of fingers. A small gray window appeared, with a white input field and flashing cursor.

"Where's the password?" she asked.

"There was no password," he responded. "Peter told me to take the backpack. I found the flash drive and tourist items. Nothing else."

"Do you have the bag?"

He pulled the blue and silver backpack from inside his own. The woman dumped the contents onto the center armrest, letting them spill to the floor. She explored the insides of the pack with her hand, pinching her thumb and forefinger along the seams.

"There's a knife in the glove box."

He found the pocketknife and handed it to the woman, who made an incision along one of the seams. She took a small white cylinder from inside the fabric, unrolling it to reveal a narrow strip of paper. A sequence of tiny characters was typed out.

"Read it to me," she said.

He read out the alphanumeric password as the woman typed it into the window on the screen: 8MNT232z9e4E91MQ2i.

The screen resolved into a new desktop. Two file icons appeared, one a document, the other a file with an extension he didn't recognize. Susan opened the program revealing a page written in Cyrillic alphabet. Russian.

"What's that?" Dave asked, leaning forward between the front seats.

"A steganography program," the woman replied.

"What?"

"A means of encrypting messages by scrambling data and hiding it in non-text files. Usually a photograph."

She opened the second file. The page was blank except for a hyperlink to a popular photo-sharing website.

"You're not getting Wi-Fi out here," Dave said.

"Hand me the bag on the floor."

From a black leather bag she produced a cellphone attached by a cable to a sleek black box. She slipped the device into the extra USB port on Barrett's laptop.

"Now we have Wi-Fi. Over satellite."

"Very cool," Dave said, impressed.

She turned to him as she was clicking on the file link. "These are commercially available."

"Oh."

"The connection is slow. It will take a few minutes."

"Maybe you can tell us what's going on?" Barrett asked.

The low light of the laptop's screen threw her features in sharp relief, the effect both exotic and fearsome. *I could tell you but then I'd have to kill you* came to his mind.

"The man on the eighteenth floor was in charge of Iran's nuclear weapons program."

"So you whacked him," Dave offered.

Easy, Dave. The woman ignored the remark.

"He was meeting a man trying to sell something."

"The bookish man in the hallway," Barrett said.

Susan inclined her head, as if she hadn't understood

him. "Who are you talking about?"

He explained the terrified man with the glasses and receding hairline who darted for the emergency exit. As Susan processed the information, he could sense her choosing among different alternatives.

"I was talking about someone else."

"You still haven't explained why we're being shot at," Dave reminded her.

The computer indicated the photo was now fifty percent downloaded.

"Whatever the Kazakh—the seller—had, we intercepted it. Jacob—Peter—gave it to Mr. Ross. That's why you're being shot at."

"What is 'it'?"

"Something the Iranians think will help them."

The Mossad agent, for that was what she had to be, was sharing a lot of information. A tingle started at the nape of his neck.

"Why are you telling us all of this?"

"I thought about taking the flash drive," she said, "and leaving you."

He wondered if Dave was having the same mental image. The two Americans, sprawled in the moonlight on the rocky plateau, neat little holes in their foreheads.

"I can't leave this country easily," she explained, "and I don't have a consulate to run to."

"You want me to keep this?"

"Peter thought you would get it to your intelligence people. I learned long ago to trust Peter's judgment."

"Is there something else we should know?"

"You must understand what you're up against. The Iranians may assume you're part of my team—only posing as Americans. Either way, they know what you look like."

"You're saying the Iranians just attacked the United Arab Emirates?" Dave challenged from the rear.

"You're both ex-military? You know of Hezbollah, Iran's proxy in Lebanon. They have proxy forces throughout the region. Supervised by senior operatives."

"Iran has agents on the ground? Here in Dubai?" Dave asked.

"This is Iran's backyard. We're less than seventy miles from their coast. The Qods Force is not constrained by the sort of legalistic considerations you Americans worry about."

Barrett knew the FBI had foiled a plot by Qods Force operatives to assassinate the Saudi ambassador to Washington in 2011. The plan involved blowing up a trendy Georgetown restaurant—and killing many Americans in the process. A friend in the Bureau told him it was sheer luck that one of the bad guys contacted their undercover agent to buy the explosives.

The computer beeped. Filling the screen was a picture of a sun-dappled stream flowing beneath trees, bordered by giant beds of white and yellow tulips on the bank. A tourist's snapshot of a botanical garden in Europe.

Susan imported the photo into the program, and a new icon popped on the screen. Opened, it revealed a single page of Arabic text.

After scanning it, Susan spoke.

"Parts of this I'm not sure of, but these are directions. Roads and distances from a reference point. The destination is a mine or tunnel of some sort."

"What's located there?"

"I have a theory."

"Just so we're all on the same sheet of music . . ." he said.

"Alizadeh was the man in charge of getting a nuclear warhead on top of Iran's missiles. They are having difficulties with their program—"

"Yeah, their scientists keep getting killed," Dave said.

"—and if they enrich their uranium to weapons-grade quality, they know they risk a preemptive strike."

"And?"

"They're looking for a shortcut. They want to steal uranium that's already highly enriched. The Kazakh was ex-KGB, and he found a way to get his hands on it. The location might house one of the unaccounted warheads scattered throughout the former Soviet Union. Or simply HEU—highly enriched uranium—sitting in storage."

"The Iranians would take these chances for that?"

"If the Iranians can make one warhead, in secret, it changes everything. Attacking their facilities is out of the question if there's risk of nuclear retaliation. With one bomb made from stolen uranium, they'd be free to enrich their own uranium for multiple warheads."

A hundred questions were popping into his head.

"Why don't you just email the file to yourself, from here?" Dave asked.

"I will, but—"

The top of the canyon wall in front of them lit up with bouncing circles of light. Headlights jerked back and forth across the rocks, but they were dropping, too, as the angle flattened. Through their open windows they heard the stillness of the night pierced by the high-pitched revving of engines as the pursuing vehicles slammed back to earth in their jolting race up the mountain road.

9

Susan threw the car in gear and gunned it forward, sending the vehicle fishtailing and fighting for traction as it headed toward the canyon wall. The headlights behind them were catching outcroppings of rocks lower down the hillside. The lowering trajectory of the lights told them that the pursuers were approaching the lip of the plateau.

As Barrett bounced and rolled in his seat, he fumbled to pull the flash drive out of the USB port without snapping the metal connector. When he had it free, he stuffed the drive and his laptop into his daypack. A glance back showed two pairs of headlights a hundred meters away.

Susan was driving without the lights on, negotiating the terrain in the ambient light of the trucks behind them.

"When I stop, get out!" she yelled over the noise.

As the car approached the cliff, Barrett saw it was not a continuous wall of rock. Instead, a steep promontory rose closer to them, but between it and the farther wall ran a wadi that angled down to the right. Susan swerved the car around the bend and followed the dry streambed downhill. Not far ahead, the route deteriorated into a narrow ravine, impassable by car.

"Take the phone from the black bag," Susan said to Dave. "I'll contact you."

She slammed the brakes and shouted, "Go!" even as the car was still skidding. Barrett threw his door open, tried to hit the ground running, and tumbled. Susan sped off, with her lights on now.

"This way," he shouted, crossing to Dave and leading them toward the rock wall. The men sprinted for about twenty meters and threw themselves into a shallow depression behind a pile of boulders stranded at the base of the cliff.

No sooner were they down than the roar and light of the pursuers were all around them. Two big SUVs careened around the turn to follow Susan's headlights into the wadi's dead end, spraying the hidden Americans with dirt and pebbles.

"Let's go," Dave said in his ear.

"Which way?"

Dave pointed back in the direction of where they were parked a minute earlier.

"Dubai is that way, southwest."

The two ran, crouching. As they left the entrance of the wadi, they avoided the open area where they'd sat in Susan's car, and veered farther to the right, staying in the low ground at the base of the cliff. Past the open area, they found and followed a boulder-strewn draw that led west between two spurs coming off the heights. Barrett hit his watch light: 0503. He stole a glance over his shoulder. The sky was just hinting at lightening in the east, less than half an hour until sunrise.

They were breathing hard now, jogging uphill. They slowed only to negotiate the trickier sections of jumbled rocks. Dave was huffing.

"Watch your ankles," Barrett warned, then softened his voice. "I can't carry your fat ass."

"Gee, thanks, brother."

The draw widened and flattened. The ground on both sides fell away as they crested the top of the low ridgeline. He took a knee, and Dave stopped beside him. Before them lay the Al Hajar range. A maze of cuts and draws between the peaks formed a darker black in the gloomy premonition of day. Above the hills an amazing array of stars had not yet been washed out in the growing light.

Turning, they could see the vehicles stopped in the wadi, about a kilometer away below them. The tops of the large white SUVs were barely discernible in the predawn gloom, but Susan's car was spotlighted in their headlights.

Crack!

A shot reverberated from the floor of the canyon below, followed by two, then three more. Controlled, aimed shots.

The good feeling he'd just had, the sense of accomplishment that came from negotiating the rough terrain, evaporated.

"Christ," Dave muttered.

"Dave, we're armed."

"We're armed with two pistols and a handful of rounds," Dave said. They'd ditched the rifle at the ambush site before getting into Susan's car. After all, they couldn't walk around Dubai with a rifle.

"I don't like it," Barrett said, but it was too late. The decision to stay together, the three of them, should have been made twenty minutes ago.

"She has a better chance of getting away on foot than we have of going back and surviving," Dave responded. "I have the feeling she's done this sort of thing before."

"I'm running too," he said, half under his breath. A

bitter taste spread across the back of his tongue. "Running away."

"What?" Dave asked.

"Never mind," he said. "Let's go. We'll move hard for thirty minutes. Then we can stop and figure out our location and plan a route."

"That sounds better," Dave replied. "Anywhere away from here."

Barrett checked the wadi layout again before he stood, shouldered his pack, and faced the mountains. He broke into a jog, picking a path through the sharp rocks in the dim light.

The ghostly white blip in his viewfinder disappeared behind the cold black rocks near the top of the ridge. His men had missed and the woman was gone. Safavi lowered the thermal scope from his eye.

"Sir, should we pursue?" A team leader awaited his order.

Safavi wanted to strike the man in the face. "No. We leave before the Arabs investigate the gunfire."

They had found the empty car high-centered on a rock. Beyond, they spotted the woman climbing the hills on the north side of the ravine. At that distance, darting in and out of the rocks, she was not an easy target for his men, even with their night scopes. The two Americans were nowhere to be seen. His teams had fanned out through the wadi and the open ground above, looking for evidence of their trail.

The woman was clever, he would give her that.

He had not foreseen the Israelis would leave anyone behind. His source reported the involvement of an American, maybe two, at the hotel. Two men who were not part of the group of suspects the police were compiling. Two men who fled the hotel in the early morning hours. One, the police source learned after the fact, possessed a backpack which didn't belong to him.

How close had he been? If Amir's men hadn't been idiots, starting a firefight on the highway, he would have them now.

Then the woman surfaced, snooping around the hotel, asking questions. They almost lost her trail, until the startled goat herder pointed them in the right direction.

Were the men truly Americans? Was the United States conspiring with Mossad in its assassination plots? Or were the Israelis brazen enough to use forged American passports? In either case, the men had what he needed. Safavi understood that now, and he would track them down.

The security forces of the U.A.E. would help. While the Arabs drew the net tighter around the fugitives, Safavi would wait and pluck them from the trap at the last minute. Once he had what he needed, the Arabs could have their bodies.

Something was odd, though, about these Mossad confederates. The Dubai police were compiling passport photos and travel itineraries for eight suspects, not including the "Americans." The two assassins in the hallway, posing as Poles, were killed by his men. But six others had been posing as Brits and Spaniards, including, maybe, the woman who'd just escaped over the hill. One wounded man was in police custody. Four Jews, three men and a woman, were unaccounted for, hidden somewhere, no doubt.

So why did the two men with American passports get in their car and attempt to flee along the most obvious route?

They were amateurs.

Safavi smiled to himself. Americans, yes. Operatives,

no. He felt the truth in his gut. They had no support, no network, no safe houses. Being Americans, and amateurs, they would think of only two courses of action. Turn themselves into the local police, or make their way to the American embassy.

The teams were coming back to the vehicles. He pulled out his phone to set the operation in motion.

"Hessaby?"

"Sir," came the response from his deputy, managing the operations center from the private compound near the airport.

"The Americans are on the run. They have our item, I am sure of it."

"Do you want the other team sent to you?"

"No, not yet. We are going to implement the plan we discussed last night. I will call Amir next."

"What about the Kazakh, Ismagulov?" Hessaby asked. "The police found him bound and drugged in one of the Israelis' room. He is still in custody at the Dubai central station."

"Has he told them anything?"

"Only that he was on holiday and was attacked. His backpack was stolen. Should we eliminate him?" Hessaby asked.

"No. If the Americans don't have all the pieces, we may still need him."

Hessaby acknowledged this.

"The Scientist, though. Get him on the next plane to Tehran. He is to continue with the rest of his mission as planned."

"Without the item secured?"

"I'm confident I will have it soon," he said, "and I don't want to be waiting on the Scientist when I'm ready. Is that understood?"

Receiving Hessaby's assurance, he hung up and got

into the lead SUV.

"Go," he said to the driver. "Dubai." The vehicles backed up along the dry riverbed until they reached a space wide enough to turn, and raced back down the slope toward the highway in the growing light. He punched another number into his phone.

"Amir," the man answered.

"Your men were worthless this morning."

"I—"

"No excuses," he said. "It is time to redeem yourself."

"We will do—"

"Shut up and listen. This is what you will do."

He spent the next fifteen minutes explaining in detail what he wanted, and how he wanted it done. After making Amir repeat the key points, he folded the phone, breaking the link. The Arab should understand his own survival depended on success this time.

Amir's men would begin the work by phone, by email, by quiet meetings with men of a certain disposition. They would form the nucleus. Around this they would gather the disgruntled, the poor, the criminal element. This time Safavi's own men would be present. To fan the flames, when needed, and to lead the timid. They would ensure the proper outcome.

There had been setbacks, but success was still probable. Likely, even. Soon, the Americans would stumble into his trap. He would put this distraction behind him and push forward with the real mission.

10

The two friends had been pushing themselves for an hour when they stopped at a large flat rock lying in their line of travel. Barrett pulled the laptop out of his backpack and knelt next to their improvised tabletop. Using the satellite phone and access device Susan gave him, he soon established a Wi-Fi hot spot.

Dave located their position with the GPS on his smart phone while Barrett pulled up Google Earth on the laptop. They found the little road north of Fujairah where Susan had turned off the highway. Barrett marked their current position with a pushpin icon. For the next twenty minutes the two men hunched over the computer screen, zooming in and out of the satellite imagery, using the distance and elevation tools built into the program.

"Sixty-four miles to the U.S. consulate, straight line," Barrett noted.

"Sixteen miles through these hills, up and down, before we break out into flatter desert," Dave said. "Look at all these ascents and descents. This is going to kick our butts."

"Let's do it," Barrett said. "Highway 89 is twelve and a half klicks from here. Let's shoot to intersect it here, across from this town. From the high ground on our side of the highway, we can figure out the best way to get around it."

Dave grunted. Twelve and a half kilometers. Eight miles in a straight line, which meant they'd walk ten or more. He was already sweating, and the sun was barely over the horizon. It was shaping up to be a long, hot day, but neither of them was ready to move toward a road and flag down a ride. Not this close to where they'd fled from the white SUVs.

The next three hours were like being back in Ranger School. A combination of Desert Phase and Mountain Phase, all rolled into one. It wouldn't have been bad if he was still twenty-two. He was in shape, sort of, but not this kind of shape. They kept gaining elevation, but their progress was broken by frequent and steep descents, forcing them to slide down rocky hillsides, only to climb back up to regain the elevation they'd lost. Sometimes they'd land at the bottom of wide wadis, easy to travel, but then would have to climb up and out, or be thrown too far off their intended route. The best movement, flat and easy, was on top of the ridgelines, but there again they were forced to abandon one ridge after another, to avoid being pulled in the wrong direction. It was tempting to follow the easy line of drift, but without a map in hand, they needed to stick to a straight line. Otherwise, they'd end up walking in circles.

The entire morning was a refresher course in pain. At ten o'clock, drenched in sweat, they paused to drink some of their water. He had to force himself not to gulp everything he had. He looked over at Barrett. He was dripping with sweat too, but he looked a whole lot better than Dave felt. He'd always been a fitness nut, even for an infantry guy.

He sidled over and knelt next to his friend, who had the laptop opened again, this time keeping it inside his pack to shade the screen from the bright sunlight. They compared the lat-long of their target intersection with Dave's phone's GPS coordinates. They were close to the high point in elevation along the route they'd plotted. After a minute, the two men packed up and continued moving.

Two hours later, they crested a rise and saw a wide valley running down from the North. While the floor of the valley along their route of travel was hidden from view by the intervening terrain, to the north he could see the thin ribbon of blacktop bisecting the valley. Highway 89. For the next two hundred meters the pair slowed their rate so they wouldn't expose themselves to view from the small town or the road they expected to see up ahead.

When the town came into view below them, they saw no more than a loose collection of walled compounds, spread out just beyond the highway. From their map reconnaissance, he knew that level ground lay for two miles past the town. After that, they'd have another stretch of serious terrain while descending the backside of the Al Hajar range before hitting the open desert.

"Dude. We've gone about seven and a half miles in five hours," he said. Their rate of march was pitifully slow.

"I know. These hills are brutal."

Dave wiped the sweat from his eyes. He could feel the abrasiveness of the salt crystals on his sunburnt skin. The temperature was in the high nineties now, and they'd soon be at serious risk for heat injuries.

"Going downhill is not going to be much more fun than going up."

"How much water do you have?" Barrett asked.

"One unopened liter bottle, plus the one I'm working on. Which is almost gone."

Barrett indicated he had about the same. "I think we should stop now, see if we can find some shade and rest."

They backed away from the crest of the hill and descended the side of a knoll where they'd seen some vegetation. At the bottom, three small trees stood. They were scrubby things like the trees he'd seen in African safari pictures, with giraffes standing beneath them. These were shorter cousins, their stunted forms pushing up through the rock and sand to a height not much taller than a man. The limbs were close together and leafy, so by sitting close to the small trunks, he and Barrett were able to maneuver their upper bodies in the shade.

As he sat down, the seat of his cargo pants stretched across the raw, chafed skin of his buttocks—a result of the morning's prolonged exertion in trousers damp with sweat, and the remorseless friction of skin on fabric, and skin on skin.

"Guess what?"

"What?"

"I've got a serious case of monkey-butt."

"Nice," Barrett responded. "Just be glad you're not humping a fifty-pound rucksack on your back."

"Those were the days," he said, a smile cracking his chapped lips. "Giant green tick strapped to your back, sucking out your life force."

He peeled off his socks, inspecting the ugly blisters on the tips of his big toes and balls of his feet. His hiking shoes were broken in, but his soft civilian skin was no longer accustomed to this sort of wear-and-tear.

"Dave," Barrett said, "call Amy. Let her know you're okay."

Amy was relieved to hear from him, but she was fighting to remain calm. The police chief—Al-Hashimi—and his ugly sidekick had pounded on her door two hours ago and interrogated her about the Americans' whereabouts. Ever since she'd been frantic with worry.

"No one is telling me what the hell is going on, but they're talking about you and Barrett like you're criminals."

He explained the checkpoint and the ambush. He could hear the sharp intake of breath, but she held it together.

"Where are you?"

"We're fine. We're making our way to help. But I want you to be able to say that you don't know where we are, the next time you're asked."

Amy was not crazy about this response, but he convinced her to call a friend to pick her up from the hotel and drive her back to her apartment in the city. She should call Emirates Airlines, too. Their legal department would help with the police. Reluctantly, they said their goodbyes, and Dave promised to call again that night.

Hearing his girlfriend's voice had a wonderful calming effect. Whatever craziness had ensured over the past few hours, and whatever his own predicament, at least he knew Amy was safe. It was apparent that Barrett, however, had no such support.

"Barrett, whatever happened to the girl from Lillington? Jess?"

Dave remembered the girl well. She was a small-town girl from North Carolina, a smart young woman with a dazzling smile that had been wary of Barrett and his friends when they first met at a Raleigh club. But he and the pretty schoolteacher had started to see a lot of each other during his last year at Bragg.

His friend hesitated. "After the Advanced Course, I got orders for Lewis, but knew my brigade was deploying soon. It made sense for her to stay where she was. When I came back from Iraq, I was making plans to get out of the Army. We spent some time together as I was transitioning, but it didn't work out. *I* didn't work out."

After a few more seconds, his friend continued. "She was a very sweet girl. She was the best thing going on in my life at the time, and I made no effort."

Friendships formed in the military were strange, Dave thought. You served with a guy for a few years and felt almost like brothers. You could go your separate ways, but when you got back together, you could pick up conversations like you'd just talked the day before. Until you realized that below the surface level, you really had no idea what had been going on in their lives, or the things they'd been dealing with.

"You know, the Iranians aren't going to find us out here," he said. "But we're not getting to the consulate anytime soon, either."

"I know," Barrett said. "I'm thinking about that town, too. We'll have to wait until nightfall, and even then, how far around do we need to go to avoid alerting every dog in the place?"

Barrett might be able to gut it out, but Dave's own body wasn't going to take much more of this, not without more water and some serious attention to his feet. The conclusion was clear in his mind.

"I think it's time to call for a ride."

As Barrett became aware of his surroundings, the overriding sensation was that his feet were being roasted. His legs, from the thigh down, extended out beyond the shade of the tree, and the sun was beating down on his jeans and hiking boots.

It was so bright now that everything beyond the trees was a washed-out shade of tan. He squinted at his watch. 1:57.

He'd fallen asleep thinking about Jess. Or rather, the

way he had treated her. She was ready to follow him around, whether it was in the Army or out. And he had simply pushed her away.

The scary thing was his realization that that was exactly what his dad had been doing to those closest to him for the last several years. His dad had always been quiet. But the man who was able to land his mom, vivacious and the life of the party, bore no resemblance to the man his father had turned into. Life was hard, and his younger children were a disappointment to him, no doubt. But Barrett wondered if what bothered Henry Ross the most wasn't some unfulfilled dream, an unrealized promise or sense of wasted opportunity. Their father had worked hard for thirty years in the same small community, doing all the right things, and it was his son who got to leave, go to college, live the life he wanted to lead. His dad had gone from reserved to bitter, and somewhere along the way had taken a turn toward clinical depression.

How different things had been when Barrett was a kid. They'd spent a lot of time together, on camping trips, hunting, simply hiking through Oil Creek State Park. His life had really revolved around that relationship. Everything, the good grades, the sports, getting into college, had come almost naturally, but deep down it was because he needed to please his parents. Dad, especially.

And Barrett had turned his back on the people who cared the most about him. Not just his parents but his brother and sister. Jess, too.

The cellphone rang near his ear, and he fumbled to answer it.

"Mr. Ross, my name is Samantha Carr," the clipped voice announced. "I am the administrative officer in the U.S. Mission to the United Arab Emirates."

"Thank you for calling back."

As if to dispel any confusion about the word

"administrative" in her title, the woman added, "I am the third most senior officer here at the embassy and report to the Ambassador and the Deputy Chief of Mission."

Oh. Ms. Carr seemed to be waiting for an appropriate response, but he wasn't sure what that would be.

"Mr. Ross, where are you right now?"

"I'm in the middle of the desert. Actually, the Hajar Mountains. Near Highway 89 and a town called Masafi."

He could tell the woman was taking notes.

"Is Mr. Allen with you?"

"He is." Dave leaned in, trying to hear the other half of the conversation through the cellphone.

"Mr. Ross, what are your intentions?"

Odd question. "I called the consulate because I need to speak to an American official. My friend and I have gotten ourselves into a jam that needs straightening out, and I have something I want to hand over to the authorities."

"You seem to be a master of understatement, Mr. Ross," Carr said. He wasn't sure if the tone was exasperation or condescension, or some combination of both.

"You realize, of course, you're wanted by the Dubai authorities in connection with the deaths of three Iranians, one of whom had diplomatic status? As well as six UAE police officers?"

"Dave and I had nothing to do with that," he said, "other than being in the wrong place at the wrong time."

"I'd like to believe you," Carr responded, "but your passport pictures are being broadcast along with those of several suspected foreign operatives. The police have released still photos from hotel security cameras, which place you in the hallway at the time the Iranians were killed. You were taken into police custody and disappeared after those police were murdered."

"I walked into the hallway after the shots were fired,"

he explained. "Since then Dave and I have been trying to get to the consulate."

"Colonel Al-Hashimi says you stated you had no further information you could provide him."

"I decided I needed to talk to American officials, not Emiratis."

"Why didn't you call before this afternoon?"

"We were trying to get to the consulate when we were pulled over by the police."

"What about your involvement in the event on the highway?"

"The police were ambushed. Dave and I escaped in the confusion."

He thought about Israeli woman's belief that the attackers were Iranian proxies. It didn't sound like he had much credibility with Ms. Carr yet, so it didn't seem prudent to throw this theory out there. Not yet. Maybe Carr and her bosses would figure it out.

"Listen, Mr. Ross. Not only are you wanted by the authorities, but your personal well-being is in jeopardy. Al Jazeera and every other media outlet in the Gulf are running continuous coverage. If the Sheikh and his government are outraged by another Israeli operation on their soil, the common citizens are even more up in arms over the deaths of their policemen. You, Mr. Ross, and Mr. Allen, are being lumped in with the Mossad as prime suspects. Crowds are starting to form outside the consulate in Dubai—a disturbance we've never seen before. All Western embassies are advising their nationals to stay off the street and exercise caution—"

"The attackers of the police were a paramilitary force," he threw in.

Carr ignored this. "The media speculation has centered on whether you and Mr. Allen are Mossad agents using forged American passports, of if you're American operatives working a joint operation with the Israelis. Neither allegation is tenable from the standpoint of the Secretary of State. Who is visiting in less than two weeks' time."

The woman's inability to listen was starting to piss him off.

"Ms. Carr, you didn't seem to hear when I said. Dave Allen and I haven't done anything wrong. We're trying to turn ourselves in to the embassy to get this sorted out."

"The role of the U.S. embassy, Mr. Ross, is not to shelter Americans sought by the police in connection with a crime. The appropriate step is for you to turn yourselves in to the UAE authorities. The embassy will ensure you receive all standard due process under Emirati law."

He looked at Dave. His friend was rolling his eyes.

"You just said emotions were running high and our safety was at risk. You want me to walk into the nearest village and turn myself over to the local traffic cop?" Barrett demanded.

"Well, I—" she began.

"Ms. Carr, I'm happy to talk to the police, but I want to come into the consulate and speak to your security personnel first."

"The RSO, the Regional Security Officer, works for me," Carr explained. "If your case is simply a matter of wrong place-wrong time, I'm not sure how it pertains to his function."

"Ms. Carr, I'm ex-Army. I'm a military analyst. Trust me when I say I need to speak to your security folks. I think the Station Chief will want to listen in as well."

Carr was silent for a moment, the first pause since her opening salvo. Maybe his reference to the senior CIA person at the embassy caught the woman's attention.

"All right."

"We've been on quite a walk this morning. If you could

send someone to meet us, it would expedite the whole process."

"I'm going to have one of my people contact you. A man named Sheehan will call to coordinate your pickup."

"Thank you, Ms. Carr."

"Upon further reflection, Mr. Ross, if you're in a secluded spot, stay put. Wait for Sheehan's call. We'll do our best to get you and Mr. Allen inside our compound without further incident."

11

As promised, Mark Sheehan called within fifteen minutes of Samantha Carr's hanging up, introducing himself as the PSO, the Post Security Officer, for the U.S. consulate. He sounded harried and uncertain, so Barrett took the initiative in talking through the linkup procedures.

Two hours later, Dave spotted a dark green SUV pulling off the highway to park on the shoulder, just as Sheehan called to say he was at the agreed-upon coordinates. Sheehan got out of the Jeep Cherokee and stood by the hood so they could confirm the vehicle. Barrett and Dave left their concealed position overlooking the highway and picked their way down the long, steep slope, taking care not to slip and fall on the jagged rocks.

They piled into the back seat, luxuriating in the blessed air conditioning. Sheehan introduced himself again as he turned the vehicle back on the highway in the opposite direction. He was a big man with a large head of red hair, shaved close on the back of his neck but piled in unruly curls on top. He looked, Barrett thought, like he was a year out of college.

"You're going to meet with my boss, the RSO," he explained as he handed them each a large water bottle from the seat next to him. "Mr. Massey works out of the main embassy in Abu Dhabi, but he'll meet us at the consulate."

"How long will it take to get there?" Dave asked.

"An hour forty-five, maybe two hours. The traffic could be interesting today with the crowds."

Sheehan fell silent. No one felt like small talk. Barrett leaned back and closed his eyes, taking a mental inventory of his bumps and bruises. He was looking forward to treating the blisters on his feet and getting some lotion on his sunburn. The water offered by Sheehan would help, but he was dehydrated. If he was still in the Army, he'd head down to the aid station and let a young medic get some practice by sticking him with an IV drip, a nice rehydration shortcut.

He remembered something that might be an issue. Dave had his eyes closed, so he tapped him on the thigh. He pointed at the pack at his feet, forming his hand in the shape of a gun. Dave nodded, yes, they both still had the pistols taken from the ambush.

"Not until we see the Marine guards," Barrett said, trying to keep the message low and vague. Sheehan's eyes appeared in the rearview mirror, but he didn't say anything.

Barrett lay back and closed his eyes. How did he get into this mess? He might very well be on his way to a lengthy jail term, even if he was eventually cleared of the violence at the hotel and the roadside ambush. Would he still have his job when he got home?

He was too old to be playing this kid's game—being a secret agent. It'd been a dream of his, in one of his childhood phases. Along with Olympic athlete and astronaut.

The childish dream that had stuck, the phase he hadn't outgrown, was war hero. Army general. Silly as that sounded, he knew plenty of grown men that built their life around that dream.

Fresh out of ROTC, he'd believed he was doing the most important thing in the world—leading men, getting things done. Accomplishing the mission—that was the mantra. For him, after a few years in the service, his goal had taken the more realistic form of becoming a lieutenant colonel, or colonel, with command of a battalion or brigade of soldiers. For an aspiring young officer, that target was both very far off but still within the realm of possibility. It *was* the most important job, and finding that he was actually good at leading soldiers, he'd cherished the belief of *just maybe*. Whatever its other faults, the system had one thing going for it—even a poor kid from nowhere could rise based on merit, no strings attached.

Yet when the canned exercises and meticulous training plans gave way to hard choices, he'd learned that things could go wrong, and people could get hurt. For some, the natural response was finger-pointing and ass-covering.

Like his last boss. An idiot who looked like a sausage stuffed in BDUs. A yeller with nothing to say. Amazing how one incompetent man could ruin everything Barrett had set his sights on.

Snap out of it.

The disillusioned-soldier-back-from-war thing was cliché, Barrett reminded himself. It had been years ago, anyway. And as more time passed, he wasn't really sure if he was pissed-off at the Army, or with himself for quitting.

Barrett noticed Sheehan's eyes in the mirror again. This time, however, the PSO wasn't looking at the backseat, but to the highway behind them. He turned and there, two hundred meters behind them, two green and white police

SUVs were following, side-by-side, preventing traffic from coming between them and the embassy vehicle. He tapped Dave again, who followed his gaze to the rear window. Looking forward, he saw they were also being escorted by two police vehicles in front. Again, no intervening traffic was allowed between them and the police escort.

"Looks like you were followed to the link-up point," Dave said, with an edge of professional disapproval.

"Yes," Sheehan said.

"Wait a second," Barrett said, becoming alert. "The deal was the consulate first. Then we go over to the police. I thought I had an understanding with Ms. Carr."

"Nothing's changed," Sheehan said. "You're going to the consulate, and like I said, you'll be debriefed by Mr. Massey."

"What's with the police, then?" Dave asked.

"Given the circumstances, we couldn't just sneak you into the consulate without giving the Emiratis a heads-up. With our assurances you intend to turn yourself in."

Barrett fumed. He didn't like weak plans, and he didn't like plans changing without being informed. He didn't like amateurs, either, not when his life or lives of his people were on the line. Not even if that person was the third-ranking American in Dubai.

Poor planning. Last-minute changes. Just like fucking Iraq. Staff flunkies who directed combat operations using PowerPoint slides instead of detailed orders. Barrett had acted according to what he understood, what he knew, was the commander's intent. When his guys were hit by the IED, though, all of a sudden the second-guessing began. No one questioned the half-assed nature of the overall strategy, or lack thereof, which came from higher headquarters. Just blame it on the guys on the ground.

The mountains had long since given way to the flat sands of the desert, punctuated here and there by dusty shrubs and high-tension power lines. As they crossed the Dubai Outer Road, the desert expanse gave way to more frequent and denser areas of development. The silver spire of the Burj Khalifa dominated the skyline, and soon they were cruising past shopping malls and office space. Everywhere new construction mushroomed. They made a wide turn to the north, passing the wide marshy expanse at the end of Dubai Creek, its waters dotted with pink flamingos.

Inside the city proper, the traffic was heavy, but in a few minutes they were taking a stretch of highway running between a row of foreign embassies to the west and Dubai Creek on the east. The water was teeming with moored yachts, and shiny office towers stood on the far bank.

They turned onto a smaller road, 3rd Street, lined by more embassies and government-looking buildings. The serene, orderly cityscape of Dubai disappeared and was replaced with chaos. Fifty meters past the turn their police escort slowed to a crawl as it reached the trailing edge of a massive crowd. Barrett strained forward, scoping out the congestion. From one side of the street to the other a solid wall of people had formed, so massive he couldn't see the far side. The noise and emotion of the people blocking the street were palpable even inside the car. Soon, the small convoy was at a dead stop.

Sheehan picked a two-way radio. "Duty Officer, this is Sheehan."

"Go ahead."

"Hey, we've just turned in on 3rd Street, and we're stopped. We're not even level with the Saudi embassy yet. This crowd is huge."

"We're aware. Be advised, stick with your escort and stay inside the vehicles. We'll be waiting when you get to the gate."

"Roger."

"I've never seen anything like this in Dubai," Dave said.

The police vehicles in front inched forward, the drivers laying on the horns and gesticulating through their open windows, nudging people out of the way with their front grills. The crowd parted for the police, but upon seeing the SUV with the diplomatic plates, driven by an American, they surged back, screaming and pumping their arms.

"I wish our windows were tinted," Dave observed.

As if to emphasize this last point, a man brandishing a blurry photo ran up and assaulted Barrett's window with his fists. A glossy of me, he thought. The man was joined by others, but a uniformed arm wielding a baton beat the rioters back. Several officers from the vehicles behind came up along the embassy vehicle. They were sporadically successful in creating a small space around the Jeep.

"This is hairy," Dave said. His hand was inside his pack.

"In case something happens," Barrett said, addressing Sheehan, who was gripping the steering wheel, "where exactly is the consulate?"

He couldn't tell where the center of the massive crowd was, but he assumed that's where the main gates to the American compound were.

"Nothing's going to happen," Sheehan responded, but his tone fell well short of confidence. He added, "The consulate is about three hundred yards ahead, on the right. The vehicle gate and personnel entrance are side by side. The Marine security detail will be keeping out of sight, but they are staged to come out and get us through when we get there."

Not caring now what Sheehan heard, he turned to Dave. "Worst-case scenario, we're forced out of the vehicle. Let's exit out of the same side, and stick close.

Keep the weapons concealed but ready."

Sheehan looked like he was going to ask about that, but the police cars in front advanced as a small pocket in the crowd opened up. He lurched the Jeep forward to close the gap.

The melee was getting ugly fast. The press of people was overwhelming the few dismounted police who'd positioned themselves around the embassy vehicle, and Barrett could see fear on the cops' faces. They never experienced unrest in tranquil, tolerant Dubai. More and more people on the periphery were becoming aware the police were trying to shield a car with Westerners. The focus of the entire mob was beginning to turn on them, as ripples of recognition flowed out from around their vehicle and reverberated back as hate and fury. Placards pasted with passport photos were shaken in fury everywhere. He saw his face, Dave's, and the Israelis from the hotel. Banners scrawled in Arabic and English were now turned toward him so he could read them. *Death to the Murderers.*

The mass of people crushed in around the Jeep, the clamor increasing so they had to shout inside the car to hear each other. The police were receiving shoves, jostling begetting blows, and could do nothing. The vehicles in front wouldn't have the horsepower to move through the press of people now, even if they'd been willing to run people down.

"All right, brother," he yelled in Dave's ear. "I don't know what's going to happen, but we're not getting to the embassy anytime soon."

"Yeah," Dave shouted back. "If we end up outside, run back the way we came."

"Lot of embassies around here," he yelled, louder this time to surmount the increasing din. The car was starting to rock as the crowd on either side figured out how to work together. "Look for a friendly flag."

Dave opened his mouth to respond, but any words died with the explosion of glass as a huge piece of masonry demolished the windshield and crashed into Mark Sheehan's chest.

12

Sada sat in a blue Toyota Yaris on the corner of Za'abeel Road and 3rd Street. Her hair was wrapped in a dark purple scarf, and large wraparound sunglasses shaded her eyes. She wore a long gray tunic over beige slacks, striking the right tone for a moderate Arab woman in the UAE. A full abaya would have provided complete concealment, but would have looked odd for a woman driving her own car.

She'd repositioned the vehicle once already to avoid drawing unwanted attention, moving farther away from the American consulate as the crowd in front grew larger and rowdier. Young men walking by stared through the window, but she kept her eyes averted, as if she was studying the journalist's notebook propped in her lap. Her doors were locked. If the crowd's edge extended behind her, she'd move again. The closer she could get, though, the better. When she knew the Americans were safe inside their embassy, she could worry about making her own way out of the country.

She watched the crowd swirling and chanting, Her

skin began to crawl in a mixture of anticipation and fear. She had seen her share of riots up close, beginning with the Second Intifada in 2000, when she was a young field medic straight out of basic training. Later, as an infantry soldier in Gaza. And more than once, since joining the Institute, she had been disguised, as she was now, as a local woman in head covering or full burqa. Watching from the sidelines as a mass of angry men coalesced into a monster, the raw and visceral frustration and hatred carried by each individual feeding off the mob's raw, violent energy. Her only safety lay in the ability to go unnoticed.

If she survived this, escaped Dubai without being imprisoned for the rest of her life, she would never put herself in this position again. She made that promise to herself more than once before, but each time had reneged. It went against so much of what had been instilled in her. Now the likelihood of having the chance to fulfill it seemed very slim indeed.

The mob was like a hurricane, gaining power as it spins at sea, a growing force that dissipates only after pounding some exposed shore. Landfall for this storm would be the American consulate. But it wasn't a natural phenomenon, was it? Emiratis weren't known for violent rioting.

People continued to pour into the street from surrounding roads. Many held placards pasted with photos of her team and the two Americans. The media had been running the story nonstop since it broke, but someone was ahead of the news cycle. Hundreds of signs had been printed and distributed to the rioters, within hours. The groundswell of popular resentment against foreign interference might have been legitimate, but this was a well-organized event. Not a spontaneous eruption of anger. Iranian influence, she judged, was at play.

Two police cars passed her post and applied their horns to part the stragglers who were still moving down the middle of the street to reach the concentrated mass. Behind them, a dark green SUV, American make with diplomatic plates, followed bumper to bumper. Two more police cars trailed the Americans.

The convoy did not get far before their progress was stopped dead. The situation deteriorated from that point, the mob surging toward the American vehicle, attempting to flip it. She left her car and jogged toward the mob.

She tried to skirt the edge of the crowd, looking for an open path to the vehicles in the center. As she shouldered her way through, she could hear the grumbling from the men around her. The complaints turned to resistance, and hands reached out to pull her back. The crash of shattering glass came to her from up ahead. The police were being overwhelmed and pushed aside. Through a sea of yelling, bobbing heads and bouncing shoulders she caught a glimpse of a green SUV door being wrenched open.

She reached into her handbag and pulled out a modified Heckler & Koch P2000SK. She led with it, palm out, barrel up, letting the pistol gain the attention of the startled men she was pushing aside.

Reaching the vehicles, she shouldered through to the inside edge of the circle of violence. Blows were being thrown, she could see arms swinging, a tumult as bodies went in for the attack, stumbled, fell. Placards were ripped off stakes, the stakes used to pummel their victims. The press of bodies was compacting, pressing in on their victims.

"Move!" she shouted in Arabic.

"What are you doing?" a man said, pulling at her. The men in the immediate circle of the attack were emboldened by the frenzy, suspicious of this female interloper. They couldn't see or didn't care about her gun.

She pointed the muzzle of her weapon into the air and pulled the trigger. The men closest to her dove for the ground while those farther away, less sure of the source, crouched down in response to the others' reactions. The men beating the Americans were unaware of the shot.

Sada pushed forward again, stepping over and on the prone bodies before her. She fired again. A man with a bloody stick, holding one of the Americans by his collar, spun around. The American was the one called Ross. Another body, with shocking red hair, lay on the ground next to the front tire of the green vehicle.

The wielder of the stake wasn't Arab, or some poor Pakistani day laborer, either. He saw her weapon and darted to the left, trying to drag the American deeper into the crowd. She aimed at the side of the Iranian's head and killed him. Men all around were shouting and pushing back from the vehicles. The situation had been dangerously altered.

She ripped a blue and silver backpack up from the dead Iranian's grasp and pulled the American to his feet.

"Is the flash drive in here?" she yelled into his face. Dazed and bleeding, he gave no response.

She repeated the question, shaking him.

"Yes!"

She pulled him in the direction of her car.

"Dave!"

The American had spotted his friend, visible now that many of the rioters cowered on the ground, or were fleeing the area. Three battered policemen were on their feet, shoving the American into the backseat of the lead vehicle. The vehicle began moving, the horn blaring.

"The police have him. Come with me!"

The dash back to her car meant running a gauntlet of confused, scared, and sometimes hostile faces. She fired twice into the air to part the crowd, and once into the chest of a burly man who moved to intercept them. The American staggered as he followed but was able to run under his own power.

They reached the car at the end of the street. Jumping in, Sada backed into a hard J-turn, and raced out onto Za'abeel Road heading south.

13

Barrett's heart was pounding, fear seeping in to backfill the receding adrenaline that had flooded his body during the fight and subsequent escape. His mind said he should control his emotions, to keep his wits about him because this wasn't over. He reached up and touched his face. His nose was broken and his lower lip was split. He felt bruised all over. The bastard with the wooden stake had gotten a couple of whacks in before he could get his arms up. The man had paid for it in the end. He looked over at the woman who shot his attacker.

"You saved my life," he said. He tried to affect a tone of nonchalance. If the woman thought it false bravado, he didn't care.

"Yes," she said. "Clean the blood off your face."

He pulled his visor down with a shaking hand. Finding a water bottle in the door side pocket, he used the corner of his undershirt to tend to his cuts and scrapes.

When he had removed the most telltale signs, he sat back in the seat and allowed exhaustion to wash through him. The fear eased away, and he felt a strange contentedness, a simple pleasure in being alive. Then guilt. He was safe, for now—but what about Dave? A wave of unease overwhelmed him, stemming from his inability to answer the question, *what the hell is going on?*

He thought of asking where they were going, but decided against it. The woman seemed to have a plan. As they crossed the river and zigzagged through busy city streets, Barrett began to see the English word *Deira* repeated on many of the signs and storefronts. The area was one of residences and small shops. Foot traffic was light, and the people on the sidewalks were Arabs wearing a mix of traditional and Western attire. These people strolling along the shop fronts were blissfully unaware of the chaos on the other side of the city.

Susan spoke on her phone in a language he didn't recognize, while making a series of turns that kept them driving through the same series of neighborhoods. She was driving to kill time, he thought, or she was checking to ensure they weren't being followed.

"I'm going to drop you in front of a building," she said. "There'll be an electronics shop and a door just to the right of it. Use that entrance and go upstairs to the third floor. On the landing, go right, to the end of the hallway, number 34. Don't knock, just go in and lock the door behind you."

"Where are you going?"

"I'm getting rid of the car," she replied. "I'll meet you in twenty minutes. Keep the door locked until I get there."

They turned onto a larger road, headed north. He knew this because the road paralleled a strip of beachfront facing the Persian Gulf. On Barrett's side the road was lined with more shops and apartment buildings. Susan abruptly pulled over to the curb and stopped behind a parked car.

"Here."

He glanced at the bright yellow facade of the store and

its blue neon signs in Arabic and English. Cameras and other electronics gear filled the display window. He got out of the car and without looking left or right he crossed the sidewalk and followed Susan's directions into the apartment building.

Going up to the third floor and passing through the door marked "34," he found himself inside someone's home. He wasn't sure what he'd expected, but if this was a safe house, it was a well-lived-in one. The main room was neat but not uncluttered. The furniture looked comfortable and worn. The long bookshelf covering the left wall was a reader's library, stacks of titles in many languages. On a different day, he would have spent time perusing the titles. A light was on in the small kitchen straight ahead and dishes sat in a drying rack by the sink. He sat down in a chair at a small wooden dining table, feeling like an unannounced houseguest.

In the corner opposite the bookshelf sat a TV. He found the remote and flipped channels until he found the English-language version of Al Jazeera. A correspondent was standing with the Al Batinah Resort in the background, wrapping up the story of the suspected Mossad hit. The screen changed to a graphic with photos and national flags. The sight of his passport picture caused him to take short, shallow breaths. There he was, Dave too, reduced to two grainy black-and-white headshots alongside ten other people. The Israelis from the bar, Peter and Susan, were posted, and others. He and Dave looked as much like tourists, or Mossad agents, as the other individuals. The segment ended with a cutaway to footage of the demonstration outside the U.S. consulate, but the commentator provided no description of the attack on the embassy vehicle.

How was Dave? he wondered once again. The police had him. That was better than the crowd, surely. What could he do for his friend? Call the embassy again? This whole cluster-fuck was a result of his call to the embassy, starting with Carr sending an inexperienced security guy by himself. The police escort was a huge red beacon for the people waiting at the consulate. *Here we are.* He hoped Sheehan was alive, but whatever happened now, he wasn't going back to the diplomatic corps for help. He would have to figure out a lot of this on his own. Or, maybe not on his own. What was the Israeli woman going to say when she arrived?

Fifteen minutes had elapsed when he heard the soft knock at the door. Susan announced herself. He unlocked the door and let her in.

"How badly are you hurt?" she asked as she took off the scarf and sunglasses.

"Nothing serious."

"Let's eat while we have time," she said without further preamble, and began pulling leftovers from the fridge, peeling back foil and plastic lids to see what was available. She produced two large water bottles from a pantry.

"Is this your place?" he asked.

"No, it belongs to a friend. A helper," she said. "He'll never come back, but he'll be taken care of."

They were silent as they microwaved plates of rice and vegetables and something Barrett guessed was lamb. He was famished and tried to recall when he'd last eaten a meal. Or had a real night's sleep.

"Someone tracked our movements," he said.

She shook her head. "They lost you in the desert. But they knew you had only one place to go. The Iranians apparently had the foresight to track the movements of your embassy personnel. The police escort didn't help."

Susan drank from her water bottle and set it down, tracing the rim of the bottle with her fingertip. Her brow was furrowed in thought.

"The Iranians are a step ahead of the police. I think they have more than a proxy force here. They have someone feeding them information."

"I'm not going back to the consulate," he said, thinking aloud.

"We need to get you and the flash drive out of the country. But you won't get through an airport. Even if I devised some sort of rudimentary disguise, papers are an issue."

He hadn't thought ahead that far. "What do I do next?"

"We need someone who can move about," she continued. "The man who owns this apartment is not the right person for this sort of thing." The Israeli woman settled her gaze on him. "The woman at the pool with you and your friend—"

"No way."

"We need a vehicle."

"I'm not dragging her into this," Barrett said. "She's been questioned by the police anyway. She'd be under surveillance, right?"

The woman resumed eating.

An idea was forming in his mind. With Dave in jail, and Amy off-limits as far as he was concerned, the list of people he knew who could help was very short.

"I might have a way," he said at last. He told Susan about his contact with Tommy McCowan, and the businessman's corporate jet.

"Absolutely not. No more civilians."

Her tone was dismissive, and it was clear that she lumped him into those "civilians." She thought she was baby-sitting him. Could he blame her? So far he'd depended on her for everything he knew about the situation, not to mention his actual survival.

Barrett did not like the idea of being a burden. Or a

helpless civilian. The attack at the consulate meant that getting the file into American hands was not going to be some passive undertaking. It was time for him to contribute to this ad hoc partnership.

"You were willing to involve my friend's girlfriend."

"Only to drop off a car. Not to join in escape plans."

"This man's the best shot we have, given the circumstances," Barrett replied. "He would have a security clearance working for the U.S. government. He understands how to handle sensitive information."

Susan walked to the sink and stacked her dishes. She turned, leaning against the counter with her arms folded.

"No. It's not possible. You know about this operation because Jacob thought it was the only way to safeguard the information. Better for it to land in American hands than Iranians. But you were to go to your government. The embassy. The CIA. Not some businessman."

"You need to listen to me. This guy's not your average civilian. He told me this thing involved the Iranians before you did. And he has a plane."

The woman's eyes locked on him. He couldn't tell what was going on in her mind, but she seemed to be weighing the options. Carefully.

"We won't tell him the details," he said. "Just that I need a ride home."

When she spoke, her tone relented a tiny bit. "So how do you convince a man you barely know to fly you out, to break the law, without disclosing why?"

He fished Tommy's business card out of his wallet. "I think he'll listen to me. He places a lot of stock in being a patriot."

"Tell him nothing about the file."

"Understood. I should call Dave's girlfriend as well, let her know he's in police custody."

"No. Just call the man with the plane," Susan replied.

She turned her back to him, spreading her hands on the counter. "I don't know how long this apartment remains viable for us."

Dave was taking stock of his situation when someone charged into the room, slamming the door against the wall.

If the man intended to make a grand entrance, it was lost on Dave. His eyes were swollen shut. He managed to force a slit open in his left one, and through the teary lashes he saw a dumpy-looking policeman, his gut straining an ill-fitting uniform top. One look at the man's face, and he knew the guy was one of those types. He let his lids relax back to their puffy closed position. His whole face was battered, and he could feel the bruises extending all around his neck and shoulders, but he tried to put on his best don't-give-a-damn look.

He heard the man walk around the metal desk and stop by his side. He was seated on a stool with his hands cuffed behind his back, one ankle shackled to an eyebolt sunk into the concrete floor.

"What is your name?" the man barked.

"Dave Allen." The man knew this. The cops had taken his wallet and passport as soon as they got to the station. Looked like it was time for amateur hour.

"I don't believe you. You are an Israeli spy, a Mossad assassin."

He opened his mouth to speak, but Tough Guy cut him off.

"Where are your papers? Where is your passport?"

"You have it—"

"Silence! No lies!" the man shouted. "Where is your accomplice?"

"I don't have accomplices, because I didn't commit a

crime," Dave replied. His first impression was spot on—this guy was a puke who needed a punch in the face. "If you're talking about my friend, I haven't seen him since the mob attacked us."

"Mob," the man hissed. "That mob was the Sheikh's faithful followers protesting your insidious plot. A plot that killed six of my brother police officers."

Dave tried to say something, but the bastard cuffed him on the side of the head, hard, but not enough to topple him from the chair. He prayed for the opportunity to meet this man someday, unbound, and with his eyesight clear.

"Where is the other assassin?" the man barked.

Dave clamped his mouth shut. The man walked away a few steps. Squinting again through one eye, he saw the man rummaging through a shallow cardboard box on the edge of the table. He recognized his wallet as the policeman picked it up—his personal belongings.

"All right, Mr. Allen," he crowed, "let us see what we can find out about your *friend*."

The man held up Dave's smartphone, a look of confusion on his face. He'd be trying to find Barrett under the R's in Contacts. Apparently, he finally found him under B, for the man took a notebook from his breast pocket and began scribbling. What the hell was he going to accomplish with Barrett's U.S. phone number?

The door opened again and another officer came in, two junior policemen in tow, one of them armed with a tape recorder. One stood by the door, while the other came around and removed the cuffs from Dave's wrists.

"Captain Rafai, will you be sitting in on the interview?" the second officer inquired.

"Yes, sir, if you don't mind," the first responded, slipping Dave's phone into his pocket.

The new man regarded Dave with detachment but not hostility as he sat in the chair across the table. He was older, neat and trim, and looked professional.

"Mr. Allen, my name is Colonel Al-Hashimi. I am the chief of the Criminal Investigation Division. I am heading the investigation into the murders at the Al Batinah hotel."

This was the guy who was supposed to be doing the questioning. The officer who had questioned Amy, and Barrett, too. Who was the fat dickhead freelancing a moment ago? An over-eager subordinate, trying to earn his stripes.

"Captain," the senior man said in English, for Dave's benefit, "while we set up, could you please get a cup of water for the suspect?"

"Yes, sir," the one called Rafai responded, and left the room. Dave chuckled to himself. Trusted subordinate. One who's sent away to get a glass of water.

But the bastard's still got my phone in his pocket, Dave realized.

Rafai ducked into an unoccupied conference room. He'd been trying to think of an excuse to step out of the interrogation room when the old fool gave it to him. He dialed a number on his cell and waited.

"Yes?"

"I have it," Rafai said. He read out each of the phone numbers and the address for the missing American, Ross.

"Good," Amir said. "I'll pass that along to our friends."

14

The businessman picked up on the second ring. "McCowan here."

"Mr. McCowan, this is Barrett Ross. We met a couple of days ago at the resort."

The pause was so long, Barrett feared the man would hang up. "Of course, I remember. You're all over the news, you know."

"Mr. McCowan, I need to ask a favor."

"Okay," the man said, drawing out the two syllables to invite further explanation.

"Are you available to meet?"

"Uh, Barrett, maybe you oughta give me an idea of what you want to talk about."

"I was wondering when you were flying home. And if you had extra seats."

He'd thought the direct approach would be the best bet, but now he wasn't so sure. He'd shared a nice chat over coffee with the man. That was it.

"Well." Pause. "I'm scheduled to fly out at the end of the week," Tommy answered.

Bartlett was mulling over the best way to handle this, how to meet Susan's requirement for secrecy but still secure Tommy's help.

"Tommy, what you've seen on the news—my friend and I weren't responsible for any of that. On my honor."

"You didn't step in a great big pile of steaming manure?"

"I can't say that. But it wasn't our fault. Or our choice."

"Barrett, I need to understand this a little better. I'm country, so talk slow."

The Mossad agent's lips were set in grim steadfastness. She could hear Tommy's voice coming through over the phone, and she looked like she was ready to knock it out of Barrett's hand. He described for Tommy the events of the past thirty-six hours since they'd shared coffee, without spelling out the cause. He told of his attempt to get to the consulate, the arrest, the ambush, and the attack by the rioters. But nothing of the backpack, its contents, or Susan's theory.

"So the police are just looking for the wrong man," Tommy offered.

"Not exactly." He frowned at the woman. She might not like it, but he had to give the man something. "It's more of case of something falling into my lap. Sensitive information. With security implications."

"We? I thought your friend was in custody. Or do you mean we, as in the U.S. government we?"

"No, it's not like that. I have another friend who's helping."

"Who is he?"

"She. Listen, Tommy, I know I'm asking you to take a real leap of faith here. But the issue is not about me staying out of trouble, or even my personal safety. With your background—your previous employment, I mean—and the events of the past few days and who was involved, I'm hoping you can take me at my word. Without me being more specific on the phone."

"I'm starting to connect some dots. The 'she': is she American, Emirati—?"

"Neither, but she's a friend." Susan was watching him intently. They hadn't spoken about it, but if he was getting out of the country, he assumed she needed a ride also. "I owe her my life."

"Okay," Tommy said. "I'm not the sole owner of the plane. Let me make a call to check on moving the departure date."

Barrett thanked him and gave him the number of the cell phone.

"One thing, though," Tommy said, "I might be able to fix it so you leave here under the radar, so to speak, but we've got to land in Europe. We have to change planes to fly to the States."

Bartlett liked the fact that Tommy was doing some future planning. That meant a commitment. "Where in Europe?"

"Right now we're flight-planned into Frankfurt International. I don't know how you get past German customs."

"That's okay," he replied, "I'll figure it out. With a little luck, we won't need to bother you for a ride to the States. I've got a friend in Germany."

He hung up. Susan sat down at the table across from him and looked at him hard.

"You put a lot of faith in a man you've known for one day."

"Almost as long as I've known you."

The woman's lips formed a smirk, but it was humorless.

"Maybe at this point you have little choice in your associates. The difference is, I'm a professional." She picked up her phone and walked into the adjoining bedroom, shutting the door behind her.

Fine. Barrett had another call he needed to make, anyway. Amy would be worried sick about Dave.

Since talking with Amy, Barrett had taken a shower, cleaned his wounds, and tended to his feet. His old shirt was in the trash, replaced by a lightweight button down hanging in a closet. He took a pair of socks from a drawer to replace the ones destroyed by the walk through the desert, but the best he could do for pants was to beat out the dust and dirt from his own pair.

He'd told Amy everything he knew, and tried to reassure her that Dave should be safely in police custody. Amy promised to harass the American embassy to take action, and vowed she would not leave the police station without seeing her boyfriend. Barrett left unsaid what his own plans were, and Amy knew not to ask.

After cleaning up, he sat down on the sofa to think. The Israeli woman had not reappeared from the bedroom, but he heard the constant murmur of conversation, with the occasional spike in volume.

What kind of woman was she, this person he'd been thrown together with? Beautiful, yes. Determined, yes. Wired different than normal people? It seemed that way. He'd been shaking after his near-death experience at the hands of that mob, much more scared than he'd been at the ambush, probably because the ambush happened so quickly. But this woman was unflinching. Apparently, she killed for a living. Pulling out a pistol and dropping an enemy with a single bullet while on a dead run.

But he had just challenged her about calling McCowan, and she had backed down. For whatever reason, he'd been confident he could reason with her. Was she being reasonable, or did she feel desperate, in her willingness to go along with his plan?

Now he needed to think beyond the next step. When, if, he got back to the States, he wanted to get this information to the right people as soon as possible. He'd also like to avoid being hauled in as a suspected international criminal. A friend with the right connections would help.

Barrett found the main number for the J. Edgar Hoover Building in Washington, D.C., on the Internet. It was close to 9:00 p.m. or, with the time difference, almost one o'clock in the afternoon there.

He dialed the number, and after working through the automated directory, he asked a human voice to be directed to Mitchell Kane, spelling the last name out. No, he couldn't remember the name of the correct department. After a minute he was patched through to a line that rang twice before being picked up.

"Law Enforcement Coordination."

He gave his own name and asked for Mitchell. If he was on a wanted persons list, the woman betrayed no recognition. She asked him to hold.

As he waited, he pictured Mitchell sitting at a government-issue metal desk in a starched white shirt and conservative striped tie. Mitchell was short, stocky, and pugnacious, a fireplug of a man. He'd tended toward stoutness but carried it well. He'd been a standout on the Penn State wrestling team. They'd been roommates one year and good friends for the entire four years. After graduation Mitchell had gone off to be a tread-head in an armored division, and so their paths never crossed on active duty. From good buddies at school, the relationship drifted over time to the occasional catch-up email. Mitchell was reassigned to FBI headquarters a year ago, but the two had connected only once in person since his move to the capital.

"Barrett, how the hell are ya?" Mitchell came on the line, pleased to hear from his old pal. He had not, Barrett concluded, seen the Middle East portion of the morning news cycle.

"Good. But I'm in a bit of a fix," Barrett responded.

"Oh?"

"Sorry for calling out of the blue and getting right to the point. Can you plug my name into some system of yours? See what pops out?"

"I can, but—"

"Need a favor, Mitch," he said. "Put my name in and I'll explain."

The sound of Mitchell tapping the keyboard came through, followed by a pause, more typing, and silence.

"Christ, Barrett, whaddaya been up to?"

He gave the agent a run-down, finishing with the attack by the mob outside the U.S. consulate and his escape, but skipping over the involvement of the Israeli woman.

"Barrett, are you working for the government now?"

"No. Just a private citizen. This is all circumstantial. Wrong place, wrong time."

"Where are you now?"

"Still in Dubai, at a friend's house. Can you see the status of Dave Allen?"

"Says here he's in police custody. U.S. embassy aware of it, and coordinating."

"Listen, Mitch, I need somebody I can trust. Can I meet with you?"

"Barrett, you know I'd do anything for you. But traveling to Dubai is not in the cards. If this is all a big mistake, the best thing you can do is turn yourself in. Get back to the embassy, or call the police. From what I understand, the force over there is professional. I'll make calls."

"Mitchell, I'm not going back to the consulate. The embassy security folks had their shot, as far as I'm concerned. I don't trust the police, either. Besides, I'm talking about meeting you in D.C."

"Barrett—brother—there's no way in hell you're getting out of the country. Even if you did, you're not getting past Customs and passport control when you get here."

"I'll worry about that. Will you meet me?"

"Sure. I'll do whatever I can. But I can't help much if you run and get caught. I'm not even sure I understand what you want me to do."

"I'm not sure what I'm caught up in, but it involves national security."

"I'm listening."

"Mitchell, think about it. Media are saying this is another targeted killing by Mossad. The target was an Iranian connected with their nuke program."

"Yeah, I see that."

"Bodies are stacking up over here. First the hotel attack, then the highway, then the consulate. I didn't contribute to that body count. But somebody's gunning for something, and I think I know what it is."

"What?"

"I'll explain when I get there."

"When?"

"The next day or two. I'll call you when I hit the ground. What's your cell?"

Mitchell gave it to him, then continued, "Like I said, Barrett. I want to do whatever I can for you, but why'd you call me? I coordinate with local law enforcement inside the U.S. My department doesn't do international."

Barrett thought a second. "Mitch, I don't know a lot of special agents by name. I need someone who is going to take what I say at face value and put me in front of the right person."

"Who would the right person be?"

"Maybe CIA. Maybe your own WMD division."

"Okay, I see." In a different tone, the agent asked, "Barrett, is there an imminent threat to the United States?"

"No, I don't think so. But I've got a computer file that might show the Iranians with their hand in the cookie jar."

"Email it to me."

"I can, but you're going to need Russian and Arabic speakers to look at it. Are you sure you want me sending this via un-secure email?"

The question gave Mitchell pause. "When do you think you'll get to D.C.?"

"Two days, tops."

"We'll do a physical hand-off then. But stay in touch and let me know your ETA."

He thanked his old roommate and hung up. Now all he had to do was come through on his optimistic two-day timeline.

The door of the bedroom opened. Susan was wrapping up a call. The conversation must be in Hebrew, but whatever the language, it was clearly heated. The final exchange was terse and angry. She looked at him as she lowered the phone.

The Mossad agent wiped tears away with the back of her hand.

15

There was a soft, sustained knock at the door. Sada walked over and asked in Arabic, "Yes?"

"It's Tommy McCowan," the muffled reply came through. The American businessman had called forty-five minutes earlier, saying they could leave immediately if they were ready.

The American in the opened doorway was a large man, standing with his hands clasped in front of his ample girth. The face was plump, bespectacled. The face of a cheerful simpleton. This was the man Ross expected to get them out of the country? She stepped aside and McCowan entered the apartment.

Ross greeted the new arrival awkwardly before introducing McCowan to her. Was he second-guessing his decision? At a minimum, he should be worried about endangering the newcomer. Whatever McCowan's past role in the American government, or his connections now, he was putting himself at grave risk. If not from Iranian agents in the Gulf, then from laws of more than one country if he was caught smuggling criminal suspects across international borders. Did he understand that? Did he understand this was not a game? Did Ross understand that?

"Here's what I've got," McCowan said. "I called C-Flights, the operator of the plane, and was able to push the departure to one o'clock this morning."

She looked at her watch. It was just after ten o'clock local. Almost too much time—she was not comfortable staying in one place for too long.

"What about getting us on the plane? How much of an issue are we going to have?" Ross asked.

"My vehicle will take us right to the steps of the cabin door."

"What about the crew?" she asked.

"The pilot's an old Navy aviator I've flown with him a number of times. I'll have a quiet word with him, and we should be good to go."

She had her doubts about the smoothness of that undertaking but held her tongue. The overweight American's nonchalance scared her.

"But," McCowan continued, looking between both of them, "I'm not sure I understand your plan once you get to Germany. You're going to be scooped up by the German authorities when you step off the plane if you're not put on the manifest. I assume you're willing to accept that? That it's better than staying in Dubai under the current, ah, circumstances?"

"That's correct," she said.

McCowan turned in surprise that she had answered.

"What about you?" Ross asked the man. "We appreciate what you're doing, but what will happen to you and CarbonTec?"

McCowan's grin was a little forced. "I'll make up some cock and bull story about exigent circumstances. You showed up planeside, recognized me as a fellow

American. Said you were being chased by crazed killers. Matter of life and death, so I had no choice but to stow you away."

Maybe not so far from the truth, she thought.

"Besides," McCowan said, "I own the company, and I'm the one paying the tab for the C-Flight contract. I won't get much flak."

"When do we leave?" Ross asked.

"Now."

"What?" she asked. This was unexpected and unwelcome. "We're only a few minutes from Dubai International."

"We're not flying out of Dubai," McCowan explained. "I didn't want to change the departure airport. I thought it might be a yellow flag for anyone looking for something out of the ordinary."

"Where are we flying from?" she asked.

"I'd planned another day at Al Batinah after the conference. We're leaving from where I flew into. Fujairah Airport."

Fujairah was two hours away, at least. Back in the direction of the police checkpoint where the Americans were caught. Back in the direction of the firefight between the police and the Iranian proxy forces. The route would lead them straight into the area, she had just learned on her call, from which an Iranian special forces unit was staging its operations.

She'd reached Avigail at headquarters, where her friend was working in the operations center, barred from fieldwork indefinitely while undergoing her treatment. She had passed the information about the Iranians. The men in the wadi weren't just proxy forces, some group of semi-trained radicals. The man she killed outside the consulate, the one trying to drag Ross and the backpack away. Not an Arab, either. An Iranian, she had guessed, and Avigail confirmed it.

An element of the Qods Force deployed from a base in north central Iran the day before, traveling under civilian cover, destined for Fujairah. A shadowy group inside the IRGC's special operations wing, whose capabilities and missions the Institute knew almost nothing about. An element that was unusually aggressive, with a leader that was proving to be a risk taker.

Avigail had passed everything she could, and then the Director himself came on the line. The threat was too great to risk further compromise, he argued, and ordered Sada to break away from the American and exfiltrate the country immediately. He demanded. Threatened. It was clear that her career was over, and punitive action awaited, if she didn't heed the Director's order immediately.

That order Sada was refusing to obey. Not until she knew how this arrangement with McCowan, and Ross's plan for getting back to his country, were going to work out.

She was really alone now, with no help to be expected from her former colleagues, unless she meant to go back to Israel. And her self-imposed mission was morphing into something that she could not be entirely sure of. What exactly was she trying to do? Secure the file? Keep the American alive until he could reach safety?

Either way, Sada had an uncomfortable feeling she might soon know more about this special Iranian force than Avigail, the Director, or any of the Institute's experts could tell her.

Barrett lay in the back of the Suburban, the curve of the Israeli woman's hip pressed against his leg. The two were squeezed beneath a shell of empty cardboard boxes and a plastic tarp. Around them, boxes filled with CarbonTec wares and promotional materials formed a framework to keep the empty boxes in place above them. Anyone taking a cursory look through the windows would see a filled cargo space. Barrett kept pushing the tarp away from his face, using his hand to create a gap between the plastic and the back of the seat so they wouldn't suffocate. Even with Tommy cranking the A/C, their combined body heat in the cramped space was making the drive through the city a stifling experience.

"We're in the open desert now," Tommy said. "Very little traffic, if you want to poke your heads out."

Barrett and Susan pushed the tarp back and carefully arranged the boxes so they could sit up against the back seat, but still pull the facade back down over them quickly if needed.

Their departure from the safe house had been quick, with very little further discussion once Susan understood the timeline. Barrett thought part of the haste might have been Tommy's way of making himself go through what would he otherwise would have considered a harebrained undertaking. Despite his down-home charm, he seemed like an executive used to making prudent decisions. Barrett also wondered what exactly the man was concluding about Susan and her role. Tommy was the sort of person to figure out a lot more than he might let on at first.

"Tommy, back at the hotel, why did you say the shooting must be connected to the Iranians, and not Hamas?" Barrett asked.

"Dead Iranian scientists have been popping up all over the place the past couple years. A prominent physicist is walking down the street in Tehran. Two men pull up on a motorcycle and shoot him in the head. A senior official's stopped in traffic. Next thing he knows, he's got a sticky bomb slapped to his car door. That sort of thing. Everyone assumes it's the Israelis."

Barrett remembered the police chief's comment about the dead including a senior official from a neighboring state.

"That," Tommy said, "and the conference I was attending."

"Iranians were at the conference?"

"The U.S. has been pushing the U.N. to get serious about sanctions on Iran for years. One sanction was a travel ban on scientists involved with their nuclear program."

"I don't get it. Then why would they be here—"

"Like any U.N. resolution, it got watered down. The travel ban doesn't apply to IAEA–approved events. It's a way for Iran's senior people to mingle at 'peaceful' nuclear industry gatherings."

"Of course."

"Might be a double-edged sword. If everyone knows it's the only way for them to travel outside their country."

Barrett wished he could see the Israeli woman's face more clearly in the dark.

"You're really up-to-speed on all this," he said.

"It's part of my job. You mentioned nonproliferation the other day. As an American, I don't want to sell my parts to someone who's going to turn around and sell centrifuges to Iran. Or other wackos."

"You make centrifuges?"

"We make the rotors that go into the centrifuges. Out of carbon-fiber composites," Tommy said. "They're lighter and stronger than metal alloys. That's a key issue: faster centrifuges, with less chance of structural failure."

"That's the big concern, isn't it?" Barrett asked. "That's why we hit the Iranian centrifuges with the computer worm."

When the Stuxnet cyber attack damaged Iran's

uranium processing plant a couple of years ago, the Iranians had immediately accused Israel and the U.S. of unleashing the worm. Both countries denied involvement, but the sophistication of the attack pointed to the resources of a major state. A leak from within the U.S. government later confirmed it.

"Yep," Tommy responded. "It's a big hurdle for any country wanting nuke power. Or a bomb."

"Why so hard?"

Tommy turned his head over his shoulder. He was warming to his subject.

"Uranium ore is crushed and processed to separate the pure uranium from the rock. But naturally occurring uranium—"

"Can't sustain a chain reaction." Barrett was starting to remember some of the details.

"Right. U-235, the type of atom you need, makes up less than one percent of natural uranium. It takes a concentration of five to twenty percent for a good fuel."

"A centrifuge does this?"

"Spinning forces the heavier, unusable U-238 atoms to the outside," Tommy said.

"Separation in a single centrifuge is negligible, though," he continued. "You have to pump gaseous uranium through thousands of these things. The good U-235 keeps getting pulled out and pumped forward. The U-238 gets pumped backward. Eventually, at the end of the line, you get a high enough concentration of U-235 gas. Then, presto, you convert it back to a solid that can go bang."

"What did Stuxnet do?"

"These centrifuges are big machines—tall, heavy cylinders that rotate over 100,000 rpm. Think of your washing machine when it gets unbalanced because all the towels are lumped to one side. Now, imagine your washing machine is forty feet tall and spinning at the speed of sound. Stuxnet attacked the software that kept the centrifuges balanced. Crash."

"You think Iran's going the whole way to build a nuke?"

"You only need five percent enrichment for reactor fuel. The Iranians are building the ability to ramp up to eighty to ninety percent enrichment. That's weapons grade."

"Just a matter of time, then?"

"Stuxnet and assassinations aside, I think the only thing really holding the ayatollahs back is fear of what Israel's willing to do when it really gets fed up."

Tommy's technical assessment jived with the few papers on nuclear proliferation that Barrett had read at the think tank. It also mirrored, quite eerily, the sentiments that this representative of Israel, seated beside him, had professed only a night before. Iran was trying to build a nuke, and Israel was not going to allow it.

He found himself, for the second time that night, desperately wanting to see the woman's face. Seeing how she reacted to Tommy McCowan's conclusions was just part of the reason.

Barrett and Sada had repositioned the empty boxes to conceal themselves. The smooth ride of the previous two hours gave way to an increasing number of stops, turns, and speed bumps. They arrived at a gate, and Tommy rolled down his window and explained his destination and purpose. The vehicle started forward again and traveled for a few minutes before stopping.

Tommy swung the cargo doors apart and removed the empty boxes.

"Quick," he said, "I sent the customs guy off looking

for some shipping forms."

Barrett and Susan unfolded themselves out of the back and stretched their limbs. The warm night air felt refreshing after the cargo compartment.

Barrett did a three-sixty. The parking ramp was located between opposing rows of large hangars and was crowded with planes, large commercial liners taking up most of the space, while a cluster of business jets, like the one next to them, were arrayed in neat rows on the remaining quarter of the tarmac. On one side of the parking area, a taxiway led out to the main runway, its length outlined by white landing lights.

This corner of the airport was quiet. The only visible activity was the loading of a sleek white business jet several parking spaces away from them.

"Come on," Tommy said, "let's get you two inside, and I'll deal with customs."

As they were ascending the steps, a sedan pulled up and two men in caps got out carrying pilot bags and briefcases.

As arranged, Safavi and Hessaby met the customs man at an access gate on the north side of Fujairah Airport, near the large maintenance hangar that serviced the airliners. Moving around the perimeter of the parking ramp between the planes and the buildings, they followed the man's truck as he guided them to the Falcon's parking spot.

Every time one door is shut, another is opened. One must remain flexible and adapt to changing circumstances, in order to seize the opportunities that presented themselves.

Such philosophical musings did not make Safavi any happier about the other American slipping through his grasp. It should be only a matter of time before the police caught the man, though. If that happened, the police would find the memory stick, look at it, find nothing, and forget about it. Amir's contact would pull it out of the American's belongings, and Safavi would be able to continue with the mission.

But this American who bumbled into the way, he was not simply a tourist. Safavi learned he was a former soldier. A professional then, of sorts. For all their propaganda about peace and diplomacy, the American people had no shortage of experience in war. While lecturing others about human rights, they were the most warlike of all. Safavi would not make the mistake of dismissing the American out of hand. Especially now that he was teamed with the Mossad woman.

What was the expression the American general had written in his book? No plan survives initial contact with the enemy. Yes, that was true.

Contingency plans could make the difference between failure and success. However remote, the possibility existed the American could evade the UAE authorities and return to his country. Safavi would have said it was an impossibility, except the man was partnered with a trained operative now.

The cost would be high: diverting a two-man team at a critical juncture. But if the American turned the file over to his government, that would be mission failure.

He was certain of his course of action.

The vehicles pulled up next to the plane. The flight crew were beginning their preparations, while his two men were loading their gear into the cargo hold. This was a task requiring care and circumspection, and so Safavi would brief the team in person before they departed.

Safavi stepped out and motioned for the team leader to come over. The customs man and Hessaby went to speak with the pilot.

Having been summoned off the stairs by the crew, Barrett stood by the SUV trying to look unperturbed by the chain of events. Susan was staring off at the Fujairah city lights beyond the airport. After a few minutes the copilot went up into the cockpit to begin the preflight checks, and soon the whine and whir of the APU kicked in, giving power to the plane's systems.

Barrett heard, distinctly, a "No way, Jose!" from the gray-haired pilot. The older man had his captain's hat in one hand, the other on his hip, the uncompromising posture evident even in the dim light. Tommy was trying to reassure him, but it didn't look like he was making any headway.

The younger copilot stuck his head out of the cabin door, looking for his left-seater.

"John?" he called. "Mr. McCowan?"

"Over there." Barrett raised his voice over the aircraft's whine, pointing forward of the nose.

"Let them know we're ready when they are," the copilot said. "Are you joining Mr. McCowan? If so, I need to see your passports or photo ID to send an adjusted manifest."

"That remains to be seen," Barrett replied.

The copilot shrugged his shoulders and ducked back in to complete his preparations.

The customs official, while willing to make certain exceptions for his Iranian business partners, was otherwise a stickler for details. His contempt for laxness made him an inveterate checker-of-things, which irked his three young subordinates. Now he noticed the plane several parking spots down had people milling about, and not one of his customs vehicles was present. Where was Faruk?

Finished with the Iranians, he jumped in his pickup and headed over to investigate.

Sada saw a pair of headlights switch on and swivel in their direction. She edged closer to the vehicle, putting the bulk of the SUV between her form and what she saw now was an airport pickup approaching.

"Barrett!"

McCowan called out to Ross, and the American jogged over to join the businessman and the captain. Sada hadn't had time to process and react before the American moved from her side. The pickup was pulling right up to them, the sound of its approach masked by the spooling up of the Gulfstream's engines. As it stopped, the pickup turned to park with its headlights bathing the immediate area around the plane's steps, and Ross, who was just crossing the space. Ross turned and looked at the vehicle.

Sada saw the whole thing unfold as if in slow motion. She pulled her weapon out and ran around the SUV to close the twenty-meter gap to the passenger-side window of the pickup truck.

The customs man sat stunned, hit by a flash of recognition. He knew that face. It was all over the news for two days now. He looked at the two men standing by the nose of the aircraft, one in a pilot's uniform. A movement out of the corner of his eye caused him to turn his head. A woman, her arms extended, was pointing a gun at him.

The vehicle leapt forward, careening into a tight left turn

as the driver struggled to control it and not clip the wings of the aircraft parked in the adjacent row. The truck straightened out and raced away between the lines of planes. Damn! She should have fired.

Sada yelled at the stunned men. "We need to go! Now!"

Safavi couldn't believe his ears. He wasn't sure how the customs man understood to come to him first instead of reporting the Americans to airport security, but he did. Praise be to Allah.

"Follow me," he yelled to Hessaby and the team, "the American!" He pulled out his concealed sidearm as he ran, cursing at the realization his men had just packed their rifle cases in the cargo hold. How had the American arranged this? In about sixty seconds it wouldn't matter.

Susan ran over to them. "What are we waiting for?" she yelled.

Barrett knew the driver of the pickup saw his face. Airport security would be here soon, and they might shoot him on sight.

"Listen!" he shouted, pushing himself before the pilot. "You've got to trust me. This is a matter of life and death, and national security. I need you to get me and this woman out of here now!"

The captain hesitated. He was grizzled, with an old-fashioned crew cut, the same one he'd worn since he'd done his first carrier landing off the coast of Vietnam in '69. The set of his jaw indicated he did not suffer stupid bullshit.

"Are you working for the government?"

Barrett was tempted to lie. "No, but that's only because

the government doesn't know what's going on yet. I tried to meet with the embassy yesterday, but was stopped. I've got a linkup set with the FBI, but I need to get to the States first. Will you help us?"

"Ross!" Susan shouted at him. She then leaned out around the back of the Suburban and fired her weapon across the parking ramp. Even over the Gulfstream's whine, Barrett heard the cracks and pings of the return fire as bullets ripped through the sheet metal body of the SUV. Rounds chipped the concrete around them.

Barrett ran crouching to the side of the SUV's nose, putting the engine block between him and the attackers. "Get over here!" he yelled, pulling the woman beside him.

He shifted over and they both fell into the prone position, looking beneath the vehicle and around the tires. With only a few floodlights high atop the adjacent hangars, it was hard to discern anything among the shadows of the parked planes stretching before them. As his eyes adjusted, though, Barrett thought he saw two or three darker spots on the tarmac, fifty to seventy-five meters from them. "There," he whispered, pointing to three spots.

"Yes," Susan acknowledged.

"Cover me," he said. He ran back to the pilot and Tommy, who were lying next to the plane's front wheel.

He was back in twenty seconds. "What was that about?" she asked.

Barrett started to explain but was drowned out by the roar of the opened throttle as the plane, passenger steps retrieved, began rolling, heading toward the taxiway.

The woman looked him in the eye but didn't say anything.

They directed their attention back along the flat expanse of the tarmac. As if in response to the receding aircraft, three figures jumped to their feet, sprinting toward Barrett and Susan, firing in an attempt to strike the aircraft with weapons that weren't effective beyond fifty meters.

"I've got right, you take left!" Barrett shouted. From his firing position beneath the Suburban's engine block, Barrett aimed at the approaching rightmost target. He squeezed off two rounds. By the time he indexed his weapon to the left, the middle target was already down, whether in response to the sound of firing or because the woman took him out, Barrett wasn't sure.

"Now," Barrett yelled, and standing, he yanked open the passenger door. He slid across behind the steering wheel and fired the ignition with the key Tommy had just passed him. Susan jumped in beside him.

The vehicle roared to life, and the headlights caught the form of a man twenty meters away, ducking his way in and around the landing gear of the other aircraft. He'd been flanking them. The man knelt next to the front wheel of a Cessna and aimed.

"Get down!" Barrett yelled, and they missed cracking each other's skulls as they threw themselves below the dashboard. A round shattered the driver's-side window. Two subsequent rounds tore through the side and rear quarter panel of the SUV, as the shooter corrected his initial mistake and fired lower. But Barrett was already powering through a quarter turn, driving while aiming in his mind for the spot where the Gulfstream had been parked. He straightened the vehicle and gunned it as more rounds impacted the rear of the SUV. After a second, Barrett raised his head enough to peer over the dash. He lashed the steering wheel to the right to avoid a light stanchion at the corner of the ramp, almost flipping the Suburban but regaining control in time and pointing it down the taxiway. He raced the two hundred meters to the end of the taxiway where the jet waited, passenger stairs deployed once more.

Barrett slammed on the brakes and the vehicle skidded to a stop a few meters from the jet. With a quick glance back, the two dashed for the steps to the plane's cabin. Susan had just thrown herself inside and Barrett was halfway up, when Tommy, positioned at the top of the steps to help them in, began shouting forward into the cockpit, "Go, go, go!"

PART 2

Critical

Q: How concerned are you about the potential leakage of nuclear material from the former Soviet Union, from Russia?

A: Oh, I'm very concerned. I think we're lucky that there haven't been large losses so far, as far as we know. I think that reflects well on the Russians who are responsible for this material, their discipline and their commitment. But they are in a chaotic situation. It's a race really between efforts to improve the situation and the black marketers. And as far as we know, nothing really major has happened and that's been amazing good fortune.

Q: But we don't know what we don't know.

A: Of course, we don't know what we don't know and, you know, it could be that we will find out that there have been thefts and they've been going to Iran or someplace like that.

Ultimately there is a market and the invisible hand works, unfortunately, in all areas. And we've got to be concerned, of course, about this because nuclear weapons are very small. They are very destructive and a loss anywhere in the world can result in a nuclear explosion anywhere else in the world.

When we were engaging in this craziness, which was the nuclear dimensions of the cold war, we never figured that one of the nuclear weapons states might collapse and then we'd have a situation where there were tens of thousands of nuclear weapons and the nuclear materials *equivalents up for grabs.*

The cold war may be over, but the threat from the cold war is far from over.

— PBS Frontline interview with Dr. Frank von Hippel, former Assistant Director for National Security in the White House Office of Science and Technology Policy, professor at Princeton University, and Co-Chair of the International Panel on Fissile Materials.

16

The three of them slumped into the beige cushioned chairs. Susan and Tommy sat across a table from each other on one side of the cabin, Barrett along the other, his chair swiveled toward the aisle. No one said much while the plane climbed, other than Tommy making a quick check forward and coming back to explain the pilot had gotten emergency clearance after alerting the tower he'd been fired upon. With luck, the Fujairah Airport security force were responding to a suspected terrorist event and sweeping up the attackers.

The big man, flushed, wiped his brow with a napkin from the table and broke the silence.

"Friends of yours?"

"Iranians," Susan responded.

"It wasn't the Dubai police we were really worried about," Barrett added.

"Why are Iranians trying to kill you?" the executive asked. "The ambush, the mob, now this. Are you trying to impress me?"

Barrett knew the man was putting two and two

together, making an educated guess as to Susan's occupation. Barrett caught Susan's eyes.

"I want to give Tommy the background."

"No. There's no reason to. Soon you'll be in the United States. You can give everything to your authorities."

"Or, I'll be arrested by the *Polizei,* and find myself trying to get a twenty-two-year old from the embassy to listen to my story before the Germans put my ass back on a plane for the UAE. If I do get to the States, I'm going to need to do some fast-talking to convince an old friend to go to bat for me. I need to understand what we've got, and Tommy can help us."

"I don't like widening this further than it has to."

Barrett sensed the woman was listening to him. Not lecturing a pupil, as she had in the safe house.

"I'm sure Tommy's clearances far exceeded anything I ever had. Yet here I am running around with a secret people are killing for."

Barrett saw her wavering. The hardness in her expression at the safe house was also gone. She nodded slightly. Barrett turned to the CarbonTec CEO.

"We have an electronic file that seems to pinpoint the location of an illicit source of highly enriched uranium. Either an old warhead or bulk HEU from a Soviet stockpile. The Iranians were trying to buy these directions from a Central Asian operative," Barrett said.

"Why would they do that?" Tommy asked. "Everyone knows the Iranians can enrich their own HEU if they want to."

"With consequences," Susan reminded him.

"What does the file say?" Tommy asked.

"I still need to translate it," Susan said. "I merely glanced at it the first time. At the apartment I was...focused on other things."

The Mossad agent was holding back. That was clear.

All the time in the other room in the safe house, talking with her people. What did she find out that she wasn't sharing?

Barrett took the laptop and flash drive out of his backpack and set them on the table in front of her. She accessed the program and opened the file. The cabin fell silent for the next half hour as the Israeli agent sat hunched over the keyboard, staring at the screen, and typing her translation.

When she was finished, she turned the laptop around to face the men.

"It's probably ninety-five percent correct."

Barrett came over to stand next to Tommy and the men read through the translation on the screen.

```
WHITE SEA
Site COLLIERY


From HICO on Road #60, go south/southwest on
Road #19 for 7.4 kilometers. Turn left onto Road
#5, and follow it for 600 meters. Turn right,
and immediately bear left onto the Station Road.
Follow this road for 4.9 kilometers. It will
wind through a series of switchbacks to the
Bridge. From the south end of the bridge, follow
the road for 1.8 kilometers. The road will make
three switchbacks, the third of which is at the
1.8 kilometer point. From this point, move on
foot. Leave the road to the left and enter the
woods. Cross the small stream, and 20 meters
beyond you will come upon an old mining trail.
Turn left and follow the trail for 2.8
kilometers. The trail will start northward,
moving uphill for the first 400 meters, at which
point it will crest the top of the spur. From
```

that point, continue to follow the trail for the remaining 2.4 kilometers, which will lead generally southeast and then south, parallel to the river in the valley to the left. The path is covered by dense woods, and follows a gradual incline. After approximately 2.8 kilometers the path will widen out into an open area. A large portal will appear on the right, blocked by an iron gate. Continue for another 100 meters, passing an abandoned stone building on the right. The next aperture on the right is the drift mouth, which is approximately 4 meters wide and 2 meters high. This is the entrance to the cache site. An iron gate has been installed since the mine's closing. Proceed into the shaft exactly 50 steps. Along the left wall, five large support timbers are stacked on the ground. Beneath the timbers, the cache has been cut into the stone to a depth of approximately 1.5 meters. Once the timbers are removed, the top of the cache is covered with 30 centimeters of loose stone and dirt, under which sits a wooden board and then the metal container. Remove the wood board carefully. The cache container is protected by means of MOLNIYA, and must be disarmed accordingly before attempting to move or lift from the hole.

BADEN	Command
CORAX	Command
GOLD	Military
CHUTE	Military
Y12	Industrial

Tommy leaned back in his chair. "Your working thesis

is that the Iranians were going to find this uranium and...do what?"

"Make their first warhead," Susan said. "They would avoid the pre-emptive attack that enriching their own uranium stockpiles would invite."

"Where do you think this HEU is?" Tommy asked.

Susan fielded this as well. "The individual selling the information was a Kazakh, a former KGB officer. For years there were many unsecured nuclear storage sites throughout the Balkans and former Soviet republics. In addition to warheads, the source could be an old commercial reactor or scientific lab."

All vestiges of Tommy's inherent good-naturedness were gone now, his face set in an expression of dead seriousness. His voice lost much of its Southern twang.

"I don't think it's HEU from reserves or a lab. It's an actual warhead."

"Explain," Susan said.

"I will," Tommy said. "More important is the location. This site isn't in Kazakhstan or any other former Soviet republic. It's in the United States of America."

17

Safavi terminated the call on his cell phone and turned back to the window, staring into the darkness of the rushing desert as Hessaby pushed the SUV toward redlining. Taking the Dassault now was out of the question, with one of his men lying dead mere meters from it. But any questions he'd had as to next steps were gone, any previous indecision replaced with a clear path forward.

His last call was to the customs man, with whom Hessaby usually dealt. Safavi wanted to talk to the man himself, to thank him for his faithful service as well as his quick thinking on the airfield. Although Safavi understood the man must be careful not to run afoul of his superiors, perhaps the unit's plane and equipment could escape inspection by the police for a time. The customs man assured Safavi he would do everything in his power. He also promised to inquire as to the Gulfstream's filed destination.

Safavi's first call upon leaving the airport was to his team leaders. The men positioned in Dubai, Fujairah, and

Al Batinah were converging on Dubai International Airport. His second call was to the operations center at his base outside Qom, where support staff were scrambling to secure the earliest available flights for Safavi and eleven men. The teams would split into pairs, adopting the personas on their British, Indian, and German passports. They would depart Dubai en route to London, Frankfurt, Madrid, and Rome, with final destinations of New York and Washington. And Raleigh/Durham.

Safavi made calculations in his head. With luck, and a good connection, he should be in Washington, D.C., by Friday night, U.S. time. The operations specialist was to make sure that of all the team, Safavi should land in enemy territory first. He could take care of the American by himself, if need be, if the others were delayed. His team was critical for the rest of the mission, not to the handling of a single American.

Safavi's focus shifted from the blackness outside the window to his reflection in the glass, his face etched by the dim light from the dashboard. He let his focus blur, and his features slid away to reveal those of the American. That face had been framed in the windshield as the vehicle swept past him. In his eagerness he made a novice's mistake. The American was a lucky man. Still, Safavi considered, everyone's luck ran out. The Israeli woman kept showing up inconveniently as well. No matter. Maybe Safavi would find them together and eliminate them both.

Safavi's phone rang, and the operations center in Qom gave him his itinerary. Dubai to Amsterdam, Amsterdam to La Guardia, landing at 6:05 p.m. American East Coast time.

Safavi did not know this La Guardia person. If an airport was named for him, though, like JFK and Reagan, he would be no friend of Iran. Safavi knew about these men from his study of history. Great American presidents who had treated the Iranian people in ways ranging from dismissive arrogance to outright brutality. He remembered the day when he learned his two favorite cousins had died at the hands of the Americans. It was an awakening—as a boy of fifteen years—hearing the older men describe the hundreds of innocent men, women, and children shot out of the sky by the American navy.

Safavi felt his anger rising. Yes, a long list of unanswered injustices.

But, he reminded himself, although the American posed a risk, his escape worked to Safavi's advantage in one respect. General Roghani and his superiors were compelled to accede to Safavi's request to pursue, and so the mission was one step closer than it would otherwise have been. Things were going according to plan with the Scientist as well.

That part of the plan was simple because of the greatest failing of the Americans: their gullibility. No other people were so belligerent, on the one hand, yet blind to deceit, on the other. Amazing. How ironic that Americans were so often criticized as a nation of cowboys when most of them acted more like slow, dim-witted cattle.

They might one day learn their lesson.

Safavi would retrieve the file, and the device. When the call came, he would deliver the ultimatum with joy in his heart.

General Masoud Roghani, commander of the Qods Force, looked out over the brick wall and wrought iron fence surrounding his compound in the heart of Tehran. Other than the anti-American murals, not much had changed in the physical appearance since he'd stormed these walls as a young man in 1979, when the building that now served as his headquarters had been the American embassy to the Shah's puppet regime.

On his desk awaited a large brown envelope, and he carefully unwound the string tie. He pulled out the thin sheaf of yellowed onion-skin papers. Computer files were fine, but not until the Kazakh had produced these originals, complete with date stamps and penciled initials next to the Cyrillic text, had Roghani taken the possibility to his superiors.

The Soviets had been vigilant against their enemies, and their network of spies and informants pervasive. He wondered if the Americans ever learned just how pervasive.

The secret communiqué was fascinating reading, even for a man as experienced as he was in operating in the shadows. It laid out the process of deductive reasoning the Soviet agent had followed. Some anonymous foot soldier of the KGB, who no doubt had risen quickly through the ranks of the KGB based on the strength of this discovery.

The initial clue had been the blast doors.

The agent had developed an informant in an American engineering firm, which formed a "Nuclear Products Group" at the height of the Cold War. Americans were building bomb shelters in their backyards, and in true capitalistic fashion, some were determined to make money off the terror of their fellow countrymen. The company also had contracts with the American government.

In 1961, the informant reported the receipt of an order for two massive blast doors constructed of twenty-inch-thick steel. Weighing twenty-five tons apiece, they were large enough to drive trucks through and had to be shipped on special rail cars. The bill of lading read simply, "Greenbrier Hotel."

In the autumn of 1962, the agent was on site. Even as the Americans were first learning of Khrushchev's gambit in Cuba, and Kennedy was leading the world to the brink of nuclear war, the Soviet sleeper continued his surveillance of the facility. The huge construction project required thousands of tons of concrete, hundreds of mattresses, and months' worth of provisions poured into "the hole." The agent learned that the true purpose of hotel's "addition" was an open secret among the American peasants living in the remote corner of the Allegheny Mountains.

The agent made his recommendation. The Greenbrier Hotel in White Sulphur Springs, West Virginia, should be put on the WHITE SEA list. What followed were the agent's forecast for delivery of an ALPHA cache from the staging area in Juarez, Mexico. And, at the end, a carefully worded and circumspect questioning of the effectiveness of saboteurs and demolitions against the sort of hardened bunker he had just discovered beneath the hotel.

Roghani smiled to himself. In this instance the agent's superiors in Moscow were well ahead of him. They understood the lengths the Americans would go to protect themselves.

Roghani turned the paper in his hand, and his smiled faded. He had reached the end of the file's contents. They knew what the target had been, but Ismagulov had insisted on withholding the location of the cache until this latest meeting. And now Alizadeh, the idiot, had failed.

Out the window, over the wall, people were hurrying by on the opposite side of the street. He sighed. He had not wanted to send Safavi out. Not yet. But what choice did he have? Without the last piece of the file, everything was wasted.

He would learn if the wager he'd made on his young upstart protégé had been well placed. His own survival might rest in Safavi's hands.

18

Barrett was trying to make sense of Tommy's assertion that the unsecured uranium source was in the U.S.

"Tommy, how are you getting to this?" he asked. He wiped the palms of his hands on his pants.

"These code names at the bottom, followed by the words *command*, *military*, and *industrial*. What do you think those mean?"

"I didn't get that far yesterday," Susan admitted. "Reading it now, I assume they're sites associated with the HEU, or weapon storage. Maybe production sites."

"I assume this file, the original, was encrypted?" Tommy asked.

"Yes."

"Well, I think the Russians were counting on protection from prying eyes. These aren't really true, randomized code words. They're just a sort of shorthand. For people who already knew the targets."

"Targets?" Barrett asked, almost blurting out the word.

"I'm not sure what these first two places labeled *Command* are, but I have a pretty good idea of what the

Military ones are. You should too, Barrett. As far as *Y-12*, the *Industrial* site, I know what it is."

"Go on," Susan said.

"Folks, Y-12 is my old stomping grounds. It's Oak Ridge National Laboratory."

Startled, Barrett looked at Susan. The woman's face was placid, but her mind must be racing like his was.

Tommy continued, "Y-12 *was* a top-secret code word, long ago. An American one. It was the designation General Leslie Groves and Robert Oppenheimer gave to the huge plant built at Oak Ridge, Tennessee in 1942. For the Manhattan Project. It's where the U.S. processed the uranium-235 to build Little Boy, the bomb that destroyed Hiroshima."

"I'm still not sure this is making sense to me," Barrett said. "You mentioned targets."

"These directions weren't written up by a current agent. Or any would-be terrorist," Tommy continued. "I'm sure this is something stolen from the KGB's files."

Barrett glanced at Susan again. She was listening closely and wasn't arguing with the man. Turning back to Tommy, he asked, "You said the code names referred to targets. Targets of what?"

"Targets of what's in the cache site."

"You're saying the Soviets hid a weapon in the U.S.? To attack targets here?"

"Over the years," Tommy continued, "the Swiss and the Germans have located and destroyed a number of Russian cache sites filled with weapons, radios and demolitions. These were buried for use by special saboteur teams in the event of war breaking out between NATO and the Soviet bloc."

"This sounds like something out of a book."

"Nevertheless, it's true. Rumors surfaced, too, that the Soviets planted not just conventional demolitions but small nukes."

"You mean Soviet agents hiding backpack nukes on U.S. soil," Barrett challenged. Even as he said it, he realized the idea didn't seem crazy in light of his personal experiences over the past three days.

Tommy took off his glasses, rubbing the bridge of his nose. "Maybe not as far-fetched as you'd like to think. Man-portable nukes were achieved. The U.S. built and deployed its own version in the 1960s, called the SDAM, or Special Demolitions Atomic Munition."

"Why would either side bother? We had tens of thousands of land-based and submarine-based ICBMs pointed at each other."

"The original purpose of the SDAM was a small atomic bomb for taking out key facilities. Like dams and bridges. Any target too big to be handled by conventional demolitions. You have to remember, these were the days before laser-guided smart bombs and cruise missiles."

"How small could these things be?"

"The term 'man-portable' is a stretch. The SDAM looks like a fifty-five-gallon oil drum inside a giant backpack. Man portable for a few miles—maybe. The point is, the SDAM was plenty small enough to hide in a car or truck and, if needed, be carried over the final stretch by a single man. It could be carried a lot farther, too, if you had a small team of Special Forces soldiers taking turns humping it."

"Even if it was technologically feasible—still, Soviet nukes hidden in America?" Barrett knew he was repeating himself.

"The possibility has been taken seriously," Tommy said. "That's a matter of public record. Congress held hearings back in the nineties where KGB defectors testified about just such a Soviet capability—and intent—during the Cold War."

"Would such a weapon, if recovered from a cache, still work?" Susan asked, speaking for the first time in several minutes.

"Most likely, no," Tommy responded. "The bomb contains conventional explosives inside that have to fire first to initiate the nuclear explosion. These would be worthless now, or dangerously unstable. Not to mention the batteries needed for the electrical charge—they'd be long dead. Also, to ensure enough neutrons were present to sustain a chain reaction at detonation, the bomb would have a neutron source embedded in it. This component would be inert after forty or fifty years."

"Then we're back to the idea of the Iranians hoping to harvest the uranium to use in their own bomb," Susan mused.

"Or, worse, they could be planning to transfer it to a third party," Tommy continued. "A group with sufficient expertise to use the HEU to build an IND."

"A what?" Barrett asked.

"An Improvised Nuclear Device."

Dave Allen sat on the blanket his jailers had given him, the thin brown cloth folded into a square to provide some cushion against the tile floor of the cell. He'd been in the jail for at least half a day. The attack by the mob had been late afternoon. His chat with the police chief had taken place an hour or two later. It had to be early morning now, and he was exhausted but couldn't sleep.

At least no one had beaten him, not since the cuff on the side of the head. That was a positive sign.

Dave checked his wristwatch—before he remembered he didn't have it. His watch, his wallet, his clothes, were all gone. He sported the fashionable uniform of the Dubai jail system: white cotton trousers and white shirt with a wide blue stripe running the circumference of his midsection.

Besides the badly bruised eye, his inventory yesterday revealed a missing tooth, contusions all over his arms and torso, and what felt like a deep muscle bruise on his thigh. He assumed his face was a black and blue mess, but he hadn't seen a mirror yet. Overall, he'd live.

His back was propped up against the cinderblock wall of his cell. The other three sides were bars, forming a big cage sticking out from the wall. His cell was one in a series of four identical cages attached to the puke-green wall on the other side of the central walkway.

The accommodations consisted of four sets of bunk beds, a lidless toilet in the back corner, and a plastic table bolted to the floor. The problem was the cell, designed to accommodate eight prisoners, now housed thirty men. From what Dave could see, all the other cages were equally overcrowded. Most of the inmates managed to sleep, and a few played cards. They were Arabs and expat laborers, the poor Pakistanis, Bangladeshis, and Indians who filled the insatiable need for manual labor throughout the city.

A few paler faces dotted the other cells. Despite Dubai's reputation for leniency, the occasional European tourist got thrown into the poke for public displays of affection or flipping off a motorist. Generally, you had to do something pretty dumb to draw the police's attention.

Like flee the scene of a crime and try to run a police roadblock.

He'd had one brief talk last night with a harried embassy staffer who stood outside the cell's bars. Dave tried to explain what happened to him and Barrett, but the man didn't listen, just kept reassuring Dave the U.S. government would do everything it could to ensure due process, yada, yada, yada, and then the interview was over.

He wondered if Amy knew he was in jail, and had contacted the embassy, or if the Emiratis had called Carr's people. Had Amy left the hotel, and was she safe? He hoped she did as he urged, and left Al Batinah right after their phone call. He tried to figure who, beyond the police, might know she'd accompanied Dave and Barrett to the resort.

And what about Barrett?

Al-Hashimi had shut him down when he tried to ask about his friend, but clearly the police thought Barrett was alive. They were eager to find him. Dave did his best to adhere to the story as he remembered Barrett saying he'd told it to the chief during the initial interview in the hotel room. All Dave knew, he claimed in response to the policeman's repeated questioning, was his friend was desperate to get to the consulate and speak to the American authorities.

One possible ray of sunshine was that Al-Hashimi pressed him hard on the Israeli woman as well. She must be with Barrett. His friend had escaped the mob somehow. If the two of them were together, Barrett's chances would be a lot better.

Dave looked around in the gloom of the early morning light.

One of the prisoners stuck out. In the cell opposite his, a man paced back and forth along the outer bars while most of the other inmates slept. He must have come in during the night, and he hadn't been given prison garb yet. Although rumpled and soiled, the slacks and jacket he wore were of a decent cut. He wasn't a day laborer, that was clear. He was a stocky man, and his face, while not European, wasn't Arab or Indian either. This man's features had a Slavic look, with a hint of Asia as well. He could be from one of the -Stans.

He wasn't taking his incarceration easily. He should sit down and relax, Dave thought. He doubted that anyone was expedited through Dubai's jail system, even if their offenses were minor. Dave had little hope he was going anywhere anytime soon, even if the embassy got involved.

Which was an issue. Barrett was out on the lam, maybe with the Israeli, or maybe on his own. With some sort of secret that people were willing to kill for.

Or maybe he shouldn't be so worried about his friend. He might want to worry more about how he was going to get out of jail.

"I need to reach my friend in the FBI asap," Barrett said.

Tommy had gone on to explain that an IND was the worst-case scenario in the government's terror-response scenarios. The fear that Al Qaeda or some other group would get their hands on sufficient HEU, and the relevant expertise, and fashion a crude atomic device. While such a bomb would be orders of magnitude less efficient than a modern warhead in a superpower's arsenal, it could still devastate a large portion of an American city, killing and injuring hundreds of thousands. The scariest part, according to Tommy, was that the scientific knowledge required was not much beyond that gained by many physics grad students.

"What is your plan to get home?" Susan asked, interrupting his thoughts.

Barrett felt sheepish considering the rapid escalation of the situation. He couldn't deny he'd been making this up on the fly. He'd been preoccupied with just escaping Dubai with the flash drive. Even at the expense of leaving Dave behind, he realized. *I will never leave a fallen comrade to fall into the hands of the enemy.* Violated that one. He hoped, in the end, it would prove to be the right call.

"I have a friend at the air base in Ramstein who I think can smuggle me into the States."

"Room for two?" Susan inquired.

"I think so," Barrett said, "but I thought you'd be working your way back to Tel Aviv."

"Maybe it's best we stick together for a while longer."

The woman's statement came like a reprieve from a looming threat. The situation was spinning out of control, and he'd felt like he was the one on the hook for fixing it all. Until now. She was beginning to trust him, and that made the rest of the plan forming in his head seem like a possibility they might actually pull off.

"A plan," he said. "Tommy, do we have Wi-Fi on this thing?"

Tommy nodded, and Barrett took out his laptop. A quick map reconnaissance showed that Ramstein Air Base, the headquarters for the U.S. Air Force in Europe, lay about 100 kilometers southwest of Frankfurt-am-Main, the international airport.

"Tommy, how does this work when we land? Is there anyway for Susan and I to get off the plane and avoid the authorities?"

"I think the Germans are going to be pretty strict. Most European countries are. When we land, we'll taxi over to the Fixed Base Operator. It's a private terminal of sorts, separate from the main terminals. We sit on the plane until an official comes out plane-side to do the customs and passport checks."

"So we're stuck."

"Maybe not. We're allowed to open the door while we wait, and customs usually takes five to ten minutes to show up," Tommy said. "We'll be parked pretty far from the tower, but Frankfurt is a major airport. I'm not sure what their security measures are to prevent this sort of thing."

"Being arrested by the Polizei would be bad enough," Susan said, "but there's another consideration."

"What's that?"

"The Iranian hunting you has been resourceful. He's had operatives everywhere you turn. He'll know, from the flight plan filed with Fujairah, that this plane is destined for Frankfurt."

Barrett studied the map on his computer again. *Sometimes you have to get on the ground to figure things out.* It was a favorite saying of an old boss. You couldn't come up with the perfect plan by sitting back at headquarters, standing around a map. You made a tentative plan, then moved into the field and started your recon to really understand what your options were.

"Tommy, what happens if we divert to another airport? Will they allow us to land?"

"Sure, we can land. But if the crew, or C-Flights' headquarters, hasn't submitted a revised flight plan before we land, we get hit with a fine. Five to ten thousand Euros."

Barrett remained silent, and Tommy added, "I reckon it's worth not getting shot at again. Tell me where you want to go."

"Here," Barrett said, turning the computer around. The screen showed an enlarged satellite view of an airfield dotted with small private planes. "Egelsbach. A regional airport, ten klicks southeast of Frankfurt International."

"Consider it done," Tommy said, and walked forward to the cockpit.

"Now I need to call in another favor," Barrett muttered, reaching for the sat phone.

19

Barrett checked his watch. Another four hours before the plane reached the small airfield at Egelsbach. Susan had been right to avoid Frankfurt. He thought about the body count that was forming in the wake of the Iranian's pursuit of him. Barrett needed to come to grips with the fact that this man was targeting him and would not stop until he was dead.

The irony was not lost on him; he was in more danger now than he'd ever been in while wearing a uniform. Until the incident near the end of his tour in Iraq, he hadn't seen much in the way of violence and hadn't worried about his personal safety.

Most people never noticed the small camp squatting in the dust west of the main supply route. If the passersby were U.S. troops, they were too busy scanning the trash on the shoulders of the highway for suspicious objects.

The forward operating base could be spotted easily, though, by those who knew it was located at the base of the aerial antennas rising a thousand feet above the surrounding fields. The array of red and white radio masts were a vestige of the place's former life as an Iraqi communications site. Now the only purpose they served was as giant aiming stakes.

Shoot here.

The insurgents had figured that out, and on moonlit nights they'd fire one or two rounds from the bed of a pickup before racing away along the irrigation berms. Shoot and scoot, before the helicopters found them. If the antennas were giant crosshairs, the good news was that the bad guys were also bad at mortar fire. Yet one morning that had all changed.

Just before first light the camp was rocked by an explosion. Running from the command post, he'd tried to make sense of the confusion as soldiers poured from their tents, rushing half-dressed in shorts and body armor for the safety of the concrete blast barriers. The First Sergeant and NCOs were shouting, directing, trying to assess where the round landed and if anyone was hurt.

Relief outweighed embarrassment when they figured out the source of the blast. A water heater hooked to the portable showers had suffered a malfunctioning valve. The pressure built up until the tank launched itself into the sky. They found the mangled cylinder a hundred meters from the shower trailer. It was, according to the assessment of some of the men, proof positive of the stupidity of lowest-bid Army contracting. Not to mention the inadvisability of "buying cheap-ass haji shit."

There had been a few close calls, but the insurgents never managed to lob a round inside the perimeter. For the entire length of his deployment they remained incompetent long-range shooters.

They would figure out other ways of bringing the fight to the Americans. His unit already knew that, of course, but it was a point driven home right before the end of their rotation. A lesson learned in the hardest possible way.

* * *

Barrett awoke with a start. He rolled to his side and propped himself up on his elbow. The cabin lights were dimmed. Susan was asleep on the opposite divan and Tommy was reclined in a chair, snoring. Maybe he'd gotten three hours of fitful sleep, interrupted by dreams. At one point, he was shoving a hand towel into the back of Peter's leg to staunch the bleeding. Then the people and places morphed, and he was back in the Army. He wasn't sure if the dreams dredged up the memories flooding his head, or if it was the other way around.

On a night seven years ago, the sound had caused him to swing his legs off the side of the cot before he was even fully awake. Usually, the explosions were muffled *cruhmps*, like artillery impacting far off in the distance. This had been a low, guttural roar, like the start of thunder, clipped at the end with a clang of sundering steel. The sound of metal shredding.

Someone had been hit on the main supply route to Baghdad.

He pushed his feet into his boots and pulled a polypro top over his T-shirt. The night air was cool when he stepped through the tent flap. The full moon from earlier had set, and he used a small blue-lens flashlight to negotiate his way through the tent stakes, ropes, and sandbags on his way back to the tactical operations center.

As he stepped into the concrete building that housed the TOC, Lieutenant Harker was on the radio. He waited for his XO to put the handset down and brief him on the situation. Barrett listened, and dispatched the quick reaction force, which was already spooling up after hearing the blast. They'd link up with the unit that had been hit, provide security, and escort the casualty evacuation vehicles to the aid station. Lieutenant Harker confirmed that Doc and his team were standing by.

The battalion's physician assistant and half of the combat medics were stationed at his company's FOB. They were the most comprehensive medical care around for a few hundred square miles. Logistics convoys moved up and down the MSR every night, passing within five hundred meters of the camp. Anytime people got hit by IEDs between overpasses 12 and 20, the wounded came here.

The event was tracked, logged, and plotted on the map by the soldiers on shift. He checked the situation reports before they were radioed in to higher headquarters. Then he called Harker over to the large mosaic of 1:50,000 scale maps covering an entire wall, and discussed a shift in the remaining patrols scheduled before daylight. He'd have Third Platoon focus on possible avenues of approach; nothing would be found at the site itself except a divot in the shoulder of the road.

One of the routes he wanted the patrol to cover crossed into the Poles' territory. Call Battalion and coordinate up the chain?—Harker wanted to know. Hell, Barrett thought, that'd take a day and a half. *None of our vaunted NATO allies leave their camps at night, anyway.*

He was debating on another cup of coffee when the QRF leader called in thirty minutes later. The site was secured. Three casualties were en route to base, two urgent, one walking wounded. The unit that was hit, a transportation battalion, would be carrying a KIA with them back to Victory Base.

Increasingly, the attacks were being conducted with EFPs—explosively formed penetrators. Cheap and easy to make, the new weapons created hypersonic metal slugs that penetrated the heaviest of armor. They were complete overkill for light-skinned vehicles, and the insurgents were getting their hands on more and more of the things.

The field ambulance pulled up in the gravel turnaround between the TOC building and the aid station, a partially collapsed structure in which Doc worked his magic in an improvised surgery suite built on elevated cots and field medical chests. He stepped outside to find the platoon leader of the QRF and get a rundown. As he stood there, a second humvee pulled up next to the aid station.

The cargo humvee had been stripped of its benches in order to fit stretchers in the bed. Soldiers and medics swarmed around both vehicles, preparing to move the wounded into the building. The rickety aid station door was propped open, and by the yellow light Barrett could see a casualty in the back of the humvee. She was lying on a litter, covered up to her neck with a poncho liner, a tube running up from under the blanket to the IV bag held by the medic kneeling over her. She was young, nineteen or twenty, a private or specialist. Her hair was matted to her forehead with sweat, and her dirty face was blank with shock. The medic talked to her, but her focal point was up among the stars.

Four men rushed to the back of the truck. As they pulled the stretcher off and hurried to the door, one of the soldiers stepped on the corner of the poncho liner, and the cover slipped away. The girl's leg was severed high above the knee. The stump was wrapped in bloody bandages and T-shirts, and a quick-cinch tourniquet cut deep into the thigh above the wound.

The soldiers hustled the casualty into the aid station, and the door banged shut, returning the space between the buildings to moonless dark.

He never got a chance to track down the QRF leader, or think any more about the young girl who'd just lost her leg. A frantic burst of radio communications squawked from inside the TOC.

A sergeant came running out into the dark. "Captain

Ross! Captain Ross!"

When they had been waiting for Sheehan to pick them up in the desert, Dave had tried to pass the time telling old stories of their lieutenant days together. Barrett's participation was half-hearted, but his friend persisted. At one point, Dave asked, "Why'd you get out Barrett? You would have gone far if you'd stayed in."

He hadn't actually been fired, of course. Only officers that got DUIs or were caught having affairs actually got booted. But his options were effectively reduced to getting out, or hanging on for the pension. He was never going to command anything again after Iraq, not with the rating on his last report card. He would have become one of those bitter lieutenant colonels who get shunted off into obscure roles, waiting for retirement.

He saw it coming, of course, after everything that happened in the aftermath of the incident. Even so, his evisceration at the hands of the brigade commander had been a thing to behold. The write-up on his efficiency report was a classic case of damnation by faint praise. Cool, correct, indisputable. And career-ending.

But all that was behind him. A past life that had no bearing on the present. They'd be landing in Germany soon, and he needed to focus on getting back to the States, and turning over the information he carried. Mitchell Kane and his FBI superiors could take it from there.

20

As they touched down on the small airfield, Barrett and Susan said their goodbyes to Tommy. Barrett could tell from her thank-you that the Israeli woman was reappraising the big American with the southern accent.

"Listen. I know you'll be speaking with the FBI soon, but if I can help with anything beforehand, give me a call," the man offered. "You have my number."

Looking through the window, Barrett could see the little Egelsbach airport bore all the signs of the distinctly German orderliness. Next to the tower was a single one-story terminal along with a handful of smaller buildings housing what looked like a flight school or aviation club. The adjoining parking area was filled with prop-driven two-seaters and a number of small business jets.

At that time of the morning, no one was in sight when Barrett and Susan stepped off the plane and walked the twenty-five meters to the door of the private terminal. Inside the FBO, the lounge area, as well as the desks normally staffed by the charter service employees, was deserted. The two simply walked across the large room and through the sliding glass doors, and found themselves on the sidewalk outside the airport's perimeter fence. A tall man in an Air Force jumpsuit was leaning against the door of a black BMW.

Jammer, aka Ed Janokowski, had been the air liaison officer attached to Barrett's battalion in Iraq. Like all Air Force ALOs, Jammer was responsible for coordinating air strikes if the ground troops made enemy contact. But neither the rules of engagement nor the tactical situation called for the dropping of two thousand-pound bombs during their OIF rotation, so Jammer assumed the duties of the Army captains in the battalion tactical operations center. He was smart, unflappable, and a quick study. Barrett hadn't seen much of Jammer in Iraq, separated as he was with his company at the FOB. But the bonds of friendship built during training and beer calls prior to deployment made Barrett feel okay about waking the pilot up at one o'clock in the morning. When he'd reached him, all Barrett said was "I need your help," and Jammer sprang into action. It didn't hurt that he was now a lieutenant colonel and commanded one of the C-17 squadrons based out of Ramstein.

The bad news was that the first bird flying west was a C-17 bound for Dover, Delaware, departing at 2200. Ten o'clock at night. Jammer had hosted them at his bachelor's quarters and did his level best to cook an Italian dinner for them before taking them out to the flight line.

Once Barrett was sitting in the big cargo plane, he looked around the cavernous belly of the C-17. The last time he'd been in one of these, he'd been jumping from it at eight hundred feet above a North Carolina drop zone. This plane was not configured for jumping, though. The red nylon jump seats still lined the sides of the aircraft, but the center was taken up by several large pallets strapped to the floor's tie-down points. Boxes and equipment were shrink-wrapped in heavy cellophane and cinched down with yellow cargo nets. He'd guided Susan forward toward the nose of the aircraft, to stay out of the way of the Loadmaster and any other passengers who might board.

He could see his friend Jammer standing at the top of the ramp, chatting with the loadmaster, the senior airman who ran the show in the rear. The pilot and officers up front might fly and navigate the plane, but the loadmaster owned and controlled everything that happened aft of the bulkhead. It was the loadmaster who let Jammer pencil in the two newcomers to the manifest without the formality of showing military IDs.

Two lines of men walked up either side of the ramp and spread through the belly of the plane. Some were wearing flight suits, like the loadmaster's, but without any insignia. Others wore civvies, a mix of Carhartt trousers, heavy shirts, and work boots. Certain features were common to all the men—lots of facial hair, civilian ball caps with Oakleys propped up on the visors, assault packs, and black high-impact weapons cases. A few of the men glanced in the direction of Barrett and Susan, but made no indication of caring about their presence. The newcomers settled in, pulling out paperbacks and ear buds, rolling out air mattresses in the open spaces alongside the pallets.

Jammer and the loadmaster stopped one of the bearded men. From the length of the big fuselage, with the whine of the four Pratt & Whitney turbofans cranking up, Barrett couldn't hear the discussion. Jammer was pointing forward at the two of them. The bearded man nodded a couple of times, and the Air Force officer clasped his arm in thanks. Jammer walked forward to Barrett's seat.

"Dan's cool with everything. When you get to Dover, you'll hang in the back of his group while the S.P.s do the customs thing. He's even agreed to give you a lift through the front gate. After that, you're on your own."

Barrett shook his friend's hand, and Jammer hurried to deplane. No sooner had the officer cleared the ramp than the loadmaster hit the button to raise it. The tail wasn't even buttoned up when the aircraft started to taxi.

For the warriors spread throughout the plane, this was old hat. How many times had they made this trip? Barrett wondered. How many deployments, doing for their country what most Americans would never know about and few would understand? Some of these men had been at this for a decade.

Susan followed his gaze and then turned to him. Since the firefight at Fujairah Airport, he liked to think she was regarding him more as a partner, and not a burden.

"You miss being a soldier, don't you?"

Barrett hesitated. "I never did anything like what these guys do. But some aspects I definitely miss."

"Why did you leave?"

"I made a call to reposition a patrol in response to an IED attack in Iraq. Without getting higher headquarters' approval first. The patrol was hit by another IED and two of my men died."

"I'm sorry."

"It was a questionable call on my part." He'd never really articulated it that way before. He'd scarcely admitted it to himself. "My boss thought it was a horrible call."

"Losing people is never easy."

"You had compulsory service?" he asked her. "Before your current assignment?"

"I joined voluntarily, as soon as I could," Susan replied. "I was a medic first and then served three years in the Caracal Battalion. That's our mixed infantry unit—men and women soldiers."

"You said losing people is never easy. Some of the men in the hallway were your teammates, weren't they."

"Yes."

"I'm sorry."

"Unfortunately, I've experienced this sort of thing before. Ten or twelve years ago my life plan was much different that what I've ended up doing. Things changed with that loss."

The plane pivoted and braked to a stop. They were poised at the end of the runway.

"Were you close to Peter?"

"When I joined my current organization, Jacob—his real name—was the head trainer for my cohort, the one in charge of pushing our minds and bodies through the selection process. He never yelled, but we all feared him."

"I understand."

"When I left my kibbutz and joined the Defense Forces, I made my first real friends. When I graduated from the course in the desert, I joined a special group. Years later, when I joined Jacob's team, I found a new family."

He wanted to ask her more, to understand where she came from, what life in the Mossad was like, but felt he might be crossing a line. Conversation was becoming harder, anyway, as the big plane's engines spooled up to a screaming pitch as the pilot achieved maximum thrust before releasing the brakes for the takeoff run.

Instinctively, Barrett leaned toward the nose of the aircraft to counteract the steep angle of attack as the big plane lifted into the air. Why had he left the Army? The decision to get out six years ago had altered the course of his life, no doubt about it. He'd avoided much of the hardship and disappointment these men on the plane would have endured. How many of them had lost comrades, close friends? But as he looked around at the grizzled veterans settling into the familiar routine of flying home, he knew they also shared something that sustained them.

Mission. Purpose. Brotherhood. Each man might define it differently. Susan would know that feeling.

Shared sacrifice, too. That was part of it. The knowledge that you were part of a group that did the necessary business that others weren't able, or willing, to do. Susan would know about that as well.

Plenty of people made sacrifices in other, less obvious ways. Like the people in his life. The choices his parents made that gave him the opportunities they never had. Maybe opportunities that his brother and sister never really had.

His course had been much different than the men around him. Whether it had been the right choice, he still wasn't sure. But the question that confronted him was, had he done anything important with his life since getting out? Had he looked out for anyone besides himself for the past six years?

What had he sacrificed?

Barrett opened his eyes. He must have been out for hours, the effect of the Ambien offered up by the special ops medic sitting nearby. Susan was slumped against him, still asleep. Her face, this close, in repose, was softer, and more beautiful, than when he first saw her. Exotic and foreign. Not just in the sense of birthplace but also experience. He felt like he had gotten merely a glimpse of what she had done in her life. Where was she going next? Was she coming to the U.S. to make sure the flash drive went where it needed to go, or because this was the easiest route back to Israel? The weight of her body against his arm was warm, comforting even.

The woman stirred, her head rolling off his shoulder in the other direction, coming to rest against the seat back. Barrett checked his watch, then reset it for the six-hour difference between Germany and the East Coast. Just past midnight in the States, and they'd be landing within the hour at Dover. Back in the U.S. after what felt like a month, but in reality had been, what, five days? Soon this affair would be out of his hands, and he could focus on getting his life back on track.

Barrett rubbed his eyes. His head ached, no doubt from the lack of caffeine. His body expected several cups a day, and right now he would kill for a good cup of coffee. He fished his Thucydides out of his pack and flipped to Pericles' funeral oration, but lost his concentration after a couple of pages. Restless, he stood up and moved aft toward the loadmaster's station to stretch his legs, stepping over and around the poncho-wrapped forms asleep in the aisle.

On the way back to his seat, Barrett spied an abandoned newspaper in one of the jump seats and grabbed it. The *Stars & Stripes*, Europe edition, from the day before. As he sat back down, he skimmed the headlines. Each article was an update of the news from a week ago. The economy, of course. The unfolding train wreck that was Europe's debt situation. The *Stripes*, however, paid particular attention to the war in Afghanistan, and he read the main articles. He flipped through the remaining sections. He was getting ready to put the paper back down when small article on page ten of the "In the World" section caught his eye. The word "Iranian" was in the headline. The AP article was accompanied by a small photo of a bespectacled young man being greeted by a throng of people.

Something was odd, or familiar, about the picture, and so he read the article.

```
Chapel Hill, NC — Jubilant supporters greeted
Karim Hoveyda as he arrived at the Raleigh-
```

Durham Airport today after a harrowing two-month ordeal as a prisoner in Iran's notorious Evin Prison. Hoveyda, a doctoral candidate in physics at the University of North Carolina-Chapel Hill was imprisoned by the Iranian authorities and accused of spying upon his return to Tehran in May to visit his family. His imprisonment garnered international recognition, and became a cause célèbre among many groups, including the American Society of Physicists, which sent a letter to Iranian Supreme Leader, Ayatollah Ali Khamenei, protesting the young Iranian's imprisonment.

"The charges were just ludicrous," said Robert Spencer, Hoveyda's doctoral advisor. "Karim is an extremely bright and dedicated scientist, and it's a shame his own country has treated him this way."

Hoveyda, 28, is an Iranian citizen who has pursued postgraduate studies in Great Britain and the United States. He is widely respected as a young scientist of considerable promise, a colleague noted.

No reason was given by Iranian authorities as to why Hoveyda was released now, without charges. U.S. officials were surprised, given the often hardline stance Iran takes with citizens and foreign nationals it accuses of espionage.

"We don't understand it, but we are very thankful," a source quoted family members in Tehran as saying.

It's thought the many petitions calling for Hoveyda's release may have pressured an Iranian regime which is feeling increasingly isolated in world opinion. Mr. Hoveyda would not comment directly on his ordeal, but a representative for the university stated that Hoveyda is happy to put this behind him, and is eager to resume his research and teaching responsibilities at UNC this fall. Hoveyda is pursuing his doctorate in nuclear physics.

Barrett was going to reread the article, but his eyes locked on the accompanying photo instead. The thin man had wire-rimmed spectacles and a bookish demeanor. He was walking through a waiting area crowded with people....

Barrett recognized the face.

"Susan, wake up. I have something here."

The woman pulled herself upright, instantly alert. Barrett folded the paper in half and held it out to her.

"The Iranians say they just released this nuclear physicist from prison."

"Yes?"

"He wasn't in an Iranian prison. This is the man I saw in the hallway of the Al Batinah Resort. This is the other man I told you about, the one who ran from Alizadeh's room."

Susan grabbed the paper and studied the news story. "Are you sure?"

Barrett replayed in his mind the two of them locking eyes, the sheer terror on the other man's face, the change in his expression and his relief when he realized he wasn't about to be killed.

"Yes. It's him."

"A trained physicist, reportedly imprisoned by the Iranians, was instead meeting with the head of Iran's nuclear weapons program. As well as the man selling the whereabouts of a warhead."

"Tommy's remarks about terrorists making an IND—the main stumbling block is getting the HEU. But they'd also need a person with the right scientific background."

"It fits," Susan answered. "Maybe not the assumption about giving it away to a terrorist group, though."

"What do you mean?"

"The Iranians are trying to get their hands on the nuke at the cache site. It seems they've already obtained a scientist with the requisite knowledge to convert the HEU to an improvised bomb."

"You think the Iranians intend to build an IND themselves? In the U.S.?"

"I think," she said, "that while you meet your FBI friend and alert the American intelligence bureaucracy, I'll make a visit to the University of North Carolina."

21

Barrett pushed west across the Delmarva peninsula, the teardrop shape of land encompassing Delaware and Maryland between the Atlantic and the Chesapeake Bay. He drove along the rural routes as fast as he thought prudent in the early morning hours—he didn't need to be stopped by a Maryland trooper when he had an unregistered weapon in his backpack.

They'd touched down in Dover around one in the morning. The Air Force security police conducting the customs inspections on the special operations unit assumed he and Susan belonged with the crew, even without ID. Two hours later they were clear of the base, and Dan gave them a ride in one of his Econolines to the rental place just outside the main gate.

Barrett's plan was to hit the Chesapeake Bay Bridge and U.S. 50, which would take him through D.C. to his house in Arlington. Somewhere in the dark, Susan was driving another rental. At the Beltway, she'd veer south for the six-hour drive to Chapel Hill, hoping to arrive as people were showing up to work at the university.

Before they split up, Susan shared what she'd learned from her colleagues in Tel Aviv about a new, shadowy Iranian unit. Ansar-ol-Mahdi. The men at Fujairah airport must be part of this group. He should not underestimate these guys, she said. But while he could see the wisdom of avoiding the scheduled landing in Frankfurt, he knew there was no way anybody could have traced their route via the Air Force flight to Dover. Besides, he was going to meet with a bunch of armed federal agents. He'd be very secure, very soon.

Susan would call as soon as she learned anything, and Barrett could relay the information to Mitchell. She hadn't offered up what her plans were after that.

Barrett realized that he'd probably seen the last of the Israeli operative. Once the file was safe in the hands of the American authorities, she would report back to her superiors and resume her normal life.

Normal. Did she know what normal was, or was her whole life a series of events like this? Of being constantly alert, on edge? He couldn't imagine.

Barrett let his mind go blank. The rest of the drive was uneventful, given the hour and the light traffic. He took 50 right through the heart of the city, around the Mall, and crossed the George Mason Bridge into Crystal City, headed for Arlington. He entered the Aurora Hills neighborhood, where he'd been lucky to find his house, a two-bedroom white clapboard on a quiet tree-lined street. Lucky, because it listed for substantially less than the million-dollar brick homes right around the corner. As he turned down his street, the sensation of coming home was strong. Reinvigorating even. As soon as he handed this business off to Mitchell, he was going to call Amy again and focus on doing whatever he could to clear Dave and get him out of jail. He'd call his boss at the think tank and ask for another day before heading back to work.

As his house came into view, however, he had a nagging doubt. He fought the impulse to slow down and instead drove past his driveway. He headed to the end of the long street, checking his mirrors and peering into the early morning gloom outside his headlights. Nothing. When he reached the end, he made a couple of lefts to put him on a parallel street and completed a rectangle.

As his house came into view the second time, he saw a car was now parked in the gravel drive. He'd called Mitchell when he was still an hour out, and seeing the driver's silhouette, he felt a sense of relief. As he pulled in between the other car and the hedge bordering his neighbor's yard, Mitchell Kane got from behind the wheel. Dark suit, conservative tie.

"Mitch, thanks for coming."

"Sure thing, my friend. Glad to see you home."

"As I mentioned on the phone, this is a bigger deal than we first thought," Barrett said, walking to the front door. "Come in and I'll show you what I have."

"Do you want to hop in my car? We can hang out at headquarters until people come in this morning."

"It's not even five o'clock," Barrett responded. "If it's okay, I'd like to put coffee on, show you what I have, and hit the shower. I'll go in with you then if you think it's still necessary."

Mitchell looked like he was going to argue, but conceded to the reasonableness of the request. "All right." He followed Barrett up the walk and through the front door.

Barrett pulled his laptop out and put it on the small table in the dining area, setting the open backpack on the floor next to his chair. While he pulled down the coffee and filters from a kitchen cabinet, Barrett gave Mitchell a blow-by-blow of the events since the previous Tuesday, starting with meeting the British tourists by the pool. He got to the discovery of the bloodbath in the hallway, and the call from Susan warning him to get out, before Mitchell broke in.

"Where's this woman now?"

For some reason, Barrett hesitated to tell Mitchell that Susan was en route to track down Hoveyda. "We split up outside Dover Air Force Base. I'll get to that in a minute. I assume she's working whatever connections she has to return to her country."

"Barrett, you came close to abetting a foreign agent here," Mitchell muttered.

"Mitchell, what was I going to do?" Barrett responded. He hit the button on the machine to start the brewing. "Use my special police powers to arrest her? For what? By the way, she's saved my life two or three times over the past few days."

"You're a big boy, Barrett," his friend said. "Don't dismiss the possibility you're being used. Would she have helped you if she didn't need you alive?"

Barrett passed over a cup of coffee.

"I trust her, Mitchell. For a while I didn't have any choice. But now I trust her."

Barrett completed the rundown of events, including the most recent discovery of the news article about the Iranian physicist, as well as his presence at the hotel shootout. He opened his laptop and connected the flash drive, inputting the password from the crumpled scrap of paper. He demonstrated the steganography program for Mitchell, importing the photo just as Susan had done.

"Like I said, you'll want some Russian and Arabic speakers to take a look at this, but here's a translation the Israeli woman put together," Barrett said, pulling up the other file.

"Why Arabic, if the intended buyers were Iranian?"

"The Israelis assume the Kazakh was originally trying

to find a buyer in Al Qaeda."

"I think—"

Mitchell's statement was cut short by the splintering of wood as the bolt in the front door was kicked through the jamb. A figure rushed through the door and stopped when he saw he already had a straight line of sight to Barrett and Mitchell standing in the dining room. The man pointed an assault rifle at them. A split second later, glass shattered behind them. Barrett pivoted his head. A short series of steps next to the dining nook led down to the bottom half of the split level, the living room, where a hand was now reaching through the broken glass and unlocking the sliding glass door that lead to the patio. The second man came through, armed like his colleague in the front room.

The man in front was large and fit. His dress slacks and open-collar business shirt was incongruous with the silenced rifle pointed at the center of Barrett's chest. The man in back moved closer to the wall on his right, to get a cleaner angle at Mitchell's back, and put himself out of the potential crossfire from the man in the front room.

"You have a computer memory device," the man in front said. The English was not native but passable. "And a password. Put them on the table."

The laptop on the table was turned so the Iranian couldn't quite see it. But Barrett saw the man's eyes dart to the table, recognition showing on his face. The man knew Barrett had the program, and the password, right there in front of him, and was showing it to Mitchell. Barrett had another moment of clarity. This was the man from Fujairah, the one kneeling by the plane's landing gear, pumping rounds into the side of the Suburban.

The man in the front room said something in Farsi to the man behind.

Then Barrett felt himself falling to his left, his shoulder slamming into the base of the wooden bookcase that lined the wall hidden from the front room. He realized he'd been shoved by Mitchell as spits of silenced gunfire filled the air around him. Chunks of drywall and wood erupted above him as he fell back to the floor, little visual explosions disembodied from the deafening noise of an un-silenced weapon firing. Through the metal legs of the dining table he saw with one good eye Mitchell crouching, weapon raised and firing into the front room. Then the balustrade behind his friend exploded into wood chips, rounds thumping into his friend's body. Mitchell grunted and fell still. Something was flowing into Barrett's left eye. The dark form of a man came into his limited field of vision, stood over the table, swept the laptop into a satchel, and barked an order in Farsi.

The first man disappeared. A pair of legs appeared beneath the table, the second man who'd come up the steps from the den below. The legs turned, dress shoes pointing at the slumped form of his friend. A single silenced shot ripped into Mitchell's body.

The legs turned and moved left to come around the table. Barrett rolled his head to focus his good eye on the approaching killer.

Another shot, close, loud and nerve shattering. The man above him fell to the floor like a puppet cut from its strings by a scythe, arms and legs splaying as the torso fell straight through its center of gravity. Barrett saw the pistol in his own outstretched arm. He lowered his arm, and his gaze, saw the red spreading out from beneath the body.

He waited for the first man to come back, knowing he would die now. Instead, he heard the distant wail of a police siren many, many blocks away, and the screeching squeal of tires as a car raced away on the next street over.

He struggled to focus. His friend was dead. The Iranian had his computer. The Iranian had the file. The police would arrive at his house in minutes.

Hope ebbed from his body as the blood poured down his face. All this way, and all he'd accomplished was to get Mitchell killed. The sirens grew louder, accusing him. How would he explain an FBI agent gunned down in his kitchen? Who would listen to him now?

Barrett lurched to his feet and fled his home.

22

The campus of the University of North Carolina at Chapel Hill was beautiful in the morning sunlight. The massive oak trees shaded grassy quadrangles set off by diagonal sidewalks connecting the neo-gothic buildings. Today, the paths were mostly devoid of people, since the undergrads had departed for their summer break a month ago.

Sada found a visitors parking lot just down the street from the famous Old Well and walked across the street to Phillips Hall.

If her life had turned out differently, she would have spent more time in a place like this, albeit one with palm trees lining the sidewalks. Her father—her real father—had been a professor at Tel Aviv University. But her mother's choice had been different, and so Sada found herself growing up in the barren Judean desert, an unhappy teenager looking for the first opportunity to escape the life of the religious kibbutz.

After her dereliction of duty, or so her superiors would deem it, she might be returning to the farm on the outskirts of Petah Tivka, north of Tel Aviv. If it hadn't already succumbed to real estate developers. Maybe she'd find the old grove where her grandfather had raised Jaffa oranges, the ones he'd let young Sada pick and eat straight from the tree. She would find a man who was not a soldier and raise her own daughter in a life full of soft sunshine and sweet oranges.

Shaking off the brief idyll, she walked up the broad steps to the brick and stone edifice, and entered a wide hallway with classroom doors opening off each side and a broad stairwell leading to the upper floors. Sada was looking for a directory for the faculty offices when an elderly gentleman walked down the hallway toward her, rifling through a stack of loose papers.

"Excuse me, can you tell me where I might find Karim Hoveyda?"

The man beamed. "Ah, Karim. I'm not sure if he was coming in so soon after getting back. But if he did, he'd go straight to the TUNL."

"The 'tunnel'?"

"T-U-N-L," the man explained, "the Triangle Universities Nuclear Lab. It's located on Duke's west campus. It's a facility shared between ourselves, Duke, and N.C. State. Is there something I can help you with?"

"Oh, thank you," Sada said, smiling. "My name is Susan Howell. I'm a freelance writer. I wanted to meet Karim and see if he was interested in telling his story."

Sada listened to the directions and thanked the professor. After the twenty-five minute drive northeast on U.S.15, Sada found herself cruising past the Duke campus. Another prestigious institution of American higher learning. Iranian higher learning, as well, she thought. How many scientists and engineers employed by the IRGC, Hezbollah, the Chinese People's Liberation Army, and other organizations with purposes antithetical to the values of the West had graduated from the West's top universities?

After stopping at a visitors center for a campus map, Sada pulled into a small triangular parking lot outside a dark, squat building fabricated with slabs of concrete stacked one upon the other, like a child's wooden blocks. The place looked deserted, but as she started toward the front door a young man with straight sandy-brown hair, dressed in khakis and a long-sleeved Oxford, approached from the other end of the parking lot. She asked after Hoveyda and the young man offered to take her to the director's office to inquire there.

Inside the front door, they walked past a large doorless room stacked from floor to ceiling with electrical panels containing switches, lights, and screens. Just past the control room, the man opened the door to the small office of the director, Dr. Pearson. The director was a short, balding man with a full white beard. He came around the desk as Sada introduced herself as a freelance writer and requested to meet Hoveyda.

"We haven't seen Karim since he came back," the director explained. "He emailed saying he expected to be in some time by the end of this week, so maybe that's today or tomorrow. No sense rushing, though, after the ordeal he went through."

The director apparently didn't want his visitor to walk away with the impression that Karim Hoveyda was the type to shirk his research responsibilities.

"I went to the UNC campus first," Sada said by way of conversation.

"Of course. I'm a member of the UNC faculty myself. But our larger projects and experiments are done at this joint facility. It's a world-class lab," the director said, beaming.

"What was Mr. Hoveyda working on, if I may ask?"

"He's part of a team conducting a long-term study using gamma ray spectroscopy to measure reactions involving radiative capture."

"I'm sure it's fascinating. I can tell I'll be hard-pressed to put this in terms the general reader can understand. Is there anyway I can talk to Karim now? Would it be possible to get a phone number for him?"

"I'm sorry," the director said with an apologetic smile, "university policy, you know. I can take your contact info and pass it to Karim when he comes in."

The sandy-haired young man who'd escorted Sada inside burst into the director's office after a preemptory knock.

"Dr. Pearson, can I speak with you? Outside?"

The Director apologized and followed the young man out. Through the smoked-glass window set in the door, Sada could tell the younger man was speaking with great urgency. When the director returned, his cheeks were flushed, and he didn't make eye contact with his visitor.

"Ms.—?"

"Susan Howell."

"Ms. Howell, if you want to leave your info with the office next door, someone will be sure to contact you. I'm sorry to be so abrupt, but a serious matter needs my attention."

"Of course, I understand. I hope everything is all right."

The director was ushering her to the door. "Unfortunately, a sensitive piece of equipment has gone missing. Hard to believe, but it appears we may have suffered our first theft of equipment since opening the facility." Putting on a brave smile, he said, "Thank you for your interest in Karim's ordeal. He's a promising young physicist."

In the hall outside the director's office, Sada debated

what to do next. She could find a position outside to survey the front door, hoping to spot Hoveyda when he arrived. That plan had only a low probability of success, considering he might arrive any time over the next two days. Also, the lab had a number of entrances. She decided to leave her cover contact info with the administrative assistant, as the director suggested. Of course a journalist would want to write a follow-up article on the man at the center of an international news story. At worst, a cautious Hoveyda would simply ignore the message, but it shouldn't arouse any particular suspicion on his part.

Sada thanked the secretary in the admin office. She was striding through the main hallway, headed for the front door, when the sandy-haired grad student appeared again, this time in earnest conversation with another young man, also a grad student by the looks of it. Sada walked past and stopped several paces away, just within earshot, making a pretense of searching her bag for car keys.

"I can't believe it," the second man, with an Indian accent, uttered in an awed tone.

"It's gone. The lab was locked when Thiesen got here this morning, but the initiator was gone."

"Stolen? Who?"

"It wasn't just misplaced. You know that thing is bolted to the tabletop."

"Who has access to the lab?"

"Me, you, Thiesen, Hoveyda, and the director are the only ones with keys."

"I wonder how much a neutron generator costs?"

Sada had heard enough. She hurried out into the North Carolina sunshine. Dashing down the front steps, she replayed the conversation with Tommy McCowan on the flight from Dubai. A terrorist group needed three items to build an improvised nuclear device. The most difficult to obtain was uranium, sufficiently enriched to be of weapons-grade quality. If Tommy's guess was right, the Soviets had buried such a source, in at least one place, on American soil forty or fifty years ago. The Iranians were desperately seeking the directions to that site. Second, someone had to have a baseline of scientific expertise, and Hoveyda's curriculum vitae fit the bill. Third, Tommy said to ensure a proper detonation, the bomb should be equipped with a neutron generator.

Hoveyda was missing, along with just such a piece of equipment from the lab he worked in. An Iranian physicist based in the United States was ideal.

Sada felt the goose bumps standing out on her arms despite the rising temperature. No terrorist group, no third party, was involved here. This was entirely an Iranian operation. The cache directions were the one piece missing from their plans. Barrett Ross was the only obstacle in their way.

Sada broke into a run, pulling out her cell phone as she sprinted toward the parking lot.

23

Consciousness came with a throbbing in his head and bright light battering his eyelids. Barrett squeezed his eyelids tighter and turned his head away. The sudden movement was worse, sending arcs of fiery pain circling around his skull. Facing the dark, he forced his eyes open. As his vision adjusted to the contrast, he saw empty terra cotta flowerpots stacked in a corner. He was sitting, legs outstretched, with his back against an uneven wall and a fine layer of grit sliding between the hard floor and the palms of his hands.

It took Barrett a full minute to realize where he was and why. The sunlight striking his chest and side of his head was coming through a small, dingy sliding-paned window near the top of the shed. As he peered into the gloom past the thick shaft of dust mote-filled light, he saw the rakes and shovels hanging on the corrugated aluminum wall, and a lawnmower next to his feet.

Barrett felt a cloth on his head. He pulled and the towel, or his skin, yielded with thready tendrils clinging to the clotted wound. He held the blood-soaked cloth in the light and recognized it as the dishtowel he'd yanked off the refrigerator hook as he ran from the house.

He brushed his hand on a pant leg and explored the wound with the pad of a single fingertip. He found raised edges, unsure of what was torn tissue and what was dried, crusty blood. He was alive, and thinking, which was a clue to the severity. Conclusion—a bullet had creased the top of his head, left of center. The wound was shallow at the front and back, just a scrape, but deeper in the center, a trough where the projectile's flat trajectory plowed through his scalp. His skull was intact, but he'd have an ugly gouge in the skin.

Zipper head. Nice.

Barrett checked his watch and realized he'd been in the shed for close to five hours.

Then he remembered—Mitchell Kane was dead. His old friend had saved him, sacrificing himself in the process. He'd responded to Barrett's request for help and paid for it with his life. The man woke up like any other morning, kissed his sleeping wife goodbye. Then he died in Barrett's kitchen.

Quicker than Barrett, Mitch had realized they were at an endgame. Without even knowing the stakes, the FBI agent understood the enemy's next move when they realized the flash drive and password were right in front of them. Mitchell knew he had nothing to lose, and his split-second decision saved Barrett's life.

He couldn't remember pulling his weapon out of the backpack, but he'd survived because the Iranians assumed he was incapacitated or dead from the initial exchange of fire. The second man expected to step around the table and deliver a *coup de grace*, as he did in murdering Mitchell.

Barrett tried to stand. A wave of nausea welled up inside, and instead he bent over and threw up into a flowerpot. Feeling enervated, he slumped back against the shed wall. He tasted the salty tang as the first tears rolled over his cheeks and into the corners of his mouth.

Barrett remembered stumbling through the shattered sliding glass door onto his patio, crashing through the lawn furniture in the early morning with blood streaming down his face. He'd pushed aside a board and crawled through the fence into his neighbor's yard. He skirted along the line separating the rows of backyards, somehow climbing over a series of fences and hedges, until he found this unlocked shed. He was only a few houses away from his home, where the police and the FBI must be crawling over the premises.

Should he stumble back there? Turn himself in, answer all the questions he could to help them find the attacker?

No. Barrett had nothing but a crazy story. Had Mitchell told anyone he was meeting him? Either way, Barrett would look complicit in the death of another man, this time a federal agent. He had no flash drive, no computer file, and no evidence.

Just a face.

The man in the front room who gave the orders. He was also the shooter at the Fujairah airport, the face in the window as Barrett wheeled the vehicle around and sped after the Gulfstream. He'd had a fleeting glance then, but now the man's image was seared into his brain.

Who was this dickhead? Who was this guy running a paramilitary op inside the U.S. and killing federal agents? Whoever he was, he'd followed Barrett from Fujairah, lying in wait at his house. He must have been surprised when Mitchell showed up first, but that didn't stop him.

Determined fucker.

Barrett Ross could be a determined fucker, too.

It was time to stop feeling sorry for himself. Time to stop expecting others to step up and fix his problems. And time to stop ignoring things he didn't want to face.

His cell rang. He grappled for it in his pants pocket to shut off the ringer, even though the sound was muted in the dusty, confined air of the shed.

"Hello?"

"Barrett, this is Susan. Have you met with your FBI friend?"

"He's dead, Susan. The Iranian, the one at Fujairah, he and another man were waiting at my house."

"What happened?"

Barrett recounted the attack, Mitchell's death, and the Iranian escaping with the flash drive before the police arrived.

"Where are you?" she asked.

Barrett surveyed the clutter of lawn and garden implements. He explained his situation.

"We need to meet. I'm on the highway, leaving North Carolina."

"I'll be waiting."

"Don't do anything rash."

"Like what?"

"Don't contact the authorities."

"No, I'm not going to do that. What I'm going to do is find this Iranian. And take him out."

The woman was silent for a few beats.

"Okay. Good," she said. "There's something else now. The scientist Hoveyda is missing from the university. Along with a piece of lab equipment that generates neutrons."

"What?"

"Do you remember what Tommy told us, about the feasibility of using the Soviet warhead?"

"He thought a halfway sophisticated group could build an IND if they had sufficient HEU, someone with an appropriate physics background, and—"

"And a source of neutrons to ensure the atomic core

went supercritical at the point of detonation."

The news filled him with alarm. "Susan, come get me."

"I'm on the way. Barrett—?"

"Yeah?"

"My name's not Susan. It's Sada. I wanted you to know that."

Safavi pulled into the parking lot of the drab hotel just after eight o'clock in the morning. Hessaby had chosen the type of American hotel frequented by construction tradesmen with their work trucks and vans. The presence of Safavi's team and their vehicles, even if they stayed several days, would not arouse suspicion. The location, near the juncture of the interstates numbered 64 and 295, northwest of Richmond, Virginia, was situated between each man's arrival airport and the next leg of their journey.

Safavi called Hessaby's number. His deputy appeared at a door on the side of the T-shaped building, where he handed Safavi two keys. Inside, the stark hallway reminded Safavi of a military barracks more than the typical American hotel. Which was appropriate.

"Gather the others in your room in ten minutes," he said in English as he stopped before his room door.

"Yes, sir," Hessaby said

Safavi gave him a sharp look. His men were to dress and act like minor businessmen, maybe salesmen, but not soldiers. He knew their appearances and accents would mark their birth as foreign, but the miraculous thing was, this did not matter to the Americans. As long as they spoke English and acted with the crude and informal manners of this country, they would draw little attention to themselves.

"Sorry," Hessaby said, with casualness achieved through effort, and moved to alert the others.

Safavi put his overnight bag on the bed and sat at the desk. The mission was at a critical stage, balanced on a tipping point between past actions and future outcomes. Overall, he was confident of success, but he could not say the scales had tipped decidedly in his favor. Too many deviations had happened so far. He would not fool himself in believing the outcome was inevitable.

The interception of Ross at his house had gone poorly. Safavi had taken only the one man, that fool Taheri, which should have been sufficient even if the American was armed. The rest of the team had been dispatched: most accompanied Hessaby to this staging point, while two men met Hoveyda in North Carolina to secure the essential pieces of equipment. But another man arrived at Ross's house, and Safavi could tell from where he watched the man was an agent of some kind. He'd been forced to confront them together rather than risk the flash drive slipping from his grasp again.

The second American was dead. So, too, he presumed, was Taheri. The last shot was from a handgun, not the soldier's silenced rifle. Safavi had waited in the vehicle long enough to know Taheri wasn't coming.

Taheri would never succumb to American interrogation techniques, but Safavi would prefer that he was dead. Nothing would identify him as IRGC or Ansar-ol-Mahdi: his clothing was bought in America, the weapon and ammunition stolen long ago in Mexico. No, the real concern was the American. Did he die along with Taheri, or was he still alive? Did he speak to the American police, the FBI, or CIA?

Safavi left the room and walked three doors down. Using the key Hessaby had given him, he entered the planning room. Hessaby and the six others were sitting on the edge of the bed and in folding chairs around a low coffee table, waiting for him. A road map of the southeastern United States was spread on the tabletop.

"Where is Ardabili?" he asked, in English still, as the door closed behind him. He sat down in the cushioned chair at the foot of the coffee table, and Hessaby brought his commander a cup of rose-flavored Persian tea from the kitchenette. Ardabili was the senior man of the three escorting the scientist, Hoveyda.

"Everything went well. He reports they were loaded and moving by three o'clock this morning," Hessaby reported. "They are in position now and awaiting arrival of the materials."

"Are we prepared, vehicles and equipment, for the next phase?"

"All is in readiness, other than pinpointing the exact location."

"Then let us do that." Safavi took the American's laptop and flash drive out of his bag and put them on the table. Simultaneously, Hessaby reached into a portfolio briefcase. He took out a second map, unfolding and spreading it out next to the computer. This one was a 1:24,000 scale U.S. Forestry topographical map, and the legend in the lower right corner read "New River Gorge National River—West Virginia."

24

The air inside the metal shed had become stifling. There must be no trees along the fence line to shelter it from the full brunt of the midday sun. On the positive side, no one had come into the backyard, neither kids nor dogs, and Barrett felt it was safe to crack open the door a little, knowing Susan would not complete the drive up from North Carolina for four hours.

Sada. Not Susan.

Of course Susan wasn't her real name. Sada. He said it again, sounding it out in his mind, testing it.

Barrett tried to push Mitchell's death out of his mind and concentrate. But he could not ignore the glaring fact that the call to his friend—out of the blue, and after how many years?—that the call had led to his friend's death. This loss, and all the others, had to mean something. Stand for something. But it was up to him to make that happen, wasn't it?

He spent the rest of the wait trying to figure out both what he and Sada knew, and what they were going to do next. Did they even know what the Iranians were really trying to achieve? He tried to picture the translation Sada typed out on Tommy's plane.

A Road #60 had appeared at the beginning of the directions. Interstate 60? Highway 60? Tommy was certain Y-12 was Oak Ridge National Laboratory in Tennessee. Two other sites were labeled *military*, GOLD and CHUTE. Tommy said Barrett should know what they were, and Barrett was pretty sure he did. GOLD would be Fort Knox, Kentucky, historical home of the Army's tank units, but also the site of the federal gold bullion depository. CHUTE would be Fort Campbell, home of the 101st Airborne Division (now Air Assault), positioned astride the Tennessee-Kentucky border. He recalled two more code names on the list. Maybe Sada would remember them. Maybe the nuke was hidden somewhere in Kentucky or Tennessee, but that didn't narrow down the search much.

The other name he remembered was the top of the document. WHITE SEA. Displayed like a code word for the entire subject matter, that's what it would have indicated at the top of an American secret document. WHITE SEA registered in his mind because he wondered if the Soviet author, working at the height of the Cold War, had intended the irony. Few Americans, except those with a military history background, would have even heard of the 1918 American "Polar Bear Expedition" to the White Sea, when Woodrow Wilson sent five thousand U.S. troops to the port city of Arkhangelsk, Russia. Where American troops had fought against the newly formed Red Army.

His phone rang.

"It's Sada. I'm on the street parallel to yours. Come out, I'll be looking for you."

Earlier, he'd worried about how he'd look walking out of someone's back yard with blood all over his head and clothes. Now he just wanted out of his personal little sauna-hell. He held the bloody dishtowel to his head, crossed the backyard and passed through a side gate, stopping under a large shade tree next to the sidewalk. He hadn't seen anyone. A green late-model Pilot was pulled over to the curb, about thirty meters up the street. It began backing up to him.

"You're a mess," Sada remarked as he slid into the passenger seat. She was already driving.

"Here," she said, reaching into the back and handing him a water bottle. Barrett gulped down the contents of the first bottle, let the empty fall to his feet, and turned to grab another from the opened case.

"Where are we going?" he asked.

"That's a good question," she said. "We don't know, do we?"

Barrett shared his speculation about Fort Knox and Fort Campbell, narrowing the search to the adjacent states of Tennessee and Kentucky.

"Tommy's company is based in Knoxville. I think Oak Ridge is nearby," he said. "That's the eastern half of Tennessee. Fort Campbell is farther west, on the Tennessee-Kentucky border. Fort Knox is in the northern half of Kentucky, close to Illinois. I'm not sure, but I'm guessing those three points are separated by hundreds of miles. So is the cache close to one of these places, or centered between them?" he wondered.

"The Russians wouldn't have tried to hide the cache right next to a well-guarded facility."

"Right. Man portable, but most likely delivered by a car or truck. Carried the last stretch through the woods, through a security perimeter, by a man."

"Two more targets were labeled *command*," she said.

"The Soviets probably meant what we call C2. Command and Control. Headquarters sites."

"But not necessarily military," Sada offered, staring out at the road ahead of her. "National command and control."

"The Pentagon? White House?" Barrett wondered. "Neither of those is close to the three targets we just mentioned."

"By the sixties, the Soviet Union had more than enough intercontinental ballistic missiles targeting your capital, including the Pentagon, the White House, and Capitol Hill. I think we're looking for something else. A command and control target they'd want a saboteur team to destroy before hostilities began, before a full-scale exchange of nuclear missiles."

"A decapitating strike," Barrett ventured, running his fingertips over the wound on his scalp. Despite the throbbing ache in his head, there was nothing he wanted to do more than solve this puzzle. Find the cache. Find Mitchell's killer.

"We need a map, the internet, and a place to think."

"Let's go buy a computer," Sada responded.

Two guards came to the cell late in the evening and motioned him forward. His hands were cuffed in front of him, and one guard led the way while the other guided with a hand on his arm. At the end of the hallway, they turned right and Dave was escorted into a conference room.

Amy jumped out of her seat as soon as she saw him. She started to rush around the table, but the guards made it clear she was to stay on her side of the table. They guided Dave to a metal chair opposite her and stepped back a pace or two.

"Oh, sweetheart, your face," Amy began. She began to laugh and cry a little bit.

"Pretty bad, huh?"

"I'm just relieved you look as good as you do."

"How did you manage this?"

"I have been an avid petitioner to the police chief here. Also, I asked Hamid at work for his help. His family is very wealthy. Very connected."

"How'd you find out what happened?"

Amy paused, and then said, "A good friend I just met this week." Her eyes darted to the guards standing behind Dave.

Barrett. He'd called Amy. Dave thought the guards probably didn't know a lot of English, but it still didn't make sense to be too open. He felt silly, trying to talk in code. "I hope he's still got the same girlfriend."

"Yes, they're still an item." Good, the Israeli woman was with Barrett.

Amy told him she had indeed called his parents in California, and his dad had called a congressman and the State Department. No one knew how long extracting Dave from this mess would take, and his dad has asked Amy if he should fly over.

They had talked for only a few minutes when one of the guards stepped into Dave's line of sight, spoke, and raised two fingers. It was the two-minute warning.

"Amy, I know other people are working on this. But I need you to keep the pressure on. Call the consulate and ask for a woman named Carr. She's a high-up muckety-muck, third-in-charge or something like that. She botched the rendezvous that Barrett and I had planned."

"What do you want me to do?"

"Pester her until she agrees to come and meet me. I need to see her, not one of her understudies."

The guards began chattering, easing Dave off the seat with a hand under each arm. They were being fairly decent, but he still hated to turn his back on his girlfriend. Amy called out her love and promised to call the woman at the consulate. The door to the conference room shut behind Dave.

Back in his cell, sitting on his little brown blanket, Dave pondered the situation. It was good knowing that Amy was on the case. And the fact that Barrett was teamed up with the Mossad agent was good news as well.

Dave reviewed everything that had transpired over the past—what—forty-eight hours? He tried to remember what the Israeli woman had said in the car before he and Barrett escaped from the wadi. The attack at the hotel had turned into a bloodbath because more Iranians had shown up than the Israelis had expected. She also said a former KGB agent was implicated, a rogue operative selling nuclear secrets to the Iranians.

The man's name escaped him, but she had said he was a Kazakh.

In the cell opposite, the nervous pacer was finally still, sitting against bars with his head drooping between his knees. Inexplicably, he was still in his street clothes, and not a jail uniform.

Dave couldn't see his face, but remembered his earlier thoughts about how different the man looked from most of the inmates, like he could be from one of the –Stans. Uzbekistan. Tajikistan.

Kazakhstan.

The hair clippings fall into the sink as Barrett gripped the counter, bracing himself whenever the electric clippers skimmed the edge of the wound. Sada had cut back the hair around the laceration with a pair of barber scissors. Now she was shaving the stubble to the scalp.

In a strip mall just west of the Beltway, twenty minutes from his house, they'd found a drugstore and he waited in the car while she bought the barber tools, hydrogen peroxide, gauze bandages, and the strongest over-the-counter pain killer she could find. Across the street at a mall department store, he'd waited again as she purchased a pair of jeans and two golf shirts to replace his bloodstained clothes, along with a baseball cap. The final stop was an electronics store, where she reemerged after a short time with a new Apple MacBook Pro laptop. They found the hotel on the edge of Tysons Corner.

"Hold on," she said. "This will sting."

He felt the cool liquid on his shaved skin, and the flaming sensation as the hydrogen peroxide pooled in the open wound and foamed.

"Lucky for me, you were a medic."

"Actually, I learned things like this when I was just a girl."

"A hard life?"

"An isolated one."

"You said you left as soon as you could. Do you ever go back?"

"Not to the kibbutz. That's my stepfather's life."

Sada rinsed his wound again with the hydrogen peroxide, mopping up the rivulets of fluid with a hand towel. "And you?"

"I used to see my family twice a year, every leave I had in the Army. It'd been three years since I went back, before my Dad's funeral."

"Why?"

"My family is a mess. I guess I was afraid of saying things to my sister and brother like the things I did end up saying."

Sada didn't respond, but washed and dried the wound one more time before taping a large square gauze over the site.

"What did you mean, that was your stepfather's life?"

"I grew up in Tel Aviv until I was twelve. My father, my real father, was a professor at the university. When my parents divorced, my mother remarried to a Haredim, an ultra-orthodox immigrant from Canada. We moved to a religious kibbutz in the middle of the West Bank."

"Joining the IDF was a way to escape?"

"Most of the girls on the kibbutz took the religious exemption from military service. It was expected. I refused, to spite my mother and stepfather. And joined up as soon as I was old enough."

"You said before something changed. You hadn't planned on the life you have now."

"As a young soldier, I had much different plans. After my two-year term of service, I was going back to school. And starting a new life with my fiancé."

Sada's ministrations ended. The bandage was in place on Barrett's head.

"He was killed in the Second Intifada. When the Institute came around to my unit for the second time, recruiting female soldiers, I had no reason not to try out."

Sada left Barrett and closed the door. He changed into the new clothes, throwing the bloody ones into the trash. He put the cap on his head and checked in the mirror. It covered the bald spot and the bandage, but didn't do anything for his busted nose and lip. Or the uneasiness in his gut.

Sada had the laptop out of the box and running when he emerged from the bathroom. He sat down on the couch beside her and saw she was in the process of downloading Google Earth. When it was complete, she turned to him.

"Here. It's your country."

"Let's see what we can remember from those directions," he replied.

Barrett typed Oak Ridge National Laboratory into the search field. The blue orb of the earth, suspended against a starry black background, spun and zoomed in until the satellite imagery showed a campus of buildings surrounded by the verdant Tennessee woods. He used the marking function to place a yellow pushpin on the electronic map and labeled it "Y12." He did the same for Fort Campbell, Kentucky, labeling it "Chute," and Fort Knox, Kentucky, labeling it "Gold." As the program zoomed in on both military bases, he recognized the outlines of training areas, firing ranges, and drop zones he'd experienced firsthand.

The three yellow pushpins marked an isosceles triangle with Campbell at the westernmost point, Knox to the north, and Oak Ridge at the southeastern point. The distances between each point, which Barrett found using the ruler function, were 120, 160, and 180 miles, respectively.

"We could assume the cache is located somewhere between these," Sada said. "But this area covers more than a third of the state of Kentucky."

"We need the two command and control targets," Barrett replied. "They were at the top of the list. They'd be higher priority for the Soviets than these three. Wouldn't the cache be closest to the primary target?"

Barrett swiped the Google Earth program into the background, pulled up a search engine screen.

"One of the sites started with a C," Sada said. "Try Covax."

Barrett input the word into the search engine as she spelled it, but nothing promising turned up.

"Let's try this route," Barrett said, and he typed in the phrase "command and control facilities."

The first item listed was a generic Wikipedia article. The summary description of the second link caught his eye.

"Look, I've heard of this," he said as he clicked on the hyperlink entitled "Raven Rock Mountain Complex." The

Wikipedia article described the site as an alternate C2 facility to replicate the National Military Command structure in the Pentagon. The location was also known as Site R, and was reputed to be 6.2 miles north-northeast of Camp David, Maryland.

"This might be promising," he mused. Back in Google Earth, he inputted, "Camp David, MD" into the search window and got a laundry list of possibilities. Most were unrelated places with similar names, but one identified the "Naval Support Facility Thurmont (Camp David)." He selected it and the program zoomed in on the site, an isolated area surrounded by woods, with several house-like structures, tennis courts and paths. This was where the President vacationed. He zoomed back out. Using the ruler function, he drew a straight line 6.2 miles long, angled northeast from Camp David. His line stopped just across the Pennsylvania border. He slid the map back and forth a little to look at areas away from built-up areas. He settled on a large rounded section of woods encircled by a road. As he zoomed in, Google Earth popped up a little green icon, shaped like a mountain and labeled "Raven Rock Mountain." If this weren't confirmation enough, as Barrett zoomed in farther, the screen became populated with numerous photo icons, each a link to photos people had uploaded and tagged with GPS coordinates. Clicking on the first photo revealed a complex array of communications antennas on top of the bald crown of the mountain, seen from a low-flying plane. Each of the other photos gave clear overhead views of the large, concrete tunnel entrances leading from various points along the perimeter road into the heart of the mountain.

"Unbelievable what you can see on the Internet nowadays," Barrett said. He marked the map with another yellow pushpin.

"Corax, not Covax," Sada said. "That was the second

target."

A search revealed Corax was the Latin word for the common raven. Site R. Barrett labeled the push pin on Raven Rock Mountain with the code name Corax, and zoomed out to see the relationship with the other targets.

"Corax's a good five hundred miles from the area we were looking at," Sada said. "It just widens the area for our potential hide site."

"We need the first code name on the list," he said.

"I'm thinking."

"Baden." Barrett surprised himself. That was the word beneath WHITE SEA.

Back in the search engine, Barrett typed in the word. "Baden" was the name of a state or region in Germany along the Rhine River, based on a city called Baden-Baden, but none of the possibilities presented a clear connection for him.

Barrett went back to the screen with his original search for command and control facilities. The third link down was to a private security firm which had compiled a listing of command and control facilities that included the White House, the Pentagon, and Site R, which they already knew about. But at least fifteen other locations followed, several Barrett had never heard of, including a place called Oakville Grade. It sounded similar to Oak Ridge, so he clicked the hyperlink, but was disappointed to see the site was in Napa, California.

"I don't think we're interested in the West Coast," Sada said.

He almost clicked away when he saw the text below the Oakville Grade name. The website said the facility was related to "continuity of government in the event of nuclear war."

"Of course," he said. Opening a new tab, he typed, "continuity of government" into the search engine.

"Raven Rock wasn't an ordinary C2 site," he explained to Sada. "It meant to provide 'continuity of government' in the event of war. An alternate site from which to conduct the key functions of government, if the normal location was threatened or destroyed. In the case of Raven Rock, it was the alternate site for key Pentagon personnel, where they'd go to survive a nuclear strike on D.C."

The first link led to another Wikipedia article, this one describing the history of continuity of government planning for several countries and their associated facilities. For the United States, Raven Rock topped the list, followed by Mount Weather, which he was not familiar with. Next was Cheyenne Mountain, Colorado, which he knew was the site of NORAD, the North American Air Defense headquarters. Then STRATCOM, the U.S. Strategic Command at Offut Air Force Base, Nebraska. Near the bottom was a placeholder for an as-yet unidentified spot labeled simply as "Unknown."

"Unknown ——> United States Congress. (The Greenbrier was used until 1992.)"

The accompanying text described a place called the Greenbrier Hotel. Barrett hit the link, and he and Sada read about the Bunker, an underground facility built beneath the exclusive Greenbrier Hotel and Resort, located in White Sulphur Springs, West Virginia. The article described how the secret bunker was built in the years 1959-1962, a facility large enough to safeguard and support the entire U.S. Congress and selected staff members in the event of nuclear war. The bunker was built under the cover of the hotel's aboveground expansion. It had remained operational (although never tested) until it was exposed by a news reporter in 1992. Afterward, the government removed the site from official service and turned the lease back over to the hotel owners, who now offered their guests guided tours of an interesting Cold

War relic.

"Look at the dates," Sada said.

Barrett nodded, but he was thinking of something else.

"It says here the Greenbrier has been renowned for centuries for its mineral spa, the white sulphur spring waters for which the nearby town is named."

"Yes?"

"I'm pretty sure Baden-Baden is a famous spa town in Germany."

Barrett found the website of the modern Greenbrier Hotel, copied the street address and pasted it into Google Earth, marking it with yet another yellow pushpin. "Baden." This time the target was 250 miles from the Y-12 pushpin marking Oak Ridge National Laboratory.

Seeing everything take shape on the map was reassuring. He knew how to do this. This had been his former life. Looking at maps, analyzing terrain, figuring out course of action. With Sada, he had a shot at stopping the Iranians.

As he zoomed out from the resort, he switched from satellite imagery to map view. As the map pulled back to a smaller scale, the increased coverage of the geography captured on the screen caused the push pin to appear to sit right next to a yellow line marking a major road.

"Look," he said, pointing. Near the yellow pushpin marking the once-secret Greenbrier bunker was the white shield symbol identifying a non-interstate U.S. highway.

"U.S. 60," Barrett said. "I think we're in the ballpark."

25

Karim Hoveyda surveyed the warehouse. The space was small but more than adequate for their purposes. Good lighting overhead and no windows. Hoveyda and the two soldiers could construct the assembly in private, with no prying eyes, and they had the requisite power for the electronic components. The building was situated in a small compound, with a loading dock and parking area inside a high chain-link fence, with easy access to the street. It was near the center of the city, close to the financial district. Hessaby's scouts had done well. Apart from whatever decision led to this city, the building was ideal.

The tower would go there, along the wall, he decided. The other two men had already laid out the planks and frame for the scaffolding set they'd rented. His equipment could go on the long table, there, and they would tape the heavy-duty cables to the floor, where they ran to the electrical box on the far wall.

"Professor." Two soldiers had accompanied Hoveyda to help him. The senior of the two drew his attention to the roll-top door opening onto the loading dock.

"The metals have arrived."

Hoveyda nodded his assent, and the soldier pulled the chain hand over hand to raise the door in its tracks. Outside, a brown UPS truck was backing up to the dock. The brake lights came on, and the driver hopped out of the cab and jumped up onto the dock. He lifted the door and walked over with his digital signature pad. Hoveyda signed for the delivery.

"Got a lot of packages for you," the man said with a smile. The two soldiers stripped down to their T-shirts and began to carry the cardboard-wrapped sections of aluminum into the building.

"I almost didn't find you," the driver said. "The system tried to send me way south of town."

"Well, thank you," Hoveyda said.

"Whachya making?" the man asked as he took the signature pad back and entered a couple of keystrokes.

"I work for an energy company," Hoveyda said. "My colleagues are building a scale replica of an oil derrick, for use at a trade show."

"Happy building," the driver said, touching the brim of his cap, already striding back to his truck. The soldiers watched the truck leave the fenced parking area and went out to close the gate and secure the heavy padlock, before coming back and lowering the warehouse loading door.

Hoveyda had to see if these two knew what they were doing. Aluminum was extremely difficult to weld, but Hessaby assured him the two soldiers had trained for many hours to do this. If so, maybe the simple structure would be no issue for them. Hoveyda would supervise to ensure the directions were followed and the tolerances met for every measurement. Although this would never be used, Hoveyda took pride in the knowledge it could work.

Would work, if anyone were mad enough to let it go

that far.

Hoveyda had thought about it for a long time. He was a son of his country. An ardent patriot, he longed for his homeland to resume its rightful place among the powerful nations on the world stage. But he did not hate the common people in this country. Only their imperialistic, arrogant government. He'd studied here too long, met too many people, and he knew many Americans, especially his academic peers, distrusted their own government. If he could play some role in thwarting the aggressions of this militaristic superpower, and its lapdog Israel, then he was helping not only his own people, but in a way, all those in America who championed peace as well.

"Lay all of the pieces out on the floor. Ensure you do not nick or dent anything," he instructed the two soldiers. It felt strange giving orders to men whom he would have shown total deference to on the streets of Tehran, or risked a real visit to Evin Prison. It helped they were not wearing their Revolutionary Guards uniforms. It also helped that Hessaby briefed the two that the Scientist was in charge.

Hoveyda pulled up the plans on his laptop. Soon his part would be done and the waiting would begin.

Hoveyda was not stupid, though.

He knew the plan could go wrong. Whatever message was delivered, everything depended on the military man, Safavi. Hoveyda did not trust this ambitious man. He couldn't say that, but when he was recruited he asked about safeguards. General Roghani brushed aside his concerns. Hoveyda wished he enjoyed the general's confidence. But something about this IRGC colonel, Safavi, wasn't quite right. Hoveyda couldn't quite put his finger on it, but he was never at ease around the man.

Anyway, he was the scientist. Only he understood the theory behind what they were doing. He'd decided from the start that, while he would do this for his country, he also promised himself it would only go so far. If Safavi, or anyone else, decided to take the unthinkable last step, Hoveyda would have his own safeguard in place.

"When I say my name, their tech guys are going to be all over this number, pinning down our location," Barrett said.

"This phone's not traceable," Sada assured him.

Barrett wanted to give the Feds everything he and Sada had figured out, but he wasn't ready to spend the next several weeks in a padded room while they figured out if he was telling the truth. The pros would stop the Iranians—if they believed Barrett's story. But this Iranian prick was finding this location right now, and Barrett knew what the man looked like. As long as he gave the FBI all the information, assumptions, and guesses he and Sada came up with, he wasn't going to accomplish anything else by turning himself in. He needed to believe he and Sada had a larger role to play, somehow. In any event, he planned to keep looking for the man who killed his friend.

Barrett realized he was dreading this call. He would be talking to a colleague of Mitchell's, a man or woman who'd consider Barrett the foremost suspect in the death of a brother agent. Anything he said would be regarded as a self-serving lie.

"Law Enforcement Coordination." The voice was subdued.

"My name is Barrett Ross. Can I speak to Mitchell Kane's supervisor?"

The woman paused, and said simply, "Hold."

A few seconds later a voice said, "This is Special Agent in Charge Darrell Hascomb."

"This is Barrett Ross."

"Mr. Ross, we need to talk to you right away."

"More than you realize," Barrett said. "That's why I called you."

"I think the FBI understands its priorities when it loses an agent," the man responded.

The tone was flat, but Barrett appreciated the effort the man must be making. This Hascomb was a cool character.

"Mr. Ross, your activities overseas, and the death of Special Agent Kane in your house, put you in a very unfavorable light. We need you to come in to straighten out this matter. Now."

Barrett almost said, *That's not going to happen*, but decided on a less confrontational tact. He needed to build some credibility so the agent would listen to him rather than fixate on getting Barrett handcuffed in an interrogation room.

"Do you know who the other dead man in my dining room is?" Barrett asked.

"I'm not discussing details of our investigation with you," the agent said. The unspoken challenge was out there, though. Say something, convince me.

"You won't identify him, not anytime soon. The man's Iranian. He's a member of the Islamic Revolutionary Guard Corps. Part of their special operations wing, the Qods Force."

"You know this how?"

Hascomb's tone was unmistakable. *I've encountered more than my share of nut-jobs in two-plus decades of doing this job. So, impress me with how crazy you are.* But Barrett wasn't about to tell the FBI he had a Mossad agent sitting next to him, providing intelligence on their Iranian adversary.

"Listen to me, Agent Hascomb, please. I'm sure by now you've pieced together my movements in Dubai. First, do you think I stumbled into this situation, or do you think I caused it?"

"You've touched upon some of the issues we'd like to

talk to you about."

"This isn't the first time the Mossad has targeted someone in a Dubai hotel, Agent Hascomb. I just happened to find the bodies. Do you think I work for the Israelis?"

"Why didn't you cooperate with the UAE authorities?"

"I did. What looked like me running away from the authorities was me running from this Iranian group."

"Mr. Ross—"

"No, listen to me. Check some of these facts. The Israelis knocked off an Iranian diplomat named Alizadeh. But he was one of the main men in Iran's covert nuclear weapons program. The hit went bad because the Iranians had a security team on the ground the Israelis didn't anticipate."

"You seem to have a lot of insight into Mossad operational planning. For an innocent bystander."

"I've learned a lot in the past few days. When I stumbled on this operation, one of the Israelis passed me a device. He knew I was American and ex-military. He was desperate. This morning I tried passing this device to Mitchell."

"What device?"

Barrett laid it all out for the agent—and for the recording devices and anyone else who might be listening in. He explained the flash drive and the steganography program, the hidden directions, everything Sada had shared about the Iranians and their proxy forces, his recognition of Hoveyda and the scientist's subsequent disappearance. As well as their conclusions about the locations of the five Cold War targets.

"So let me get this straight. You think the Iranians have a covert force operating inside the United States, whose purpose is to locate a Soviet tactical nuclear weapon, from which they are going to use the uranium, and equipment stolen from a university physics department, to build an improvised nuclear device?"

"Exactly."

"Sounds a little farfetched, Mr. Ross."

"I know. But no one expected the Qods Force to be running around the U.S. last year trying to assassinate the Saudi ambassador, either," Barrett said.

Hascomb didn't concede the fact, or say anything else in reply.

"Ask the CIA to talk to the Israelis," Barrett added, "see what they think is far-fetched."

"We'll check out this Hoveyda person," Hascomb allowed. "But where's this cache supposed to be?"

Barrett gave as much of the text of the directions as he remembered, listing again the five target code names and their conclusions about the locations, and the reference to what they thought was highway U.S. 60.

"I'm not looking at a map right now," Hascomb said, "but I think those five locations cover a pretty large area."

"It doesn't matter. What's important is finding the cache site. What about approaching the Russians?"

"What?" Hascomb laughed.

"Why not?"

"Even if the U.S. intelligence community were to take your hypothesis at face value, what do you suggest we do? Ring up the Russians and say, 'Where are your nukes? You know. The ones you hid in the U.S. We're sure you just forgot about them, or you would have told us sooner.' Something like that?"

"I don't know how you would do it!" Barrett snapped. "Get the right people involved. Have the President make some phone calls, for chrissake."

That came out harsher than intended. Barrett could sense the man bristling on the other end of the line.

To his credit, Hascomb came back coolly, but with a

different angle. "Why are the Iranians doing this?"

"They fear the Israelis are going to try to put a couple of bombs down the smokestack of their nuclear program."

"I'm no foreign relations expert, Mr. Ross. But it's not clear to me how setting off an IND in the U.S. achieves anything for the Iranians, except massive retaliation."

"Not setting off. Threatening with it, as blackmail."

"Why?"

"Who else is going to rein in the Israelis besides the U.S?"

"You're saying the Iranians want to hang an IND over our heads? To pressure the Israelis to hold off from a preemptive strike," Hascomb concluded.

"That's it."

"I need you to come in, Mr. Ross."

"I can't do that," Barrett responded. "You've got everything I have. Find Hoveyda. Start talking to the Russians. I'll call you again to see if you have any questions I can answer."

Barrett hung up on the FBI. He was sweating. It felt like those few other occasions in life where he'd knew he was making a huge decision. He'd just committed to a course of action. Doors were shutting behind him. He hoped Hascomb and everyone listening in from the alphabet soup of federal agencies were as scared as he was. Would they move fast enough?

"What do you think?" Sada asked.

"I don't know," Barrett said. "But we're not going to sit around this hotel room waiting to see if they figure it out."

He was beginning to feel a real partnership with this woman, and trusted her implicitly. How far would she trust him?

"Tell me, Sada, what does the KGB call itself nowadays?

26

SVR. That was the answer to Barrett's question. *Sluzhba Vneshney Razvedki*, the Foreign Intelligence Service, was the successor to the KGB's First Chief Directorate. Sada knew the change was little more than a rebranding. The senior personnel, missions, and methods of the new Russian agency were a direct carry-over from its Soviet predecessor.

A man was standing midway across the small pedestrian bridge that arched over Rock Creek. He pushed away from the rust-red iron railing as Sada and Barrett approached on the path. He was a tall man, big because of his height, with a gangly body tending toward pear-shaped. His head was long and bald, like an egg, and square rimmed spectacles perched on his nose. Dimitry Vasilievsky was not the film version of a Russian spy posing as a diplomat. More like a middle-aged businessman in a rumpled suit, weary from too many days on the road.

The FBI's rebuke of Barrett's suggestion to contact the Russians only strengthened the idea in the American's mind. If the FBI wouldn't make the call, he would. Not Barrett Ross, exactly, but someone with access to that world.

The options to find the cache were limited. When Barrett pitched the idea, Sada consider it only briefly before placing a call. Forty-five minutes later, her Avigail rang back from the Institute. Since Sada was refusing to return to Tel Aviv, Avigail was taking a big risk by helping out in this way. But her friend worked her magic, convincing a colleague in the U.S. to call in a chit. Sada secured an appointment with Vasilievsky, the SVR Rezident in Washington: 7:30 p.m. in Rock Creek Park, the beautiful preserve of green woods and sun-dappled streams located north of the city between Chevy Chase and Silver Spring.

"Miss Di-Nur?" Vasilievsky asked, extending his hand.

Sada shook his hand and introduced Barrett. The Russian's hand was soft, but the grip was that of a self-assured man, comfortable in his power.

"I was not aware you had a colleague coming with you," Vasilievsky said, eyeing Barrett. "Who do you work for, Mr. Ross? American, I presume."

"Yes. But I don't work for anyone. Not State, FBI, or CIA, if that's what you mean. I used to serve in our Army, but now I'm a private citizen."

The Russian raised his eyebrows but made no remark. He was willing to go along with this statement even if he didn't believe it. Sada knew it didn't matter to Vasilievsky who Barrett was, because he didn't expect the conversation to go anywhere.

"Thank you for agreeing to meet on such short notice," Sada said, drawing the Russian's attention back to herself.

"A mutual acquaintance suggested it might be of interest for me to hear you out," Vasilievsky said. He looked at his watch. "I do have another pressing engagement this evening, so perhaps we can speak as we walk."

Vasilievsky took off his jacket and hooked it over his shoulder with his thumb as he walked. Sada fell in step beside the man as they traversed the span over the creek and the path leading deeper into the woods, while Barrett fell in behind them.

Neither agent was inclined to begin the conversation. Sada considered the surrealism of the situation, strolling through this gorgeous park with its sticky humidity and tiny gnats swarming around her hairline, juxtaposed against the reason for this meeting. The odd-looking Russian walking next to her might offer the best hope of preventing a nuclear confrontation.

"What can I do for you, Ms. Di-Nur?" Vasilievsky asked.

"We have reason to suspect an element of Iran's Islamic Revolutionary Guards is operating inside the U.S. It's in the final stages of constructing an improvised nuclear device."

That startled the man. "That would be horrible," Vasilievsky said. "For many reasons."

Sada was about to volunteer more but caught herself. The Russian's face showed he was processing the information, anticipating the ramifications. Threat or opportunity. Exploit or withdraw.

"So many questions come to mind," he said, "but I guess the obvious ones are: why are you telling me this? Why are you not speaking to the American authorities?"

"We have," Sada answered, "but unfortunately, they are somewhat skeptical."

Vasilievsky glanced over his shoulder at Barrett as they continued to walk. A breeze rippled the leaves in the trees above them, but did little to ease the sweltering conditions on the trail. Facing front again, the Russian's eyes shifted back and forth to the tree line on either side of the path, as if trying to reassure himself that his security personnel from the Rezidentura were in position. Sada assumed they were being photographed and recorded with a series of parabolic microphones.

"What do you want from me?" Vasilievsky asked.

"The fissile material the Iranians have obtained, or will obtain, is from a Soviet weapon."

"A nuclear weapon," Vasilievsky snorted, "belonging to the Union of Soviet Socialist Republics? Preposterous."

In the ensuing silence the only sounds were their footfalls on the gravel path.

"Is this your friend's theory, Ms. Di-Nur? Do not be deluded by the conspiracy theorists and the tabloids. The accusations of lax controls on our weapon stockpiles were the paranoid fantasy of American alarmists. I assure you, the former Soviet Union, like the Russian Federation of today, did not make a habit of losing control of its strategic assets."

"She didn't say you lost control of a nuke," Barrett said from behind them. Sada could tell he was hot at the Russian's dismissive attitude. She raised her hands to ward him off, but the American plowed ahead.

"You staged a tactical nuke inside the U.S. as part of your Cold War battle plan. The target was the congressional bunker under the Greenbrier Hotel in West Virginia. We need the location of that cache."

"I don't know what your purpose is, but I don't have time for this game." Vasilievsky stopped, facing them. He was in the process of putting his jacket back on. "I'll ask you to leave me, or I will find the park police and inform them you are harassing a senior diplomat of the Embassy of the Russian Federation."

"Mr. Vasilievsky, does White Sea mean anything to you?" Barrett asked.

Just the slightest wrinkling of skin between the man's eyebrows, a hunch in the fold above the bridge of the nose, which caused his glasses to bump up, betrayed Vasilievsky.

"Ask yourself, Mr. Vasilievsky, how would we know that?" the American pressed. "Where would we have seen 'White Sea'? I'll tell you where we saw it. We saw it with a steganography program, written in Russian, and supplied by a former KGB officer named Ismagulov."

"Absurd," Vasilievsky said with less conviction this time.

"That document was in our possession, and now the Iranians have it. The FBI isn't listening to me now. But when the Iranians blackmail my government with an IND planted in an American city, you know as well as I do that the full resources of my country will be focused on neutralizing the threat. After that, the next step will be a full-scale investigation to figure out how it happened."

The Russian might take the American's assertions as idle threats, but Sada realized their only hope was to press this line of reasoning.

"Mr. Vasilievsky," she broke in, "this situation, the Iranians gaining possession of a nuclear warhead—it cannot be tolerated. You know my country's leadership considers that possibility as nothing less than an existential threat, even if the first target is America. It will be perceived as an attempt to limit Israeli freedom of action in response to Iranian weaponization of their nuclear program. That is unacceptable. Israel, which possesses much of the raw intelligence backing Mr. Ross's claim, will throw its full weight behind the American effort."

Vasilievsky drew himself up stiffly. "Such wild accusations can be checked and refuted," he said, his language more stilted than before. Then he added, "Where can I reach you?"

Sada gave him a number, which he jotted down in a small notebook he pulled from his breast pocket.

"This is all nonsense," the Russian repeated, but Sada sensed his statement was made more for the benefit of those listening and recording. As if in confirmation, Vasilievsky muttered sotto voce, "I will contact you," before striding off by himself in the direction of the footbridge over Rock Creek.

Darrell Hascomb scanned his yellow legal pad, folded over to the third page of scrawled notes and conjectures. He referred back to the computer screen, which displayed the official military personnel file of one Barrett N. Ross, honorably separated from the United States Army at the rank of captain.

It was pushing eleven o'clock. Normally he'd be worried about catching hell from his wife (mild hell, to be fair) for working ungodly hours and not being home to eat with the family and help out with homework. Eighth-grade algebra was not his wife's strong suit. But tonight, and this week, she would understand, even if she didn't know all the reasons. What she understood was every agent in the Bureau's headquarters was looking for a way to help out in the investigation of Mitchell Kane's murder. People in random departments all across the building, even if they couldn't directly contribute, would be sitting at their desks long after their normal departure time, frustrated and hurt, not wanting to walk out of the building while the people assigned to the case were busting their humps around the clock.

Lack of ways to participate was not Hascomb's problem, though. Because Mitchell had been a part of his team, he wasn't assigned to the investigation. Partly, this was standard protocol, but also because Hascomb's expertise dealt with coordinating state and local law enforcement agencies, not counterespionage and anti-terrorism. Nevertheless, he now had a mission.

Hascomb couldn't believe merely seven hours had elapsed since Ross called with his crazy story and then hung up on him. At least it had seemed crazy until he kicked the matter up to his assistant director. He was surprised to find Ross's allegations were not met with the same level of disregard he'd expected. The AD, while reminding him the murder investigation was under the direction of the seventh floor, asked him to review the tape and write out every possible lead from his conversation with Ross. The AD also suggested that he stay by the phone a little longer this evening in case Ross called back. The tech guys set it up so if Ross did call, Hascomb needed only to click one button on the computer screen to initiate a trace downstairs.

Not long after talking to the AD, Special Agent in Charge John Dunlop knocked on his door with two colleagues in tow, younger agents with serious expressions. Dunlop identified himself as the senior Bureau representative with the National Counter-Proliferation Center, WMD Security Issues. He asked Hascomb if he had a moment.

"How can I help?" Hascomb asked the trim man.

"First, you understand our role at the NCPC?"

"Joint and interagency task force, designed to combat the proliferation of weapons of mass destruction. You partner with the CIA, Defense, Homeland, I'm sure all the other players in the community."

"That sums it up."

"So you're taking this guy Ross seriously?"

"Let me ask you, Agent Hascomb, what do you think? Did this guy sound completely off his rocker? Or just confused about something he saw or overheard?"

Hascomb had thought about that exact question. The electronic personnel record on his computer, and the accompanying photo of Captain Ross standing ramrod straight in his Class A uniform, told him a lot.

"He didn't sound crazy. The story sounded crazy. The man sounded tired and under stress. He sounded like a professional talking about a serious problem. Like you or I would."

Dunlop nodded. One of the junior colleagues was taking notes of everything being said.

"The things he said we should check out," Dunlop began, "well, we started checking." He turned in the direction of the young woman, who opened her portfolio.

"Iran has confirmed one of the victims of the multiple murder in Dubai five days ago was Jamshid Alizadeh, a high-ranking diplomat and scientist, and deputy head of their nuclear power program. The Israelis insist his real job was chief of Iran's covert nuclear weapons program. The CIA concurs."

The woman continued.

"Second, the embassy in Abu Dhabi has confirmed Ross and his friend"—the young agent referred to her notes—"Dave Allen did contact the embassy. They met with a security officer from the consulate. Unfortunately, the vehicle carrying the three men was attacked by the mob outside the consulate. A girlfriend, an Australian national, was questioned and released."

Dunlop stepped in. "Through back channels the UAE have expressed a belief the rioting was not spontaneous, but was instead provoked by third-party influencers."

"Influencers?" Hascomb repeated.

"The UAE has been concerned for a long time with the growing strength of Iranian proxy forces within their country."

The female agent picked up the summary.

"The UAE also stated they don't believe Ross had direct involvement with the killings, but they want to question him further as a material witness. The head of police is portraying this as a Mossad hit on an Iranian scientist, with subsequent Iranian retaliation. Ross and Allen got mixed up, and may have been mistakenly targeted, by the Iranians as Israeli operatives.

"Further, the UAE police confirm the incarceration of a man of Kazakh descent, named Ismagulov, who was present at the hotel at the time of the shootings, although his involvement is unclear."

"What about Ross's claim he found the location of a Soviet nuke from directions embedded in a picture file?" Hascomb asked.

Dunlop picked up the narrative again. "Things are quiet on the AQ front. No chatter, no ripples, no movements. Nothing right now."

"But what about his claim this is a nuke already hidden somewhere in the States?"

"The story of 'suitcase nukes' in the U.S. is not a new one," Dunlop said. "Back in the early nineties a couple of junior congressmen tried to make names for themselves by hauling KGB and GRU defectors before a series of televised committees. These guys made a bunch of allegations about Soviet saboteurs and nukes. Some of the claims panned out. Stolen Soviet archives led to the discovery and destruction of saboteur caches throughout Europe. But they were all conventional materiel—definitely not nukes. I was with NCPC at the time. We spun round and round chasing supposed leads from this congressional rumor mill. Big circus, but we found nada."

"You believe Ross is well-intentioned, but someone's feeding him bad info?"

"It may not be that simple," Dunlop said. "The most worrisome thing Ross said, that we confirmed, is that the

Iranian-born physicist and doctoral candidate Karim Hoveyda is unaccounted for. Unusual circumstances. People expected him back to work, but now he's gone, and his lab is missing some radiological equipment. The university hospital has also reported the loss of some cesium-137."

"This is the scientist Ross claims was present at the incident in Dubai?" Hascomb asked, although he knew the answer.

"We can't confirm that. The UAE don't have security photos to corroborate it. But for someone just released from Evin Prison, it's odd he's disappeared again, out of contact with his family, friends, and colleagues."

"So what's your take on all this?" Hascomb asked.

"The supposed Iranian connection is sketchy. But we are looking hard at Hoveyda. With his background and access to certain materials, he could be part of a group attempting to build an RDD."

"A what?"

"A radiological dispersion device. A dirty bomb."

"Shit."

"Yes, shit," Dunlop said. Then, "You've reviewed Ross's history?"

"I've got it right here."

"He was no slouch in the Army."

"Until his last report card, which is probably why he got out."

"We need to talk to Ross. At the same time, I don't think he is going to give up his own search. He's on the ground, and has been figuring things out on his own. He may be the guy who leads us to the nut-jobs we're looking for."

"What do we do?" Hascomb asked.

"You should stay available for this guy," Dunlop answered. "Mitchell Kane was a close friend of his. You were Kane's boss. Now you're Ross's contact here. I've talked to the AD, and you are on this full-time. Welcome to the team."

"Okay, thanks."

"As a first step, put your local law enforcement connections to work. From what Ross told us about the supposed targets, we know the general area where he'll be looking. I don't think this guy is going to give up until he finds something."

Dunlop marched to the door, followed by his colleagues. He paused with his hand on the doorframe and turned to Hascomb. "Find Ross."

In the quiet of the holding area erupted the loud scraping of the door at the end of the hall. Dave assumed the guards were getting ready to turn the overhead lights out. Instead, a white man, a big guy, was pushed through the door, his hands cuffed behind him and each arm held by a jailer. The guards propelled the man forward until they stopped at the cell across from Dave's, removed his cuffs, and pushed him inside. The new prisoner found an open space and slumped to the floor with his back against the bars. Apparently, he was no stranger to spending a night in the clink. He closed his eyes to go to sleep as if he hadn't a care.

The guards left again, and a few minutes later the lights were turned off. Dave closed his own eyes, willing himself to fall asleep, but knowing that it would be a long time before his swirling thoughts allowed him.

The lights were on when Dave opened his eyes. The swelling in the one eye had come down quite a bit, although the edges were still puffy. He stood up, a welcome change from lying on the hard floor. A team of jailers were already making their way down the line of cells with a push cart loaded with trays. Each contained the daily institutional fare of rice covered in yellow sauce, and a single hard-boiled egg rolling around in the tray. The food wasn't horrible, but no one would gain weight here.

A commotion broke out across the way. Dave and his cellmates moved like a school of fish, pushing forward against the bars to see what was going on. Any deviation from the tedious routine was good. In front of the opposite cell, officers were shouting at the thirty or so inmates who retreated to the back half of the cell. All except one man, who lay facedown on the floor close to the bars along the center aisle. The clothes showed that it was the man from the -Stan, the nervous pacer from the day before. The cell door opened. A team of guards, batons in hand, pushed in and fanned out in a semicircle around the body.

Amid more shouting, more guards hurried through the door that connected to the main area of the police station. Two senior officers arrived, evidenced by their peaked hats and gold braided epaulets. Dave held his position along the railing as the men in his cell jockeyed for a better view. One of the jailers tried to find a pulse on the body.

A man in a white coat rushed in, followed by a rolling stretcher. The doctor bent by the man's side, but quickly lost his sense of urgency. He concluded his exam by speaking to the senior officer standing on the other side of the bars.

The jailers ordered two of the inmates to lift the dead prisoner onto the gurney. As they did so, the man's head flopped to the side with gruesome flaccidity, as if his neck were deboned.

The prisoners started chattering in their various dialects until a barked command silenced everyone. The police pulled prisoners out by ones and twos, leading them down the hallway, no doubt for questioning about their cellmate's death. As the first small group was lead away to the interrogation rooms, the body was wheeled out. The cell was relocked and the remaining prisoners fanned back out to occupy their former positions in the overcrowded cell.

Dave examined the first set of prisoners being led away for questioning, then checked the cell, searching the faces. He moved along the bars fronting his cell, to get a different vantage point. Not there.

The white guy, the big European who'd been dumped in the cell just before lights out, was nowhere to be seen.

<h1 style="text-align:center">27</h1>

Another soulless American motel, this one catering to unwashed truck drivers. Safavi knew he and his team were not blending in here, in the backwoods and small towns, as they did in the city of Washington. No matter. Let the rude idiots stare. They were by nature suspicious, much as the peasants in his own country. But they did nothing. Safavi remembered how his confusion had turned to amusement when, on his previous trips in America, he met the suppressed hostility in the poorer, rural areas. The common people tried to hide it. The authorities, the men in the large hats and mirrored sunglasses, made a point of acting indifferent to his foreign appearance and accented speech. Safavi knew many in this country cherished such laxness. An astute warrior, though, thought of ways to exploit this American blindness.

Safavi lay in the bed and stared at the dark ceiling. Soon he would leave this miserable place. Hoveyda and his minders were in position. Ardabili was in position. He was waiting only for Hoveyda to call and report the structure was complete. He did not want to dig up the source material until he was sure he could deliver it, have it inserted into the device, and report to Roghani that all was ready.

The operation was progressing. But what were the Americans doing? What had they surmised from recent events? Two separate investigations would be launched, each of which posed the risk of the American agents and police finding his trail. The events in Dubai and now the messiness at the American's house. A drawback of killing that fool Amir, although he deserved it, was that now Safavi had lost his conduit of information in Dubai.

Hessaby would have the man's number. He called his second in command, and in a minute had the number to the special cell phone that Amir used to talk with his police informant.

The phone rang and Safavi asked in Arabic, "Do you know who this is?"

The man on the other end hesitated, so Safavi spoke again, "This is Amir's friend. His employer."

Safavi sensed the policeman was unsure, perhaps fearful a trap was being set.

"Yes, this is unusual," Safavi continued, "but I have given Amir another assignment. For the time being, I will communicate directly to you. Is that clear?"

"Yes, sir."

"Amir was providing updates on the investigation into the Israeli assassination plot at the resort hotel. I am calling to learn of the progress of your office."

The man gave Safavi the current status of tracking down the identities of the suspected Israeli operatives, as well as the unidentified men in police uniforms at the site of the shoot-out along the highway. The police were making little progress in either case.

"There has been another development," the policeman said hesitantly.

"Don't waste time. Tell me."

"The Kazakh, Ismagulov, who was apprehended at the hotel. He has been killed here in the jail," the man said. "He was found at first light, two hours ago."

"Ismagulov? Killed?"

"Yes, sir."

Someone has saved me the trouble of cleaning up that item, Safavi thought. "Did your interrogation get out of hand, or did the pig get into a fight over cards?"

"We had nothing to do with it. We think it was another inmate, a Russian. The Kazakh's neck was broken."

"Who is this Russian?"

"We don't know. He's disappeared."

"What do you mean?"

"The Russian was arrested for public drunkenness and brought to the jail. Later, before dawn, the station commander received a call directing the Russian be released. A call from very high up—he won't share with me who the call came from. Only after sunrise, when the inmates were forming for breakfast, was Ismagulov discovered dead."

"Curious," Safavi replied. "But this information is useful. Remind me of your name?"

"Rafai."

"Very well, Rafai. Keep your eyes and ears open. I may call from time to time."

Safavi hung up and pondered this development. In one way, Ismagulov's death was beneficial, for it severed a link between Ansar-ol-Mahdi and the Russian source of the weapon. But Safavi did not trust in happy coincidences.

If Ismagulov had represented a loose end for Safavi, he also posed a threat to another group, of course. He was ex-KGB. He was not far removed from the current intelligence service of the Russian Federation. If his complicity in this operation was discovered, the Russians would be hard pressed to deny their role in placing nuclear weapons on American soil. They would not be able to claim those were the long-forgotten war plans of the previous Communist government. Ismagulov would demonstrate the continuity between the KGB and the SVR. It made sense the Russians would dispatch the man. Safavi should have anticipated that.

If the Russians knew about Ismagulov's involvement, though, it could mean only one thing. The Americans were making inquiries. The soldier, Ross, must have convinced the authorities. Or the Americans were taking no chances. In either case, they had contacted the Russians. The Russians would have denied everything, of course, and begun a program of cleaning up. Silencing Ismagulov was step number one.

Safavi frowned. For the first time he was worried, truly worried. Success—after so much preparation—could slip through his fingers.

When would Hoveyda call? Safavi's impatience was turning to anger, and he fought it down. He picked up the hotel phone next to the bed. In clipped tones he ordered Hessaby to wake the remainder of the team and have them gather in Hessaby's room; he would come in five minutes. He hung up the room phone and dialed a number on his cell.

"Ardabili."

"It's me. Are you in position?"

"Yes, I am ready."

"Make your delivery."

"Sir?"

"We are going forward with the contingency. Good luck to you."

"Yes, sir. Thank you."

Ardabili sounded shaken, but Safavi had no doubt he would perform his duty as he had been trained. He might even survive. Many people would survive. That was fine, though, because panic was what Safavi wanted. If the Americans were closing in on his trail, he would give them what they expected, what they feared.

Having made the decision, Safavi felt better. He even allowed himself the faintest trace of a smile as he settled back on the mattress. He smiled wider as he reflected on how easy this part was. The Americans were so helpful. Months and months ago, as the plan and all of its possible permutations formed in Safavi's mind, he spent countless hours conducting research. The openness of the Western Internet was amazing. The U.S. government's own websites were the most helpful, the ones related to weapons of mass destruction security and counter-proliferation. Many commercial and academic sites competed to show their expertise in advising the American government on how to manage these threats.

Overwhelming amounts of information were available, even conjecture about where to obtain the materials, the relative lethality, and long-term effects. Strontium, cobalt—so many nasty byproducts from nuclear reactors. Many of these dangerous radioisotopes were manufactured for industrial and medical uses. Safavi's smile widened. One think tank even published a lengthy report including an Appendix #2, listing all hundred nuclear research reactors in the world and the radioactive isotopes they produced.

How fortuitous, then, that one of the few American research reactors involved in medical radiology happened to be the sponsoring university of his own Professor Hoveyda. The means for Safavi's best contingency plan were stored in a basement right next to the building where Hoveyda worked. When the scientist reported on the security measures, Safavi was at first incredulous. No armed security guards, no cameras? The university relied on nothing but locks and keys, and the assumption that everyone with access could be trusted.

That's why Ardabili, dedicated warrior of Ansar-ol-Mahdi, now possessed several grams of a silvery-white powder called cesium chloride, the primary form of the highly radioactive isotope cesium-137.

Yes, now was the time to move. Hoveyda would be ready soon enough. While Ardabili moved to create the diversion, Safavi would lead his unit to the cache site before sunrise, conduct his reconnaissance, and put in place the necessary equipment and security. He would have the device by this time tomorrow, while the Americans chased their tails elsewhere.

Find Ross.

Those had been words of Agent Dunlop, the NCPC man. Nothing could be accomplished after talking with the NCPC man around midnight. But this morning, as the rest of the world returned to work, Hascomb was intent on making that happen. He picked up the phone and dialed a colleague.

"Hey, Nancy. Listen, I'm going to shoot you an email with the particulars on a guy named Barrett Ross. We want him in connection with Mitchell Kane's murder."

"Okay, send it right over."

"Listen, can you get this on Law Enforcement Online right away? I want every small town cop and sheriff seeing the alert first thing when they get to work this morning."

"We can do that."

"I'm going to nominate this guy up through the Criminal Investigative Division for the Most Wanted List, but that will take a while."

"Send me the email. Every cop in the country will have his name and picture."

Hascomb thanked the woman and put the finishing touches on the email. It included Ross's headshot, cropped from the photo in his Army personnel file. Several hundred thousand local law enforcement officials would soon have the information on their desktops. The problem with the system, of course, was it featured thousands of criminals, with new alerts broadcasted every day about bad guys ranging from petty thieves to hardened murderers. Local cops were busy. Unless they knew they should be on the lookout for a certain guy in their area, they were going to focus on local problems, not email alerts coming over LEO. He needed to figure out where Barrett was going, and contact the appropriate FBI field office.

Ross claimed the Iranians were after a nuke hidden somewhere in West Virginia, Kentucky, or Tennessee. Pretty large area. Would he go there? By his own admission, he didn't know where this supposed nuke was located. Would he go to ground? Who would he turn to for help? Ross had a buddy, the other American who was mixed up in this thing. Hascomb found his notes—the U.S. Embassy in Abu Dhabi confirmed the incarceration of one David Allen in Dubai, held in connection with the shooting of several UAE policemen.

Maybe Allen could shed some light on what his friend's next move would be.

Hascomb did a search and found the homepage for the U.S. Embassy in Abu Dhabi. He guessed they were eight or nine hours ahead of him. He picked up the phone and dialed the main line from the website.

"U.S. Embassy."

"Hi, this is Special Agent Darrell Hascomb with the FBI. I have some questions regarding a U.S. national named David Allen, who is being held by the Dubai police. It pertains to an investigation we're running here on a colleague of Mr. Allen's. Can I speak to someone about this?"

Several minutes passed before the call was picked up by the appropriate office in the building.

"This is Samantha Carr, Administrative Officer, U.S. Embassy," said an exasperated voice.

Using the mirror, Barrett removed the gauze dressing and surgical tape from his head. He wadded up the old dressing and threw it in the wastebasket. He'd let the wound air out a little bit, then ask Sada to put on a fresh bandage.

It was almost nine o'clock in the morning. Exhausted, they'd fallen asleep as soon as they'd lain down the night before. Barrett had opted to sleep on top of the covers of the king-size bed.

The surge of hope and expectation he'd had when they met the Russian spy was dwindling fast. Waiting to see if Vasilievsky called was useless. Barrett was sure now that the Russian wouldn't. The little charade he put on yesterday in the park, being taken aback by the code word, the offer to call them back, none of it meant anything. The spy was just playing them in order to make a clean exit.

Had he failed again? Why did he think he could just sit here and hope Hascomb was able to convince the intel community to do something?

A thought formed in Barrett's mind. Would the Russian agree to another meeting? Would Sada be willing to make that call again? Barrett still had his weapon in the backpack. If the Russian agreed to meet, Barrett could take him at gunpoint, go somewhere, force him to speak, maybe...

The idea presented a few problems. Barrett knew nothing about interrogations. Sada would probably not assist him in kidnapping the SVR's senior spook in the U.S. Even if he could get the Russian alone, how would that lead to retrieving the file? It's not like the Russian would have the file on him.

Perhaps the situation was out of his hands. The FBI knew everything he and Sada did. They were the experts. They had the people, the sensors, and the computers to track down this Iranian asshole and his team. They could pinpoint the radioactive signature of a nuke, couldn't they, even if it was still lying in the ground somewhere?

"Barrett," Sada called from the other room, her voice rising at the end of his name. "Come in here."

She was sitting on one of the beds, cranking up the volume on the television remote. The truth hit him all at once. Something was badly wrong. The Iranians had already made their attack. He understood it in the nervous, distracted movements of the Headline News anchorwoman, even before he read the large text banners at the bottom of the screen. *Possible Terrorist Attack*, the main banner read, the obligatory *Live* in the lower right corner. A smaller red banner, too, with yellow lettering— *Large Bomb in Dallas, TX*. The lack of a video linkup contributed to the anchorwoman's distress as she attempted to remain calm and detached while, no doubt, producers were shouting in her ear and scraps of data were flashing on the computer monitor embedded in the desktop in front of her. No photos, no video, this was just emerging.

"Local authorities are confirming a large explosion has occurred at the Dallas-Fort Worth International Airport..."

"...said he would not speculate at this time..."

"...Unconfirmed number of injuries, but reports are indicating it was a massive explosion...considerable damage..."

"...Possible Al Qaeda connection..."

"...Let's turn to our terrorism expert, Colonel Spanaway, thank you for joining us this morning..."

Barrett sat beside Sada on the edge of the bed, numb, watching as it unfolded. The feeling was disturbingly like the emptiness that had overwhelmed him and everyone else standing around that television in the barracks dayroom, twelve years before, their morning routine interrupted, their lives suddenly changed.

Soon, a camera shot appeared from somewhere outside the airport, a jerky telephoto lens aimed across a tree line to a terminal building, where black smoke was rising into the sky. The woman reported that the explosion did not occur inside the terminal, but outside, on the road leading to the terminal. A car or truck bomb, they were saying. The news station began receiving the first shaky images and audio from camera phones of witnesses in the nearby terminal.

"What is this?" Sada asked herself, aloud.

"What do you mean?" he asked.

"That's not a nuclear explosion," she said. "So is it coincidence, or is it the Iranians?"

Barrett made an effort to shake himself free of the screen. Many people had just been injured or killed by this attack, but he needed to think. If this terrorist event was unrelated to the events of the past week, then it was a calamity, but not one that changed his situation. He would be no closer to figuring out where the Iranians were. No closer to persuading the FBI to look for them.

"...Reports are coming from first responders that this may be a dirty bomb. Indications of unusually high radiation signatures...." The anchorwoman had her finger to her ear, puzzled, trying to speak and absorb information at the same time.

"Holy shit." Barrett leaned forward, cupping his chin in his hands. What was going on here?

For forty-five minutes, the news people and pundits repeated the same information over and over. It was hard to tell what was being reported from the site, and what was pure speculation. The general consensus was forming, though, that this was a terrorist attack, a truck bomb. Most likely, a dirty bomb, detonated by Al Qaeda or its sympathizers. Sada flipped between all the major news channels, but the coverage was identical, with the same video feeds and handful of still photos.

The anchor returned on screen. "Officials on the ground at the site, in conjunction with Dallas police and Homeland Security, have confirmed they are treating this as a, quote, 'attack with a radiological dispersal device,' or 'dirty bomb,' and have begun implementing procedures to evacuate a large area around the site of the bomb detonation."

The anchor turned to another expert. A graphic was overlaid on the screen with concentric, oblong shapes overlaid on a map of the Dallas metropolis, with bright red in the center giving way to orange, yellow, and gray ellipses stretching to the southeast. Not circles, but elongated, to account for the direction and strength of the prevailing winds as they spread the radiation. The anchor and the expert speculated about numbers of people affected and at risk, how many would be displaced, and the economic costs to the state and nation.

Sada rested her hand on his leg and said, "I'm sorry."

Barrett pulled his eyes away from the television. "This is the Iranians."

"Why? What are they trying to do?"

Barrett's mind was racing, grasping for an answer. He knew what his intuition was screaming. He was just cross checking to see if it fit, if it made sense.

"It's a diversion. They've figured out we've told everything we know to the authorities. Maybe Hascomb and his bosses have initiated some protocols. The Iranian realizes precautions will have been taken. An investigation started. Counter-WMD assets put on alert."

"And?"

"Now all of those specialized assets, all those people and systems, are being focused on one place. Dallas, Texas. I wouldn't be surprised if DoD and Homeland had a bunch of people in the air right now, flying to Dallas to respond, investigate and clean up."

"The Iranian is throwing your government off his scent," Sada said.

Barrett was about to answer when her phone rang.

28

Sada picked up her phone off the bed spread.

"It's me."

Sada recognized Vasilievsky's voice and mouthed his name to Barrett.

"Are you watching the news?" she asked.

"Yes, I've made the connection. Which is why I decided to call. Do you have an email address?"

Sada gave him a throw-away address.

"A colleague of mine will send you a file. As you've seen it before, but translated into English."

"Thank you," Sada said. This is where the quid pro quo would come in.

Vasilievsky continued, "This is sensitive, obviously. As a fellow professional, I hope you can understand my position. No one from the American government has contacted my government. But I fear the danger you and your friend alluded to has become...shall we say, possible."

"You don't want a Soviet nuke blowing up in the United States," Sada summarized. "That's a reasonable stance."

Vasilievsky was probably wincing at the words *Soviet nuke* spoken over an unsecured line, but Sada was not concerned about his sensitivities.

"My point is, we've had no official contact from the Americans on this matter. Just you and Mr. Ross. If such a device was discovered, we would like the appropriate people to bear in mind the cooperation provided by the Russian Federation. Our efforts to prevent further tragedy."

"You want the Americans to overlook the fact your country buried the thing in the first place?"

"Miss Di-Nur, this discussion would normally occur between my government and the appropriate representatives of the American government. But since we are interceding to thwart a danger they are unaware of, that is hardly possible."

"But if Mr. Ross and I are unsuccessful, or if the existence of the device remains unproven because the Iranians can't find it, or because it has long since been paved over by a parking lot, you won't have gone on record as warning the Americans of its existence."

"Ms. Di-Nur. All I am asking is, if and when it should come up, you and Mr. Ross inform the Americans how you were able to move forward from this point."

"Of course."

"You will have an email of the text within the next five minutes. Goodbye."

Sada heard the abrupt click. Something more was going on with the Russian, but she couldn't figure it out right now.

The American had pieced together enough of the conversation to know they'd be able to move soon. He was throwing his few belongings into his backpack.

"We good?"

"We should have the file in a few minutes," she

answered. Then what? A race against the Iranians to the cache site. How many, and where were they? At least two had invaded Barrett's house in D.C. One of those was dead. A team in North Carolina had assisted the physicist Hoveyda in stealing the neutron generator and, she suspected, radioactive materials. They had at least one operative in Dallas.

But she was no longer operating alone, either. She hadn't been since Fujairah, she realized. The American had turned another corner. His insistence on pressing for the meeting with Vasilievsky had paid off. In the wake of the Dallas attack, the fruits of that interview were giving them their only chance to stop a much worse disaster. For Sada was sure Barrett's soldierly instinct on this was correct, too: what they just saw was merely a diversion.

Barrett was proving to be a reliable and brave comrade-in-arms.

Was that all that she thought about this man? Sada had to remind herself of the promise she'd made to herself—that her future held no more room for soldiers and agents. When the day came to start her new life, she would find an ordinary man concerned with ordinary affairs.

"One thing's for certain," Barrett muttered.

"What's that?"

"The next place the Iranians pop up, it won't be in Texas."

The file came through Sada's email ten minutes later. When they were sure they had saved the text to the computer's hard drive, they picked up their bags and walked out of the hotel room. The trip from Tysons Corner to White Sulphur Springs, West Virginia, was a good 240 miles, and would take close to four hours.

They headed west out of D.C. along I-66. After an hour

they turned southwest to cut through the Shenandoah Valley on I-81, which they'd follow for the next hundred miles, before turning west again on I-64 toward the once top-secret Congressional war bunker. If the Greenbrier Hotel was the easternmost of the Soviets' Cold War targets, maybe the cache site was somewhere west of the resort. Barrett assumed—hoped—the Greenbrier, being the primary target, was going to be the site closest to the cache.

While Sada drove, Barrett studied the deciphered text, looking for additional clues in the KGB's directions. From his internet search in the hotel room, he knew the route to White Sulphur Springs would have them leave I-64 and travel on U.S. Highway 60 for a couple of miles before they reached the hotel. Somewhere along U.S. 60 was the fixed reference point, HICO, the start place for the rest of the directions. Barrett read the text again:

```
WHITE SEA
Site COLLIERY


From HICO on Road #60, go south/southwest on
Road #19 for 7.4 kilometers. Turn left onto
Road #5, and follow it for 600 meters. Turn
right, and immediately bear left onto the
Station Road. Follow this road for 4.9
kilometers. It will wind through a series of
switchbacks to the Bridge. From the south end
of the bridge, follow the road for 1.8
kilometers. The road will make three
switchbacks, the third of which is at the 1.8
kilometer point. From this point, move on foot.
Leave the road to the left and enter the woods.
Cross the small stream, and 20 meters beyond
you will come upon an old mining trail. Turn
```

left and follow the trail for 2.8 kilometers. The trail will start northward, moving uphill for the first 400 meters, at which point it will crest the top of the spur. From that point, continue to follow the trail for the remaining 2.4 kilometers, which will lead generally southeast and then south, parallel to the river in the valley to the left. The path is covered by dense woods, and follows a gradual incline. After approximately 2.8 kilometers the path will widen out into an open area. A large portal will appear on the right, blocked by an iron gate. Continue for another 100 meters, passing an abandoned stone building on the right. The next aperture on the right is the drift mouth, which is approximately 4 meters wide and 2 meters high. This is the entrance to the cache site. An iron gate has been installed since the mine's closing. Proceed into the shaft exactly 50 steps. Along the left wall, five large support timbers are stacked on the ground. Beneath the timbers, the cache has been cut into the stone to a depth of approximately 1.5 meters. Once the timbers are removed, the top of the cache is covered with 30 centimeters of loose stone and dirt, under which sits a wooden board and then the metal container. Remove the wood board carefully. The cache container is protected by means of MOLNIYA, and must be disarmed accordingly before attempting to move or lift from the hole.

BADEN   Command
CORAX   Command

GOLD   Military
CHUTE   Military
Y12   Industrial

He had the laptop opened to read the text of the cache directions, but without Wi-Fi, he was reduced to using the road atlas spread across his lap. Once they reached West Virginia, they could pick up a local road map from a gas station. He stared at the page for West Virginia, tracing the length of U.S. 60 as it cut across the state from east to west. At one point, before the completion of the interstate system, this was the main thoroughfare across the state. He checked back with the written directions. The map showed an intersection of U.S. 60 with U.S. 19. That could be the 19 from the directions. Whether through the inconsistencies of translation, or simple oversight, the Russian author had referred to roads when these were, for those times at least, major American highways.

"Sada, pull over where we can get Wi-Fi. Find a Starbucks or something."

Fifteen minutes later, they were inside a coffee shop in a small mall just off the highway. Barrett zoomed in and out, and rolled around the virtual terrain of Google Earth.

"That's it, we've got it," he said. He pointed to a little circle with the name Hico near the intersection of the two highways.

"HICO's not a code word. It's a town. No more than a crossroads."

Barrett kept switching between the text and the map program, plotting a path on the satellite imagery, zooming in and out, backtracking and making several corrections.

"Have you pinpointed it?" Sada asked.

"This area is the New River Gorge. The bridge that spans the gorge, carrying U.S. 19 across it, is famous. It crosses six hundred feet above the river. You see it all the time in ads for the tourism industry down there."

Barrett frowned. The directions and the reference to the bridge didn't make sense. Yet soon the answer came to him.

"I got it now. This cache was buried in the late fifties or early sixties, right? The New River Gorge Bridge wasn't even built yet. So, here," he said, pointing to the imagery on the screen.

A little gray rectangle, indicating a much shorter bridge, spanned the narrow bottom close to the level of the river.

"This old bridge is the one they would have been referring to. Here's Station Road."

Sada peered over his shoulder as he traced his finger over a thickly vegetated piece of the imagery.

"This area, right here, this is it. No trails visible with all the trees, but when we get to the bridge, we should have no trouble finding it."

"Let's go," she said.

Back in the car, Sada was soon pushing their speed over eighty-five mph, passing the heavy semi-trailer traffic in the right lane.

Having pinpointed the site as close as they could from a map reconnaissance, they had to consider what they were going to do once they arrived.

"How many do you think there are?" he asked.

"Somewhere between five and ten. They'll want to be as small as possible to avoid detection. But they have some heavy lifting to do. They have to dig up and carry the device out."

"The Iranian will have men for tactical security," Barrett said.

"We need to get local law enforcement involved," Sada said. "We need to shut down the road networks, start looking for the Iranians now."

"How do we do that? I'm liable to be arrested if I show my face in a police station."

"I can try to convince them."

"The Iranian has a head start on us," Barrett said. "How do we risk taking the time to convince someone of our story?"

"He still has to get the device to wherever the scientist Hoveyda is waiting with the neutron source."

"Sada, if we don't stop this group here, at this cache site, then that's just another location we'd have to figure out. And we have exactly zero clues to that."

Barrett knew what she was thinking. The odds didn't favor them. But getting there first might be the only chance they had.

"We have the two of us, and we're both capable. If we handle it right, we'll have the element of surprise," he said. Sada was quiet.

"We can't risk letting the Iranian pull that thing out of the cache."

"Yes. We go straight to the mine," Sada concluded.

She turned, and he caught her look. He was afraid he would see doubt. Instead, in those eyes he met with what seemed approval and encouragement.

"We'll get boots on the ground," Barrett said, "and figure it out."

Dave sat on his little square of folded blanket, inspecting the pipes and sprayed-on insulation of the ceiling high above him. He'd been confined three days now. How long could they hold him without charging him with anything? Forever, for all he knew. That flunky from the embassy who'd visited him wasn't accomplishing anything.

Dave dropped his view back to the immediate confines of the cell, brought out of his musings by the excited murmuring of his fellow prisoners. A guard had just deposited another ward of the state in the cell. As the guard walked away up the hall, the inmate searched out an acquaintance and began chattering. News rippled out from this epicenter. Soon everyone in the cell who spoke any Arabic was murmuring. Some were shaking their heads. A few grinned, but the smiles disappeared when they noticed Dave watching them.

"Anybody speak English?" he asked the room in general.

An older man, with several days stubble on his weathered face, came over and knelt beside Dave.

"I speak English," the man said in a heavy accent.

"What is everybody talking about?" Dave asked, circling the room with his hand.

The man looked at him with clear eyes. "I am sorry. Big explosion in America. Big...fight."

The old man was searching for a different word than fight, but couldn't find it.

"Do you know where?"

"Duh-Lass."

Dulles Airport.

"Was it a bomb?"

"Yes, yes. A bomb."

Oh, Christ. Another terrorist attack on American soil. A sickening feeling of mingled rage and helplessness turned his stomach.

"I am sorry for you."

The man lowered his eyes and withdrew to his group. Many of the inmates were watching Dave. More than a few sympathetic glances were cast Dave's way, but a few hard, covert looks as well. Fuck you, he wished to the second bunch.

He needed more information.

Just then the door at the end of the hallway opened. A

guard came down the wide aisle between the opposing cells. When he was close to Dave's cell, Dave stood and raised his hand to the bars.

"Wait. Please. Do you speak English?"

"Yes. What do you want?"

"Was there an attack in America? A terrorist attack?"

The policeman's face softened a bit. "Yes. Very bad. It is crazy."

"What happened?"

"A bomb. A, ah, truck bomb."

"Are you sure? Not a nuclear bomb?"

The man looked surprised by Dave's question. "No, no, no. A truck bomb, but dirty. Many killed and hurt. Radiation…" The man made a gesture with his arms to indicate a billowing explosion.

"In Washington, D.C.?"

The guard again regarded Dave oddly, as if wondering how, if Dave had heard the information, he was getting it so garbled.

"No. Dallas. In the state of Texas. The airport of Dallas, Texas."

The guard walked away, and Dave went back to his blanket along the side wall. Think. Think.

Dave was not the type of guy who thought the world revolved around him. But the circumstances were strange. A series of events like this couldn't just happen unless they were somehow connected. His best friend stumbles into an international espionage plot. They get shot at by militants working for the Iranians. They link up with a Mossad agent, and find out the Iranians are trying to buy uranium from an ex-KGB agent. He and Barrett were attacked a second time.

The night before, a Russian-looking guy shows up just before lights out. In the morning he's gone, but the guy matching the Mossad agent's description of the Kazakh go-between is dead. Murdered in his sleep, his neck snapped. Now a terrorist attack in the U.S. A dirty bomb, using radioactive materials.

The woman, Susan, said the Iranians were trying to buy uranium so they could complete their first warhead, without having their own plants bombed to hell. But what if the Iranians weren't the buyers? Or they bought it only as middlemen, to sell to Al Qaeda or some other group?

No. The Iranians who bought the uranium, they didn't sell or give it away. They used it. They wrapped the uranium around conventional explosives and detonated the bomb to spread radiation to kill and sicken Americans.

What the hell? They must think they could get away with it, deny any involvement. But how? Why?

Where the hell was Barrett, and this woman Susan? Were they thinking along the same lines? Had they warned the CIA, the FBI? Were Barrett and Susan even alive still? God, he needed to talk to someone in the embassy, now, and someone above the rank of coffee-pourer.

"Hey! Hey! I need to talk to someone!"

Dave shouted for three minutes until one of the jailors came through the door, brandishing his billy club.

"Quiet! You must be quiet!"

"The colonel who questioned me when I came here. I need to talk to him. I have something to tell him I didn't say before."

The guard lowered the billy club and turned to walk away.

Dave didn't know what he was going to say to the police chief, but it needed to be good enough to earn him a meeting with someone higher up in the American embassy.

29

At two o'clock Sada pulled off Highway 19 onto a small two-lane road winding back into the rolling green hills north of the New River Gorge. The fast-running river and the spectacular rocky bluffs on either side attracted whitewater rafters, rock climbers, hikers and campers from all over the world. The town of Fayetteville, West Virginia, south of the river, and many of the homes they were passing on the winding back roads were connected with the area's focus on adventure tourism. ATVs were parked in driveways. Off-road vehicles with canoes strapped on top, and blue school buses pulling trailers stacked with rafts, lined the road shoulders.

The day was sweltering, with the temperature in the high nineties. Despite the mugginess, Barrett rolled down his window.

"The Station Road" described in the cache directions ended up being Fayette Station Road. It did indeed cut back and forth through a series of hairpin turns as the road dropped down the side of the gorge until they were far below the highway and the clustering communities up top on the rim of the gorge. After a turn they made a long, gradual descent as the road hugged the steep side of the mountain. Barrett said, "Look up."

Sada slowed and looked through the sunroof. Five hundred feet above them, framed in an opening of leafy boughs, were the massive bolt-studded steel girders of the New River Gorge Bridge, its rust-red undercarriage dark in its own shadow. That was the main passage, via U.S. 19, across the river.

At the end of the descent, they made a right and broke free of the treeline, coming upon the much older and smaller Fayette Station Bridge, built a century before its larger neighbor. The good news was, it was still serviceable, used now and then by the local traffic. Crossing the river, Sada noted the odometer reading. At 1.1 miles, which corresponded to the cache direction's mark of 1.8 kilometers, they entered a hairpin turn. The sharp curve bent to the right with a loose gravel pullout to the outside of the curve. A ramshackle little home rose just beyond the turnout, connected to the main road by a gravel drive. Sada drove another mile ahead, and they started gaining elevation again, climbing the south side of the gorge. At another pullout she veered over and parked behind a car.

"God, this reminds me of home," Barrett said. "I spent a lot of time roaming hills just like these with my dad."

They walked back down the road. Barrett felt the sweat beading on his forehead and his shirt sticking to his back, even though they were strolling downhill.

"When this is all over, I've got to go back," he said to himself. "Sort everything out."

He noticed Sada was looking at him oddly. She wasn't the type to talk to herself, he would venture.

As they neared the previous turnout on the hairpin curve, Barrett appraised the situation.

Where the road came up the hill into the curve, the woods stood close to the shoulder, but the terrain dropped precipitously just beyond. The only easy way off the road, in the direction they wanted to go, was to walk down the private drive for fifty meters before cutting left into the woods. Staying clear of the property would mean scrambling down into a deep gully and working back up to the level of the path the cache directions indicated were somewhere in the woods before them.

Barrett had visions of his up and down walk in the desert, but with the added complications of interlocking brambles and mountain laurel.

"Come on," he said to Sada, hiking his pack higher on his shoulders, heading down the drive for a break in the leafy undergrowth.

"Hey there!" a voice called out from the home.

Barrett turned but couldn't see anyone. The structure at one time had been a simple trailer home, but now was an agglomeration of additions tacked on over the years, so the original form was all but hidden. Then he saw a form rise from a chair that was hidden in the shade of a dirty, striped awning spread from the side of the trailer out over a makeshift wooden deck.

"This here's private property, sir," the man yelled. The effort he made for his voice to carry was a strain, but the belligerence in the last syllable was unmistakable. The man was now standing at the railing of his deck. He had to be ninety, if he was a day. Despite the heat, he was wearing a long sleeve checkered shirt and work dungarees.

"Sorry about that," Barrett yelled. "We heard there was a hiking trail with good views up this way."

"Plenty of public trailheads 'round here, but this ain't one of em. Go back to the ranger station and git a map."

"OK, will do."

But Barrett kept following the driveway for a few more

feet until he spied the trail leading off into the woods. No time for niceties. Just as he thought, this trail was much more gently sloping, and they soon hit a stream that ran down through the draw. Large boulders broke it into a series of cascading pools. The stream at this point widened into a large, shallow pool, with numerous stepping stones. Just beyond, the path led back up into the dark tree line. They climbed this stretch for twenty meters or so before running into a larger path, just wide enough for an off-road vehicle.

"I think this is it," he said. "The old mine trail from the directions."

"All right, 2.8 kilometers from this point."

"Let's go."

Sada stayed him, touching his arm. She didn't say anything but reached into her pack. She pulled the slide back on her Glock, making sure a round was chambered in the barrel. She dropped the magazine to make sure it was full before sliding it back into the weapon. She zipped the bag back up, but slung it only over one shoulder, clutched in her non-firing hand. Barrett repeated the check with his own weapon, and they resumed walking.

"I don't think the Iranians will do anything until nightfall," Sada said. "But just in case."

"There is one thing I worry about," Barrett said as he fell into stride.

"What?"

"If I was the Iranian, and I made it this far, I'd put security on the site. If the plan were to come back in hours of darkness, I would put an observer in place to overwatch the mine entrance."

Sada considered this. "We could try to go around, come to the back side through the woods..."

"I thought about that. But if someone is already stationary in a hide site, our blundering through the woods will draw attention to ourselves. We won't surprise anybody."

Sada agreed with this observation, and they continued onward. The grade was fairly easy, but they were pushing themselves. They were both beginning to breathe heavily with the exertion.

"On the other hand, if we just walk up and look around, maybe take some photos, maybe we'll look like tourists out hiking."

"Unless they recognize our faces," Sada said.

Barrett chose to ignore this complication. "We need to look at the mine site, see if it's been breached. We have to know if the cache is still buried. If the surveillance man is hidden well, he'll be too distant to pick out our faces."

"He'll have binos, or a scope."

"It's not a perfect plan. But can you think of anything better?"

She had no response.

Twenty-five minutes later they reached the site of the old coal mine. The dappled light along the leafy trail gave way in front of them to the bright afternoon sunlight of an open space. At its edge was a building, and the trail bent around it to the right. The building was a large stone and masonry structure consisting of several large open rooms, its long axis diagonal to the path. The roof was long since gone, as were the doors. A plaque placed on the side of the trail by the Park Service identified the building as the Fan House, which once held the extensive machinery needed to ventilate the mine complex.

Continuing around the bend, they stepped out into the open. The trail widened into a large plateau cut into the side of the hill, which rose up on their right. The flat ground, like the bottom of a shallow bowl, spread for two hundred meters in a lazy crescent, curving around the inside of the terrain. The area was at most fifty meters wide in the center. To the left the ground dropped off again, heading toward the river bottom of the gorge. Half a dozen other stone buildings dotted the area, as well as several concrete pads that at one time had served as foundations for heavy machinery, as indicated by remnants of structural iron bolted into the concrete.

Barrett and Sada edged along the path, curving through the center of the wider grassy area. Not far past the bend with the Fan House, they spotted the first mine opening. It was set back a short ways into the side of the hill, a black hole cut into solid rock. A metal grate, like the portcullis of a medieval castle, shut off the entrance.

Farther on, in the center of the crescent shape, and up against the hillside, they passed another roofless square structure, identified as the remains of the Lamp House, where the miners collected their lamps before descending into the earth. Even after fifty years of disuse, the structure was solid. The metal-reinforced concrete apertures where the door and windows had been reminded Barrett of battlefield bunkers.

To maintain their fiction of a pair of hikers, they stopped and read the displays put up by the National Park Service, which described the history of the mine. They sauntered across the grounds, glancing over at a second mineshaft that opened on the other side of the Lamp House. They avoided it for the time being, but a large black metal grate blocked its entrance, just like the first shaft. At the far end of the grassy crescent, a set of modern wooden stairs led all the way to the valley bottom, passing more rusting infrastructure that once had carried coal down to the waiting rail cars on the tracks along the river. Just past these stairs, the open area narrowed back down to a path, passed a narrow two-story stone building, and curved back into the woods and around a bend.

A plaque by the top of the stairs gave more history of the difficulties and dangers in mining. This particular mine ceased full-time operation in the late 1950s and was closed for good in 1961. Barrett wondered if access to the mine entrance had been easier for someone back then. Did the Russians count on someone sealing off the mine to prevent prying eyes?

Below them, the river was obscured beneath a thick canopy of maple and oak, but the swishing of nearby rapids came up to them through the woods. Barrett reached out and put his arm around Sada's waist, resting his hand on her hip. The way his arm nestled in the curve of her lower back felt quite natural. Sada turned her head toward him.

"To stay in character," he said mildly.

"Of course." He felt her arm encircle him, and she inclined her head to his shoulder.

After a moment, in silent acknowledgment, they turned and walked back in the other direction. This time they turned off the pathway and approached the second mineshaft. This, too, was set back several yards from the grassy plateau, cut into solid rock. A section of narrow-gauge track still protruded a short way beyond the opening. At its end the dilapidated, rusty hulk of a derailed coal cart lay tipped on its sides. Barrett moved up to the grate and felt the cool air pouring out of the dark mine. It was like standing in front of an open refrigerator on a hot summer day. The stream of air rushing out of the depths of the earth caused goose bumps to jump out on his sweaty arms.

The iron grate was composed of several flat, four-inch wide beams embedded in the rock surfaces at top and bottom, with two-inch-thick horizontal bars spaced a foot apart and stretching across the width. Barrett rested his hands on the grate and peered into the darkness. The light of the outside world penetrated a short way before succumbing to the dark. Within that short space he could make out wooden timbers bracing the sides and ceiling, along with a few ancient, corroded lamps. Nothing had disturbed this place in decades.

They wandered away from the mine entrance.

"Let me get a picture of you," he said. Sada stood in front of the blocked entrance. They spent a few more minutes strolling around the area, taking pictures of each other. Barrett made sure they had a few photos that gave a good sense of the general layout of the area and its ruins. Finally, they returned to the trailhead leading down the mountain.

They walked for ten minutes before stopping.

"If we're in the right place, the Iranians haven't gotten in yet," Barrett said.

"What next?"

Barrett had been mulling that over as they walked. "The FBI and everyone else are focused on Dallas. There's zero chance of getting them out here on what they think is a crazy hunch of ours."

"We have to persuade someone to open that mine and search it," she said. "Police, Park Service—someone has to listen to us."

Barrett was searching back up the trail.

"You expect the Iranians to be watching the mine?" she asked.

"If they've located it, it would be SOP."

"Now we've located it, but we're walking away. When we come back, we'll be blind."

"I know, but I'm not sure I like the alternative," Barrett said.

"You go get the police. I'll stay here and watch it."

"I don't know."

"Why not?"

Barrett knew what she was saying made perfect sense. He struggled to think of a reason not to agree.

"Okay. We stay in regular contact. No heroics."

"You forget. I'm a professional." She gave him a quick smile.

They worked out the details of a simple contingency plan, agreeing on telephone contact at least every three hours. If Barrett didn't return in twenty-four hours, and they lost comms, she would leave in daylight and try to convince the local authorities of their story herself. Barrett felt like he was stepping out of a patrol base, exchanging a five-point contingency plan with a Ranger buddy.

"All right. Go," Sada said, but then she grabbed his hand and pulled herself close, kissing him on the cheek. She turned away and walked up the trail.

Barrett waited until she disappeared around an outcrop of granite before he turned and jogged down the other way. He would have to think about what just happened—what it meant.

If it meant anything. Just a reaction to the stress? An acknowledgment of the bond of a shared mission. Whether or not it meant anything close to what he hoped, he was glad it happened. No matter what the next few hours held.

He made good time to the bottom, where the little offshoot trail took him back across the shallow ford site, and he quickly navigated across the flat boulders. He was determined to reach the car as quickly as possible, and he headed back along the trail to the old man's driveway. He hoped the old coot didn't have a dog waiting for him.

Barrett was pushing through the vegetation on the edge of the gravel drive when he almost ran into a dark brown patrol car. A big yellow sheriff's star was emblazoned on the door. He managed to catch himself, but he found himself pinned under the gaze of a serious young man with aviator's glasses and a broad-brimmed Smokey hat.

30

"Sir, could you come over here for a moment?"

The sheriff's deputy was pointing to a spot on the opposite side of the patrol car. The deputy backed up to give Barrett room to walk around the trunk. As he did so, the officer rested his right hand on his black utility belt, not quite on the grip of his holstered side arm. The crisp creases in the man's uniform, and the bulge of the armored vest beneath his shirt, communicated a sense of all-business.

"Sure," Barrett said, and complied.

Another officer was in the front yard, speaking to the old man.

"That's him, that's one of em," the old man said, pointing a gnarled hand toward Barrett.

The other deputy, voice lowered, was trying to reassure the man the situation was under control. The sheriff's office was on the case. Finally, the old man turned back to his trailer, and the other deputy approached Barrett. The second deputy was a bit older and paunchier than the first, and his close-shaved head showed white-gray stubble.

"What's your name, sir?"

"Barrett Ross."

"Do you have ID, Mr. Ross?"

"I left it in my vehicle."

"Where is the woman you were with earlier?"

"I guess somewhere along the river. We just met up hiking. We were both looking for the mine trail, and I came back after looking around. I think she took the long stairs down to the river."

"So you didn't know her?"

"No, sir."

The older deputy gave a curt nod to his colleague, who asked Barrett to turn around and place his hands on the vehicle. A thorough pat-down ensued, and Barrett's hands were cuffed behind him. The deputy turned him around and leaned him against the patrol car.

"Well, now, what have we got here?" exclaimed the second deputy, kneeling beside Barrett's backpack. He suspended the pistol in air with a ball point pen through the trigger guard.

"Let's go," the man said, and the first deputy was already pushing Barrett's head below the frame of the backseat door.

The sheriff's office, along with the county courthouse, was located in a large red brick building in the center square of Fayetteville, West Virginia. Barrett was escorted into a drab room on the second floor and placed in one of the two metal folding chairs arranged on either side of a wooden table. A deputy, not the one who apprehended him, stood just inside the closed door. The painted cinderblock walls were adorned only with an institutional clock with skinny black hands. The lone window had its dirty cream-color blinds tightly closed.

An older officer and the deputy who apprehended Barrett came into the room. The older man took a seat across the table from Barrett.

"Mr. Ross, my name is Sheriff Johnston. It's a pleasure to make your acquaintance."

Barrett thought it best to keep his mouth shut.

"Here we were, thinking Old Man Scruggs was just being his usual pain-in-the-ass self. Seeing foreigners everywhere, and all keyed up about the Dallas explosion. He kept calling us every half hour, claiming all sorts of strange people were traipsing across his property."

The sheriff measured Barrett up and down. He referred to a manila folder in his hands which contained, at most, two loose pieces of paper.

"Deputy Ainsworth and me, we assumed it was some of the local kids checking on their pot plants in the woods. Or worse, setting up a meth lab in one of the caves up there."

Sheriff Johnston paused, seemingly to see if Barrett would comment.

"So imagine our surprise when we find a bona fide criminal. On the FBI's most wanted list, too."

Barrett shifted his gaze to the unflinching stare of Deputy Ainsworth, who was leaning against the corner.

"Armed, too," Johnston added. He looked back at the file. "Wanted in connection with the murder of an FBI special agent, and in connection with various matters related to United States national security," the sheriff read aloud.

"It'll be a while before the FBI get here, Mr. Ross, so why don't you just go ahead and explain what you got goin' on in our peaceful little West Virginia town?"

* * *

Here goes nothing, Barrett thought. He started chronologically, with his arrival in Dubai six days earlier. His admission, right off the bat, that he was fresh from a trip to the Middle East caught the attention of Johnston and Ainsworth. Barrett was counting on that to sustain their patience through what would sound like a long-winded explanation of his presence in their town. Barrett took particular care to explain his bystander role in the shooting event that resulted in the death of the Dubai police. Arabs or not, law enforcement professionals were law enforcement professionals, he assumed would be the sentiment in this room.

"So you say the FBI agent killed in Virginia—"

"Mitchell Kane," Barrett supplied the name.

"—you say he was a friend of yours," the Sheriff said. "How did you know Special Agent Kane?"

"We were classmates and ROTC cadets together in college."

"ROTC. Huh."

Barrett explained they had both served several years on active duty after school.

"What did you do in the Army?"

"I was an infantry officer for eight years. My first assignment was with the 82nd Airborne Division at Fort Bragg. Later, I deployed with a Stryker Brigade to Iraq."

Deputy Ainsworth straightened up from his slouch against the wall in the corner.

"Who were you with in the 82nd?"

Barrett named his battalion and regiment. A flicker of recognition crossed Ainsworth's face. Not surprising, given the number of soldiers Barrett worked with over the years who'd left the service to join the local force back home. A very high percentage of cops in small towns and rural areas like this were former soldiers or Marines.

The sheriff drummed his fingers on the metal table top, as if absentmindedly, but Barrett had the feeling that a quick mind lay behind the aw-shucks demeanor.

"So, you stumble into the middle of something bad. You get passed a computer program on a memory-thingy. Bad guys start chasing you, and the body count skyrockets. The bad guys even follow you to the United States and kill an FBI agent. Now, I know the Iranians are a bunch of crazies. I remember the embassy thing in '79. But invade the United States of America? We're not like we were back under Jimmy Peanut—wouldn't they be worried about a massive American smack-down? What's on that memory stick?"

Barrett tried to fill in the gaps. Describing the sequence of events was problematic enough, but piecing together the information provided by Sada and her contacts, the perspective of Tommy, the conclusions surrounding Hoveyda's disappearance and the stolen neutron generator was hard to weave into a coherent picture on the spur of the moment. He had to admit, even to himself, it sounded far-fetched.

Sheriff Johnston sat still until Barrett finished speaking. He leaned back in his chair with his hands clasped behind his head.

"Mr. Ross, I think you're crazy. I hope you're crazy. The Iranians digging up an old Russian nuke. In West Virginia. Because of the Israelis."

Barrett knew he needed to take a different tack, a way to get the ball rolling.

"Listen. Forget about my story," he said. "Let's go back to your original suspicion. If you think I was checking on pot plants, or scouting a meth lab, then okay. I admit it. Take me back up the trail. Let me show you where the stuff is."

"That's not going to work, Mr. Ross. I believe you're mixed up in something worse than pot. This FBI sheet tells me so." He waved the manila folder.

"You said yourself, it's going to take the FBI a while to get here. In the meantime, take me back up that trail. It can't hurt to look."

The sheriff pushed back from the table.

"Wait," Barrett said. "Maybe I'm crazy, Sheriff Johnston. But once upon a time I took an oath to defend this country. I still believe in that. I'm hoping that buys me some benefit of the doubt."

The two men were staring hard at him, looking for any signs of a fraud. He met their gazes, more confident in that statement than anything else he'd said in a long while.

"You just sit tight, Mr. Ross," the sheriff said as he stood. He walked out into the hallway, followed by Deputy Ainsworth. Barrett didn't know if Johnston was trying to be cute, but the advice was unnecessary, as he was still handcuffed to the chair.

Ainsworth came in alone a few minutes later.

"All right, Mr. Ross, you've got your chance. The sheriff has some time on his hands. Looks like the Feds aren't going to make it to town anytime today."

Safavi took the battered kettle off the burner and poured the water over the loose tea leaves and crushed rose petals in the infuser. The reconnaissance went well, the equipment was in position. His man was watching. Hessaby came to his hotel room to discuss the next phase of the mission, which would have him move to a separate location as the unit extracted the device from the cache site.

"What does Ardabili report from Dallas?" he asked his subordinate.

"He has not moved from his room, but he watches the television all day. The Americans are calming down. They think it was a crude and amateurish attempt at terrorism."

"This is good, they reassure themselves. Our ploy worked, and we are in position."

"Sir, you wanted to discuss the next steps?"

"Yes," Safavi said. He took the cups and saucers down from the cabinet and poured the strong, dark tea. He handed a cup to his loyal second-in-command before he sat down in a chair opposite him.

"We must limit our communications to a bare minimum from this point on. Let's review our plan, shall we?"

Hessaby sipped his tea. "Of course. When you tell me to depart—"

"You will leave immediately, after we confirm the details."

"—I will take the train north to New York City. There I will stay at the designated safe house. I will await General Roghani's communication, either by phone or email."

"What if you are not contacted?"

"I will wait thirty days. If I have not heard from the general in that time, I will contact you."

"How?"

"From my disposable phone to your disposable phone. No other way."

"What if you cannot reach me?"

"I will wait for another thirty days. I will make no attempt to return to this area and find you."

"After that?"

"After that, I will contact our operations center, again on the disposable phone. They will either give me new instructions or tell me to return to base."

"Good. What will you do if captured?"

"I will maintain the same cover story of our business

appointments in the U.S. I will contact the lawyer in New York. He will relay my status to you."

Safavi drank his tea, appraising his subordinate. Hessaby was calm, confident in his abilities.

"When General Roghani contacts you, what steps will you take?"

"I will call each of the major news outlets in New York City and the major television networks. I will deliver the warning."

"Review the points."

"I will state we are religious warriors fighting for the legitimate rights of the Islamic Republic of Iran. I will inform them we possess a nuclear device, which we will detonate in a major American city if either the United States or Israel conducts a military strike against Iran. I will deny any connection to the government or military of Iran."

"Go on."

"I will describe the nature of the weapon, and where we found the uranium. I will encourage the journalists to question the American FBI and CIA to check the veracity of our claims. I will encourage them to go to the mine site and see for themselves."

"What else?"

"I will say the weapon is equivalent to fifteen kilotons of TNT, much like their weapon over Hiroshima. If detonated, the death and devastation would be similar to that meted out to the Japanese."

"But it can all be avoided if the Americans refuse to allow the Israelis to take their premeditated criminal actions," Safavi added.

"Yes. I will hint at the probability of a high loss of Jewish-American lives should they force us to carry out our threat."

"Good. Remember to discuss the Kazakh to lend

credibility to the threat. I don't care if the Russians are embarrassed. If you can insinuate an Al Qaeda connection, so much the better."

Safavi drained his cup. Hessaby did likewise, in expectation that his commander was preparing to dismiss him to depart on the next leg of his mission. Safavi stood up and smoothed the wrinkles in his slacks.

Hessaby bolted upright, but sat back down awkwardly. A look of surprise crossed his face, and he raised his hand to his forehead.

Safavi leaned over the coffee table and picked up both saucers and cups. Hessaby reached up to his neck as if to loosen a tie, but he was wearing an open-collared shirt. Safavi dumped the dregs of both cups down the drain in the kitchen sink, and dropped the cups and saucers into a lined trash bin.

Hessaby's breathing was becoming labored, alternating between frantic gasps and wheezing. Safavi washed his hands with the dish soap, lathering and scrubbing well up to the middle of his forearms. From his rear he heard the coffee table being pushed across the carpet and then a thump as his old friend fell to his hands and knees.

Safavi dried his hands and returned to the small room. Lying on his side between his chair and the table, Hessaby was curled almost in a ball. He was staring dully at a point beneath the sofa. His heart had shut down. His life was gone.

"You have performed your duty well, Second Colonel Hessaby. As you always have. But I fear you would never have received that communication from General Roghani."

From the beginning, all through the deliberations and months of preparations, Safavi knew in his heart the truth. The clerics would never have the will to strike this blow.

"And so, this last step is one I must take alone.

PART 3

Prompt-Critical

"With modern weapons-grade uranium, the background neutron rate is so low that terrorists, if they have such material, would have a good chance of setting off a high-yield explosion simply by dropping one half of the material onto the other half. Most people seem unaware that if separated HEU is at hand it's a trivial job to set off a nuclear explosion...even a high school kid could make a bomb in short order."

— Luis W. Alvarez, American physicist and Nobel Laureate

31

Barrett had been loaded in the patrol car again, his hands cuffed behind him. Ainsworth was driving and Sheriff Johnston sat in the passenger seat. As they backed out of a slanted parking spot in front of the county courthouse, Barrett asked:

"Where are the others?"

"Who?" Sheriff Johnston asked, not turning around.

"Your backup. I told you, we think that anywhere from five to ten men are involved here. They'll all be armed."

"Mr. Ross, I appreciate your concern. But if I've learned anything in twenty-seven years of law enforcement, it's not to overreact. Not when you don't have to."

A few seconds later, Johnston added, "I don't expect to come up against a squad of enemy soldiers in a national park in the middle of the day."

Barrett couldn't see his watch with his hands pinned behind his back. But it was going on seven o'clock in the evening. A couple hours of light remained, but who knew what the Iranians' timeline was like.

Seven o'clock was coming up on the three-hour window he and Sada had agreed to contact one another. Somewhere, back in the sheriff's office inside a desk drawer, sat his phone. Along with his pistol. Was there any way he could communicate with her once they got to the site? What could she do? He just hoped Sada found a good vantage point, and he and the other men weren't walking into an ambush.

They approached the turnout on the road next to the unauthorized trailhead and parked in Old Man Scruggs's drive. If he was looking out through the dirty curtains, he must have been satisfied by the sheriff's presence, because he didn't come out to complain. Deputy Ainsworth removed the cuffs from Barrett's wrists. He took up a position behind Barrett and the sheriff, with his self-loading police shotgun carried at the low ready.

"After you, Mr. Ross," the sheriff said, indicating the gap in the foliage.

If anything, it was hotter now than earlier in the afternoon when he'd made the first ascent with Sada. Although the shade under the trees was deeper, the air was still and oppressive. Barrett was sweating after the first few minutes of walking. He wondered how the officers felt in their body armor and starched uniforms. The woods were quiet, simmering, waiting for the relief of a cooler evening.

Barrett wasn't sure what he expected, but when they reached the crescent-shaped plateau cut in the side of the hill, the sight was anticlimactic. Like the path, the site of the old mine ruins were deserted and quiet. With the bowl in the hill opening to the east, the sun was almost down behind the tall hill above them, casting a long shadow over most of the stone buildings. Barrett led them over to the second mineshaft entrance, near the truncated track and its toppled coal car. Nothing had changed in the past three hours. The iron grate across the mouth of the shaft remained undisturbed. The sheriff even went so far as to grab the cross bars and shake them. The iron bars, despite their age, were still thick, substantial, and sunk deep into the rock around the shaft's opening.

"Well, Mr. Ross, if your old nuke is in there, it's safe for now."

"It wouldn't be impossible to cut through that grate."

"No. It wouldn't be impossible. Not if someone was willing to lug up the right equipment," the sheriff conceded. "But I think we're safe for tonight. If the boys from the FBI want to check it out after hearing your story, I'm sure they'll have everything they need to satisfy their curiosity."

Maybe the sheriff was right. In any case, he wasn't prepared to go through the trouble of opening the mine to check out Barrett's story. Maybe the only thing to do was to convince the Feds, and leave Sada in hiding to provide warning if anyone moved in. Of course, if Johnston didn't believe Barrett, he wasn't going to respond well to a 9-1-1 call from a woman hiding in the woods in the dead of night.

Barrett followed the sheriff to the middle of the open space. He stopped, waiting behind the older man, who surveyed the hillside, then the bluffs on the far side of the gorge. The setting sun was burnishing the steep slope east of the river with a dazzling display of light and dark greens, slashed horizontally by long stretches of exposed red rock.

Barrett realized the sheriff was not looking far into the distance, however. From the perspective of where the three men were standing, the old Powder House was framed beneath the white safety sign spanning the main path. Beyond it the plateau narrowed back down to the width of a trail and disappeared around a bend. The hill's shadow, lengthening as the sun set, had not yet reached the small stone building at the southeast end of the open area. The sheriff advanced toward the structure, which Barrett remembered from his reading earlier in the afternoon was the building the miners used to stored the bulk black powder and fuzes necessary for blasting rock down inside the mine. The Powder House was built of stacked stone with an angled slate roof. No more than twenty feet by twenty feet, it was built against the side of a wooded slope. It gave the impression of being taller than it was wide. A short series of steps led to a small landing just before the door, several feet above the path.

The sheriff was eyeing the door. It was closed, but an incongruous glint of shiny metal reflected in the angled sunlight. As they drew near, Barrett noticed a modern padlock hung from a hasp to secure the door. The lock was dull from exposure to the elements, except for the end of the U-shaped shackle, the part that should have been concealed inside the body of the lock. Johnston climbed the steps and slipped the open lock off the hasp. Barrett and the deputy cautiously followed him up and into the dark building. All three men needed a moment for their eyes to adjust, but then they saw a cloth-covered bulk filling the corner of the otherwise empty building.

Ainsworth came from behind them and pulled a small tarp off the shape. The first thing Barrett could make out was a series of white circles suspended in the gloom. He and the sheriff stepped forward, and the form became clearer. A handcart, with two sturdy rubber wheels, supported two large gas tanks, like air tanks for scuba divers. Not air, though. These were industrial, and bigger. One, a dull gray, was taller than a scuba tank. The other, squatter than the first, was covered with dark chipped paint. The white circles turned out to be the gauges, which connected to a series of valves and fed a red hose which ended in a long wand-like device of three metal tubes capped by a nozzle.

"That," the sheriff said, with doubt rising in his voice for the first time, "is a cutting torch."

Deputy Ainsworth knelt down beside the tanks. The shotgun rested butt-down on the stone floor while he wiped grime away from the tank labels.

"Oxy," he said, using the shorthand for the oxyacetylene fuel mixture. "This will burn at six-thousand degrees and cut through just about anything. My brother-in-law has one in his shop. I've seen him cut through four-inch steel with one of these in seconds."

The sheriff turned an appraising eye on Barrett.

"Okay, Mr. Ross," Johnston said, "let's have another look around."

Sheriff Johnston led the way outside. Barrett was halfway down the steps when Johnston pitched backward, his head striking the step just below Barrett's feet. He saw the vacancy in the man's eyes, heard a *phfftt*, felt a passing sensation, and saw a section of the wooden banister near his left arm disintegrate. He was throwing himself over the banister, landing hard on the sloping ground, even as he heard Ainsworth let out an *oomph*, followed by the clatter of the shotgun hitting the floor of the Powder House.

"Shit, I'm hit," the deputy reported.

Barrett was sliding down the short incline under the stairs, about to emerge in full view of any shooter who had a bead on the steps. He turned over on his stomach, got both feet under him. He used the timbers on the underside of the steps to pull himself forward until he caught the corner of the stone building and was able to pull himself up from under the steps and around to the side of the building facing the hillside. Another *phfftt*, and dead leaves a few inches from the corner of the building kicked up in the air. As if in response, three shots were fired, but these were not silenced. Not a rifle either, but a pistol. Sada had located the shooter's position and was trying to suppress his fire.

"Ainsworth, are you okay?" he shouted. "Are you inside the building?"

"Yeah. Yeah. I'm okay, I think," the deputy responded.

Johnston was dead, he was almost sure. If the bullet hadn't killed him, striking his head so hard on the stairs had incapacitated him. Ainsworth said he was okay, but might be in shock or unaware of the extent of his injury. Best-case scenario, he'd taken a round in the body armor and just had the wind knocked out of him. At least one shooter out there, with a rifle, probably scoped. Sada had found his location and returned fire, but that was a mismatch. How many were there?

A frightening realization crept over Barrett, and it had nothing to do with the physical danger of a sniper in the tree line. The Iranians were no longer worried about a covert operation. This had just turned into an open battle on American soil. Any plans the enemy had for plausible deniability were slipping away.

The game was up. If the rest of the Iranians were nearby, they'd come with guns blazing.

"Ainsworth, listen to me. I've got a friend out in the woods. Those were the un-silenced shots you heard."

"Okay."

"Thing is, we need to get out of here ASAP, or we're all dead. You with me?"

"Yep," the deputy grunted through his pain.

With that cutting torch the Iranians could breach the gate blocking the mine in about three minutes. Depending on where they set up their staging point, the enemy might be a few minutes away from getting their hands on a nuke.

Barrett, Sada, and the wounded deputy were all that stood in their way.

32

God damn Safavi. General Roghani slammed the receiver down and swept the phone off his desk in utter disgust. He would castrate that man if he ever got his hands on him. He walked to the window and looked out over the compound's wall to the traffic on Taleghani Avenue.

The shifting sands of the constant power struggle between the clerics, the armed forces, and the politicians were complicated enough. He did not need a rogue officer pursuing his own mission. If one wasn't nimble in the current environment, he could get crushed. Roghani had no intention of getting crushed.

Word filtered out from the secret councils. The Supreme Leader was siding with the Majles this time, listening to the parliament's politicians who advocated new rounds of talks with the Americans. Roghani had no doubt the Ayatollah would manage to twist these to his advantage, but the point was, Roghani's plans were no longer in line with current thinking. His superiors in the IRGC had called many, many times over the past two days to make sure he understood the situation.

Hadn't he ordered Safavi to return with all his men and leave the device undisturbed?

Now the man was out of contact. Would not respond to the secured calls or encrypted emails sent by Roghani's operations staff. Neither could Hessaby, his second in command, be found. The bombing in Dallas, with radioactive materials stolen from the same American university where the scientist Hoveyda worked. Coincidence? No.

Screws were being twisted. Roghani's superiors, the big generals in the IRGC, were fielding uncomfortable questions from the Supreme National Security Council. The Americans believed the Dallas attack was attributable to Al Qaeda, or its sympathizers, but the Iranian leadership knew the truth. The remnants of Al Qaeda's senior leadership were guests of Tehran. While gleeful over the attack in America, they admitted to having no prior knowledge of it.

The man had gone mad, crazy with the power entrusted to him. Power entrusted by Roghani.

This man would not be his downfall, not after all he'd accomplished in his time. Better for the Americans to find and kill Safavi before this was traced back to Roghani's failure in judgment.

Roghani swiveled around to his desk and picked up the phone. His friend in VEVAK, the Ministry of Intelligence, would help.

He explained the situation. "I need to communicate a message to the Americans, but they must not know it comes from us. Make it seem as if...make the Americans think they have intercepted messages between our Arab friends."

Roghani explained the nature of the threat facing the unsuspecting Americans. "Where? Washington, D.C., is the target."

Roghani remembered Safavi's remark during planning, about the irony. A nuclear weapon once destined for the U.S. Congress's secret hideout would now be turned against them to hold them hostage on Capitol Hill.

Safavi was no longer interested in blackmail, though. Or hostages, or strategy. He was trying to start a war.

Before the guards came by with the standard morning breakfast fare, two policemen came to the door of the cell and called for Dave by name. He was not handcuffed this time as he was ushered out of the cell and down the hallway through the door separating the holding cells from the main police station. In the nicer hallways of the office area, the two guards approached and spoke in quiet voices to an older police officer.

Al-Hashimi again.

The police chief didn't turn in the direction of the interrogation rooms, as Dave expected, but headed toward the offices. Through small windows he saw officers sitting at desks, typing on computers. Plaques on the walls, pictures of family on desks, filing cabinets and office chairs. Normality.

Al-Hashimi turned the corner and opened the door of a conference room. One of the guards motioned for Dave to precede them inside. Seated at the table were two Americans. One was the young man from the U.S. Embassy who had visited him a few days ago but refused to listen to Dave's story. Next to him was a woman, middle aged, wearing a gray suit and a frown on her face.

"Ms. Carr," Al-Hashimi said, walking around the conference table to shake her hand. Quick introductions were made between Colonel Al-Hashimi and the junior embassy staffer, whose name was Jenkins.

"Mr. Allen, my name is Samantha Carr. I'm the administrative officer for the U.S. Embassy and represent the chief of mission here in the UAE."

"It's good to finally meet you," Dave said. "I wish I could have said that days ago."

"Let me assure you, Mr. Allen, your situation has never been far from our government's concern."

"I don't think your colleague here," Dave indicated the young man, "took seriously the things I was trying to tell him about my friend Barrett Ross."

Carr pursed her lips, as if she was about to launch into a lesson to an errant schoolboy. "From time to time our citizens get into legal trouble here in the UAE, and we take seriously our duty to ensure they receive fair treatment and due process under the laws of this country. Which they always do," she said, nodding in acknowledgment to Al-Hashimi.

Al-Hashimi sat, noncommittal, watching the testy exchange between Dave and his government's representative.

"However," Carr continued, "the duties and responsibilities of United States representatives cannot come to a complete halt to focus on one individual's legal difficulties. The secretary of State is due to visit his highness, the foreign minister, next week. Now, with the attack in Texas, we are all scrambling to rearrange schedules and...other considerations."

"Listen to me," Dave said, raising his voice, "what I was trying to tell your colleague here, and what he ignored, was Barrett Ross and I aren't common criminals. We got involved in a serious matter related to national security. Barrett was carrying information about an Iranian group trying to steal a source of uranium."

Carr looked back at Dave with a blank expression. Startled, Al-Hashimi leaned forward in his seat.

"Gee, do you think there might possibly be any connection to the dirty bomb attack in Dallas?" Dave asked.

"Why didn't you make this information known to me when I first spoke to you?" Al-Hashimi demanded.

Dave realized it was a fair question. How much should he reveal in front of Al-Hashimi now?

"Barrett was passed something. It was recommended—he thought it best, since it pertained to U.S. security, to safeguard the information until he could get it into the hands of American intelligence personnel. Which is why we were trying to get to the consulate," he said, looking at Carr.

"I've spoken with the FBI," Carr said, as if avoiding the insinuation of professional malfeasance. "Barrett Ross is wanted in connection with the murder of an FBI agent in DC."

"Bullshit. Barrett Ross is a patriot. Not a killer of American federal agents."

"I'm just telling you—"

"What happened?"

Carr relayed the circumstances of Mitchell Kane's death and Barrett's subsequent flight.

"Mitchell Kane was a close friend of Barrett's. Sounds like after you guys at the embassy blew the link-up, Barrett made it back to the U.S. somehow. He was meeting a guy he knew inside the FBI. Sounds like he was attacked again."

A suspicion was tickling the back of Dave's brain. Yes, the attack killed the FBI agent. How was Barrett, though? Alive, apparently, the way this woman talked about him. But it was another in a series of attacks on his friend, all to get that goddamned backpack and the flash drive. First the ambush in the desert and the phony cop who'd tried to grab the pack before he was shot. Then the mob forming in front of the consulate just as he and Barrett were driven there. The police escorted them right into the middle of the riot. Then Barrett was followed back to the States and attacked in his own home. What was the common denominator? How could the Iranians always show up at the right place at the right time? Because they knew Barrett had the backpack. Had known it, right from the get-go, because…

Because Al-Hashimi, this man acting so calm and composed right there in front of him, saw the backpack in Barrett's room when he questioned him the first night.

He focused his glare on the senior policeman.

"Funny how my friend keeps getting targeted by the bad guys, like they always know where he's going. I wonder how they knew he had the backpack and the flash drive in the first place?"

Carr's jaw dropped open and the younger staffer averted his eyes to the notepad in front of him. Al-Hashimi blanched at the challenge.

"Mr. Allen, that is absolutely uncalled for," Carr sputtered, embarrassed before the Emirati policeman.

"Is it? You tell me my friend has been attacked again, and I don't know what his status is. But the common denominator seems to be our entanglement with this police department."

The color returned to Colonel Hashimi's face. He stood, turning to Samantha Carr. "I'll leave you now to talk with your countryman."

The colonel strode out of the conference room, but the two guards remained positioned on either side of the door.

"Mr. Allen—"

"You listen to me," Dave interrupted. The young staffer sitting next to Carr was positively blushing now. "I tried to warn you, tried to tell you people. Barrett tried to make you listen when he called you the first time from the desert. Now we have more bodies stacking up in the U.S., plus a terrorist attack, someone using the uranium we tried to tell you about."

The man named Jenkins looked up from his notepad. "Uranium?"

"Yes! That's what I've been trying to tell you. Barrett was handed a flash drive with a secret file. It pointed to the location, somewhere in Russia, of a stockpile of Soviet uranium. The woman with us, the Israeli, she said the Iranians were trying to buy it off of a Kazakh, an ex-KGB agent. She thought the Iranians wanted it for the nuclear program, since they were getting into so much hot water over their covert program. They feared the Israelis were getting ready to bomb them. I'm pretty sure I saw this Kazakh guy murdered in the jail cell across from me two nights ago."

The two Americans from the embassy looked nonplussed. Dave decided to sum it up for them.

"So, an ex-KGB agent is trying to sell uranium to a group of Iranians, and he gets whacked inside a UAE jail. Somebody uses the uranium to make a dirty bomb and attack the USA. No connection?"

"Wait a second," the young staffer said. "The dirty bomb in Dallas didn't use uranium."

"What?"

"The RDD detonated at Dallas-Fort Worth International was laced with cesium. A radioactive isotope someone stole from a research reactor. Not uranium. The experts confirmed it was cesium-137."

"So maybe there is no connection with your friend and this information, after all," Carr concluded hastily.

This made a hash of some of his assumptions, Dave could see that. But no way was this all some big coincidence. Too many connections ran through that flash drive, if only he could sort it all out.

"I doubt it. All this means is there's a second attack being planned. This time with uranium."

Carr looked frustrated, harried, and one hundred percent like she didn't want this being dumped in her lap. Not now, not with the SecDef coming and everything else on her plate. Dave could see the bureaucratic equivalent of the Heisman stiff arm coming.

"The guy you said you talked to at the FBI, you've got to warn him," Dave said. He needed to capitalize on any momentum he'd built with these two. "Tell him about the connection with the Kazakh being murdered over here. Tell him there's a police leak here feeding information right to the Iranians. These Iranians are going to sell that uranium to someone, if they haven't already."

"Mr. Allen, I will call the FBI back and relay your concerns."

"When?"

"In due time. They are eight hours behind us in D.C., so I will call Agent Hascomb back when he arrives at his office in the morning."

"There's no time for that. Call the FBI, have the duty officer wake the right people up. Something is going on right now, I can feel it."

"I appreciate your sense of urgency, Mr. Allen. But we are worried about a good number of other things right now, including the personal safety of the Secretary of State. We'll be in touch," she said. She stood and strode primly to the door. The young staffer nodded at Dave, as if acknowledging some sort of shared burden in having to deal with the prickly, self-conscious officer from the embassy.

Dave Allen found himself sitting alone, except for the two guards standing by the door, in a conference room in a police station seven thousand miles from his best friend, wondering how the hell he could help him.

33

Barrett ran through the situation in his mind. Ainsworth was alive but shaken, maybe wounded. He would at least be bruised under his armored vest, if not suffering cracked ribs. The police vest was designed to protect against slow-moving handgun bullets, but Barrett seemed to remember that suppressed rifle rounds were subsonic, too. Lucky for the deputy.

The shooter must be positioned on the hillside looking down over the mine complex. That meant the only door to the Powder House was exposed to his line of fire. Even if the shooter was alone, it'd be impossible for Barrett to get in, or Ainsworth to get out, without presenting an easy target. Whoever the man was, he was trained and had a scope on his weapon. That's why he hadn't engaged the sheriff again; he could see his first shot killed Johnston.

Barrett needed to talk to Sada.

"Deputy Ainsworth?"

"Yeah?"

"Can you reach anybody on your radio?"

"Not this far out. I'd have to get back to the car. But I

have my cellphone."

"Okay. Call your office. Get backup out here. Have them hold up farther down the trail. I don't want them blundering up here until we can give them more info on the sniper."

"Okay."

"And tell them to bring my pack, with my phone and pistol."

Barrett heard Ainsworth calling in, explaining the situation; he was hit but okay. Two civilians, one armed, were working with him. At least one assailant, armed with a high-powered rifle. Possibility of five to ten other armed men due to arrive on site. Ainsworth told the deputy on the other line to come as soon as they could get the tactical gear together, but to hold in a position five hundred yards north of the mine complex.

When the deputy hung up, Barrett knew he had to make a move now. How much light did he have left? Hour and a half, two hours, tops. The first step was to coordinate with Sada.

"Hey, Ainsworth. I've got a plan."

"Shoot."

"I need your phone and your weapon. But watch the doorway."

"I hear you. I can throw them out past the steps, along the berm. You're still going to have to expose yourself."

"Throw the phone out, then the shotgun."

Barrett heard Ainsworth shuffling around inside the building, maybe getting up on a knee to gain enough leverage. Barrett heard a ripping sound, some grunting. Soon the cellphone landed in the leafy dirt on the slope just forward of the corner of the building. Barrett hoped it was concealed from the shooter's position by the stairs and the small trees on the incline leading up from the flat open area before the Powder House. Next, the shotgun came sailing out past the corner, with a cloth tied around it. Barrett darted around the corner, grabbed the phone, then slipped and fell on his side as he tried to backtrack. The shotgun lay a little to his right, not quite back under the stairs. This time Barrett heard the muffled retort of the Iranian's weapon, the shredding of leaves not far above his head. He lunged for the shotgun, grabbing it in his right hand, twisting his body and rolling over so he faced back downhill and crawled the last few feet back to his position behind the stone structure.

Now Barrett understood the flapping cloth. Ainsworth had shoved a strip of a white T-shirt into the muzzle of the weapon, to prevent dirt getting into the barrel. Another, wider strip of T-shirt was wound around the stock, covering the shotgun shell holder and the seven spare shells inside it. Barrett removed the pieces of T-shirt and dialed Sada.

"Yes," she answered, whispering.

"Sada, it's me."

"Are you hit?"

"No. But the sheriff I brought here is dead. His deputy is pinned down, maybe wounded. I've got his shotgun. We found a cutting torch in the Powder House. What's your situation?"

"I'm about fifty meters left of the shooter, to the north but lower," she answered. "He's almost directly above the mine entrance, thirty meters up the hillside, if you were standing in front of it. He knows I'm here, but doesn't feel good about trying to move against me."

"I want to try to outflank this guy, move up through the woods along the spur to the south of the open area. Do you have him pinpointed?"

"I can't see him. I can't engage him effectively from here. The best I can do is keep his head down. I'll know if he moves, though."

"Right. Provide suppressing fire when it makes sense. Be aware I'm moving east to west, uphill toward him. Let's make sure we don't get into a crossfire."

"Right," she whispered. "Be careful."

"I'm moving."

Barrett hung up the phone.

"Ainsworth."

"Yep."

"I'm moving. Once my partner and I have flushed him out, we'll come get you and move to link up with your guys."

"Good luck, Ross."

Barrett backed away from the Powder House, facing it, keeping the solid structure between him and his best guess of the shooter's position. If he stepped a little to his right, he'd be back on the main path curving around the bend to the south side of the spur, but he'd also be exposing himself to the shooter. He quick-stepped to a point where he was running out of room before he stepped onto the road, like backing into the narrow corner of a pie slice. Here goes.

He darted to his left, entering a patch of saplings and undergrowth on the edge of the woods proper. If the shooter saw him, he didn't feel the shot was a high-percentage one. If Barrett was lucky, maybe his move went unobserved. After fifteen or twenty meters walking south, fighting through brambles, Barrett reached the crest of the little spur that sloped down toward the path as it curved around the bend. Turning right, he followed the crest uphill, to the west. Within about a hundred meters, he estimated, he'd be near the Iranian. If the man hadn't taken up a new position.

The brambles and undergrowth were thinner on top of the spur, almost a deer path, but Barrett didn't want to skyline himself. Still walking, he allowed himself to slip off the centerline of the spur, so the line of highest ground would remain between himself and the shooter's position. On the side of the hill, the loose rocks and leaves combined with wait-a-minute vines to make his advance difficult without making a racket. He slowed down, picking each spot for the next step, balancing himself with the shotgun held out in front of him. After five minutes, he paused and took a knee. Barrett scanned his immediate vicinity, waited, and listened. He texted Sada.

has he moved

no, came the reply.

Barrett slipped the phone into his pocket, rose slowly, and crept forward again in a crouch. He grasped the shotgun in a ready position, looking right over the barrel. Soon he came to a thick wall of mountain laurel stretching to the top of the spur. He skirted around to the left, going downhill. When he cleared the thicket, though, he was met by an insurmountable obstacle. The southern slope fell off in a sheer drop to a jumble of boulders at the bottom. He'd have to travel a significant distance down and around if he kept to the left, with a long trek back up the other side to regain his elevation. No time for it.

He worked back to his starting point in front of the laurel thicket and passed it, moving up toward the crest of the spur. He might pop up within sight of the shooter at any point, but how far away would he be? Barrett knew his effective range with this shotgun was twenty-five, thirty meters, maybe less depending on the load and the choke.

He stopped and texted Sada again.

will be exposed soon

out of room

She replied:

ready

will suppress and move

Barrett put the phone away and inched forward, crouching. He was on top of the spur now but saw nothing but trees. To his right, the ground was sloping down again. Somewhere in that direction was the bottom of the bowl with the second mineshaft, and the Lamp House, but Barrett couldn't see any of these through the darkening woods.

Barrett picked up one foot and placed it, then the other. If the man had shifted position without Sada seeing it, Barrett could be a sitting duck.

There. An anomaly, something out of place up ahead. Through the trees, no more than twenty meters away, to the right of the line he was walking, a light brown, not the gray-browns of the tree bark everywhere around him. A slight movement that was not the random fluttering of a leaf in the breeze.

Barrett picked out a large tree four steps away as his next concealed spot. He was two steps into his maneuver when the air was rent with the nasty, soft ripping of the Iranian's rifle shots. Wood splinters fell on his head as he dove forward to the base of the tree. Two more shots, spaced apart—Sada trying to keep the man occupied from the other side.

Another large tree five meters to the front left of this one.

Do or die.

He rolled to his left, came up to his feet and fired the shotgun in the direction of the Iranian. My God! He was closer than he thought. He had a fleeting glimpse of the man's face before he dropped to the ground behind his new tree, flattening himself into the dirt.

Scrambling noises. Sada coming from the flank? No, the man was moving. Barrett peeked around the wide base of the tree, saw haunches and the soles of hiking boots, as the man fought to gain a purchase on the leafy litter of hillside. Barrett saw the Iranian's predicament before he understood it. The sniper/observer had boxed himself in, having chosen a hide spot at the bottom of a steep section of the hill. Barrett was approaching on relatively flat ground, compared to the grade the enemy had to scramble up to get away.

Barrett pushed up to his feet, ran five meters, fired. The man, struck by the pellets, turned and fired his own weapon. Barrett made a feint to duck behind a tree, but saw the man was turning back to the hill again and ran forward in pursuit. Closing the distance to ten meters, he fired a last time. The man's body slackened, then toppled over and slid backward down the leafy slope for a foot or two before stopping.

Barrett took a knee, chest heaving, sucking the humid air into his lungs. He was fumbling to pull the phone out of his pocket when Sada emerged, panting, from the trees to his right. She spotted both him and the Iranian.

She fired two shots into the prostrate form before advancing on it. Without hesitation she grabbed the man's rifle and spare magazines. She retreated through the little depression where the Iranian had hidden himself and emerged with a camouflaged kit bag.

"You did well," she said, congratulating him. "Now let's go."

Their flight down the hill was headlong, driven by an urgency to clear the open area before the rest of the Iranians arrived. In three minutes they reached the Powder House to fetch the deputy. Then they shuffled across the exposed area one more time, Ainsworth hobbling with one hand on Sada's shoulder, Sada carrying the Iranian's kit bag, and Barrett draping the sheriff's body across his shoulders in a fireman's carry. Halfway across the open area, he realized there was no good reason to carry the Sheriff's body out—they weren't on a foreign battlefield.

He'd just acted on instinct not to leave a comrade behind.

When they reached the start of the trail near the Fan House, Barrett stopped. He lowered the sheriff to the ground.

"Keep going, I'll catch up," he said, switching out the shotgun with the Iranian's rifle Sada was carrying.

"What are you doing?" Sada shouted.

"Whatever I can to slow them up."

He sprinted back to the Powder House. Inside, he fumbled with the valves and regulators until he heard the loud hissing of released oxygen. The other tank was capped, and in the dark he couldn't figure out what to do. In frustration, he hoisted the heavy acetylene tank on his shoulder and lumbered down the steps with it. He reached the area in front of the second mine shaft and placed the heavy tank upright on the rusty flank of the old coal cart before running back toward the Fan House. As he approached the trailhead, he slowed to a walk, and forcing deep breaths, willed himself to calm down. He reached the curve in the path next to the Fan House and turned, raising the rifle to his shoulder, sighting in the acetylene tank. He timed the squeeze at the bottom of his exhale, squeezing the trigger gently so as not to pull the round.

The gloom erupted into blinding white light, and shards of hot metal left hissing sounds in the wake of their paths around him. The concussion had knocked him to the ground. He regained his feet, looking away to regain vision. He picked up Johnston's body and ran after his colleagues as the fireball rose into the air.

34

Sada led the three in the run down the path, holding back a little because she knew the deputy was still struggling to take full breaths. She'd checked the man while waiting on Barrett—she found no visible wounds under the vest. Barrett took up the rear, with the body of the slain sheriff across his shoulders. Ainsworth said his colleagues would approach on this path but stop several hundred meters before the first structure.

After a few minutes, she stopped and dropped the Iranian's kit bag.

"We're a thousand meters from the open area," she gasped.

Barrett set the sheriff's body down and Deputy Ainsworth collapsed along the side of the path.

"Ainsworth, when will the others get here?" he asked between breaths.

"Should be soon," the deputy said, though he didn't sound so sure. His breathing was getting stronger.

"We need to decide if we wait for them, or go back by ourselves," Sada said.

"I know," Barrett responded. "What do we have in the kit bag?"

Sada unzipped the canvas bag and listed the contents: food, water, a poncho, a jacket, explosives—consisting of several sticks of C-4, det cord, time fuze, blasting caps—spare ammo, and binos.

"If the observer had demo," Barrett muttered, "then the rest of his group will, too. Blowing the acetylene tank may not have bought us much time."

Barrett was thinking clearly, she could tell. He seemed unflustered by dangerous assault on the Iranian's position and the physical exertion afterward. The American tourist who had been reluctant and unsure of himself in Dubai was still transforming before her eyes. Whatever he thought his shortcomings had been, whatever decisions haunted him from Iraq, and the years of shame and guilt that followed, he was proving now to be a natural warrior. The kind of man she was surrounded by daily at the Institute, the ones who had been her teammates. She realized with a start that he reminded her of the best qualities about Jacob, her mentor.

If they succeeded, and lived through this, would Barrett Ross return to his army, or work for his government? He'd be welcomed back as a hero. Did he crave such acceptance, the sense of belonging, as she herself had once sought solace among a surrogate family?

She caught herself with a mental shake. Whatever happened in the future would happen. Today, and tomorrow, for as long as it took to stop the Iranians, Sada would join this man. She would do everything possible to help him finish this task. Only then would she consider other possibilities.

So much had changed in the span of five days, so many things she thought she was sure of, about her future. Now, when she returned to her country, she would face disciplinary action. She might even be imprisoned for disobeying direct orders, not once but twice, and jeopardizing state secrets. The life she had gradually been losing confidence in was gone now, beyond her ability to salvage it.

She was about to speak when the sound of a vehicle, maybe a motorcycle, came from down the hillside, rushing up the path.

The explosion rattled the tree limbs around them and reverberated across the valley.

"Go!" Safavi yelled at the point man. "Move!"

The point man turned to Safavi, startled by his commander's shouting instead of the normal whispered commands. The fool doesn't understand the situation has changed, Safavi thought.

The unit was moving in single file down the narrow track they'd picked out during the previous hours of darkness, when Safavi had conducted his reconnaissance of the site and his men hid the heavier equipment. He wouldn't risk accessing the mine site using the same trails as the tourists and hikers. Instead, they'd stationed their vehicles on a deserted road near the flat summit, and worked their way along a wooded spur running from the top of the hill down to the open area in front of the mine entrance.

The men began jogging, for the point man finally had understood his commander's urgency.

The call from Beheshti came as the unit was staging at the vans at the end of the secluded road, conducting final checks of their weapons and equipment. They would have completed their preparations and waited in the vans until well after nightfall. Beheshti had fired on the three men, and at least one had been killed. Yet Beheshti had not responded to Safavi's calls for ten minutes, well before the explosion.

Had the American, Ross, caught up to them? How many others were out there? The Israeli woman? Soon enough the woods would be crawling with police from the nearby towns, along with their dogs. Maybe helicopters, if the locals had them. No need, or time, for stealthy creeping now. Safavi would storm the target and shoot anything that stood in his way.

The unit hit the flat trail at the southeast end of the open area. Breaking into its task-organized elements, each sprinted to their assigned positions. One two-man team pivoted off and moved around the bend to guard the path from the southern approach. The other two-man security team led the sprint across the open area. After clearing the Lamp House and Fan House, they would establish security to the north. Both would find positions commanding the longest possible stretch of kill zone. With their M249 machine guns, they would have more firepower than any local police force. Remarkable, Safavi thought, what a private citizen could buy in America with a little ingenuity and discretion.

Two men ran to the closest stone building and cleared it. The cutter, Pesian, reemerged empty-handed. Safavi realized what had happened. The explosion, and the sputtering fire by the mouth of the mine—the American had destroyed the acetylene tank for the cutting torch. No matter.

"Use the charges," he instructed the cutter. "We're not worried about noise now."

"Find Beheshti," he said, turning to two of the men still by his side. They were the carriers. When they weren't busy carrying the heavy load, they would provide security and dig. In addition to Falasiri, the ordnance specialist, his ten-man unit was complete. Nine men, he reminded himself, if Beheshti was dead.

Pesian began rigging the small cutting charges on the iron bars of the grate blocking the mine entrance. Each charge was small, less than two inches long, pre-wrapped in adhesive. They were molded in a V-shaped cross-section that would concentrate the explosive force to slice through the metal bars. Pesian placed the charges in a pattern, connecting them to ensure simultaneous detonation. The result should be a doorway big enough for two men, stooped, to pass through together.

"Sir, I am ready," Pesian announced, waiting next to the series of interconnected charges with the igniter in his hand. Safavi and Falasiri moved to the safety of the Lamp House to the right of the shaft opening. Pesian removed the safety and tugged the pull ring on the ignitor. A wisp of smoke emerged at the juncture of the ignitor and green time fuse. The explosives man knelt to observe the smoke in the waning light, checked the time fuse was not looped over itself anywhere, and laid the ignitor on ground. He jogged to Safavi's position. The three men stopped their ears with their fingers, opened their mouths, and leaned into the building.

A moment later, the sound and shock wave passed around them. A piece of iron grate hung for a second in the newly cut portal, before falling forward with a thud into the grass before the mine entrance. Falasiri was already running into the mine, reaching up to switch on his headlamp.

Safavi called the carrier team on their radio. "Come back to dig."

He called each security team, who both reported no change in status. The two carriers appeared out of the woods near the stone structure and informed him Beheshti was dead, found a few meters from his original position, his weapon and equipment bag missing. Safavi flipped on his own headlamp and led the two men into the mine.

So close. But the next task would take some time.

Safavi saw the lights ahead of him and marched forward, careful to guard against striking his head on the low rock ceiling. This was the tricky part. He hoped the Kazakh knew what he was talking about. Falasiri had spent months training to overcome the Russian booby-trap system, but the explosives and circuitry involved were fifty years old. They came upon Falasiri. The other two men came forward to begin moving the heavy wood timbers stacked against the left side of the tunnel. If they were not careful, or if Ismagulov's information was faulty, the Molniya device would splatter Safavi and his men against the rock walls. Which was not how he meant to achieve martyrdom.

Rafai was uneasy. It was all very well to do the Iranian's bidding when they were in the country, telling him what to do. Well, at least Amir had been available to answer questions, to provide reassurance. Now the Iranians were gone, and he hadn't been able to reach Amir since Thursday night. He felt much less sure of his position than he had three days ago. He felt exposed.

Peering through the cracked door of his office, he watched as Al-Hashimi entered the conference room at the end of the hallway, followed by the American and two guards. Rafai knew the American woman from the embassy had already gone inside. She was a high-ranking official. Rafai had seen her plenty of times when she visited with Al-Hashimi, usually to intervene in the punishment of some American drunkard. How they could allow a woman to serve in such a position he would never understand. Perhaps his sentiment was too obvious, though, because Al-Hashimi never invited him to sit in on these meetings with the Americans.

The door to the conference room closed, and Rafai withdrew farther into the office and shut his own door. He must consider this development. Why were the American officials now paying attention to this man Allen? What was going on in America? The terrorist bomb, of course. Were his Iranian friends involved in the attack on the American airport? If so, good, God be praised. Another strike against the arrogant superpower.

But if the Iranians were involved...the Americans would not rest in their search for the perpetrators.

How closely tied was he to the Iranians? He talked only to Amir, usually, but that had changed. Amir had disappeared, and the Iranian commander called him out of the blue.

Rafai had reached his current position by being a competent police officer, not through the patronage of the royal family. So, like a good policeman, he knew what a criminal should worry about. Where were his fingerprints? What clues connected him to recent events? The Iranians took a peculiar interest in the Americans, especially the man named Ross, and the backpack he carried. The Iranians disappeared, and the attack occurred in the city of Dallas, Texas.

Rafai scolded himself for being a woman. He pushed the fretful thoughts from his mind as he picked up a large stack of files and paperwork from his inbox. Al-Hashimi valued him as a trusted assistant. To maintain this trust, he ensured the station ran well and his commander looked good. The UAE's was a modern police force. Like any modern organization, those who mastered bureaucratic tasks were granted power and access. He did his work with care, and freed his commander from the burden of mundane administration. And because all the paperwork and emails destined for the commander came through

Rafai, he could better serve his Iranian masters.

Rafai plowed through the paperwork and his commander's email inbox for an hour and a half, but could not shake the worried feeling in his gut. He stood up at last and poured himself a cup of coffee. Walking to the window, he stared through the blinds at the city lights. Maybe he should wait until morning. Maybe he was overreacting.

No. He was tied to whatever the Iranians were doing. They were searching for a backpack. Rafai had spotted it in the American's hotel room and provided this information to Amir. When the Americans informed Al-Hashimi that Ross and Allen were coming to the consulate, Rafai had recommended to the chief they insist on an escort for the American vehicle. Rafai had provided the information on the convoy's timing and route to Amir. When the Iranians wanted to know where the American lived in his own country, Rafai had accessed Allen's phone and provided the information to the Iranians, again through Amir.

Did they kill the American, Ross? Is that why Al-Hashimi and the American embassy woman were meeting with the American prisoner now?

Rafai wondered where would he go to live, if staying in Dubai meant imprisonment. Would the Iranians give him a position? Or would they shoot him and dump his body into the shark-infested waters of the Strait?

Rafai unlocked the bottom drawer of his desk, reached beneath a stack of manila folders, and pulled out a cellphone. Turning back to the window, he dialed a number from memory.

The phone rang several times but went to voicemail. A computerized voice requested him to leave a message. Still no Amir.

Rafai pondered his predicament. He had served them well, and he was not about to be cast adrift in his own time of need.

Maybe Amir was no longer his contact. The Iranian, the one called Safavi, had called him just this morning. When this affair all began, Amir told him in no uncertain terms, Rafai was to speak only to him, never to try to contact the Iranians directly. But Safavi was pleased with Rafai's information about the Kazakh's fate.

To hell with Amir.

Rafai searched his phone's memory of incoming calls, found the one from America. He dialed the number and after two rings a voice blurted something in English. Rafai could not make it out, but then realized the man was not uttering a traditional greeting, but announcing something, maybe the name of a hotel. But Safavi would not be traveling under his own name.

"The man from Middle East," Rafai said in halting English.

"Okay," the voice said with a snicker, "I guess that's Room 214." The room phone rang.

Rafai let the phone ring fifteen times before he turned away from the window and slammed the cell phone down on the desk.

Hunched over his desk, Rafai found himself looking at a pair of polished shoes and creased trousers. Lifting his gaze, he was confronted by the withering stare of his commander, Colonel Al-Hashimi.

35

Two men were in the seats and two more were squeezed into the cargo area of the Gator ATV racing up the path at them. The deputies were outfitted with tactical gear for their SWAT contingencies, wearing black body armor and helmets, M-4s with scopes and taclights slung over their shoulders.

The faces of the four new arrivals reacted with a mixture of fear and resolve as they focused on Sheriff Johnston's body. Barrett imagined the aftermath of Ainsworth's desperate call. The information would have rocketed through the small sheriff station that the sheriff was dead, another officer down. Not to mention two civilians in a running gun battle with a terrorist group in the woods.

The deputy who'd arrested Barrett along with Ainsworth, a stocky middle-aged man named Simmons, seemed to be the senior officer in the group.

"What we got?"

"Iranian terrorists," Ainsworth said. Then, indicating Barrett and Sada, "These two have information that an atomic bomb is hidden inside the Kay-moor mine. The Iranians found out about it. They're trying to dig it up."

The barrel of his Simmon's rifle dropped toward the ground, just as his facial muscles slackened. His jaw didn't quite drop open.

"I know," Ainsworth interjected before Simmons could say anything, "a half hour ago I would have been with you. But someone did that," he pointed at the sheriff, "and this," indicating the tear in his shirt and damage to his vest.

"Where's the shooter?" Simmons asked.

"These two, they took out the bad guy. Mr. Ross is ex-Army and Ms.—

"Hempstead," Sada added.

"—appears to have some special training."

"How many up there?" Simmons asked. He was fighting to get a handle on everything.

"We don't know for sure," Barrett said, speaking for the first time. He needed to take the reins of this operation. "The man we killed was an observer, watching the target for the rest of his unit. We think the Iranians planned to wait until tonight. Now all that's changed. The bad guy had comms, and would have reported his situation before we took him out. His commander has to move the mission forward, or abort. I'd guess they're moving right now to secure the site."

"How many?"

"We think five to ten men, maybe as high as twelve," Sada said. The men turned to her, appraising her.

"They may not be there yet. We don't know—"

An explosion rumbled down the hillside, sending a small animal scurrying through the undergrowth near them.

"I guess that's our answer," Barrett said. "They're on the target."

"What're they doing?" asked the youngest officer.

"The device is in the second mine shaft. I think that explosion was them blowing a hole in the iron grate."

"Oh, shit," someone muttered.

"We still have time, but not much," Barrett explained. "The cache is buried and booby-trapped. The Iranians need to deal with the Russian security measures—"

"Russians?" a deputy interrupted.

Barrett plowed on: "—and they have to carry the device out. It's man-portable, but won't be easy to move in this terrain."

"We need to cordon off the area. Call in backup. We need to get the Feds in on this," Simmons concluded. He was thinking containment, standoff, law enforcement.

Barrett stared hard at the man. "How are we going to cordon off the area? I see only seven of us. If the Iranian and his team get this bomb, they are going to hump it through the woods, either up the mountain to a waiting vehicle or down to the river. For all we know, there's a raft waiting for them at the bottom of those long stairs."

The deputies chewed on this possibility as Barrett pressed on. "The Feds aren't coming, not anytime soon. I can guarantee it. The people trained to deal with this sort of thing, all those national level assets—they're in Dallas, gentlemen. Something needs to get done in about the next ten minutes. And we're it." Barrett spread his arms to encompass the little group.

"Let's go," said one of the deputies who'd been silent up to this point.

"Yep, but wait a second," Barrett said. "We know the bad guys are on target. But we don't know how many or where they're positioned. If you go charging up the trail, you're going to be cut in half before you ever see the mine."

"How's that?"

"Deputy Ainsworth said Iranian terrorists. Forget 'terrorist.' Think instead, 'military unit.' A special operations unit. A trained enemy force, with the money and resources to operate inside the U.S. Not amateurs."

"Okay," Simmons conceded for the group.

"Their leader is a professional soldier. He's going to have security posted, as much as he can afford. The primary avenues of approach, like this road, are going to be covered. I'd be surprised if he doesn't have automatic weapons."

"Machine guns?" Ainsworth asked.

"At least light ones," Barrett responded. "Something they could hump through these woods without slowing down too much."

"So what do we do?" someone asked.

"A lot of American lives depend on us doing something, now. How many of you are ex-military, Army or Marine?"

Besides Ainsworth, Simmons and the deputy named Collins indicated they were prior service.

Now was the time to take charge.

"We don't know the enemy disposition, but we have to move. We're going to conduct a Movement to Contact," Barrett said, bending down to sketch out his plan in the dirt. "Here's how we need to think about it."

He'd forgotten a hundred things and others he didn't have time to worry about. He'd covered the basics, and hoped the training from long ago would kick in for the former soldiers. Element in contact, get down and return fire. Establish a base of fire. Communicate. The element not in contact, move to a position to put flanking fire on the enemy. He was relying on the KISS principle: keep it simple, stupid.

They were moving in an inverted wedge, a loose V-shape sliding around the trees. At the front left, Ainsworth led a two-man team of himself and Collins, the other prior service deputy. Barrett expected they would make contact first. Collins walked behind and to the left of Ainsworth. The plan was for Collins to attempt to handrail the path, while staying up the hillside in the woods as far as he could while still spotting the trail. That might put him twenty to thirty meters off the trail.

Higher up the hill, to the right, Simmons led a two-man team of himself and Fitzpatrick, the young deputy with no military background. Simmons led, Fitzpatrick trailing as his wingman ten to fifteen meters behind and to the right.

Between and behind the two lead teams, Barrett walked in the center. He could just make out either team through the foliage. Behind him, the trail team consisted of Fernandez followed by Sada. Barrett asked her to take Fernandez's radio, and keep her head on a swivel for rear security. From his position in the center of the V, armed with the dead Iranian's assault rifle and Sheriff Johnston's radio, Barrett hoped to coordinate the fire and movement of the two lead teams. He'd also be able to flex Fernandez, sending him to reinforce whichever element needed him most.

Barrett felt alert and alive, like never before in his life. Part of him knew it was the adrenaline high from being in charge, that extra surge of energy one found when leading others. But the feeling he had was stronger than he'd ever experienced in his time in the Army. It wasn't overconfidence. He put the odds of his surviving at thirty-seventy. But he was doing something that mattered. He didn't have the time to second-guess himself. They needed to act, and they were. They had a simple plan, and they were executing it. The risk of failure from not acting was off the table.

Barrett thought he knew where the Iranians would set up a security element. The torn-down remains of the Fan House made perfect sense, and that's where he would have put it. The heavy stones of the foundation and partial walls would provide ample cover and concealment. The building's placement this side of the bend meant it would have a decent line of sight down the trail. He'd briefed Ainsworth and Collins on it, and shared the pictures from Sada's camera, but the big question was how close they could draw before the Iranians heard them. The closer they could get before the Iranian reacted, the shorter the distance Simmons and Fitzpatrick would have to move to assault the Iranians' flank. With the few people he had, they had to find and neutralize the Iranians' security element first. They couldn't afford to bypass them only to get fired on from the rear. The other element he worried about was Simmons, moving through the rough terrain, succumbing to the gravitational pull of the hill. He might angle down into the way of Ainsworth's team. Barrett didn't want to meet the Iranians on a narrow front where a single gun could pin down his entire ad hoc force. Barrett could use the radio to nudge the teams back into position, but he had to be careful the noise of a mike keying wouldn't expose the men up front.

Any time now.

He didn't want to be conducting this assault in the dark. No doubt, the Iranian and his men would have night-vision goggles. Of course, he might be dead before nightfall. He realized he'd taken charge of a group of men that he might be leading to their deaths. He might get Sada killed. He acknowledged those concerns but dismissed them. Not recklessly, but with a conviction this was what he should be doing.

A staccato burst, ten to fifteen rounds, rent the air

beneath the tree canopy. Three shots answered in return, sounding insignificant in response to the automatic fire. Barrett dropped instantly to his belly, then heard Ainsworth firing the shotgun. Another burst from the machine gun. Barrett heard the thwacking of rounds impacting the trees below him.

"Contact, contact!" Ainsworth found his radio mic. "Light machine gun. Two enemy."

Barrett crawled forward on his belly, peering over a hump in the ground.

"Ainsworth, try to keep them pinned down. Simmons, are you moving?"

"Uh," was the response, Simmons keying his handset too late.

"Sada, pull forward with Fernandez, but stay behind me."

"Got it."

Barrett shut up and let the situation develop.

Another burst, sounding just like a SAW, an M249 Squad Automatic Weapon. Someone cried out. He crawled on his belly, aiming for a large tree he thought would put him about forty meters up the slope from Ainsworth.

"Collins is hit in the leg," Ainsworth reported.

"Where are you?" Simmons shouted, out of breath, through the radio.

"Cross-talk," Barrett urged. He considered pushing Fernandez up to Ainsworth and Collins, but didn't think the man could get there without getting hit.

Ainsworth fired several spaced shots and asked Simmons if he saw his fire. After a couple of minutes of Ainsworth trading shots with a rifleman in the enemy position, the Iranian SAW gunner let loose another burst. Simmons came back with a hushed, "I see them."

Barrett listened to Ainsworth and Simmons coordinate. On a count of three, Ainsworth and the wounded Collins picked up a steady rate of fire toward the Iranians. Barrett couldn't see Simmons and Fitzpatrick until the last second when they popped out from behind a copse of scrub pine. They were firing down the hill into the remains of the Fan House.

"Lift your fire!" Barrett yelled over the din to Ainsworth.

Simmons and Fitzpatrick darted out of sight, firing into the square of the Fan House walls. The skirmish was over in another ten seconds.

"Come up," Simmons shouted.

"Sada, hold with Fernandez on the slope. Orient south and west."

Barrett rushed down to Ainsworth, who was tending to Collins. Ainsworth had the pants leg ripped apart and was applying a trauma bandage from Collins's gear. The man's leg below the knee was mangled, a round having entered by the knee and traveling along the bone to exit by the ankle.

"Bring him to the building when you can," Barrett said, and rushed down the hill.

Fitzpatrick was standing in amazement, not knowing what to do. Simmons had already pushed a body away and was bent over the machine gun, repositioning the weapon to point out past the stone foundation in the other direction, and changing out the ammo drum with a fresh one from the cloth bandoleer hanging around the dead Iranian.

"Follow me," Barrett said to Simmons and Fitzpatrick. He scooted around the bend in the path, exposing to his view the large open area in front of the mineshafts and the Lamp House and, across the intervening low ground, the Powder House. On the far side of the curved plateau, two men, one carrying a SAW, ran past the Powder House on the trail heading east. Barrett stopped, raise the rifle and fired four, spaced shots. The targets were less than a hundred and fifty meters away but running. Barrett knew he hadn't hit either of them, but the men dropped out of view. Simmons himself dropped to the ground to establish a steady base for the SAW, and laced a nine-round burst across the intervening space. The tracers kicked up debris near the base of the Powder House.

"I can't see them from the prone position," Simmons reported.

"Let's move up," Barrett said. He crawled through the high grass on the inside of the path, with Simmons and young Fitzpatrick in trail. Just past the Fan House's foundation, another structure had once stood, but all that remained now were the concrete pad and piles of masonry in a rough rectangular shape on the downhill side of the path. Simmons crawled to the front and chose a firing position with an unobstructed line of sight to the far side of the crescent, including the Powder House but not as far as where the path disappeared around the bend. Barrett crawled up beside the deputy. To the right, Simmons could see the toppled rail car, but the entrance to the mine shaft itself was blocked from view by the corner of the Lamp House. Somewhere to the left, the two enemy with the SAW had gone to ground, hidden behind debris or tall grass.

"You're my base of fire. Keep that SAW team pinned down. Keep them from moving toward the mine. We'll leave Collins in the Fan House. I'm taking Ainsworth, Fernandez, and Hempstead. We'll move around to the right, through the woods on the high ground. We'll come down there," Barrett said, pointing to a spot in the treeline above the Lamp House.

"Got it."

"You," he said, tapping Fitzpatrick on the shoulder, "watch our rear."

Barrett crawled backward several meters, turned, and ran back to the building. Ainsworth had pulled Collins into the shelter of the Fan House's northern wall.

"How is he?" he asked of Collins.

Ainsworth pulled Barrett aside. "He's okay for now, but he needs a doc within the next hour or two."

"It'll be over by then."

Barrett knelt beside the wounded deputy. "Hang in there, Collins. We'll get you to a doc as soon as we can. Simmons and Fitzpatrick are just around the corner."

Barrett called Sada to warn her that he and Ainsworth were moving toward her position. When the four of them joined together, he laid out his plan. When he got to the point of saying he and Ainsworth would make the final assault, Sada interrupted.

"No. I move with you to the mine."

No one questioned her. Without further discussion, Barrett began the steep ascent up the hill. He wanted to loop around in the woods and come down the hill on top of the Lamp House, which would put them right next to the mine opening. At some point they'd be exposed to the SAW in the vicinity of the Powder House, at a range of seventy-five meters. Were other Iranians waiting in the woods in front of them?

Barrett advanced on the left side of their formation. Sada, armed now with Collins's M-4, crept up the slope to the right. Fernandez followed ten meters behind Barrett, and Ainsworth trailed Sada. After several minutes, Barrett could see the ground in front of them was beginning to rise, and he could sense the line of drift he was on was curving to the left. They were at the bend in the hillside where the mine area curved back to the east. The Lamp House and the mine shaft—and the Iranians—were directly below him.

Barrett stopped and took a knee, Sada followed suit,

and so did the other two. Barrett pointed downhill, fingers extended and joined, thumb pointing down, indicating the enemy location. Sada nodded.

Barrett waved for the other two, and when Ainsworth and Fernandez came up, he whispered his instructions. He was going to put them in a base of fire position, oriented along the eastern sweep of the open crescent, back toward the Powder House. The problem was, they wouldn't get far down the slope before they were exposed on the hillside. So they'd still be a good twenty-five meters up. The steepness of the slope would prevent them from taking good covered and concealed positions. He left them in a position just short of the point at which they would break through the leafy tree line, and instructed them to move farther down once he and Sada passed. He went back and collected the Israeli woman. Barrett checked the taclight on the M-4, making sure the pressure switch activated the light on the barrel when pressed. Sada was doing the same.

Barrett placed his hand on her shoulder.

"Ready?"

"Of course."

"Let's go."

He stepped down the hillside with his rifle at the high ready, moving to the right of Ainsworth's and Fernandez's positions. As they broke through the foliage, he scanned left and right, expecting the enemy SAW team to open up at any point. Ainsworth and Fernandez were moving forward on his left, forced to give up what little concealment they had in order to have any chance of supporting Barrett and Sada if they made contact. At fifteen meters above the path, the greenery became so sparse Barrett knew they were in no man's land. He ran, slipped, scrambled the rest of the way, landing just beside the roofless shell of the old Lamp House, his weapon trained on the mine entrance which was an oblique black sliver a few meters away. No firing yet, but the fear of being cut in half by a burst from the hidden machine gun wanted to drive him to the ground. Training kicked in and told him to get out of the kill zone. He ran the last few steps and ducked down to clear the entrance cut into the iron grate. Darkness engulfed him. He flashed on the taclight, his finger starting to squeeze on the trigger in anticipation of a brief, deadly exchange of fire at close range.

Nothing.

He felt Sada just off his shoulder. She added the beam of her light to the tunnel.

Barrett edged forward. The cache directions said what, fifty meters? Inside the entrance, the roof of the mine rose a bit, but both of them moved in a stooped fashion to avoid the irregular stone and the iron I-beams supporting the ceiling.

Barrett's throat constricted.

He was alive, when a moment earlier that outcome had been in doubt. But the reason was that no one remained in the mine to shoot at him. Instead, a jumble of large timbers spread across the floor of the mineshaft, throwing irregular shadows on the surrounding walls. On the floor against the left side of the tunnel lay piles of dirt, gravel, coal, and shovels. Wiring and canvas satchels were tossed to the side. Metal glinted in their lights. Barrett and Sada stepped to the edge of the excavation.

The harsh cones of the taclights revealed the rectangular outline of a metal container, a large box with its hinged lid thrown back against the side of the hole. The box was OD green in color, the sides thick, maybe a quarter of an inch. The dimensions were such that a man could have fit inside, and it was at least four feet deep. The ragged remnants of a thick plastic liner hung out over the sides, and the heavy-duty waterproofing had been sliced open with a knife. Scattered inside the container were a few odd-shaped blocks of wood and rubber straps, materials for bracing the dangerous cargo during transportation.

The warhead was gone.

36

The guards returned to Dave's cell after breakfast and escorted him again to the main part of the station. This time they turned neither toward the interrogation rooms nor to the conference room, but took him to the end of a hallway and stopped before a wooden door. While one of the guards knocked, Dave read the gold nameplate, *Colonel Al-Hashimi, Commander*, spelled in English below the Arabic script.

A voice responded from inside. The guard opened the door and motioned Dave forward. The door closed behind him, and Dave was surprised to find himself alone with the police chief.

"Please, sit down, Mr. Allen," Al-Hashimi said, waving at a chair.

The colonel sat behind a large polished wooden desk, clear of everything except a notepad and an expensive pen. The man had his hands folded together and resting on the tabletop. He was wearing a dress uniform, his shoulder boards glittering with crossed swords of golden embroidery, a leather cross-strap running from under one shoulder board diagonally across his tunic.

"Mr. Allen, I am releasing you on your own recognizance."

Dave didn't know whether to thank the man, ask why, or just keep his mouth shut and not question his good fortune. Maybe Carr had accomplished something, after all.

"I am convinced you know nothing more about the murders at the Al Batinah Resort. I am positive you were not the cause of the deaths of my officers on Highway 89."

"Thank you for seeing that," Dave said.

"Of course," Hashimi continued. "I would consider it a matter of personal honor"—here he paused, and looking at Dave said—"you were an officer in the American Army, no?" to which Dave nodded. "I would ask that you honor my request to stay in Dubai to be available for further questioning, should we require it. Also that you seek my personal approval before traveling outside the UAE."

"I can live with that," Dave replied. "May I ask what changed your mind?"

"Mr. Allen, you made some accusations in our last meeting impugning the integrity of this office, and by extension, the entire Emirates police force. Some men might have taken those statements to heart, held them against you forever. I, however, had cause to reflect and to investigate certain peculiarities."

Dave watched the man struggle to come to grips with how much to reveal of his reasoning. He was waiting for another shoe to drop.

"I feel your entreaties with Ms. Carr went unheeded," Hashimi said. Dave realized the colonel was deflecting the conversation, steering it away from why he was now releasing the American.

"She's a bureaucrat. Nothing can be done outside normal business hours in her world. I hope my fears are overblown and she's right."

"Mr. Allen, I would not second guess yourself right now."

Dave was puzzled at Al-Hashimi's sudden interest in his theory.

"I, too, find Ms. Carr's reluctance to investigate your fears…unusual, given the events of the past week. However, I am now privy to some information she does not have."

"May I ask what?"

"Your insinuations, whether by reasoned judgment or through what you Americans call 'gut feel,' were not unfounded, Mr. Allen. While I was not the culprit, it appears a leak did exist. I uncovered an informant working within my department."

"What do you mean? Who?"

"The name is not important to you. He will be taken care of."

Hashimi ripped off the top page from the ruled notepad, folded it in half, and leaning forward, slid it across the desktop. Dave opened the paper and saw three international phone numbers neatly printed on the page. The last one had the first three digits of 001, indicating a U.S. number.

"What are these for?"

"The informant has been communicating details of this investigation to outside forces. As you surmised, this has compromised your safety and that of your friend, Mr. Ross, on more than one occasion. I will also reveal this information to your embassy, but they seem more preoccupied with routine matters at present."

"I'm still not sure what these phone numbers are."

"Mr. Allen, if your officials are too busy to help your friend, perhaps you can. Those three numbers are the last phone calls made by the traitor in my office to his contacts.

It appears at least one is an American number."

Dave needed to call Barrett right away. "When can I leave?"

"The guards outside the door have instructions to take you from my office to a room where you will be given your clothes and personal items."

"Thank you, Colonel."

"Also, your Australian friend Ms. Caldwell has been most persistent in asking after you. I have taken the liberty of contacting her. She is waiting in front of the station for you."

Al-Hashimi stood and Dave rose as well. The policeman extended his hand. "Good luck to you."

"How the hell did they get past us?"

Barrett was looking down into the empty cavity of the box. Ainsworth joined him, while Fernandez moved back to join the other deputies.

"They knew how to defeat the booby-trap mechanism," Sada responded. "Once they breached the iron grate, they executed with a purpose."

"They took the entire warhead."

"They'll disassemble it later and harvest the uranium components."

So that was it. Later that night, or the next day, the world would witness another unspeakable horror. Would he see the blast, feel the heat? How many would die? Barrett felt sick to his stomach. His thoughts were a jumbled confusion of fear for the unknown people who were going about their normal lives, unaware. Fear for the fate of the woman beside him. A longing, if the worst happened, that he could be with his mom, and Jamie, and Nathan, and make everything right first.

Sada was walking toward the entrance to the mine,

and he followed her, just as Fernandez ran up to meet them.

"We have to get Collins to the hospital."

"We're done here," Barrett said to the deputy. "Do what you need to do. Get Collins down the hill."

"What about you?" Ainsworth asked as he handed Barrett his backpack. Simmons and his team must have brought it in the ATV.

"I have a contact with the Feds. I'm going to try to convince him to get people out here and take over the search for these Iranians. Maybe Hascomb will listen to me now."

The darkness had become complete. Ainsworth was yelling to the other deputies, and the chatter from their radios rebounded across the grassy open area. Fernandez had been dispatched down the trail to retrieve the ATV. Soon its headlights were seen pulling up alongside the Fan House to load the wounded deputy.

Ainsworth came running back over to them.

"Simmons and Fernandez are taking Collins down the hill to meet the ambulance on the road. I need to get back to the office and try to start coordinating a search for these guys. We'll have checkpoints set up on every major road as soon as we can. Fitzpatrick is staying here. We'll put up lights here in case the Feds show up and want to look in the mine at that box."

Barrett nodded. Ainsworth ran off after the ATV, which was already starting down the path.

"What do you think the chances are the local cops and sheriffs pick up the Iranians at a checkpoint?" he asked.

"Not high," Sada responded.

"I don't know what to do. Other than call Hascomb."

"Call him. I'll be thinking about what to do next."

Barrett reached into his pack, felt his pistol, his book, and pulled out the cellphone Sada had given him ages ago.

He dialed the number. Hascomb was still in his office.

"Mr. Ross, looks like we owe you an apology."

"Agent Hascomb, we found the cache site. But the Iranians got here first. They have the Soviet warhead."

Hascomb disregarded that news. "Ross, listen. The Iranians have made their attack. The RDD, the dirty bomb in Dallas, we figured out the connection. That's what I meant. We don't think you're crazy anymore."

"What do you mean?"

"We found the guy who set off the dirty bomb. We got lucky, but we found him. We're pretty sure he's linked to your man Hoveyda, because the cesium he used for the bomb matches the stuff stolen from UNC."

Barrett was starting to lose his patience. "You don't understand, that's not it."

"The guy we have isn't talking yet, but given the connection to Hoveyda, and his supposed stay at Evin Prison, we'll be asking some tough questions of the Iranians."

"Hascomb, listen to me. The RDD was just a diversion. A diversionary attack."

Hascomb for the first time didn't sound so confident. "Diversion for what?"

"So you'd all be focused on Dallas instead of a coal mine in West Virginia."

"A what?"

"A coal mine. That's where I'm at. I've just had a firefight—me and the Fayetteville sheriff's department—against an armed force here in the woods along the New River. The Iranians got the nuke they were after."

"Ross, I don't know," Hascomb said, sounding bewildered. "I don't know what to say. The bad guys made their attack. Did you see a nuke?"

"You need to get the experts out here and inspect this cache site. So you'll believe me. The container is military.

There's Russian writing on it."

All confusion was gone by now. "I'll get people down there. How do we find it? How do I find you?"

"Coordinate with the sheriff's department in Fayetteville, West Virginia. A man named Deputy Ainsworth is in charge. He's coordinating with local law enforcement to try to shut down the roads."

"Okay."

"Hascomb, we need to figure out where the Iranians are taking this thing."

"If they have something."

"Can you risk they don't? I'm telling you, we just had a firefight. There's a paramilitary group running around the West Virginia woods with assault rifles and light machine guns. A sheriff was killed and one of the deputies got hit pretty bad. Ask Ainsworth what he saw."

"Okay. Do you have any evidence on the ground there, a clue indicating where these guys are going?"

"No. It's dark and we haven't had a chance to look around. I have my Israeli friend and one deputy up here. Ainsworth went back to town to coordinate the pursuit, and they're trying to get lights set up."

"Okay. The closest field office to you is Charlotte. I'll brief my superiors and get the okay to pull them in. FBI-Charlotte will contact your Deputy Ainsworth in Fayetteville and go to your location ASAP. I'll try to get the attention of the NCPC, but I have to tell you, they're one hundred percent consumed with following up on Dallas. They're pulling all the threads they can to track down the identity of this guy and his connections."

Barrett wanted to reemphasize the threat. "I'm telling you, Hascomb, this nut has a bomb now. Or the uranium components to a bomb."

"What do you mean, components?" Hascomb asked.

"We think they are going to salvage the two chunks of

uranium and discard the rest of the warhead."

"So, you think they are making another RDD?"

"No, not another dirty bomb! I, we, think they are building a nuke. An IND. Hoveyda and his physics knowledge, the missing neutron generator from the research lab, all their preparation points to one objective."

"Okay, okay, I'll try to get the right people to listen to you."

"Hascomb, I've got a bad feeling about this. This guy, their leader, he's throwing caution to the wind. Something's changed with him and he's not concerned about covering his tracks anymore."

"What are you saying, Barrett?"

Barrett paused, and took a breath. Sada had come back over and was watching him. Barrett measured his words before continuing.

"I'm telling you, Agent Hascomb, there's an immediate threat to the United States of America. I can't prove it, but I know it. This Iranian intends to detonate a nuclear weapon on American soil. It's not a bluff, it's not a blackmail ploy, it's a mission. He's planning on destroying an American city."

Hascomb was silent on the other end of the line for a long while. "Give me the number you're calling from, so I don't have to wait for you to call me. Stay with Deputy Ainsworth so FBI-Charlotte can talk to you when they get there."

Hascomb took the cell number and hung up without further comment. Barrett looked at the phone, and back at the mouth of the mine, the black circle barely discernible against the granite rock in the fading light. It was like looking into the gates of Hell.

"Let me guess," Sada said, "he wants us to sit tight."

"He's trying to get people to listen to us. Their field office from Charlotte will be coming up soon."

"I heard what you said about the Iranian's intentions. I don't know why the man would do it, but I agree. Whatever the IRGC's intent was at the start, this man has his own agenda now. He's deviated from his mission."

"The question is whether he's left anything behind for the FBI to figure out his destination."

"It will be a city. Washington, Richmond, Charlotte, Cleveland, Cincinnati. They're all within a few hours' drive of here."

Barrett realized they needed a break, a small miracle.

That's when his phone vibrated in his pocket.

Barrett looked at Sada as he pulled the phone out of his pocket.

"Probably Hascomb calling to remind us not to wander off—Ross."

"Barrett, it's Dave."

Barrett felt an explosion of warm energy. "Where are you? Are you okay?"

"I'm good. I just got released from jail. Amy's taking me back to my apartment now. You?"

"I don't even know where to start. You wouldn't believe it."

"I hear you're tangling with our Iranian friends still."

"Yeah, but we've lost them, and they've got the device described in the file. It's also worse than we thought—"

"Barrett, listen, I might be able to help. There was a spy inside the Dubai police who was feeding the bad guys information."

"How'd you figure that out?"

"Charm and persuasion. Listen, I have three phone numbers the informant called in the past couple hours."

"Go ahead."

"Two rang through to automated voicemails. The third

one was a hotel."

"Where?"

"West Virginia."

"Fayetteville?"

"How did you—"

"Dave, I just got into a shoot-out with the Iranians in the woods near Fayetteville. What's the name—"

"The Sleep Value Inn, New River Gorge. The guy at the front desk says it's right off U.S. 19 on the edge of town." Dave read off the address as Barrett repeated it aloud so Sada could hear.

"Dave, this is awesome," Barrett said. "I'll call you back when I can."

He hefted the Iranian's kit bag and joined Sada in sprinting down the trail in the dark, willing the road and their rental car to emerge out of the gloom.

37

The Sleep Value Inn was a dingy two-story affair with an office at one end and a line of rooms with doors opening onto the parking lot or the balcony above. Sada pulled the car into an empty spot by the office.

The clerk, a young man with a scraggly beard and wearing a knit stocking cap despite the summer temperatures, had been dozing and was startled by their hurried entrance.

"Can I help you?" he asked. Sada wondered if he was drugged or just wanted to sound that way.

"We're looking for a middle-aged man, Middle Eastern descent," Barrett began. "We're federal agents," he threw in at the end, "and it's urgent."

"There've been a couple of dudes who look Middle Eastern," the clerk offered. "Do you have badges?"

Sada pulled her pistol out and pointed it at the clerk's chest. "Stand up and don't touch anything."

Frightened, the clerk raised his hands above his head.

"What room? Check."

"214."

"What vehicle are they driving?" Sada asked.

The clerk checked the registration card. "Bl-blue Chevy Impala," he stammered. "Virginia license plates."

Sada leaned over to read the license plate number. Going to the side of the desk, she motioned the clerk to come out from behind it. "You'll be fine as long as you follow our instructions. Bring your pass key."

The fear in the clerk's face was evident, but he nodded in understanding.

"We're the good guys, but we're short on time," Barrett said more kindly. "You're going to take us to the room of the Middle Eastern guy. When we get there, don't say a word. When we tell you, swipe the lock with your key card. Then move out of the way. Stay right outside and don't go anywhere. Understand?"

The clerk nodded again and managed an "O-okay."

The clerk led them up the concrete steps to the second-floor balcony and down to a room almost at the end. Sada had her weapon concealed along her body facing the building. When the young man stopped and faced a door, she switched the pistol to her firing hand. Barrett pulled his own weapon out of his belt in the small of his back. Sada touched the man's shoulder. With a shaking hand he inserted the key card and swiped down.

Sada entered first, Barrett following behind, shoving the clerk to the right before going through the door. Sada went straight, leaving Barrett to pivot right and check the bathroom. Empty kitchenette.

A body lay in the floor of the main room.

"Clear," Barrett said behind her. He stepped out to grab the clerk and pull him into the room.

Sada approached the body. The face was that of a man who could have been Iranian. The hair was close-cropped, salt and pepper gray. The eyes were vacant, and the teeth were bared in a grimace.

Barrett propelled the young man to the edge of the bed, sitting him down.

"Sit, and stay quiet," Barrett said.

"Oh, shit!" the man exclaimed, seeing the body. The body had fallen forward from the easy chair, pushing the lightweight coffee table forward, and lay sprawled between the two pieces of furniture.

Barrett put a finger to his lips, signaling to the young man to remember the admonition to be quiet. He moved around to Sada's side.

"This isn't the guy from my house," Barrett said.

"No, not the one we saw at Fujairah," Sada confirmed. "Too short and stocky."

"One of his men?"

Sada opened the closet and the chest of drawers, but everything was empty. Barrett went to the nightstand but found nothing. Sada was turning back to the body when she saw, leaning against the side of the chair the dead man had fallen out of, a slim portfolio.

"Look."

She laid it on the coffee table, opening it to reveal a notepad, pen, and several sheets of loose paper stuck in the retainer flap. Several items were handwritten notes in Arabic script. She unfolded a piece of paper and saw it was an invoice. The letterhead read Metals On-Line.

"What is it?"

"It's a purchase order from a metals wholesaler," she answered. "Aluminum for construction."

Barrett scanned the rows on the invoice. "Lots of aluminum," he said, reading. "Some of these pieces are twelve feet long, twenty-four feet long. Aluminum structural angle, aluminum channel, aluminum square pipe."

"What're they building?"

"It's got to be the IND. Somehow."

Barrett pointed at the address, a street in Charlotte, NC.

"Barrett. If the Iranian killed this man, he must have been a liability for some reason. But he didn't bother to hide the body."

"I know. Just like blowing explosives at the mine. He's not covering his tracks," Barrett said.

"He doesn't think he has any reason to," Sada answered.

Sada ran out of the room clutching the invoice, Barrett following. The night clerk sat poised on the edge of the mattress, staring at the dead body in his shabby hotel room.

Sada flew off the interchange leaving U.S. 19 and entered the heavy flow of traffic on Interstate 77 heading south, swerving into the left lane. It was just before midnight. If she could keep it up, they should reach the outskirts of Charlotte in three hours. Barrett dialed Hascomb's number from memory.

"Hascomb, we found the location where the Iranian's headed. It's an address in Charlotte."

"Ross, listen, we have a real situation on our hands now, and I have a million calls to make."

"Are you listening to me?" Barrett shouted. "We know the location of the IND. We found the address where they're putting it together."

"No, you listen. I shouldn't even be telling you this. The entire intel community is going bat-shit. There's credible intelligence of a pending WMD attack. It might be your nuke pulled out of the mine. Or another RDD, we're not sure. But it's not in North Carolina."

"Where?"

"Someone is in the final stage of launching an attack on

Capitol Hill."

After that, Barrett couldn't get the agent to listen to him. Hascomb said that unless he called back and said he had an actual visual on an atomic warhead, he needed to let Hascomb focus on what he was doing. Barrett did manage to wrest from the agent a promise he'd place a heads-up call to FBI-Charlotte, but Hascomb reminded him the field office already had one team in route to West Virginia, and almost every other able-bodied agent was surging to Washington. Then the line went dead.

Completely frustrated, Barrett found Tommy McCowan's business card and dialed the number. The man sounded relieved to hear from Barrett.

"Are you back in the States? The dirty bomb in Dallas, was that—"

"It was the Iranians, Tommy, but it was just a diversionary attack."

"Oh."

"Listen, you were right. We found the cache site for the nuke. But the Iranians got there first and took the bomb."

"Sweet Jesus."

"Listen. I'm here with Sada—Susan. We're en route to where we think they're taking it. The Feds, of course, are moving in a completely different direction. I need to know what we're up against."

"They have the warhead?"

"We assume so. At the cache site all we found was the empty shipping container. How hard will it be for them to extract the uranium core from the warhead?"

"Not hard. As long as they disable the fusing mechanism for the conventional explosives, all they'll have to do is remove or cut away an access plate, and dismantle the breach in the gun tube."

"So how big are we talking about, Tommy?" Barrett asked. "How bad can this be?"

"The American SADM I told you about—it was built around the W-54 warhead, developed in the fifties. The W-54 could be configured for variable yields, but the biggest was one kiloton. A Russian version, who knows? Depending on when it was made, and the size, it could conceivably be as big as two kilotons or more."

Barrett hit the button to put it on speaker phone, so Sada could hear the assessment straight from Tommy.

"What does that mean? What will it do to a city?"

"I am praying you're mistaken about what's going on," Tommy said, and paused. "To put it in perspective, do you remember the Oklahoma City bombing?"

"Of course."

"When that idiot blew up the Murrah Federal Building, they estimated the force of the blast was equivalent to 5,000 pounds of TNT. It sheared off the entire front third of a huge building. Killed almost two hundred people, injured upward of a thousand. It damaged buildings in a sixteen-block radius. A one-kiloton atomic bomb is about five hundred times more powerful than the Oklahoma City bomb."

God help us. A blast five hundred times bigger than Oklahoma City, if it was only a kiloton. Not to mention the radiation.

"Barrett, the area of immediate destruction would be at least a hundred times larger than Oklahoma City."

"All right, Tommy."

"Where are you heading?"

"Charlotte, North Carolina."

"Good Lord."

"Tommy," Sada interjected. "We think the Iranians have a lot of structural aluminum. What could that be for?"

Tommy fell silent as this element was considered.

"Dragon's tail," he muttered.

"Tommy, what was that?" Barrett asked.

"When the scientists were building the first atomic bombs at Los Alamos, they worked on two designs. The Hiroshima bomb used uranium in a gun-tube configuration."

"Okay."

"For the gun-tube model, they needed a way to experiment with pushing two pieces of uranium together to form a critical mass—but without blowing themselves up. A scientist named Frisch built a device he called a guillotine mechanism. At table height he set a hollowed-out ring of uranium, a subcritical mass shaped like a donut. Suspended ten feet above it was another subcritical mass of uranium, a cylinder-shaped slug. When it was dropped, the slug passed all the way through the donut to the floor. But for a brief instant, when the slug was in the aperture of the donut, the combined mass of the uranium was just on the verge of being prompt critical—an uncontrollable chain reaction. The scientists measured the radioactivity, and this is how they made the calculations for how much uranium they needed for the bomb. They were very close to setting off a nuclear explosion in the lab. Richard Feynman, another physicist, said the experiment was like tickling the tail of a sleeping dragon."

"Where does the aluminum come in?"

"Okay, this is just a thought. One way to build an IND with uranium would be to replicate the original gun structure of the bomb. Detonate conventional explosives to force a piece of subcritical uranium down a gun barrel, slamming it into another mass of uranium. But that takes serious engineering and machining skills. Theoretically, though, you could just drop one piece of uranium on top of the other piece. Like the dragon experiment, except you stop the slug inside the donut, and it doesn't pass through."

"The aluminum is used for the support structure," Barrett said, a picture forming in his mind.

"Yes. Frisch's guillotine structure was built with an iron frame about ten feet tall with aluminum guide rails. With today's metals, you could just build the whole thing out of aluminum."

38

Safavi peered up at the tall skyscrapers outlined against the night sky as Falasiri drove along the deserted streets of the business district. Two of America's biggest banks, Safavi knew, were headquartered in these buildings. In a few hours tens of thousands of people would be crowding these offices and these streets. It was fascinating to contemplate destiny and fate. This was, he was sure, his destiny.

For the Americans, their fate had been dictated by simple reasoning. This city was large enough. It was close enough to the cache site. And it was not Washington, D.C., where others were expecting him to strike.

Falasiri made a series of turns onto side streets and slowed when he identified the address of the low, squat building. Seeing the gate to the fenced parking area was locked, he pulled the car to the curb in front of the warehouse. Getting out, Safavi assessed his surroundings. Yes, an ideal location, close to the heart of the city's financial district.

By the front door Safavi pressed a button on the frame.

From inside he heard the muted buzzing. The gray door was of heavy-duty metal construction, and no windows fronted the sidewalk. Hessaby had chosen well, as Safavi knew he would. Safavi buzzed again. Karim Hoveyda opened the door, bowing his head when he saw the military commander.

"Sir, so good to see you at last," the scientist said.

"English," Safavi reminded him.

Safavi walked back to the car, where Falasiri had already opened the trunk of the sedan. The man pulled out a small box, using both arms to lift it over the lip of the trunk. The container was a black metal cube, twelve inches to a side. Three quarters of the way up, the top section was hinged and secured with large butterfly latches on three sides, and fitted with a steel carrying handle.

Safavi opened the rear passenger door and hefted an identical container from the floor. He felt the strain, carrying the weight suspended from one arm.

They were all that was left, it dawned on him. The remainder of his unit was gone now, dispersed to various airports for their planned exfiltration. The two soldiers helping Hoveyda were gone as well. All the equipment, weapons, and ammunition, all were hidden in a series of nondescript storage units outside a small town near the highway. The rent for the storage units would be paid every month, until such time that the Revolutionary Guards needed them for another operation.

Safavi entered the warehouse with the heavy object and walked around the divider wall forming the alcove around the front door. He stepped into the main expanse of the warehouse. The ceiling was much higher than he thought from outside, at least twenty feet. The entire area was well lit by banks of fluorescent lights hanging from the trestle rafters overhead. Along the back wall, a roll-up door provided access to a loading dock. The small oval windows inset in the metal slats were boarded over with cardboard and duct tape. Hoveyda's structure rose in the back left corner of the large room.

"Please place that here," Hoveyda said, indicating a spot near the bottom of the structure.

Safavi stopped in front of the structure and put his half of the uranium core down. The shiny, latticed structure reached almost fifteen feet off the carpeted floor. Hoveyda and his welders had done well. Safavi was reminded of the derricks he'd seen at the Maysan oil fields, but in miniature form. The four long support beams formed a square at the base about five feet on a side, tapering up to a smaller square at the top, fifteen feet off the floor. The sides were braced with crosses of welded aluminum. Through the center of the derrick structure, as he thought of it, ran two vertical aluminum channel pieces, all the way from the platform on top to a thick-walled metal box on the bottom. This steel target box would contain the mated pieces of uranium, serving as a tamper for the split second required to reflect neutrons inward and ensure a complete reaction. Hanging between the aluminum guide rails was a thin steel cable that disappeared through a hole in the top platform and connected to a winch.

Next to the vertical structure, Hoveyda set up a workbench strewn with papers, electronic components, cables and a laptop. At the foot of the workbench was a large silver rectangular box, the stolen neutron generator. The multi-prong connectors on one end waited to be mated to the high-power cables snaking across the floor to the power box on the far wall.

On the other side of the structure, Hoveyda and the soldiers had erected a scaffolding of metal and wooden planks in order to complete the construction of the device and to allow access to the top of the platform.

"Put that one over there," Hoveyda said as Falasiri

approached, intercepting the man and directing him to a spot along the opposite wall.

"No sense in getting these two items any closer than they need to be until everything is prepared," he said.

"How long will it take now?" Safavi asked, not turning to look at the scientist.

"Not long at all," the scientist responded, his face betraying concern over Safavi's question. "Wouldn't it be more prudent to keep the components separate? Unless we receive General Roghani's directive?"

"Dr. Hoveyda, I understand the general's intent," Safavi said, staring at the man. "An ultimatum means nothing without a credible threat. Get the pieces in place and call me when you have completed everything."

"Yes, sir."

Safavi didn't trust the scientist. But after Falasiri was dealt with, there would be time to inspect the scientist's work.

"Falasiri," he said mildly. "Come with me. I have another task for you."

39

Even as they pulled into the complex, Barrett knew it was wrong. All wrong. The GPS on the dash said the address was just ahead, but as Sada slowed the car, Barrett knew the Iranian hadn't set up shop in this cluster of low-rent town homes. They were too far out of the city anyway. They'd followed I-77 straight through the city, and were now on the south side of Charlotte, just outside the I-485 beltway in an area called Pineville. No way the Iranian was attacking the suburbs. Stupid, stupid—they should have turned back twenty minutes ago.

"Damn it," Barrett said. He checked the address in the GPS against the invoice they'd found in Safavi's room, for the fourth time. It matched. The address listed on the invoice was on Hill Road. Barrett deleted the word Road from the GPS screen and just searched for Hill, Charlotte, NC.

The only other option that popped up was East Hill Street. Barrett selected it and the GPS pulled up a new street map. He zoomed out to get his bearings. The new address was smack in the middle of downtown Charlotte.

"Go!" he yelled.

Would Hoveyda have it ready? Safavi had been gone for no more than twenty-five minutes, but he needed to venture far enough away from the city lights so he could dispose of Falasiri without undue risk of being observed. That decision was almost as painful as the one about Colonel Hessaby, but Safavi took comfort in the fulfillment of their mission. They had become martyrs in the battle against America.

Falasiri had understood his role as staying at the site with Safavi and Hoveyda, providing both security and support. He had no scheduled flight out of the country like the others. But Safavi could not afford to have both Falasiri and Hoveyda inside the warehouse when the time came. Now he would have the simple task of dispatching the scientist. As soon as Safavi was sure everything was in order.

Safavi checked his watch. Thirty minutes to first light. Three hours from now the buildings would be filling, the streets teeming with cars and pedestrians, as the Americans began their workweek.

The warehouse came into view, and he pulled the car over before the front entrance.

Sada turned onto East Hill Street. They drove past a large office building occupying an entire block, then a parking garage, before they saw the lot containing the small warehouse in a row of rundown buildings.

"That's it," Sada said, just as the mechanical voice of the GPS announced they'd arrived at their destination on the left.

As she slowed, a vehicle turned into the deserted

intersection up in front of them, driving in their direction. It stopped in front of their destination.

"Keep driving," Barrett said. As they passed the car it pulled to the curb and its headlights went out.

"Chevy Impala!" Barrett yelled.

Sada whipped the car around. The headlights swept in an arc, catching light poles, buildings, cars, a vacant lot, a grocery store, and the back of a blue Chevy Impala, Virginia plates, no more than twenty meters away.

"That's him!" Barrett shouted. He recognized the profile, the cut of the shoulders and the head, the man from Fujairah, Mitchell's killer. The Iranian, getting out of the driver's side, turned, startled by the oncoming headlights.

Barrett pulled his weapon out.

Sada hit the gas and the vehicle surged forward. Barrett had the window down, trying to line up the shot, but the sudden acceleration and braking caused his arm to swing back and forth.

They stopped and Barrett steadied himself, but the front door of the building was already closing, with the Iranian on the other side.

Hoveyda would rot in hell for this. Safavi did not bother to look over at the scientist's body, with the neat bullet hole in the middle of his forehead. That was one sacrifice Safavi did not mind making. The last words out of the man's mouth was that everything was prepared, but that was a lie.

Safavi saw the clue earlier, when he'd set the box down containing half of the uranium core next to the steel tamper box. The piece of metal tubing lying off to the side, a fragment which didn't belong, didn't have a clear purpose.

Now, with the sweat pouring off his head and hands, the urgency of the situation making Safavi feel unsure of himself for the first time in his adult life, he pried at the obstruction with his knife.

Hoveyda had inserted a thin metal tube inside the circumference of the receiving mass of uranium. It was gray, maybe not as shiny as the uranium, but Safavi would not have noticed it if he hadn't already suspected the scientist's treachery. The insert would be more than enough of an obstruction to prevent the uranium slug above from mating with the donut. If Safavi initiated the device without removing the insert, the slug would stop at a point just touching the lip of the lower ring of uranium. The result would be a low-order detonation, a fizzle, killing Safavi and blowing the uranium apart before a chain reaction could run its course.

Damn Hoveyda. The American was outside, right now. Safavi could not wait. He would improvise, take advantage of the opportunity he had. He would still strike a great blow against the enemy.

Safavi managed to get the blade wedged between the metal side of the uranium mass and the foreign object. It was tight. His knife kept wanting to slip off the smooth surfaces. He just needed leverage to slide it up...

40

The sidewalk was clear of people, the street devoid of traffic. Barrett and Sada stood in front of the featureless building, clutching their weapons by their sides. The front had no windows, and the one door, the one the Iranian disappeared through, was steel. Barrett yanked on the heavy-duty knob. It wouldn't budge.

"We don't have time," Sada said. "He could set it off immediately."

"We need a crowbar, something..." Barrett said, sweat beading on his forehead. The terror of what might happen in the next few minutes was almost overwhelming. He fought the inclination to freeze up in helplessness.

"Shoot the lock mechanism!" Sada yelled.

"It won't work!" he shouted back. "There's no way, not with these pistols."

Think. Think. What resources? What could they do out of the box? Attack through the roof, but how to get up there? Scale the fence, look in the rear of the building? Only to find another locked door?

Of course. "The demo in the kit bag!" he shouted, and

he ran back to the trunk of the car.

Bending over the opened trunk, Barrett ripped open the duffel bag, in his desperation catching the heavy zipper on the material. The bag ended up stuck in a half-opened position. Barrett grasped the two sides and ripped it apart, feeling the cloth give way. He pushed the spare magazines of ammo aside, found what he was looking for. A stick of C-4, a one and a quarter pound block wrapped in the standard army green wrapper. He found the other item, a small Styrofoam box, two halves taped together with electrical tape. He unwound the tape with shaking hands. Inside, a single silver blasting cap.

The time fuze, a loose coil of green plastic cord, was inside a gallon-sized plastic Ziploc. God, he hoped it was time fuze and not det cord, or he'd probably just blow his hands off.

"This is it," he said to Sada, who'd come up beside him. "There's only one blasting cap."

His mind was working frantically, trying to recall the little he'd learned in training. He had no idea if a single stick of C-4 would do anything against a solid metal door. Wrap it around the door knob? It would just obliterate the knob and nothing else. The blast wave would just flatten against the door in all directions, burning off the point. It wouldn't do anything to the lock mechanism inside.

The lock mechanism. Barrett hefted the bar of explosives. He needed to direct the force of the explosion through the door, at the right spot. A shape charge.

"I need a cone, a wine glass, something shaped like that," he yelled.

Sada understood instantly. "A water bottle."

Barrett ripped off the green plastic wrapper to expose the malleable white explosive. Sada returned with a one-liter bottle, dumping the water out on the street.

Barrett cut off the top of the bottle just below the point

where the straight sides began to taper to the cap. Taking this section, he inverted it and slid it into the open end of the bottle, so the cap was pointing inside. The top of the bottle was now a concave cavity. He took a section of the black tape off of the Styrofoam box holding the blasting cap. Folding it around the lip of the new cavity, he fastened the two halves together. He cut off the bottom of the bottle so it was an open cylinder.

Sada held the bottle casing as Barrett tore off chunks of the C-4 and pushed the explosive down the length of the bottle, wedging it in the spaces between the cone of the inverted top and the sides of the cylinder. He continued to pack in the explosives, kneading the plastique into position and eliminating air pockets. He pressed the remaining C-4 into the bottom of the bottle, tamping it with his fingers.

Barrett took the blasting cap out of the Styrofoam, inserting one end of the time fuze into the hollow end of the blasting cap. He needed to crimp the metal but had no tool. Holding the explosive end of blasting cap outside his cheek, he placed the tip of the hollow end between his molars, biting down just enough to crimp the thin metal around the time fuze. If he messed this up, he'd never know it.

Barrett cut off a three-inch section of the time fuze with the blasting cap at the end.

"We need something to get this at lock height." They both cast around, looking up and down the street for something to rest the device on.

"There," Sada said. An abandoned grocery cart lay up against a fence a block down the sidewalk. She started running to it.

Barrett took his improvised charge to the door. He took a pen out of his pocket and pushed a hole into the explosive, inserting the blasting cap into this well. He pressed the malleable explosive back around it until the cap was covered.

Sada returned and flipped the cart over so the wheels were wobbling in the air. The underside of the cart was now almost at the height of the doorknob, but not quite. She ran back to the car, and when she returned, she built a block on top of the mesh of the cart made out of ammunition magazines and a thick book. It briefly registered in Barrett's mind that the book was his Thucydides as he placed the shape charge against the metal door, centered between the door knob and the jamb.

"Back up," he said.

He took the free end of the short length of time fuze, inserted it into the pull-ring ignitor, and screwed the cap back down to lock the cord in.

Barrett removed the safety wire, stuck his finger into the pull ring and pulled hard. He heard the telltale hiss. He bent close to find the small trail of white smoke where the time fuze was starting to burn at the top of the ignitor. He set the assembly down on the mesh underside of the shopping cart, and ran to join Sada. He wrapped his arm around her and pressed his face into the side of the building.

He prayed it would work, but his heart began to sink as the seconds ticked by. Mitch, his men in Iraq—his family—everyone's sacrifice was for nothing.

His brain was churning, thinking of other alternatives, when the blast wave traveled down the side of the building, assaulting his ears and slamming him in the back.

Barrett choked and his eyes stung from the residual smoke as he approached the door. He saw the ragged, charred edges of the hole punched through the steel just beside the doorknob. He lowered his shoulder and the door swung in.

Inside the door, Barrett met a wall. In the haze from the explosion he was confused until he recognized it as a vestibule. Turning right, he found and passed through the doorway into the main warehouse. Sada was right behind him, hand on his shoulder.

The main room was bright, everything laid out before his eyes in a single glance. A body lay on the floor before them. The rest of the space was empty, except for the back left corner. A metal structure, surrounded by scaffolding, reached from floor to ceiling. Next to the structure, a metal table with scattered equipment. Large electrical cables ran across the floor.

Barrett spied the Iranian. On the scaffolding, just short of the top of the shiny tower, the Iranian crouched and aimed a weapon.

Sada saw him as well. Her pistol exploded, echoing in the empty warehouse, rounds pinging off metal. Shot after shot after shot, as the Iranian returned fire from the top of the scaffolding, too. Barrett dove to his left, scrambling to put a barrier between him and the man hunkering on the scaffold, hidden behind the crisscrossing bars and plywood.

Barrett looked back. Sada was lying on her back, a look of surprise on her face. She was clutching her chest, a dark stain blossoming on her shirt.

Barrett hadn't drawn his weapon before he rushed through the door. He reached back to draw it from his belt, keeping his eyes on the platform above him. A hand reached up and seized a railing near the top of the scaffolding. The Iranian was wounded, pulling himself up to his knees. Barrett drew his weapon and stood, aiming where the man's center of mass should be, obscured as it was by the confusing jumble of rods, supports, and planks.

The Iranian didn't even turn to look at him, but instead grasped the gleaming metal tower next to the scaffolding. He was three feet from the top, where a platform held a cylindrical device and a cable winch housing. Just beneath the platform, slotted between two thin strips of aluminum, hung a dull metallic object with a tapered point.

Barrett walked forward.

"Stop!"

The man ignored him. He placed one foot on a railing in the scaffolding, pulling himself hand over hand to reach the top of the platform.

The aluminum guide rails ran all the way to the bottom of the tower, into what looked like a large metal box. The pieces connected. Barrett understood what he was looking at.

"No!"

The man on the top of the scaffolding turned to him for a split second before extending his arm to reach for the assembly on top of the structure.

Barrett lunged forward, terror a physical presence animating one part of his brain. His legs felt weak and uncoordinated, but he was running hard. He was several feet away when he heard the sharp snap of mechanical tension being released.

Barrett dove, arm outstretched, pistol falling away from his opened hand.

He was aware of, more than saw, the shiny silver cylinder plunging down the lubricated guide rails. His hand, fingers extended and palm vertical, shot through the narrow gap between the aluminum rails, but his momentum was pulled up short as the thicker part of his forearm wedged between the two metal rails. The sharp edges peeled back the skin on either side of the arm with agonizing scrapes.

The metal object was lying on top his forearm. No, it

was sticking out of his forearm. A sickening, snapping sound registered in his ears.

The heavy metal cylinder was embedded, the milled point sunk deep into his flesh at the bottom of a V-shape formed where the end of his limb cantilevered up. The heavy uranium slug had crushed his bones and pushed his arm into the donut of the uranium target.

Blood was seeping out around the metal uprights, gathering in the basin formed by the uranium donut and its tamper. He felt a strange, disturbing warmth emanating from the center of his arm, and didn't know if it was merely from the flow of blood.

Barrett reached forward with his left hand, grabbing the top of the slug, and pulled it up and out of his mangled arm. He pulled and pushed, pulled and pushed, banging against the aluminum guides, battering his knuckles, until the aluminum yielded and the slug yanked free, falling to the carpet next to his body. He was staring at the bloody metal bullet when the overhead lights began swirling around the ceiling, and then someone turned them all out.

Epilogue

Barrett walked out of the Veterans Administration Hospital in northwest Washington into the wan sunlight of a late December afternoon. It was a Friday, late enough in the day that he felt justified in heading home instead of back to work. He had to admit, he was tired. Everyone had been great, his bosses more than understanding. After six months he was back into the full swing of projects at the think tank, but the regular rehab sessions were kicking his butt. The physical therapist was nice but ruthless when it came to putting Barrett through the paces of learning to live with his new arm. He was eager to progress, to get on with life. She sensed it, and was pushing him hard as he relearned how to do the thousand daily tasks he once took for granted.

He looked down at the synthetic hand protruding from his sleeve. He was getting used to it, but if he stopped and thought about it, the device was still amazing. The myoelectric prosthesis was an advanced model, with five functioning fingers that gave him an amazing approximation of the dexterity and functionality of his original hand. Without it, the road to recovery and self-sufficiency would have been a lot longer. Technically, he wasn't cleared to drive on his own yet, not having reached that step on the checklist. But he felt so confident in the new limb, he'd been driving himself for the past three weeks. What the therapist didn't know wouldn't hurt her.

Barrett left the parking lot and looped around the complex to North Capitol Street heading south toward the center of town.

Six months. Six months and everything was back to normal, except for the loss of his friend Mitchell Kane. Dave and Amy were good. Dave had been cleared of all suspicion by Al-Hashimi's department and his superiors in the UAE. The couple suggested a reunion of sorts this summer, but somewhere in the U.S. or Australia. Nowhere their military skills might come into play.

Hascomb had reached out to him after he left the hospital in the summer. The agent was gracious, thanking him for his efforts and apologizing for the communication glitches. The two got together for beers to commiserate the loss of Mitchell, and Hascomb kept in touch from time to time with a few pieces of inside information. Barrett asked, and the agent worked diligently to honor the request, to keep Barrett's name out of the official accounts of what transpired. He was ready to go about his life, quietly. Only his mom and Nathan, who'd driven out to stay with him the first few weeks of his recovery, knew the whole story.

One other person knew the whole story, and Barrett thought often of Sada. Hascomb told him that after the Charlotte police and emergency personnel responded to his explosive breach at the warehouse, they'd found the two of them unconscious. Sada underwent emergency surgery at Carolinas Medical Center, where she remained in intensive care for weeks until she stabilized. The Israelis flew her home before he'd had a chance to see or speak with her.

Barrett turned south onto I-395 and drove through the tunnel beneath the Department of Labor building.

International affairs had settled back to a certain normalcy, although Barrett knew he wasn't privy to everything said or done between the interested parties. Iran, of course, denied any knowledge of, or links to, the Dallas bomber, or the bodies at the warehouse, the motel, or the coal mine. Depending on the month, the Supreme Leader was somewhere in the process of agreeing to, or discounting, the possibility of talks. Talks, the only purpose of which was to discuss the possibility of future talks. That had been going on for as least as long as Barrett had been learning to use his new arm, and he was making a lot more progress than the U.S. and EU diplomats.

Russia denied any knowledge of an atomic weapon hidden in the U.S. They portrayed these rumors as politically motivated Russia bashing. As part of a two-step denial, they further insinuated that if any allegations had any truth at all, then the bomb's placement could only have occurred as an illegal and unsanctioned act committed by a renegade element within the KGB. An obsolete agency of the old Communist regime, they reminded everyone, with no official ties to the security apparatus of the modern Russian Federation. For whatever reason, the U.S. government wasn't pushing the issue much. At least not from what could be gathered reading the papers.

The rhetoric from Israel about Iran's nuclear ambitions had toned down over the past six months. Barrett wondered about this. Something the American government was saying was placating the Israelis. Maybe the President had sent a message: you can stop rattling your sabers, because we've already given the Iranians an ultimatum of our own.

Barrett crossed the Potomac on the George Mason Bridge, followed the highway as it looped around the south side of the Pentagon, and took the exit to cross back over the highway heading into the Aurora Highlands area.

Pulling onto his street, he noticed a car in his driveway he didn't recognize. Barrett couldn't help but flash back to the morning when he'd pulled up to find Mitchell parked in the drive.

He pulled in and parked beside the red sedan.

Sada stood up from where she'd been waiting on the concrete steps to his front door.

"How'd you track me down?" he asked, delighted, getting out of his car.

"I'm a professional," she said. "Remember?" She smiled. It was a smile fulfilling all the promise he'd seen in her face so many months ago, in an outdoor bar on the other side of the world.

"Besides," she added, "I've visited your neighborhood before."

"Would you like to come in?"

"What are your plans for the weekend?" she countered.

"No plans yet."

"Would you like to take a short vacation?"

"My last one was cut short," he said lightly. "What did you have in mind?"

"I know a resort."

"Dubai?"

"No," she shook her head and smiled again. "A historic place. In West Virginia."

"That's fine," he said. "But then we have to go north from there. I have another place I need to visit."

Acknowledgments

I'm grateful to everyone who gave me help and encouragement along the way, but especially Mom and Dad, Tom, Linda, Allison, Christine, Courtney, and Jason.

A special thanks goes out to those who labored diligently through an early draft and provided honest feedback—Rob, Steve, Patrick, Mark, John, Kristin, and Fred.

This book would not be in the shape it's in without the invaluable guidance of John Paine, my editor.

And finally, I couldn't have kept at it without Diane's love and support.